THE ASSASSIN KING

Will Adams

Copyright © 2023 Will Adams

All rights reserved

The characters and events portrayed in this book are fictitious. Any similarity to real persons, living or dead, is coincidental and not intended by the author.

No part of this book may be reproduced, or stored in a retrieval system, or transmitted in any form or by any means, electronic, mechanical, photocopying, recording, or otherwise, without express written permission of the publisher.

ISBN: 9798858790617

Cover design by: Victoria Barbera

He lost all his carts, wagons, and baggage horses, together with his money, costly vessels, and everything he had a particular regard for; for the land opened in the middle of the water and caused whirlpools which sucked in everything, as well as men and horses, so that no one escaped to tell the king of the misfortune.

ROGER OF WENDOVER

PROLOGUE

Caversham, Berkshire

May 12, 1219

London to Caversham was ever a gruelling ride for a man of almost three score and ten, but it was more than usually so for St Maur today, what with the roads made quagmires by the endless spring rains and his favourite horse lame from an infected hoof. Yet this particular summons had been impossible to deny or even put off until the morrow, so he was mighty glad to see at last the familiar landmarks of his friend's estate, and then the Manor itself emerging from the darkness.

A pair of household knights came out to challenge them. St Maur was too weary even to answer their insolence, so he and his small escort simply clopped on by, knowing that they wouldn't dare do more than bark. A fire was blazing in a corner of the courtyard. The smell of roasting venison made his mouth water. He dismounted and threw his reins to a stable boy then strode over to the front door with such dignity as the stiffness of his joints and the chaffing of his thighs allowed.

An old crone with a livid boil on her throat answered his knock, her face and forearms reddened from standing too close to a fire. He recognised her from last time. A cousin of some kind, given her position here out of charity, yet pretending to grander status. 'You were expected hours ago,' she said.

'My men need food and drink and warmth,' he told her, handing her his wet cloak.

The great man's son came down the staircase to greet him. 'About time!' he said.

'You sent your messenger to the wrong place,' St Maur replied wearily. 'Am I too late?'

'Not yet.' The son looked strikingly like how his father had done when St Maur had first met him, out in the holy land all those many years before. He lacked his charisma, of course, not to mention his sheer size and force of personality. But that was a ludicrous standard to hold any man to. His father, quite simply, had been the giant of their age. 'Not quite.'

'Then take me to him.'

A dozen or so people were milling around upstairs, wringing their hands and whispering like conspirators. The son strode through them with deliberate rudeness, seeking to scatter them like carrion around a dying stag. They entered the bedchamber. It was grand, as befitted such a man, yet modestly furnished, as if in acknowledgement of the vows of poverty and chastity he'd avoided for all these decades, that he might enjoy his wealth and sire a family instead. It was pleasantly warm too, thanks to the fire smouldering in the grate and the small crowd gathered by the bed, surrounding the dying man not only with their grief but with their anxiety too. For he hadn't merely been head of this family, he'd been its shield and sword arm too – just as he'd been shield and sword arm to this whole land these past few years. With him gone, the chaos and bloodshed would surely return. For who'd be there to stop it?

They all heard St Maur arrive, yet pretended not to, lest politeness compel them to surrender their spot. He pushed between them anyway. A shock to see his old friend beneath the heavy bedclothes, how diminished he was from even a few weeks ago. Until that very moment, he now realised, he hadn't fully believed it. Yet those gaunt cheeks, drooping eyelids and wasting forearms were impossible to deny. England's champion had taken his felling blow at last.

His old friend saw him arrive. He brightened and even sat up a little. 'Out,' he murmured to the others. 'All of you, out.' His voice was little more than a whisper, yet somehow it retained its old authority. They left with ill grace even so, perhaps fearing he'd slip away before they made it back in, depriving them of the legacies and benefactions they'd come for.

His wife Isabel was in no mood for their dithering, however. The Lionheart himself had given her to him as a reward for services done. She'd been a mere girl at the time, and he a hardened warrior well over twice her age, yet their marriage had proved fruitful, durable and loving. She looked heartbroken by her coming loss. She nodded at St Maur to thank him for coming then shooed everyone out ahead of her, leaving the two of them alone. Or not entirely alone, for the son remained by the fire with his head bowed, intent on listening to their conversation, perhaps even on stepping forwards should his father offer too many of his estates in exchange for his immortal soul. But the great man wasn't yet so far gone not to notice. He fixed him with his eye. 'You too,' he said.

'But father I think it best—'

'Out.'

He waited until he was gone and the door was closed behind him, then gestured for St Maur to sit on the embroidered stool by his pillow. There were perfumed candles all around the bed, to mask the smell of his illness and decay. Their fluttery yellow light glittered off the saliva that kept gathering at the corners of his mouth, irritating his sores and threatening to spill down his cheeks. St Maur dabbed them gently dry for him with a linen cloth, knowing how his friend hated the indignities of age almost as much as he hated asking for help.

'It's good to see you,' St Maur told him.

'I had them bring me my shroud. The cloth looks as fresh as ever.'

'Did I not tell you?'

'Do you remember that day? The day I pledged?'

'How could I forget?'

'I think about it all the time. To fight for what one knows is right and holy. Why can't all life be a crusade?'

'All your life *was* a crusade.'

'If only.' He gave a sigh. 'Did you bring everything we need?'

'Of course. You'll be a Templar within the hour.' He hesitated, from fear of sounding too morbid, but then added: 'I've set aside that place in our church for you too.'

'I am glad. I find myself strangely fearful.'

'Whatever for? A man like you, they'll welcome you with trumpets.'

He nodded, but in a distracted way, as if he'd heard what he'd expected rather than needed to hear. His eyes grew glazed and distant, a lookout on the high seas seeking first glimpse of some new land. 'But we have done such things,' he murmured.

'Great things.'

'Terrible things.'

'*Necessary* things,' said St Maur, with extra emphasis, wanting to convince himself as much as anyone, for he too would be setting off on this last dread journey soon enough, and had been suffering these same qualms. 'We saved our land. Look at it now. It heals. It prospers. That was us.'

'Was it?' His old friend was growing visibly tired, his breathing so laboured that he could only manage a few words at a time. 'I have done so much. Far more than even you know. I sought to make things well. But mostly I made them ill.'

St Maur pressed his hand to give him comfort. 'Our good Lord sees your heart, I assure you,' he told him. 'He knows the truth of everything.'

'Yes,' said the great man, turning his face to the wall. 'That is what I fear.'

ONE

A farmhouse, the south Lincolnshire coast

The storm that had been building all afternoon and evening finally arrived in the small hours, waking Anna Warne with the fierce drum of rain against her window, the rattle of loose tiles above her head, the howl of wind and the general groaning of an exposed old house in filthy weather. She turned onto her side and tried to get back to sleep. But it was no use. Because what had really woken her was the sense that something had just gone bang, meaning that she'd left a door or a shutter open somewhere, most likely in the barn. And suddenly Uncle Dun's ghost was at her bedside, his arms folded and his best Mount Rushmore face on. *Wet equipment is rusted equipment*, he'd be saying in that rock-crusher voice of his. *Wet supplies are spoiled supplies.*

Furious with herself, she threw back her duvet, pulled on her dressing gown and slippers, then made a circuit of the house. But everything was securely locked and bolted. The barn, then. Her heart sank, yet there was nothing for it. She fetched the big torch from the kitchen then went to the front door. She undid the top and bottom bolts then opened it carefully on its latch and looked out for a moment before closing it again. Even for this stretch of Lincolnshire coast, tonight's storm was something special, as though the farm was being put through a vast car wash, turning the cobbled courtyard into a virtual lake, unable to drain the water as fast as it arrived.

The wind was so fierce that she was going to have to lock the door behind her, or it would blow open and the hall would flood. She went back upstairs for her keys. Her own wet weather gear was up in York, but Uncle Dun had kept his by the front door. She traded in her dressing gown and slippers for them. His waterproof coat fitted her like a tent. She tightened the hood as best she could then rolled the sleeves up a little way to free her hands. His gumboots were even worse. She had to make fists of her toes and shuffle along rather than walk. But they were still better than nothing. She locked the door on the latch behind her then ducked her head and hurried over to the barn. Its double front doors were closed and padlocked so she set off on a circuit. The door by the old stone trough was properly secured, as too the double doors at its far end. But the one on its far side was indeed hanging open and swinging on the wind. No wonder she'd missed it earlier, for her uncle had kept it permanently bolted back when she'd been living here. She could only think that the police had opened it during their investigation, then had forgotten to—

A glint of torchlight at the barn's far end. Anna froze. Every part of her, that was, save for her heart, which instantly began pumping so much adrenaline through her system that it left her feeling woozy. She turned off her own torch before she could be spotted, and only a bare moment before a tall, thin man dressed all in black and wearing a black balaclava appeared from behind the tractor, a torch in his left hand and rubbing the small of his back with his right, as if sore from stooping.

Sometime last Sunday night, Anna's Uncle Dun had had his skull brutally split open by a mighty blow from an old axe or spade or some other similarly blunt-edged weapon that was yet to be found. His killer or killers had then dug a pit for him where he'd fallen, in the corner of a field beside the farmhouse drive, just three or four hundred yards from here. The police hadn't yet arrested anyone, but all the talk locally and in the media was of a gang of drug traffickers widely believed to use this stretch of coast to—

The man sensed something. He raised his torch and pointed it at the open doorway, catching Anna still framed in it. His beam was powerful enough to make her blink. She put up her forearm to shield her eyes. He said something she couldn't make out and a second man appeared, several inches shorter but twice as wide. He too was dressed all in black, and was wearing a black balaclava.

There was a moment of stillness as they all gazed at one another, then the tall man took a slow step towards her, as though she were a high-strung horse he was trying not to spook. His stealth had the opposite effect. Anna span on her heel and fled for the house, only to be so hampered by her uncle's outsize gumboots and waterproofs that she stumbled and went sprawling before she could quite reach it, scraping her knee on the flooded cobbles, dropping her torch and keys. And, even as she scrambled to retrieve them, the taller of the two men came running around the corner of the barn, the light from his own torch glinting wickedly off the stiletto blade he was holding in his right hand.

TWO

The investigation into Dunstan Warne's murder was being led by Detective Inspector Ben Elias of Lincolnshire Police's Major Crimes Unit. He'd telephoned Anna himself yesterday evening to break the dreadful news. Then he himself had come to collect her from Peterborough Station that morning, when she'd headed down from York in a bereavement fug, to do whatever it was that next of kin were supposed to do in such situations.

He'd been waiting outside the newsagents, as promised, his hands wrapped around a large Starbucks coffee, drawing warmth against the autumnal chill. A touch over six foot tall and built like an athlete, though with the Zorro nose, eyebrow scars and inside-out ears of a boxer. 'Detective Elias?' she'd asked, walking up to him.

'That's me.' He was younger than she'd expected from his voice, somewhere between thirty and thirty-five. He was wearing a long black leather trench coat over a crumpled light-grey wool suit and an open-collared white cotton shirt. His hair was cut down to a fuzz, and his eyes were a very dark brown, while his complexion and cheekbones suggested dashes of Caribbean and maybe even Asian blood.

'Don't bother,' he said, when he saw her puzzling it out. 'You'll never guess. Grandparents from Sweden, Jamaica, Wales and the Philippines, would you believe? Should be able to form a one-man choir with a mix like that, but I open my mouth and the wildlife howls.' He took a final swig of his coffee then tossed the empty into a bin and wiped his palm on his jacket before offering it to shake. His grip was firm, if still a little clammy from the coffee, while his scarred, misshapen fingers strengthened her sense of him as a fighter of some kind. 'Oh, and sorry again for your loss.'

'Thank you.'

'And sorry for breaking the news to you so abruptly last night. Must have come as a terrible shock.'

'Yes. It did.'

He gazed at her intently for a moment or two, then looked her up and down. Anna felt herself turning cold. She hated being stared at in this way. It was why she'd taken to cutting her own hair, and why she didn't wear makeup anymore, and why she dressed in shapeless drab clothes bought second hand from charity shops. 'I thought you weren't married,' he said, nodding at the band on her ring finger.

'It's to keep men away,' she told him.

'Does it work?'

'Not as well as I'd like.'

He allowed himself a smile, then gestured at the black laptop bag over her shoulder. 'That all you bring?'

'I keep a set of everything at the farm.'

'Come down often, do you?'

'Not as often as I should have,' she said, unhappy at having to explain her life to a stranger. 'But Uncle Dun liked me to keep a presence at the farm. I liked it too. It made it feel like home.'

'Sure,' said Elias. 'I can see that.' He gazed at her a few moments longer then turned abruptly and strode out through the automatic doors, walking so briskly that she had to scamper every few paces to keep up. She found herself disliking him more and more. They reached short-term parking. He pressed his key fob. The lights of a tomato-red Nissan Leaf flashed orange. 'Got to do our bit, right?' he said, noticing her mild surprise, for he didn't strike her as an obviously environmentally-conscious type. 'Though it was the wife's choice, to be honest. She was fierce about that stuff.'

'Was?' asked Anna. 'You don't mean…?'

'No. Sorry. Divorce, that's all. She got the house, the kids and the decent ride. I got a bedsit and this piece of junk.' But then he sighed to let the bitterness go and climbed in. He waited for Anna to put on her belt then looked over his shoulder and reversed briskly out of his spot. A photo of two children was taped to his sun visor: a girl and a boy, each about five or six years old, their thumbs up and smiling a touch too brightly at the camera, as though they knew it was goodbye. Elias saw her looking and flipped the visor up. 'So when were you last down?' he asked, as they joined the queue at the station exit.

'A month ago. Maybe five weeks.'

'Stay long?'

'Just one night.' She hesitated again, not wanting to sound disloyal. 'Uncle Dun liked me to *visit*. But he didn't much like me to *stay*. He was a loner. He tended to get jittery after a day or two. So I kept my visits short, if I could.'

'I thought you grew up with him?'

'Not exactly.' She took a deep breath, realising again just how brutal the next few days were going to be. 'Mum got badly sick when I was fifteen. After it became clear how it was going to end, she had to decide what to do with me. She had lots of friends in Manchester, some with kids my own age. But Dun was family, and family is different. They hadn't seen each other for years, but she wrote to him anyway to explain the situation and to say it was her dying wish. So he agreed to take me in, even though I was pretty much his worst nightmare. He was *not* a family man.'

'Wasn't he married once himself?'

'To his childhood sweetheart, yes. But she died during pregnancy when she was still just nineteen. I don't think he ever got over it. Or wanted to.' He and Anna had often visited the local churchyard together, where his wife and unborn daughter were buried. When he'd talked about joining them there one day, he'd sounded almost wistful. 'He had the farm, of course. It took everything he had. Until I got foisted upon him. But he did his best for me, he truly did, considering how poisonous I was.'

'Your mum had just died.'

Tears pricked her eyes, even after all this time. 'I know. But still. Anyway, it took us both a bit of time, but we got there in the end. We grew fond of one another.' Then she added, realising the full truth of it for the first time: 'I loved him.'

They reached the junction with the road, only for the lights to turn against them. 'Seems he loved you too,' said Elias. 'We found his will already. You get the lot.'

'Yes.'

'You knew?'

Anna shrugged. 'When we were out on the farm, he'd sometimes tell me how it would all be mine one day. Anyway, we were each other's only family.'

'What about his in-laws? From his marriage?'

'He'd barely seen them since her funeral. They thought their daughter was too good for him. And it's called Warne Farm for a reason. He'd never have let it go out of the family, not if he had a choice.' Anna hadn't realised it at the time, but she'd come to believe since that this had been another reason why her mother had asked Dun to take her on. She'd always felt cheated out of her stake in the farm, and this had been a way to get it back, if only by proxy.

'So you lived with him until you left school, yes?' asked Elias. 'Then what? University?'

'Nottingham to read history and archaeology. York for my PhD.'

'Why the switch?'

She gave him a look. 'Does it matter?'

'I guess not.' The lights went green. He turned onto the road. 'So how's it going? I hear doctorates can be a bastard.'

'I study medieval history all day then I peel potatoes and chop carrots in a restaurant kitchen every night,' she told him. 'I don't have time for self-pity.' This was the first lie she'd told him. Away from work, all she did these days was lie on her sofa feeling sorry for herself. It had started, for some unaccountable reason, three or four months ago, on returning from the library with a bagful of books, only to be overwhelmed by such a profound sense of pointlessness that she hadn't even been able to look at them, but rather had hidden them beneath a blanket in her cupboard before falling into a slump, paralysed by elusive fears of falling short.

The library had emailed her three weeks later to tell her that their books were due. She'd taken out a different selection instead, only to hide those ones too. And so she'd carried on ever since, unable even to think about her thesis, let alone work on it. It was a dreadful way of life, but she hadn't been able to admit to herself, let alone to Uncle Dun, that she was a kitchen hand now, not an academic.

'You must get the odd evening off.'

'Tonight's my first since I was last down.'

'So how do you get around? You have a car?'

'No. A bike.'

'But you can drive, yeah? You can borrow a car in a pinch?'

Anna turned to gaze at him. 'What are you really asking me, Detective?' she said coldly. 'Are you really asking me whether I borrowed a car last Sunday night to drive down here to murder my uncle for my inheritance?'

Elias put on his indicator and pulled in to the side of the road, bumping wheels up onto the pavement. He popped his belt then turned sideways in his seat, the better to catch every nuance of her reaction. 'Yes,' he said bluntly. 'I am.'

THREE

Small comfort for Anna that she now had compelling evidence of her innocence to show the obnoxious Detective Elias, what with one of her uncle's likely killers racing towards her across the yard. Exoneration would be of little use if he found her already dead. She kicked off the gumboots, therefore, and slipped out of the waterproofs, then snatched up her keyring from the cobbles and splashed barefoot to the front door. The man was almost upon her. One fumble and she'd be done. Thankfully the latchkey was distinctive enough that she found it instantly. She fitted it in, turned it, slipped inside and slammed the door closed a moment before he crashed into it with his shoulder. She cried out as it shuddered, but it held well enough for her to shoot the top and bottom bolts before he could try again.

She hurried through to the sitting room for the phone. She started dialling the emergency services only for the window behind her to explode as a brick was hurled through it to come rolling across the carpet and stop by her feet. She dropped the phone and ran upstairs. She reached her bedroom, closed its door and wedged her chair beneath its handle. She flipped on the lights for just long enough to find her bag. Crunching noises from downstairs as the men trod over broken glass. She turned on her phone. Her hands were trembling wildly. She had to tap in the number with her thumb.

A creak upon the stairs. Then another. The passage lights

came on, laying a thin yellow line beneath her door. A woman answered the phone in a disconcertingly calm voice. She asked which service she required. Anna whispered for the police. Doors opened and closed as the two men came hunting. Her own handle began to turn. She watched in horror as the door opened an inch or so before the chair legs bit into her fitted carpet. One of the men called out to his companion in an incongruously posh voice. The two of them then pushed against the door, forcing the chair back inch by inch.

Anna went to help in its defence, phone clamped between shoulder and ear. A new woman came on, asked the nature of her emergency. 'I need help,' Anna yelled, there being no further point in whispers. 'Two men are breaking into my bedroom right now. They murdered my uncle. Hurry! Hurry!' She shouted out her address even as the door opened wide enough for one of the men to squeeze his hand through, feeling for the chair to pull it aside.

Two years before, while walking back to her flat after a late shift at the Nottingham pub where she'd tended bar, Anna had been abducted by a bank clerk named Harry Kidd who'd been stalking her for months, despite her three separate complaints to the police, who'd done precisely nothing, other than for one of them to use her contact details to ask her out for a drink. She had no memory of the attack itself, for Kidd had coshed her from behind, so that the first she'd known of it had been on waking up with a splitting headache locked inside the boot of a moving car, her ankles and wrists taped together behind her back, with another strip of tape over her mouth to stop her from screaming.

Perversely, this had quite plausibly saved her life, by preventing her from thrashing and yelling and alerting him to her revival. She'd had to think instead. He'd bound her feet and wrists behind her back with a single long strip of tape. She managed to pick up one end of it with a fingernail, after which it had only been a matter of time before she'd pulled it loose enough to free her hands and then her feet, and peel the tape off her mouth too.

One of Anna's duties at the pub had been to host its quiz night. By bizarre good fortune, they'd had a question several weeks earlier about emergency release levers in car boots. She'd looked everywhere for it, had been on the verge of despair when she'd found it beneath a flap of carpet. She'd forced herself to wait until they slowed for a junction. Then she'd pulled it to pop the boot and throw herself out, breaking her left wrist in the fall. To her despair, the road had been empty of other traffic. Kidd had screeched to a halt and reversed back up, his rear lights illuminating the road, and her upon it. She'd jumped a ditch then had fled blindly into some woods, before throwing herself down and hiding for hours beneath a bush while waiting terrified for dawn.

Never again, she'd vowed. *Never again*. As part of her defences, she'd bought herself a chunky keyring fob equipped with both a rape alarm and a razor sharp box-cutter blade. She removed its safety cap and stabbed it down at the man's hand, only for his black leather glove to prove tougher than she'd expected. He snatched back his hand before she could do him any proper damage, then he and his companion hurled themselves so violently at the door that they knocked the chair backwards and sent her sprawling to the carpet, banging her elbows so that she dropped both her key fob and her phone.

The shorter and burlier of the two came in first. He looked terrifying. An Olympic weightlifter, with tree-trunk legs and a barrel chest that pushed his arms out wide, like a gunslinger on the draw. He turned on the light to check that the room was clear of threat, then stepped aside for his companion, tall enough that he had to duck his head slightly beneath the lintel. Beads of rain dripped from his black acrylic sweater and trousers as he walked towards her. They looked brand new, as though he'd bought them specially. He was so gaunt that his balaclava hung slightly baggily on him, giving her a glimpse of sunken cheek. She scrambled back across the carpet until she reached the wall and could go no further. She pushed herself to her feet and looked around. But the weightlifter was blocking the door and the window was painted shut, meaning that her brass Statue of Liberty bedside lamp was her only remaining resource.

She ripped its plug from the wall, tore off its shade. She turned it around in her hands to use its weighted base for hitting with. Her phone was still on. The emergency services woman was shouting that two cars were on their way and would be with her in a minute. Bullshit. The nearest station was eight miles away down twisting country lanes. Ten minutes would be a miracle. She was simply trying to spook these men into leaving. It might even work, too, for the weightlifter tapped his companion on his arm. 'Let's go,' he grunted.

'Not yet,' said the other, in his creepy patrician drawl. He took another step towards her then pointed his torch into her eyes, dazzling her and making her squint. He raised the blade in his other hand for her to see. Not a stiletto after all, but rather a large, flat-tipped screwdriver. He drew circles in the air with it, a wizard with his wand. Her heart pounded like a steam hammer. Her brain buzzed like a maddened hive. She tasted that ugly sharp metal at the back of her mouth, so that for a moment she was back in those woods again, her face pressed into the earth as Harry Kidd walked by. The memory paralysed her for a moment but then it gave her strength. Harry Kidd had meant to rape and kill her. But she was still alive while he was long dead, having hanged himself in his own stairwell to spare himself a trial, after writing her a despicably self-pitying note of apology too.

She took an even firmer grip of her bedside lamp. She drew it back behind her shoulder like a baseball bat.

One swing was all she'd get.

She meant to make the most of it.

FOUR

Many years ago now, before joining the police, Detective Inspector Ben Elias had been an up-and-coming amateur light middleweight boxer with dreams of the big time, more than a little swollen-headed at being the youngest member of the UK & Northern Ireland's podium squad in training for the Olympics at Sheffield's Institute of Sport.

The trials had arrived. He'd been put up against the man who'd ultimately gone on to represent the nation at the Games, where he'd lost a heartbreaker of a semi-final against the Cuban gold medallist. The trial had gone great for a round and a half, with Elias jabbing and moving, bobbing and weaving and all the rest of that good stuff, using his long reach, fast hands and dancing feet to put himself so far ahead on points that he'd got complacent, he'd got cocky. Then the bastard had feinted left and smacked him with a right cross that he simply hadn't seen coming, and from which he'd woken on the mat some twenty seconds later.

He'd rather lost the heart for boxing after that.

The ghost of that wretched day haunted Elias still, every time he screwed up on a case. Which was to say, it haunted him a lot. Yet he didn't resent it. On the contrary, he welcomed it. It helped him work harder and it kept him humble too.

A peacock strutted out into the road ahead, pecking at spillage from a grain truck. He allowed it a few moments before tooting it from his path. A little further on, he had to stop again, this time for a stray lamb bleating miserably for its flock, even though Elias could see them grazing on cauliflowers in the next field. Crates of muddy potatoes and other produce were for sale by the side of the road. Haystacks gleamed golden from last night's storm. The air smelled of rot and rain. It was harvest time in rural Lincolnshire, and how he hated it, particularly on these back roads, constantly getting stuck behind combines, produce trucks and the rest, just as he now came up behind a hedge-cutter spraying twigs and leaves across the narrow lane, forcing him to slow down again, stressed by his lateness though he already was.

Elias worked for Lincolnshire Major Crimes, part of the East Midlands Special Operations Unit. His department was always understaffed, but lately it had become ridiculous, thanks to a combination of holidays, sick leave and an exploding caseload, with the county's villains all deciding to go on a spree. In just one night, they'd had a strangling in Boston, a murder-suicide in Scunthorpe and a fatal bar-fight in Lincoln. Then, to cap it all, a smouldering gang war in Grimsby had burst into violent flame, with a pair of tit for tat killings and the malicious wounding of the heroic young schoolmistress who'd tried to intervene, and who was now on life support.

Enough had been enough. Lincolnshire's Chief Constable had ordered Elias's new boss Trevor Wharton to sort it out. Characteristically, Wharton had made a virtue of necessity, putting on his dress uniform to hold a press conference outside Grimsby Town Hall with the local MP and North Lincolnshire's Mayor. He'd pounded the podium and declared that this was now his personal top priority, vowing to dedicate whatever resources it took to bring the perpetrators to justice and eradicate the scourge of knife crime from the town once and for all.

The hedge-cutter pulled into the side to let Elias pass. He enjoyed a mile or so of clear road before, to his exasperation, he came up behind a tractor hauling a trailer of Halloween pumpkins, shedding mud and stones from its huge wheels that his own tyres spat up against his undercarriage.

No one had yet known it while Wharton was giving his press conference, but Dunstan Warne had already been dead by then, killed – according to their pathologist – in the early hours of Monday morning, then buried in a corner of his own field. It was the kind of case that Wharton would normally have grabbed, what with its sympathetic victim and all the opportunities for holding press conferences and making public appeals; but he'd trapped himself and his top team in Grimsby with his overblown rhetoric, so he'd had to assign it to Elias instead, the only murder detective with any capacity at all, thanks to his being so out of favour.

He'd made a solid rather than a spectacular start, seconding a team of uniformed local officers to search for the murder weapon and go door-to-door for witnesses, none of whom had seen anything themselves, but many of whom had pointed fingers at a smuggling gang widely rumoured to use this stretch of coast to bring in product. It made sense. The shore here was fringed by salt marshes on which even a small boat might founder. Except at Warne Farm, that was, where the marsh was held at bay by the outpouring of fresh water from the River Nene. On a calm night, with a high tide and decent moonlight, a smuggler could bring an inflatable right up to the seawall with minimal chance of being seen.

The tide had been high last Sunday night. The sea had been calm and the sky clear. Perfect conditions for a shipment. And everyone agreed that Dunstan Warne had been a tough old bird, the last kind to tolerate smugglers taking liberties on his patch. So a consensus had emerged that he'd had enough. Maybe he'd sat up that night, or he'd been woken by a noise and decided to go check, setting off in his van to intercept them along his drive, grabbing a spade as a makeshift weapon to go confront them, only for his killer to wrest it from him, turn it sideways and bring it down like an axe upon his head. Then they'd buried him right there in the field, no doubt intending to return his van to the farmyard so that his body wouldn't easily be found, only to realise too late that they'd buried his keys with him. It would likely have been getting light by then, leaving them no choice but to flee, taking the spade with them to dump elsewhere. It had all fitted together very neatly – or at least it had, until their return last night. And how to explain that?

He reached Warne Farm at last, speeding up its long drive in a forlorn effort to make up time. The cobbled courtyard was still a mess from last night's storm, muddy and covered by leaves and other detritus. A pair of squad cars and a blue Scene Of Crime van were already parked by the farmhouse door. He added his Leaf to their number then wiped his feet and went inside. There were muddy bootprints on the carpet, along with yellow evidence markers. He stepped carefully around them. Frank Mason, his Crime Scene Manager, was going about his business at the top of the stairs, along with two assistants. He called up to let them know he'd arrived then made his way through to the kitchen, where a uniformed woman police constable was sitting at the table with a mug of milky coffee, tapping away at her laptop.

'Who are you?' he demanded.

'Who are you?' she retorted, taking off her headphones, jacked into a police recording device.

'Detective Inspector Elias,' he told her, showing her his warrant card.

'Oh.' She half rose to her feet in apology. 'WPC Maria Quinn, sir.'

'Quinn,' frowned Elias. 'You're the one who found Warne's body, aren't you?'

'One of them. Yes, sir.'

'You left before I got here.'

'We do have other duties.'

Elias nodded. It had become his habit, as a detective, to make swift appraisals of people he met. Their height, build, looks, complexion, clothes, hair, ethnicity, accent, tattoos, marital status and the rest, all filed securely away for future retrieval. Quinn looked maybe twenty-six or twenty-seven years old. She had bright red hair and pale freckled skin that made her look a little soft, along with a glint in her eye that invited him to try it and find out. Her uniform was freshly pressed; her shirt neatly ironed. These assessments were automatic and strictly impersonal, yet he still felt a small but undeniable pang when he saw her wedding ring. Not for the first time either. There'd been that new waitress in his favourite Nettleham café, and then Anna Warne at Peterborough Station. Anna Warne, for Christ's sake, her uncle just murdered and herself a suspect. She'd noticed too, and had given him an old-fashioned glare, provoking him into needless hostility. And now Maria Quinn gave him an equally disapproving look. 'So last night,' he said hurriedly. 'Any trace of the intruders when you arrived?'

'I didn't get here first,' she said. 'That was Anderson.'

'And? Where is he? She?'

'Gone home. His shift was over and he had to get his girl to school. But no, they'd already gone. He saw a vehicle speeding off, but it was too far away to make out, and he decided that getting here came first. Making sure Ms Warne was okay.'

'Quite right,' he said. 'Speaking of whom...?'

'Gone for a walk.'

'A walk? Are you kidding me?'

'She was badly shaken,' said Quinn. 'And she'd already given her statement.' She patted her recording device. 'I thought you'd want it typed.'

'Don't we have voice-to-text for that?'

'The software's rubbish. I'm making the edits now.'

Elias grunted. He was still wound up from his drive, but that was no excuse for taking it out on Quinn. Yet somehow he couldn't bring himself to apologise. 'Did she say where she was going?'

Quinn nodded at the kitchen door. 'I asked her to stay

within earshot.'

'Oh. Okay. Good. Well done.'

'Thank you, sir. But before you go…?'

'Yes?'

'I helped find Mr Warne's body, like you said. It was easy. His van was parked right there.'

'Yes,' said Elias dryly. 'I have read the report.'

'Sorry. It's just they're saying you think he was maybe sitting up in wait for them, or that he was woken by a noise of some kind.'

Elias checked his watch. 'Can this wait? Only I really need to speak with Ms Warne while everything's still fresh.'

Quinn flushed. 'Of course, sir. My apologies.'

He headed out the kitchen door. It was a grey, chill, damp morning, not quite sure yet whether to mist or rain. Everything was wet. The small back lawn was enclosed by flower beds and a low hedge beyond which the farm ran flat and open to the grassed embankment of the River Nene as it made its way down to the Wash, at which point it turned ninety degrees to the left and became a seawall instead. Despite the gloom, therefore, he spotted Anna Warne at once, standing in the gap between two fields, her head bowed as if in contemplation. He set off briskly towards her, his black brogues soon glistening from the dew on the grassy verge, littered with shrivelled corncobs left behind by the recent harvest. 'Hey,' he said, when he was still a dozen yards away, to warn her of his approach.

She looked up, pale yet composed. 'Detective.'

'I hear you had quite the night.'

'Still think I murdered my uncle?'

'I never thought it was you. But it's my job to make sure. Want to tell me what happened?'

'I already told your colleague.'

'She's still writing it up. And I'd much rather hear it from you. Please.'

'Fine,' she sighed.

He bowed his head in concentration as she described how she'd been woken by a loud noise and had gone out to check the barn, only to spot two men on the far side of the tractor who'd chased her into her bedroom and broken down its door. 'And then?' he asked.

'The shorter guy wanted to leave. But the taller guy was in charge, and he wasn't having it. He walked up to me, holding a large flat-headed screwdriver and a torch.'

'Which was in which hand?'

She closed her eyes for a moment. 'The screwdriver was in his right hand. Why? Does that make him right-handed?'

'Maybe. Go on.'

'I grabbed my bedside lamp to defend myself. I braced to hit him with it. He stayed just out of range. He was going to stab me, though, I'm sure of it. It was the way he tensed up as he tried to pick his spot. But then he kind of froze. His mouth fell open. I saw his teeth.'

'Anything distinctive?'

Again she paused for thought. 'He maybe had a gold filling. Back here.' She touched her lower left molar. 'But I wouldn't swear to it. And there was something weird about his lips, though don't ask me what.'

'Thin? Fat? Light? Dark?'

'What does "don't ask me what" mean where you come from?'

Elias had to fight not to smile. She made little effort to hide what she thought of him, yet he couldn't help but like her. 'You say he froze. Any idea why?'

'I'd already called you guys by then. Your dispatcher, god bless her, was saying that two cars would be with me in less than a minute. Maybe he believed her.' But then she shook her head. 'Except that wasn't the sense I got. It was more like he'd just got a shock.'

'As if he'd recognised you?'

'Maybe. Though I didn't recognise him.'

'How would you have, if he was wearing a balaclava?'

'He was very distinctively built. And I saw enough of his face that I think I'd have known if I'd met him before. Anyway, his mate tugged his arm again, and this time they left. I heard them on the stairs then driving off. I've no idea what in; I was too scared to look. I locked myself in the bathroom instead, until your man arrived.'

'You did brilliantly.'

'It doesn't feel like it. It feels like shit.'

'You're alive. That's a big win. You've no idea how much paperwork it's saved me.' Her laugh was short and reluctant, yet still good to hear. 'Any chance you'd recognise them again? From photos, say?'

'Not from photos, no. Maybe if I met them.'

'Ethnicity?'

'Both white, I'd say, though I wouldn't swear to it. The shorter one was maybe five foot eight or nine. But big, you know? Olympic weightlifter big, with a ridiculous chest and neck, and massive short limbs. The other guy, the boss, he was around six feet two or three, I'd say. He ducked his head coming into my bedroom, so you could use that as a guide. And he was really thin too. I mean cadaverously so. He made me think of that old Nosferatu movie. And not just in the way he looked.'

'How do you mean?'

'The smaller guy, he frightened me. But in a normal way. I was terrified he'd hurt or even kill me. But the taller one, he gave me the horror movie shivers. There was something just creepy and repellent about him. I can't describe it better than that.'

'Did they have accents?'

'They only said a few words each.' She closed her eyes again. 'But I think the shorter one may have been foreign.'

'What kind of foreign?'

'He said about two words, Detective, while his mate was about to stab me with a screwdriver. He may have been foreign is the best you'll get.'

'And the other?'

'Kind of plummy. But hammily so, like he was putting it on. They both might have been, to be honest.'

'Ages?'

'The taller guy, I'd say about fifty. He rubbed his back in the barn, like it was sore from stooping. The other one, maybe late thirties. But I could be way out.'

'Anything else?'

'About them? No. Sorry.'

'Not just about them. About anything.'

She took a breath. 'There is one thing. Maybe. Though probably not. I honestly don't know how to judge any more.'

'Tell me anyway. Let me do the judging.'

'Okay. It's just, Uncle Dun used to do a round of the farm every evening. To make sure everything was as it should be, you know. Shipshape. I'd go with him whenever I was here. It was a nice way to end the day. So, after you guys left last night, I did the same. Not to make sure it was shipshape, exactly, but...'

'To do him honour.'

'Yes. Exactly.' For the first time, she looked at him with something approaching warmth. He found that he liked it. 'Anyway, I came this way. See these footprints? I don't think they were here last night.'

He crouched for a better look. The two fields were separated from one another by a hedge and a drainage ditch half filled with water. But there was a gap in both the hedge and the ditch at this point, for tractors and other farm vehicles to pass between the two. It was a churned-up mess right now, thanks to the recent harvest and last night's rain, yet he could see two distinct pairs of bootprints in the mud, treading back and forth over one another as though searching for something. At first glance, they looked similar to the bootprints on the farmhouse carpet too. He took out his phone to photograph them. 'You didn't see these last night?' he asked. 'Or they weren't here?'

'I don't know. Not for sure. They might have been here, I

suppose. Though the ground was drier before the storm, so I doubt it would have taken them so well. And they'd be more washed out, wouldn't they?'

Elias circled around their other side to take more pictures. Then he stood back up. 'You're right,' he said. 'It's probably nothing. But thanks for telling me. You never know what will matter and what won't.' He put his phone back in his pocket. 'Now how about we get back to the house, eh? I'd kill for a cup of tea.'

FIVE

It was called Warne Farm, and had been ever since a local landowner by the name of Albert Warne had built it for his family home upon his marriage to Emilia Crowston, a young widow with two children. That had been back in 1826, according to the plaque above its front door, and Warnes had lived here ever since. Every so often, since learning of her uncle's death, Anna would realise that not only did it now belong to her, but that she – in some obscure way – also belonged to it.

She didn't know why she'd become obsessed with history. These things just happened. But if forced to give a reason, she might have said that history gave her a sense of her place in the world that her own upbringing had failed to provide. Her father was probably Australian. That was all she knew. Not because Mum had held out on her, but because it was all she'd known herself. They'd hooked up in a Norwich bar one Friday night a bit over twenty-five years ago. He'd made her laugh with his stories about life in Sydney and as a backpacker. They'd spent a riotous weekend together in a friend's apartment until he'd popped out on the Sunday afternoon for a pack of smokes, never to be seen again. And the address and phone number he'd given her had turned out to be duds, so who could say for sure that the rest hadn't been bullshit too?

On learning she was pregnant, Mum had arranged for an abortion. But a dream about her daughter's graduation had led to a change of heart. Mum had told Anna the story regularly, as if to make her feel special. In fact, it had merely made the world freeze for a moment or two, thinking how close she'd come.

Mum's parents had been dismayed by her decision. The farm was hard enough work already, without having a single mother and her baby to look after too. But Mum had dug her heels in. Discussion had turned to arguments and then to fights. Old resentments had resurfaced. They'd yelled increasingly unforgivable things at each other until, one morning, Mum had simply packed her bag and caught a coach to Manchester to crash on a friend's sofa.

It hadn't been easy, heavily pregnant and virtually penniless as she'd been, but she'd made a fist of it. She'd become a nurse, which she'd loved and been extremely good at. The family rift, however, had never healed – not least because both her parents had died before time could do its usual trick, her mother taken by the family curse of breast cancer and her father following a few days later, swimming far out into the Wash on his morning dip then not even trying to make it back.

The double loss had left Uncle Dun as the sole owner of the farm. By an odd coincidence, he'd been deeply interested in history too, though of places rather than of people. *This* place in particular. The Fens, the Wash, the junction of Lincolnshire, Norfolk and Cambridgeshire. In those rare quiet moments when there'd been little to do on the farm, he'd taken Anna on exhausting long walks up the coast and inland along ancient footpaths, explaining how villages had got their names, why rivers took their particular course, why some crops prospered while others failed, why certain surnames dominated particular graveyards.

Warne was one such name, with over two dozen stones in the local churchyard, including both her grandparents as well as Uncle Dun's poor young wife and unborn daughter. It had given Anna a sense of being knitted into the fabric of the place, a sense that she owed a kind of duty to it, and to all the Warnes before her – a duty that for example precluded her from leaving the sitting room window broken and exposed to the next storm, whenever it should arrive. The trouble was, she had no money. Her student debt was terrifying and her kitchen work was miserably paid. She lived from week to week, skimping on heat, on food, on clothes. Her train ticket down from York had already taken a chomp out of her emergency fund. She couldn't afford a glazier. But nor could she leave it as it was.

She plucked the remaining shards of broken glass from the frame then measured it up and went into her uncle's workshop. He'd carried out all his own repairs, so it was very well equipped. She clamped a sheet of ¼ inch plywood to the worktable then marked it out in soft pencil. She put on safety gloves and goggles, plugged in the handsaw and was about to start on it when her uncle's ghost reappeared over her shoulder with his arms folded. *Measure twice*, he told her sternly. *Cut once*. She sighed and took her tape-measure back out. 'See,' she retorted, when she came back in. 'I was right.' But it was he who'd been right, and she knew it.

She cut the plywood down to size, sanded off its edges and carried it out, then went back for a hammer and a box of nails. She tried to pin the plywood in place with her forearm while holding a nail between her fingers, only for it to keep slipping slightly, forcing her to start over.

'Need a hand?'

She rested the plywood sheet down on the cobbles and looked around. A tall, broad-shouldered, fair-headed man in his early thirties was standing in front of a white BMW 4 Series convertible with a black soft-top. She'd heard his car coming up the drive but had assumed it was just more police. He didn't look like police, though. His face was vaguely familiar, in fact, as if she'd known him long ago, though she couldn't say from where. Handsome without being beautiful, but making the most of what nature had provided with good clothes, a cheerful smile, kindly bright blue eyes and straw-coloured hair highlighted by blonde flecks, artfully arranged to make it look like it hadn't been arranged at all. 'I'm fine, thanks,' she told him, before realising that she very obviously wasn't. 'Though actually…'

'Of course,' he said, stepping forward. 'Tell me how you want me. Do I hammer or do I hold?'

'Hold, please.'

He took the board without another word, pressed it firmly against the frame until she'd hammered in enough nails on either side to keep it set. 'Thanks,' she said. 'That was great. But who exactly are you?'

He glanced curiously at her, as though he suspected his leg was being pulled. 'My name's Oliver Merchant.'

'Oh Christ,' she said, embarrassed. 'Of course. I knew I recognised you. But what are you doing here?'

His puzzled look deepened. 'Interviewing Mr Warne for a documentary. Hasn't he said?'

'A documentary? My uncle?'

'On King John and his lost crown jewels. He wrote a book on them, you know.'

Anna nodded. Yes, she did know. Her name wasn't on its jacket, but it might easily have been, for it had come out of the many, many talks they'd had together on their long walks around the county. It was a fascinating story, rooted in the collapse of the Magna Carta accord between King John and his rebel barons, and the civil war that had ensued.

The two sides had been evenly matched, so that each had cast around desperately for allies. John had won the backing of Pope Innocent III with promises of crusade, while the barons had recruited the French dauphin and a fair-sized army. Wary of taking them on in open battle, John had criss-crossed the country, emptying his castles not just of coin to pay his troops, but of his crown jewels too, and all his other treasure. In autumn 1216, he'd helped relieve a siege of Lincoln's strategically important castle, then he'd headed south to King's Lynn, some ten miles east of here.

Lynn, as it had been known at the time, had been one of the few towns left where John had still been popular, having recently granted it its charter. Its leading citizens had duly thrown a banquet in his honour at which he'd so overindulged that it had brought on the dysentery that had ultimately killed him. Before that had taken hold, however, word had arrived that Lincoln Castle was under siege once more, and needed relief. So John set off back north, though making a detour inland to Wisbech to arrange for the transport north of certain supplies.

His army had been large. Some two thousand mounted knights, and twice that number on foot, all needing food and drink and wages, along with tents to sleep in, weapons and armour to fight with, and the raw materials to mend them and make more. Then there'd been the supporting cast of smiths, farriers, cooks, servants, stewards, surgeons, advisors, whores and all the rest. It had been harvest time, what was more, so that they'd have needed stores to last them deep into winter, including cartloads of grain, barrels of Norfolk apples, pork salted in Lynn's famous pans and locally-caught fish pickled in brine.

The resultant baggage train would have been a good two miles long, lumbering slowly over the churned up autumn tracks, prey to broken cartwheels and lame horses. Hauling it all down to Wisbech and then back north again would have added a full day to the march, if not more. And Lincoln Castle couldn't wait. So John had taken the fateful decision to split his forces, taking most of his soldiers with him but sending his baggage train with a modest escort on a more direct route back across the muddy estuary of the Wash, to meet up again on the other side.

But it had all gone terribly wrong.

Two contemporary chroniclers, Ralph of Coggeshall and Roger of Wendover, described what happened next, varying a little in detail but not in essence. Despite being led by experienced local guides at low tide, the baggage train and its precious cargo of crown jewels, treasure and supplies had got bogged down halfway across, only to be caught by the inrushing tide or maybe even a freak wave. It had overrun them all, sucking them down into the vast bed of silt that underlay this whole region, so that, when the tide had gone back out again, not a single trace of them had remained, or had been found since. More to the point, all this had supposedly happened within spitting distance of, or perhaps even directly beneath, Warne Farm.

SIX

In the farmhouse courtyard, Oliver Merchant was still gazing quizzically at Anna, waiting for her to explain what was going on. She found an appropriately solemn expression before she did so. 'I'm afraid I have some terrible news,' she told him. 'About my uncle.'

He stared at her a moment. Then he looked around at all the police vehicles in the yard, only now taking in their full significance. 'Oh hell,' he said. 'I assumed it was just a burglary.'

'No. I'm afraid not. This was something else.'

'Then… when? How?'

'Last Sunday night. I'm surprised you haven't heard. It's been all over the news.'

'I've been away,' he said. 'I've been in Wales.'

'Did you know him well?' frowned Anna, for he looked too shaken to be a stranger.

'No. No. Hardly at all.' He pulled himself together. 'I spent an afternoon with him a month or so back, that's all. And we've spoken several times since on the phone. I mean we spoke just last weekend. He wanted to know what time I'd be getting here today.' There was a plaintiveness in his voice, as if this had to be some kind of grotesque mistake. 'But he was the heart of my programme. How the hell am I going to…' He stopped and held up a hand, realising how inappropriate his lament must sound in the face of her loss. 'Forgive me,' he said. 'It's just, this is my first big solo project. I've got a *lot* riding on it.' He took his phone from his pocket. 'Would you excuse me a moment? I've got a crew coming in the morning. I need to let them know.'

'Of course.' She watched him wander off across the courtyard, then banged in a final few nails before stepping back to assess her handiwork. Not perfect, but it would do. She returned the hammer and nails to the workshop then came back out to see Elias approaching up the farmhouse drive holding a long thin metal stake. She was about to go ask him what he was up to when he caught sight of Oliver and his face darkened. 'No media,' he said, marching up to him.

'I'm not media,' replied Oliver, finishing his call. 'At least, not in the sense you mean. I had an appointment with Mr Warne is all.'

'An appointment?' said Elias. He touched fingers to his temple, as if at bad news. 'Oh hell. You're O.M., aren't you?'

'I'm sorry?'

'Mr Warne had meetings with an O.M. marked in his diary for this afternoon and tomorrow morning. You?'

Oliver nodded. 'I was to interview him for a documentary on the last days of King John.'

'The Magna Carta guy?' asked Elias, throwing a bewildered glance at Anna.

Anna pursed her lips. It always irked her how Magna Carta was so indelibly associated with King John. The man hadn't been involved in its negotiation, he'd never intended to honour it, and he'd reneged on it within weeks, plunging the country back into civil war. It actually felt personal to her, for her stalled thesis was on a man called William Marshal, who – along with his best friend Aymeric de St Maur, head of the Templars in England – had negotiated it on John's behalf. Yet Marshal's contribution was forever being overlooked, even though he was one of the more remarkable figures of English history, not only a courageous warrior, a tournament champion and a paragon of chivalry, but also skilled at navigating the treacherous waters of the Plantagenet court, loyally serving five consecutive kings despite them all having been at each others' throats.

More to the point, however, it had been Marshal who'd reissued Magna Carta after King John's death, while serving as regent to John's nine-year-old son Henry III, in an effort to reunite the kingdom. And it had been Marshal's version, rather than John's, that had survived and been built upon. But Elias didn't look in the mood for a history lesson, so she said simply: 'A few days before he died, John lost his crown jewels and a ton of other treasure somewhere very near to here. My uncle wrote a book on it.'

Elias nodded and turned back to Oliver. 'And you were meant to be interviewing him about it?'

'Yes.'

'May I ask where you were last Sunday night?'

Oliver squinted at him, not sure whether to laugh or be alarmed. 'Is that when it happened? Am I a suspect?'

'You're in good company,' Anna assured him. 'He accused me yesterday of killing him for the inheritance.'

'Well?' asked Elias, unabashed. 'Where were you?'

'Christ. Is this still about your wife?'

'It's about the murder of Dunstan Warne,' said Elias tightly. 'Why won't you answer my question? Do you have something to hide?'

Oliver shook his head. 'Have it your way. I've been in Ludlow since last Friday, working on a script about King Arthur and Excalibur. You can check with the woman whose apartment I rented. I ate in the local pub every evening, including last Sunday night. It's called the White Swan. And I interviewed Professor Alun Thomas of Cardiff University in Caerleon first thing on Monday morning. Give me your address, I'll email you all their contact details.'

'Thank you. I'd appreciate that.' He handed him a card from his wallet. 'But right now I need for you to leave.' He turned to Anna. 'You too, for that matter.'

'Me?' protested Anna.

'Yes. You.'

'This is my home. You can't just kick me out.'

'Two men broke in last night,' said Elias. 'Maybe it was to do with your uncle's murder. Maybe not. But this is now all part of the crime scene, until I can work out which.'

'But where will I go?'

'I'm sure there are hotels,' said Elias. 'Or I could have you taken back to the train station.'

'You arse,' she said, for she had appointments arranged with her uncle's solicitor and undertakers, as well as the registrar, and she couldn't keep shuttling back and forth to York. But neither could she afford hotels, not for more than a night or two.

'I'm booked in next door,' murmured Oliver. 'I could see if they have any free rooms.'

Anna nodded. The property directly to their north was a hotel. The King John Hotel, no less. Her uncle had loathed the owners, so she'd never normally have considered it. But the situation was exceptional. 'Please,' she said.

He called them for her, handed her his phone. She turned her back to ask how much, for it was the kind of boutique place that could sandbag you with their prices. But it was off-season, thankfully, and just within her range, so she took it and told them she'd be over shortly.

'Fancy a lift?' asked Oliver.

'If you can give me five minutes? I need to pack.'

'Of course,' he said. 'Take as long as you like.'

Elias was still there when she went back down, glowering at Oliver as he played solitaire on his phone. The bad blood between the two couldn't have been more obvious. She stowed her bags then they set off up the drive, passing on their way the corner of the field where her uncle had been found buried. A white privacy tent had been erected over it when she'd arrived yesterday morning, and the field had been swarming with police, but both the tent and the police had now gone, leaving the site merely staked off instead. One of the metal prongs they'd used for this was missing, however, so that the blue-and-white police tape was fluttering freely in the breeze. That was when she remembered the metal stake Elias had been carrying. He must have taken it from here, for some reason.

'Is that where...?' murmured Oliver, when he noticed her staring.

'Yes,' said Anna.

Uncle Dun's van had been parked on the short strip of grass into the field when their postman had made his round early on Monday morning. Having delivered Uncle Dun's mail for nearly ten years, he'd known his habits well, and he'd never seen the van left out overnight like that before. It had been so unusual that he'd gone back on his way home to make sure everything was okay. The van had still been there, and there'd been no sign of Uncle Dun, so he'd knocked on the farmhouse door. When no one had answered, he'd taken a second look at the van. It itself had been locked, but there'd been a low mound nearby, in the otherwise neatly-tilled field, and a few spatters of what had looked enough like blood for him to call the police, who'd found her uncle's body almost at once in his shallow grave. But, save for his van being parked right there, and a conscientious postman, it was entirely possible that no one would even know yet that he was missing.

SEVEN

Elias tapped the metal stake against the side of his shoe as he watched the white BMW soft-top head up the drive. He tried not to hate, but Merchant made it hard. The car turned onto the lane and vanished from view. When he was certain that it was gone for good, he went into the barn to look for something to protect his knees. The best he could find was a roll of black bags, so he tore one off then made his way back to the gap between the fields where Anna had spotted the bootprints.

On evenings when the loneliness grew too acute for him to bear, Elias would head down to his local for a bit of banter and a few jars of something numbing. Then, on his return, he'd typically hate-watch some American police procedural or other, yelling drunkenly at all the sophisticated equipment they had at their disposal, and which he and his colleagues so conspicuously did not. There'd been an episode a few weeks back in which a cold case detective had used a state-of-the-art probe to test soil for the ninhydrin-reactive nitrogen released by rotting mammalian flesh. A cold case detective, for crying out loud! They had nothing like that in Lincolnshire. They'd once owned a pair of cadaver dogs, it was true, but they'd sold them off in the last round of cuts, and had to hire them back when needed, which was expensive and time consuming. These days, if you suspected human remains might be buried on a certain plot of land – in the gap between two fields, say –

what you did instead was you worked a long thin metal stake as deep into the ground as you could get it. Then you pulled it out again and put your nose to the hole, to see what you could smell.

The ground was muddy on the surface, yet it was hard beneath. It took a lot of effort for Elias to force his stake even a foot deep. He spread out the black bag then knelt upon it before pulling the stake back out and sniffing the hole. Nothing. But he didn't give up. Last night's two intruders had spent at least several minutes searching out here. In such filthy weather, they must have had a very good reason for doing so. From the moment Anna Warne had drawn his attention to their bootprints, Elias had had an uneasy suspicion as to what that reason was. Dunstan Warne had been found buried in the corner of a different field, after all, so who could say for sure that his was the only body?

He moved a couple of steps to his left then forced in his prong a second time, leaning his full weight upon it, feeling the burn where it cut into his palm. Still nothing. But on his third go he gagged and jerked away his head at the cheesy stench released. He stood and walked off a little way to spit it from his mouth, nauseous not just from the smell itself but from recognition of what it was. Butyric acid, no question, a product of decomposition that started around three weeks after death, and lasted for months.

Yes. Something – or surely more likely someone – had been buried here.

EIGHT

León Alessandro de Bruin was standing in the shallow end of his indoor swimming pool, teaching his beloved daughter Melanie how to swim, when Andrei Lubov, his driver bodyguard, called to let him know that he'd collected Ronan Calder as instructed and would be at Fenton Airfield in around thirty minutes; and also that he'd spoken to their pilot Victor Unwin, who'd confirmed that the Twin Otter would be ready and waiting.

'Who was that, Daddy?' asked Melanie, splashing towards him in her orange water wings, her chin held high above the water.

'No one that matters, my precious,' he told her, with a distracted smile. 'But I think that's enough for today, don't you?'

Out came her lower lip. She'd have stamped her foot if not for the four feet of water beneath her. 'You promised!'

'I'm afraid Daddy has business to attend to,' he told her. '*Important* business.'

'Don't care. You promised!'

'Work comes first, my love. How else will I afford that pony you've been pestering me for?'

'Sell one of your cars.'

'What was that?' he demanded, looking at her in mock disbelief. 'What did you just say?' He made his way through the water towards her, roaring and waggling his fingers like he was some kind of monster, making her shriek with terrified delight. It amazed him still, the pangs of paternal love that could overwhelm him at such moments. He'd never felt anything remotely like them before, nor had he even thought himself capable. He caught her and hoisted her over his shoulder, her water wings scratching his cheek and back as he waded to the steps and out. He grabbed both their towels then carried her still screeching joyfully through to the kitchen, pummelling his back with her tiny fists. He set her down on the white cushioned wicker sofa while his wife Samantha quietly seethed, like a pan arriving at the boil. 'I just had those dry-cleaned,' she said.

'It's only water,' he said.

'The chlorine stains the cloth.'

'The chlorine stains the cloth,' he mimicked. She glared at him. Husbands and wives! Husbands and wives! They'd met at Ascot's Ladies Day several years before, after his horse had pipped hers to the Norfolk Stakes. Her beauty, youth and aristocratic manner had got beneath his skin, the way she'd looked down her nose at him during the presentations, then had pointedly turned her back. He'd spent the next three months mooning around London after her, making an idiot of himself. He hadn't cared. Everything else had become utterly flavourless to him – even striking deals and making money. What was the point of wealth, after all, without a beautiful and demanding woman to spend it on?

He'd been euphoric when finally he'd persuaded her to take tea with him at the Ritz. He'd spent hours in Hatton Garden showrooms before that first date, stretching out the purchase of an absurdly expensive diamond bracelet because it was his one point of contact with her. Yet she'd only sneered when he'd given it to her, and tossed it in her bag. That sneer had lived with him for weeks. He'd never wanted her so fiercely, nor thought so highly of her.

His testosterone fug had lasted another three years. It had even survived their getting married. All she'd ever had to do was put on a slutty dress and press herself up against some stranger at a party and it would drive him crazy all over again. But then had come pregnancy and childbirth, and – for all that he doted on their daughter – he'd never once felt that glorious madness since.

A consignment of fresh apples had arrived from the orchard. He chose a D'Arcy Spice. Ugly as sin, yet with an addictive nutmeg tang. He polished it with a cloth then took a bite, savouring the juices as they washed around his mouth. 'I have to go out for a bit,' he said.

'What for?' asked his wife.

'Business.'

'*Important* business,' corrected Melanie.

'That's right, my little angel,' said de Bruin, scruffing up her hair. '*Important* business.' He went upstairs to change into an Anderson & Sheppard charcoal suit and a blood red tie, then tucked a cream silk handkerchief into his breast pocket. One needed to look good when meeting the staff. Then he headed down to the garages where he kept the cars his daughter would have him trade in for her pony. Her cheek made him smile. He couldn't help it. Entitlement in other children was repulsive, but some particular quality in Melanie made it charming. He ignored his wife's white Tesla Model Y, his silver Aston Martin DB5, his black Ford Discovery and his flame-red Lamborghini Huracan, electing to take instead his Rolls Royce Silver Shadow. Because sometimes you needed to show people who was boss.

The airfield was a ten minute drive. He parked inside the middle hangar then got out to explain exactly what he intended to his pilot. Andrei arrived with Ronan Calder a few minutes later in another of de Bruin's fleet, a gold Mercedes S-Class. 'I thought we weren't supposed to meet,' fumed Calder, getting out of the back.

'That was while you and your friends were under surveillance,' said de Bruin patiently. 'It's been called off.'

'And you're sure about that, are you?' asked Calder. 'There

was a van across the road all morning.'

De Bruin sighed. 'You persist in believing that I got where I am by some unaccountable stroke of good fortune. Haven't you seen enough yet to correct that view?'

'Even so,' said Calder. He was pompous, overweight and balding, and looked the best part of a decade older than his thirty-eight years. 'Sending your... your *goon* in to my place of business. Humiliating me in front of my staff. Who the hell do you think I am?'

De Bruin smiled thinly at him. 'That's what we're here to find out.'

NINE

Some two thousand years ago, this whole south Lincolnshire coast had been a vast area of low-lying land, overrun twice each day by inrushing tides fierce enough to knock a person off their feet. Even when the sea had been out, it had still been awash with water from the countless streams and rivers that disgorged into the Wash, bringing with them such enormous quantities of silt that it had only needed reclamation and drainage to become some of England's most fertile land.

The Romans had been the first to set about this work. An embankment on the other side of the River Nene was actually still called Roman Bank, and Roman coins had been discovered in its vicinity. Those initial works had been repaired and enhanced during the eleventh century, with more embankments being built in stages over the centuries since, pushing the sea ever further back, penning the rivers into their modern courses, and meaning that the perilous route that King John's baggage train had once taken across the Wash was now productive farmland rather than open estuary.

A vast network of ditches and dykes had meanwhile been dug, to give the rain somewhere to run off to after storms as fierce as last night's, to be pumped out into the rivers or the sea, or to be released through sluice gates at low tide. One such ditch ran between Warne Farm and the King John Hotel, its northern neighbour, all the way from the sea up to the lane behind. The hotel was still easy enough to reach along the seawall. You could even hike directly across the fields – though that meant fighting through a hawthorn hedge as well as jumping the ditch. Yet, thanks to the perverse layout of the local roads, it still took several minutes in the BMW, especially once Oliver and Anna got stuck behind a tractor hauling a huge haystack on its flatbed trailer, scattering straw like rustic confetti. With no hope of overtaking on this narrow lane, Oliver sighed and dropped back, using their reduced pace to dart puzzled glances at Anna, until finally he just shook his head. 'I have to ask,' he said. 'Have we met?'

'You don't remember?' smiled Anna. 'How very insulting.'

He shook his head, annoyed with himself. 'I'm usually good with faces. I need to be, for my job. It's just, I meet so many people.'

'Don't beat yourself up. It was years ago, and only for an afternoon.'

'How about a clue?'

'Bolingbroke Castle. There was an excavation there.'

'Bolingbroke?' frowned Oliver. 'That was the mosaic, yes? But I don't remember you, and I think I would. There was this spiky old bird who seemed furious that I was there at all, and a guy with such a terrible twitch that we had to cut him out.'

'Yes. But you only interviewed them after asking me. I pointed out that you should probably talk to someone who knew what they were doing, rather than a first year undergraduate. You assured me that knowledge was massively overrated, then suggested we have lunch together to discuss what I should say.'

'Oh hell!' he said. 'That was you?' But he seemed amused rather than embarrassed. 'In my defence, though, you should have seen yourself that day, with your face all flushed from digging. Every man there was gagging to ask you out, believe me. I just had the balls.'

'*That*?' mocked Anna. '*That's* your defence?'

'Sure, why not?' He reached across her for his glove

compartment, where he kept a multipack of extra strong mints. He took out a new tube then flipped one up for himself, popped it in his mouth. 'Got to keep the species going, right?'

'And to think I almost believed you about it being a working lunch.'

'Yeah, well. A useful lesson then. Never believe a word I say. Anyway, you spanked me pretty hard, as I recall. Couldn't sit for a week.'

Anna laughed. He'd had the kind of cocksure charm that her vanished father had apparently had, and which she'd therefore disapproved of on principle, yet couldn't help enjoying in practice. Perhaps that was why she'd rejected his offer of lunch so sharply, retorting that she was already working on one antiquity, thanks, and didn't need another. Everyone had fallen about laughing, if only from the look on his face, as though he'd walked into a wall. Then she'd done it again, when they'd all gone out for a drink afterwards, and he'd grumbled about how he kept butt-dialling people even though his phone was locked and in his back pocket; and she'd suggested sweetly that maybe facial recognition was to blame. 'Did I really?' she said diplomatically, deciding to pretend forgetfulness. 'How awful. I'm sorry.'

'Apology accepted. Slate wiped.' He flipped up another mint with his thumb, held it out to her. 'Peace offering,' he said. 'I mean you never know when you're going to be glad of having minty fresh breath.'

'Wow. You don't give up easily, do you?'

'No. Why? Do you?'

Anna took the mint and crunched it between her teeth, washing its delicious sharp sweet flavours around her mouth before swallowing it away. 'So you and Elias,' she said. 'What was all that about?'

'What was all what about?'

'Come on. You looked fit to kill each other.'

'He looked fit to kill me, you mean.'

'If you like. I still want to know.'

Oliver sighed. 'It's not a pretty story. I don't come out of it very well.'

'Thank god I was already sitting down,' said Anna. 'But you owe me more than that.'

'Fine,' he said. 'Then he blames me for wrecking his career and his marriage.'

'Jesus. And did you?'

'Yes,' said Oliver gloomily. 'I rather think I did.'

TEN

Elias stood in the gap between the fields and gazed down at the ground beneath his feet. His duty was clear enough. He needed to alert Frank Mason to the possibility of human remains being buried here so that he and his team could get to work at once. But the remains were at least several weeks old, which reduced the urgency; and while Mason was a fine Crime Scene Manager, he was also a protégé of Trevor Wharton, assigned this case in part to keep an eye on Elias and report back. Report this back and Wharton would likely use it as an excuse to abandon his thankless Grimsby knife hunt and take over here instead.

That would have been okay with Elias if Wharton had been a good detective. Unfortunately, he was barely a detective at all. His investigation technique was to hold numerous press conferences at which he'd list all the resources he was committing while hinting gnomically at promising leads. Then he'd sit back and hope that something turned up for which he could take the credit.

Elias wasn't having that. He was invested in this case now. He meant to solve it.

He returned to the farmhouse for a glass of water to wash away the lingering taste of butyric acid. WPC Quinn was still at the kitchen table, gabbing away with PC Rodgers and the Scene of Crime team. Mason toasted Elias rather sheepishly with his mug. 'They never came anywhere near here,' he said, to excuse himself. 'And Ms Warne said we were to help ourselves to anything we wanted. So we thought a coffee for the road...'

'For the road?'

'Another stabbing, would you believe? In Grantham, this time. Wharton said to call him if you had a problem.'

Elias gave a grunt. Wharton knew he'd never call. And it suited him just fine. 'Anything I should know?'

'It'll be in my report,' said Mason. 'But basically no. No fingerprints, no hairs, no DNA. Only those bootprints.'

'Any idea what they were looking for?'

'We searched the barn pretty thoroughly,' volunteered one of Mason's team. 'Maybe they'd already found it.'

'Yeah,' said Elias. 'Maybe they had.' He waited for them to rinse out their mugs and leave, then turned to Quinn. 'You finished Anna Warne's statement yet?'

'Check your email,' she said.

'Great. Then thanks for everything. I'll call if I need anything else.'

'We can go?' she frowned. 'All of us?'

'All of you,' he said. 'Though not a word about last night, please. Can't be having a media circus. And if you could arrange for a car at the top of the drive...?'

Her puzzled look cleared. She suspected what he was up to. A sharp one, that. Worth keeping an eye on. 'Yes, sir,' she said. 'I'll see to it myself.'

He waited for her to leave, ran himself a glass of water. The cheesy taste still lingered, however, if only in his mind, so he put on the kettle and checked the biscuit tin. A pair of custard creams had somehow survived the general carnage. He took them out with his coffee. The barn was a cavernous tall affair with creosoted slat walls, a pitched roof of terracotta tiles and double doors at either end, large enough for the tractor, which was parked alongside the ditch digger.

Two ploughs, a harrow, a seeder, a front-loader and various other attachments were lined up against the walls, as were a pair of rakes, a wide-headed stiff-bristled broom and several sacks of fertiliser up on wooden pallets. The brick floor was rutted from decades of wear and tear, and covered by the pebbles of dried mud that got everywhere at this time of year, and which would have made it a nightmare to search for anything small.

No way had those two intruders found what they'd been looking for. If they had, they'd have left before Anna Warne could have spotted them. So then. What was it? And what had made it worth taking such a crazy risk for? Perhaps it had some great personal or intrinsic value. More likely, though, it was incriminating in some way.

Elias had enough respect for Mason and his team to know that they'd have found it had it been lying openly on the floor. But equally those men must have had good reason for looking in the places they had. He had a good idea now why they'd been out in the fields, which offered a clue as to why they'd searched in here too. Because every crime had been committed before. A few years on the force taught you that. And this particular crime, he strongly suspected, had been committed half an hour's drive south of here, on the Norfolk side of the Great Ouse – though surely elsewhere too.

He finished his second custard cream, set down his empty mug and walked over to the side door at which Anna Warne had been standing when she'd been spotted by the two intruders. Then he paced out the distance to the other side of the tractor. A little over ten yards. In bad light and with uncertain footing, it would have taken a man in reasonable condition at most two or three seconds to cross. If they'd set off at once, and Anna had been as badly hampered by her gumboots and waterproofs as she'd said, falling in the courtyard and dropping her torch and keys, then they should have caught her easily before she got inside the house. The implication, therefore, was that they *hadn't* set off at once. They'd attended to something else first.

Elias meant to find out what.

ELEVEN

The tractor lumbered on ahead, spewing out exhaust smoke of a thickness and colour that normally announced a new pope. Anna gazed at Oliver in consternation. 'You wrecked Elias's career and his marriage?'

'Can we not talk about something else, please?' begged Oliver.

'He's investigating my uncle's murder. So no.'

'Oh god. Okay.' He took a breath then bit his teeth together. 'So I guess it started about two or three years ago now. Your mate's boss at the time was a guy called Colin Vaughn. Very highly rated, liked by everyone, and pretty much a shoo-in to run Lincolnshire's Special Operations Unit when the old Chief Constable retired and everyone moved up a notch. So anyway I was working at the time on a story about this biker gang suspected of running much of Lincolnshire's drug trade. I got tipped off to a country pub where a lot of deals apparently went down, so we set up there for some undercover filming. With me so far?'

'It's hardly *War and Peace*.'

'This is still only chapter one, to be fair.'

The tractor turned finally into a field, only to reveal why it had been going quite so slowly, for a pair of novice cyclists were wobbling all over the road ahead, forcing Oliver to slow straight back down again, scowling impatiently.

'You were telling me about Elias's boss,' prompted Anna.

'Yes. Okay. So there we were, in this pub, and guess who shows up on our second night?'

'This guy Vaughn, I assume?'

'Yeah. He was out for dinner with his wife and another couple, so it all looked kosher enough. Only he went to the loos at the same time as one of the bikers. Then it happened again. You can hardly lock him up for that, right? But it made him worth checking out. Especially as there'd been rumours for years of some kind of mole inside Lincolnshire Police. Anyway, the harder we looked, the worse it got. He was forever popping in and out of bookies, for one thing. Not huge bets, but enough to make it clear he had a problem. Plus he'd been at school with a member of this gang. I filmed the two of them conferring together in the park one afternoon. Nothing definitive, but enough to mention it to my boss when he asked me for an update, and for him to pass on to our Chairman, who happened to be golfing buddies with the Chief Constable. Anyway, it's a week or so later. News suddenly breaks that Vaughn's house has been searched and ten grand in used notes has been found beneath his floorboards, along with a baggie of cocaine. So it's handcuffs time for Mr Vaughn.'

'Quite right too,' said Anna.

'He claimed in his trial that he'd been investigating this gang on the quiet precisely because there was a mole. He claimed that they must have realised this and so had set him up. The jury didn't buy it, not least because of the evidence we were able to give the prosecution. The night of his conviction, we went large on the story. Our part in bringing down the bent cop. Then we all went out to the pub to celebrate. We'd already sunk a few when your mate comes steaming in. Marches up to our table and accuses me flat out of having framed an innocent man. And you know that thing that sometimes happens, when you're chuffed with yourself over whatever, only to realise you've screwed up instead?'

'God, yes,' said Anna.

'It was his anger that got to me. It was too righteous to

be fake. So of course I got defensive. I said maybe he was only mad because he'd been on the take too. He invited me outside to discuss it further. I bottled it. Honest to god, the one time in my life. And not because I was scared, exactly. My heart just wasn't in it. It isn't, somehow, when you fear you're in the wrong.'

'No.'

'Though I was a bit scared, to be fair. The bastard did box for England.'

Anna glanced at him in surprise. 'He did?'

'Come on. You don't end up looking like a blue-period Picasso from too many frames of snooker. Anyway, word got out about our confrontation. Policemen can't treat members of the public like that, at least not in front of a table full of journalists. I didn't press charges, of course, but it still shredded his prospects. He was enough of an embarrassment to Lincolnshire police that they tried to get him to transfer out, but he dug his heels in. Fair enough. This is where his kids are.'

'And his marriage? You wrecked that too?'

'Oh god. This makes me look even worse, if possible. So it's maybe a fortnight later. I'm in the supermarket, doing the weekly.' They reached at last the turning for the hotel, headed down its gravelled drive to the fork into its car park, pulled up in an empty bay. 'This woman comes up to me. Happens all the time when you're on TV. You nod along to the nice things they say, thank them for watching, maybe pose for a selfie. Sometimes they'll hit on you too. I'm usually pretty careful about that. Lincoln's a small town, and I've already got a bit of a reputation, for some unaccountable reason. But this woman is sexy as hell, and she's giving me the works. Fluttery big eyelashes, top buttons undone, pressing her chest against my arm. What can I tell you? I'm a bloke. A nice bit of cleavage and my brain turns to mush.'

'Ah. Don't tell me. Mrs Elias.'

'As it turns out, yes. Not that I knew it at the time. She'd taken off her ring and she introduced herself by her maiden name. But obviously she knew who I was, and about my bust-up with her husband. Everyone did. It had been all over the local papers. She was just getting her own back on him.'

'What for?'

Oliver grimaced. 'I want to be clear about this. I didn't even know she was married to him at the time, let alone that they had kids.'

Anna nodded. 'A girl and a boy.'

'That's the thing. There used to be *two* boys. Their eldest fell into the swimming pool while Elias was supposed to be watching him.'

'Oh hell,' said Anna.

'Yeah. And this was soon enough afterwards that everything was still raw. Anyway, I didn't learn that until much later. That afternoon, we went back to my place. We had fun. Enough that she took to visiting once or twice a week. She'd get her hair done and wear some sexy new outfit. It was pretty obvious in retrospect that she wanted him to find out. He is a detective, after all. Anyway, she got her wish. I walked her down to her car one afternoon only to find him waiting. There was quite the blow-up, as you can imagine. And he blamed me rather than her, accusing me of picking her up in revenge for him coming into my local that night and showing me up in front of my crew.'

'You didn't tell him the truth?'

'Never had the chance, to be honest,' said Oliver. 'Anyway, my hands were hardly clean, were they? I knew something was up. There was such sadness in her. I was just enjoying myself too much to find out why. Plus frankly I was worried for her. You should have seen how angry he was. Better all round if he blamed me. Broken marriages are brutal enough already, especially on the kids.'

'How noble of you.'

'Yeah, sure. I'm a saint.'

A tall, thin, fifty-something blonde woman in a swirling blue skirt and a battered green Barbour jacket came striding by at that moment, before vanishing into the hotel. 'Penny Scott,' murmured Anna. 'She and her husband own this place.'

'Is she the town gossip, by any chance?'

'What makes you say that?'

'Come on,' he said. 'Anna Warne books herself a room and she comes straight over. Ten gets you twenty she asks about the latest from the farm.'

'Ten gets me twenty?' scoffed Anna, popping her seatbelt. 'Ten gets me a hundred, and maybe we can deal.'

TWELVE

When León de Bruin had bought Fenton Airfield out of bankruptcy, it had been for its large plot of prime Lincolnshire land, perfect for a new housing development. True, it hadn't yet been rezoned, but he was a patient, connected and wealthy man, confident of getting that changed. As it had happened, however, the business had owned several other assets, including a pair of light aircraft: a Piper Cherokee for training new pilots, and a Twin Otter for skydiving and parachute jumping. Being the kind of man who liked to squeeze a lemon to its last drop of juice, and ever keen on new experiences, de Bruin had hired the airfield's former owner – an ex-RAF flight lieutenant named Victor Unwin – both to be his pilot and to teach him how to fly. He'd loved it from the start, circling proudly around his Tudor mansion and estate, buzzing low over Welbourn and Leadenham to repay the residents there for their endless complaints about his redevelopment plans, or circling the county to admire his housing empire and whet his appetite for more.

He typically took the Piper Cherokee, in which he'd learned to fly. But today he needed the extra space of the Twin Otter. Its original cabin seating had been stripped out and replaced by benches along either side, and its door had been permanently removed too, creating an open hatchway behind its starboard wing. A sturdy long steel platform step had been fitted beneath this hatchway for nervous parachutists to inch out onto, clinging grimly to the wing strut as they built themselves up to jump. But it also served as a step to help people climb aboard, as de Bruin did now before offering Ronan Calder a hand. But Calder brushed it irritably aside and made his own way up, before frowning in puzzlement at the block of broken masonry at the rear of the cabin. 'What's that for?' he asked.

'Ballast,' explained de Bruin. 'For when we don't have a full load.'

Andrei joined them aboard. They buckled themselves in while Victor taxied out of the hangar and to the end of the runway. They turned for take-off. Their propellers roared. They jolted along the pitted old concrete until they reached take-off speed, then lifted sharply up over the trees and banked into a turn before levelling off and heading east.

Last night's storm had largely cleared the sky of cloud, giving them a good view of the patchwork fields beneath. They quickly neared the coast. Boston appeared through the open hatchway. De Bruin tapped Calder on the arm to draw his attention to it. 'Looks so pretty from up here, doesn't it?' he said, having almost to shout to make himself heard. 'Clean. Attractive. Historic even. A lovely church, a fine market. You'd think people would be able to build good lives for themselves there, wouldn't you? Yet the way my tenants moan! A dribble of water through their ceiling, it's like they're living beneath Niagara Falls. Their boiler won't start. Put on an extra jersey, for goodness sake. And am I really supposed to go sponge mould off their walls myself?'

'People have forgotten how to do for themselves,' said Calder.

'You are exactly right, Mr Calder,' agreed de Bruin. 'You are *exactly* right. People have forgotten how to do for themselves. You and me, we're out of place in this modern age. We have *expectations*. We have *standards*. Isn't that so?'

Calder glanced at Andrei, sitting on his other side, his arms folded and gazing stolidly ahead. He'd been head of security for a dissident Russian oligarch when de Bruin had first met him, at one of his mother-in-law's London bashes. He'd been struck not just by his extraordinary physique but by the coldness he'd radiated, like walking into an industrial freezer. When his boss had fallen, jumped or been thrown from his Park Lane penthouse balcony a few months later, de Bruin had checked to make sure that Andrei hadn't been at fault, then he'd hired him to replace his previous bodyguard; because veterans of Russia's Special Forces, to put it bluntly, were rarely afflicted by the kind of qualms that sometimes hobbled ex-members of the SAS.

'I'd like to think so,' said Calder.

'Good. I'm glad. One of my expectations – you may think this is excessively pernickety of me, but it's how I am, so it's probably best you know – one of my expectations is that my employees don't try to fuck me up the arse while telling me it's a suppository.'

'But I didn't—'

'I'm speaking, Mr Calder.'

'Sorry. Sorry. I just—'

'I'm speaking,' he said again. He waited for Calder to fall quiet and drop his eyes. Then he continued. 'As I said, one of my expectations is that my employees don't try to fuck me up the arse. I don't care whether they do this deliberately or through negligence, or because they have to take their son to the hospital. The bit I object to is the being fucked up the arse. Is that unreasonable of me, would you say?'

'They couldn't get an ambulance to us in time. Ask anyone. The service has fallen apart.'

'It's a disgrace,' agreed de Bruin. 'But it's no excuse for turning your phone off.'

'That was the hospital. They made us.'

'You're not listening, Mr Calder,' said de Bruin. 'I don't care *why*. I care *what*. The reason I keep you around is to serve as a conduit between the legitimate and the illegitimate parts of my organisation. That's how a shitty little struck-off accountant like you has made himself rich. Your one job is to keep that conduit open, or at least to notify me that it might fail so that I can make arrangements, should I – to pluck an example at random – happen to get advance notice of a raid, and need to get word out. Instead I got screwed.'

'I was the one got screwed,' said Calder. 'It was me they arrested, remember? I'm the one on bail.'

'And I'm the one who has to undo the damage and foot the bill,' said de Bruin. 'Do you know how much the drugs they seized were worth? Or are you offering to reimburse me?'

'I'm sorry,' said Calder. 'Truly. But what could I do? My son couldn't breathe. He literally couldn't breathe. Check with the hospital if you don't believe me. It messes with your head when your kid can't breathe. Did I panic? Yes. Of course I did. It's what parents do. Imagine if it had been your Melanie who —'

'Don't bring my daughter into this.'

'I'm just saying, I only did what you'd have—'

'I'm warning you.'

Calder took a long breath. 'You're right. I'm sorry. That was wrong of me. I won't let you down again. You have my word.'

'That was what you told me last time we spoke,' said de Bruin. 'Yet something else went wrong last night. And what I need to know is, was that an accident, or was it deliberate?' He leaned forward to give Andrei the nod, and Andrei took a stun gun from his pocket and pressed it crackling to Calder's throat, making him twist and scream and convulse for several seconds before finally slumping unconscious, held in place only by his belt.

THIRTEEN

Elias couldn't help but notice – and be impressed by – how old all the equipment in the barn was, kept alive by Dunstan Warne long after anyone else would have given it up for dead. Only the bunded fuel tank appeared new, made from toughened green plastic and positioned near the barn wall between the tractor and the ditch digger. It thus looked by far the most promising place for Elias to start his search.

He unscrewed its fat plastic refill cap and peered inside. It looked to be less than a third full, and it smelled pungently of diesel, just as it should. He crouched down to examine the bottom of the tank. It didn't sit directly on the brick floor, but rather on a base of the same toughened green plastic. He examined its casing more closely. There were two hairline joins at the end nearest the ditch digger, the more accessible of which was scratched and scuffed up, just as if it had been prised open by a flat-headed screwdriver. He felt a flicker of irritation that Mason and his team had missed it, even though he'd never have spotted it himself unless he'd actively been looking.

He fetched a pair of latex gloves and a torch from his car, then a flat-headed screwdriver from Warne's workshop. He rested his torch on the floor, angled to give himself light, then leaned his phone against the wall to film. He forced the tip of the screwdriver into the hairline join then levered it up. The whole front section of the casing came away, revealing a pair of steel rails inside, and well oiled castors, and a pair of catches locking it all in place. He flipped these up then went around the other side of the tank and put his shoulder to it. It budged, if only a fraction. He heaved again and it came more easily. He pushed it maybe two feet until it jolted to a stop, revealing a kind of manhole cover in the floor.

He lifted this by its canvas strap, releasing a whiff of stale ammonia. It proved to be heavier and bulkier than he'd expected, made from a pair of steel disks either side of a fat layer of soundproofing foam, all held together by half a dozen steel rods. To his dismay, as he laid it down, he noticed some bloodied scratch marks on its underside, as might have been left by someone trying to claw their way out.

He did his best to put this image from his mind, then knelt beside the shaft to point down his torch. Metal rungs in the wall led down to a vault maybe seven feet square, with a cement floor and breeze block walls. There was clearly no way this could have been put in without a man like Dunstan Warne knowing. No way. He'd obviously been involved somehow. Elias felt a little sad for Anna, that her memories of her uncle were about to be so tarnished, but mostly what he felt was satisfaction that his hunch had paid off.

He lay on his front and reached his phone as far down inside as he could, to photograph the walls and floor. Then he put everything back as he'd found it. He took his laptop into the kitchen and transferred his photos onto it, to study them on its bigger screen. There were numerous elliptical stains on the vault walls, in the characteristic pattern of blood spatter, even though someone had clearly tried to scrub them off. There was graffiti too, most of which had been reduced by cleaning agent and elbow grease to an indecipherable blur; but several lines had been carved into one of the walls with a knife instead, and though someone had tried to scratch these out, he could still make out a list of Arabic names and a date.

Elias felt agitated suddenly. He stood up to pace around

the kitchen. That date, some six weeks ago, was inscribed into his memory almost as deeply as into the wall, for it had been one of the more humiliating of his career. He'd arrived at Lincolnshire Police's Nettleham HQ at his usual early time to find it already buzzing. Serious and Organised Crime – the companion unit to his own Major Crimes – had just carried out multiple dawn raids on the Lincolnshire biker gang that his old boss and mentor Colin Vaughn had been jailed for leaking information to. And because they hadn't fully trusted him, they'd deliberately kept him in the dark about it.

The raids had proved a disappointment, even so. They'd caught a good number of the bikers still in their beds, and had found considerable stashes of cash and drugs. But they'd hoped to recover far more, and their top targets had all been away, seemingly tipped off at the last minute. And what did it mean, if anything, that on the very day that the gang had either been in custody or in hiding, someone had carved names into the wall, like a memorial?

Elias sat back down again. Failure to notify Scene of Crime now would get him into serious grief if it were ever found out. Yet the few extra hours they'd gain by starting tonight wouldn't make much difference. It would, however, surely bring Trevor Wharton here, to call one of his trademark press conferences and so let last night's intruders know their vault had been discovered. That was the last thing Elias wanted. He wanted them believing all was still well. That way, with any luck, they might even risk another visit. If so, he intended to be here waiting.

FOURTEEN

Fifteen years or so ago, long before Anna had first arrived in this part of the world, the King John Hotel had been a working farm and equestrian centre run by a formidable woman called Helen Roth, who Uncle Dun had liked and much admired. But her children had had no interest in running it after her death, so they'd sold it to Gregory and Penny Scott, an investment banker and PR executive looking to downshift from their London lives.

The Scotts had duly leased the fields to one of the farming conglomerates who managed much of the land around here, while converting the barn into a home for themselves, screened off behind a line of trees. Then they'd turned the house and stables into a boutique hotel that had done excellent business over the years, thanks to its timbered charm and well-tended gardens, its all-weather tennis courts and swimming pool.

Uncle Dun had taken against the Scotts from the start, as much for their high-handed ways as for the noise and disruption they'd caused. But his initial irritation would no doubt have passed had they and their guests not treated Warne Farm as an extension of their own property, clomping across his fields and treading down his crops until in exasperation he'd planted a hawthorn hedge alongside the drainage ditch.

Anna had naturally sided with her uncle in all this, to the extent that she'd never even set foot in the hotel before, despite it being the only place within miles for a drink or a bite to eat. Yet in truth she had nothing personal against the Scotts themselves. Whenever they bumped into each other, at the shops or out on walks, they treated each other with a kind of reserved cordiality. But there was nothing reserved about the way Penny reacted when she saw Anna arrive in reception. She cried out and hurried over to hug her and kiss her on both cheeks. 'My poor dear!' she said. 'Your lovely uncle! I'm so *terribly* sorry. We're all *devastated*. Devastated and *heart*broken.'

'Thank you,' said Anna.

'Priya tells me you'll be staying here tonight.' She gestured at her receptionist, a plump, forty-something Indian woman with a sweet smile and ropes of long black hair done up in an elaborate knot. 'I told her you're to have our best free room. Our *very* best. As our guest, of course. Our *honoured* guest. We wouldn't *dream* of charging you a thing.'

'That's so kind,' said Anna, taken aback.

'Nonsense. Nonsense. What are neighbours for, if not for times like these?' She put her hand on Anna's arm. 'You must be *shattered*, absolutely *shattered*.' Her teeth were amazingly white, like from a toothpaste commercial. 'I mean they're saying that *something else* happened last night. They're saying there was a *break in*. By the same monsters who murdered your poor uncle.'

'They don't know that. Not for sure.'

'But there was a break in?'

'Yes.'

'I knew it! I knew it!' She turned away a moment and closed her eyes in what looked so like relief that Anna and Oliver exchanged puzzled glances. 'Sirens blaring at that *ridiculous* hour, waking the *entire* neighbourhood.' Her habit of stressing so many words meant that she barely stressed them at all. 'Not that I *needed* waking, of course, not with all these dreadful smugglers running loose. But you must have *been* there at the time! You *poor* thing! How *ghastly* for you! How *terrifying!*'

'It wasn't much fun,' admitted Anna. 'But I'm really not supposed to talk about it.'

'Of course. Of course. Then I'll leave you in Priya's capable hands. But if there's *anything* we can do… *anything at all*. I remember from when my own dear father passed how *gruelling* it can be. All that paperwork and bureaucracy when you only want to curl up and cry. And the farm too. I can't imagine you'll want *that* headache. You're far too young and pretty for such a life. You'd not believe the sheer *drudgery* involved! It never stops. You'd be well out of it, believe me.'

Ah, thought Anna. *So that was it.* The Scotts had done very nicely out of this place, and were forever on the hunt for new projects. 'I did live here for nearly three years,' she pointed out. 'I do have some idea of what's involved.'

'Yes. Yes. Of course. But the world moves on. Farming too. It's such a *battle* to keep ones head above water these days, especially after all these bad harvests. Even your poor uncle was having second thoughts.'

Anna frowned. 'Uncle Dun? Second thoughts?'

Penny nodded vigorously. 'He came to see us a month or so ago. He was *terribly* down. All that work for such little return. I know he loved the life, but small farms simply can't compete with the conglomerates anymore. It's crazy even trying. But he *hated* the thought of selling to them. It felt too like defeat. So he wondered if we'd be interested in a field or two. Of course we would! He was our neighbour! Anything to help.'

'How kind,' said Anna doubtfully.

There was a basket on the counter filled with brochures and pamphlets touting local attractions. Anna and Oliver browsed idly through them once Penny had left and Priya was checking them in. A stack of photocopied leaflets beside the basket bore the hotel's address and contact details, breakfast times, Wi-Fi password and the code for the front door, locked after eleven. A crude, hand-drawn map on its back showed the seawall, the local roads and the hotel grounds, with her uncle's farm marked clearly as out of bounds. His complaints had finally paid off, it seemed. It also offered a short list of items for rent, including bicycles, field glasses, metal detectors, even a dinghy. 'Fancy going for a sail?' asked Oliver, when she showed it to him.

'Sorry. Way too much to do.'

'Probably wise. My navigation skills, we'd likely end up in Belgium.'

Priya completed their check-in and opened the hotel guest book to its ribboned page for them to sign. Then, with another of her charming smiles, she selected two keys from the rack behind her and came around the desk to show them to their rooms.

FIFTEEN

León de Bruin squatted down by the Twin Otter's open hatchway, the better to savour Ronan Calder's expression as he recovered from his stun gunning. He was so groggy that it took him several seconds to realise his predicament, lying on his side on the platform step behind and beneath the aircraft's starboard wing, his arms and legs taped to the block of masonry he'd remarked on earlier, hugging it to his belly like he was a contestant on the World's Strongest Man trying to heave an Atlas stone up onto its stand. And the only thing stopping him from falling from the platform step into the sea below was Andrei holding onto his jacket collar – another source of amusement for de Bruin, as it happened, for Andrei's one weakness was his very palpable discomfort with heights.

'What's going on?' slurred Calder, sounding more confused than terrified.

They were low enough by now for de Bruin to taste the salt upon his lips and see the Twin Otter's black shadow rippling over the roiled grey water. Away to their south, he could make out the pursed mouth of the River Nene and the white dot of Warne Farm, scene of last night's fiasco. He could picture it now, Anna Warne scrambling away across her bedroom carpet before getting back to her feet and picking up her bedside lamp, her baggy white cotton T-shirt clinging and translucent from the rain, the outline of her breasts and nipples, her dark brown hair wet and bedraggled, and a look of such imperious contempt in her eye! Just like that, he'd been thirteen again. Thirteen, and in love for the first time. Her name had been Carmen Trent. She'd been in his year at school, pretty rather than obviously beautiful, a bright-eyed English rose, all vitality and flushed skin. A little plump, maybe, but savvy enough to turn that into the kind of feminine curves that had reduced him to blushing imbecility. Moderate in her use of make-up, and her silky long hair so well brushed that it had taken on an almost hypnotic swishing quality whenever he'd sat behind her in class and she'd turned her head.

Most of all, though, she'd been *kind*.

De Bruin had been an ugly child, weedy of build, with bad skin, protruding ears and crooked teeth. He'd been hopeless at games, slow to learn and with an unfortunate habit of saying exactly the wrong thing when trying to fit in. His bullying had been incessant. Perhaps it had only been because Carmen had lived a couple of doors down, and their mothers had been friends, but she'd been the one person at school ever to treat him with decency, or to stand up for him against his small army of tormentors. For that alone, he'd have worshipped her. But it hadn't been for that alone.

His body had been changing in the most confusing ways. He'd had endless fantasies of wrestling Carmen to the ground, their bodies hotly pressed, their cheeks and mouths. Walking home together after being dropped off by the school bus one afternoon, a violent summer squall had set them sprinting for shelter beneath the old oak at the foot of their street. Her cheap white cotton blouse had been drenched to a pearly translucence, clinging beguilingly to her skin, while dribbles of rain had trickled down inside her collar, causing her to undo her top buttons to brush it away. Still panting from their dash for cover, she'd put her hands on her knees to recover.

Her blouse had fallen open from the throat. Her young breasts had swung free inside her bra for a few heart-stopping moments. The shape and colour of them, the way they swelled and then sank again with each breath, the chilled rose bumps of her nipples, all framed by her frazzled long dark hair. He'd never seen anything remotely as erotic, either before or since. He'd suffered the inevitable teenage reaction. Terrified she'd notice, he'd tried to adjust himself before she looked up, only to draw attention to it instead, so that she'd caught him with his hand down his trousers, and had given him a look of such utter revulsion that it had stamped itself deep into his psyche, so that he'd never quite been able to lose himself completely to a woman since, however beautiful, unless she had about her that same sense of contempt and loathing.

An English rose with bedraggled hair in clinging wet white cotton regarding him with horror and disgust. No wonder he'd frozen last night in Anna Warne's bedroom. No wonder she'd become lodged like a splinter in his mind ever since. And, like a splinter, the harder he tried to squeeze her out, the harder he found it to think of anything else. 'Do you know where I went yesterday evening, Mr Calder?' he asked, gesturing south across the Wash.

Calder shook his head, bewildered. 'Warne Farm?' he hazarded.

'Correct, Mr Calder. Warne Farm. And do you know why?'

'You never told me. I'd have gone there myself if you'd said what for.'

'Forgive me,' said de Bruin. 'I expressed myself poorly. I didn't mean: *Why* did I go there? I meant: Why did I go there *last night*?'

'Oh. Because the police had left. Because it was empty.'

'Not exactly, no. Not because it was empty, but *because you told me* it was empty.'

'Oh Christ,' said Calder. He closed his eyes and tried to calm himself with a series of short fast breaths. 'I never actually said it was empty, if you recall. I only ever said that the lights were off and all the cars had left.'

'A little late to be revising your story now, isn't it?'

'I'm not revising it. I just—'

'I asked you if there was anyone there,' said de Bruin. 'You told me no. You told me they'd all left.'

'I meant the cars,' said Calder, in desperation. 'I mean we don't have cameras everywhere. Only on the roof and in the barn and covering the drive.'

'The time to tell me that would have been yesterday, don't you think?'

'I did, I did. I swear to god, I thought I did.'

'No,' grunted Andrei. 'You said there was no one there.'

'Oh Christ,' said Calder again, risking another glance down at the sea beneath, the white spume reaching up for him like the hands of drowned sailors. 'Please. Please. I beg you. My boy. He's sick. He needs me. His mum can't do it alone.'

'You know my policy, Mr Calder. I've always made it clear. My employees are allowed one honest mistake. I'll always forgive one honest mistake. I'm not a monster. But you've now made two. Two *serious* mistakes. Two *costly* mistakes. Two mistakes, moreover, that might almost have been designed to do me harm.'

'No. No. Never.'

'And I should just believe you, should I?'

'It's the truth. I swear it is.'

'I'm sorry,' said de Bruin. 'I don't buy it anymore.' And he gestured at Andrei to push him to his death.

'Please,' wept Calder. 'I beg you. I don't want to die. I'll do anything. Anything.'

De Bruin frowned as if undecided. Not that he was. Calder didn't have the balls to betray him deliberately, and he still had value, both as his link to the bikers and as a fall guy to toss to the police should the need arise. But he'd been careless twice now, and so he needed to be reminded of his place in the world. 'Anything?' he asked.

'Anything,' vowed Calder.

'Good,' said de Bruin. He gestured for Andrei to haul him back inside the cabin. 'I'll be holding you to that.'

SIXTEEN

A robin redbreast was trilling away in the trees as Penny Scott trudged back to her home. It was a fight song, or so she'd been told by an elderly birdwatcher who'd once stayed at the hotel, designed to warn rivals off their patch; yet Penny couldn't help but hear a certain euphoria in it too, perhaps because she herself was so buzzing that, without the crunch of gravel beneath her feet, she might have thought herself floating.

Life had been a nightmare since word had broken of Dunstan Warne's murder. Now, thank god, it was over.

It was still early, yet she'd surely earned herself a tipple. Her hands trembled as she uncapped a fresh bottle of Chardonnay and poured herself a glass, then fell still as she knocked it back. That intoxicating perfume. That delicious chill. Was there anything quite like it? She refilled her glass then took it through to the sitting room where her husband Gregory was as she'd left him, seated lumpen in his armchair, checking his portfolio on his laptop. He'd happily spend all day at it when the market was hot, explaining at tedious length why he'd chosen some particular stock over another. But a crash soon shut him up.

'It *was* our Anna Warne,' she told him.

'Ah,' he said.

'And those sirens last night *were* at the farm. Intruders.' She took another sip of her wine, now warmed enough to taste the strawberry that her merchant had told her of. 'The same ones who killed poor Dunstan.'

This time he did look up. 'She told you that?'

'Who else could it have been?'

'Yes. I suppose.'

'Is that all you have to say?'

He sighed and set down his laptop. 'What else would you like me to say, sweetheart? Then I'll say it and we can move on.'

It was his attitude that did it. She'd have bitten her tongue otherwise. But she wanted him to know the stress she'd been living under. 'Don't treat me like a fool,' she said.

'What are you talking about?'

'I'm talking about how you went out that damned night.'

'Out?' he said, feigning bewilderment. 'You're imagining things.'

'I heard you on the stairs.'

'Come on, my love. You know how this place creaks.'

'Stop it!' she cried, her fears returning in a rush. 'I *won't* be lied to. I *won't*.'

'I'm not lying,' he insisted, though his sudden pallor said otherwise. 'I assure you.'

'I heard you on the stairs and then the door opened and those damned intruder lights came on. I *saw* you. I actually *saw* you. You were going towards the shed with that wretched metal detector on your shoulder. Then you woke me again when you came back in. I heard you on the stairs. You were over there *exactly* when it happened! You *must* have been!'

'That was a different night,' he said desperately. 'That was the night before.'

'Stop it!' she cried. 'Don't lie to me. I'll tell the police, I swear I will.'

His face had drained completely of colour by now. He looked fit to collapse. 'Okay,' he said, dropping his voice to a whisper. 'Yes, you're right, I did go out. But not to that field, I swear it on my life. I'd already checked that field. I was down by the seawall instead. I didn't see or hear a thing.'

'How could you not?'

'It's a big farm. It was a dark night.'

'Have you told the police?'

'Told them what? If I knew anything, I'd have gone to them already, I swear I would. But I didn't. All it would do is put us both in the spotlight.'

'Both!' she exclaimed. 'What do you mean, both?'

'We discussed me going to check his fields. You were all for it.'

'Only to see if they were worth buying. Not for *that*.'

'And I didn't do *that*. It was the intruders. The ones who broke into Warne Farm again last night. Or have you forgotten them already?'

'Oh,' said Penny, as some measure of relief returned. 'Yes. Them.'

'Yes, them,' agreed Gregory. 'Because they're the ones who killed him. So please, please, please, not another word on the matter. Let's never talk of it again.'

SEVENTEEN

The pine rocking chair in the corner of Warne Farm's kitchen looked so old and worn that it might almost have been there as long as the house had. Elias lowered himself carefully into it, to make sure it would hold, then closed his eyes as he pushed himself gently back and forth, enjoying its rhythmic creaking as he contemplated what he now knew.

The vault beneath the oil tank had surely been used for the smuggling of both people and drugs. Dunstan Warne must have known about it, making him at least partially complicit. Last night's intruders had also known about it, as well as about the likely human remains out in the fields. They'd likely lost something at one or other of the sites, and so had come looking for it last night. It was hard to imagine them taking such a risk unless it was highly incriminating. They hadn't found it, or they'd have left before being spotted by Anna Warne. So maybe they hadn't lost it here at all, or maybe it had been ploughed into a field and was effectively gone for good.

It was also possible, however, that Dunstan Warne had found it himself and – realising that it gave him some kind of hold over these people – had hidden it somewhere safe. Elias had already had the farmhouse searched, of course. But Warne had been killed several hundred yards away, while this place had been securely locked, so they hadn't expected much. And maybe they'd been looking for the wrong things.

He stopped his rocking and pushed himself to his feet. Warne's study was the obvious place to start, a long, thin room made even thinner by the two filing cabinets and the leather armchair set against the right hand wall, and by the fitted bookshelves against the left. A battered walnut desk stood in front of a sash window with its heavy floral curtains half closed. There were books on the floor all around it, while its top was covered by a mess of pamphlets, maps, old excavation reports and correspondence, presumably in preparation for his interview with Oliver Merchant.

He checked its drawers. A plain white envelope in the bottom right contained a ticket stub for a London musical along with a hotel receipt, both for the same night. With anyone else, Elias would have thought nothing of it. But Warne hadn't been a West End kind of man. Besides, the performance had taken place only a few days after that list of names had been scratched into the vault wall.

He checked the undersides of the drawers and the cavities they left behind. He looked beneath the rugs, tested the floorboards, shook out the folders in the filing cabinets, flipped through the books on the floor and on the shelves. Finding nothing further, he went back to the kitchen and was up on a chair looking behind tins of beans and soup when WPC Quinn, the redhead with the steely eye from earlier, called him on his mobile. 'Yes?' he asked, jamming his phone between shoulder and ear. 'What?'

'Is this a bad time?' she asked. 'I can call back later.'

'No,' said Elias. 'It's fine. Just a bit distracted, that's all.' He stepped down from the chair to give her his full attention. 'Maria, isn't it? How can I help?'

'There's something I'd like you to look at, sir. But I need to explain first.'

'Sure. Go for it.'

'Okay. You know how I helped find Mr Warne? Well, it was easy. His van was parked right there.'

'I am leading the investigation,' said Elias dryly.

'Yes,' she said. 'But I'm not sure you realise *how* it was parked. The way its wheels were angled, I mean, and the tracks it left on the grass. It was only ever so slight, but they made it look like Mr Warne had been heading towards the farmhouse when he pulled off the drive, not away. As if he'd been coming home from somewhere, that is, not setting off.'

Elias froze. It was absolutely true. Yet somehow he'd missed it. 'Go on.'

'Anyway,' said Quinn, 'if he'd been coming back from any distance, he'd pretty much have had to pass through Holbeach or Wisbech or Sutton Bridge, all of which have traffic cams. It was a bit quiet around here this afternoon, so I thought I'd check.'

'And? You've found him?'

'I think so, yes. Heading south on the A17 where it joins the A151.'

Elias closed his eyes, the better to visualise. That was surely the road he'd been taking himself all week. 'That's near Holbeach, right? Meaning he'd have been coming back from Sleaford or maybe even Lincoln?'

'Exactly, sir. Yes.'

'What time was this?'

'Four minutes past three in the morning.'

'Four minutes past three? And you're sure it's him?'

'That's not what I said,' protested Quinn. 'I said I *think* it's him. The resolution on that camera is rubbish. You can't see his face properly and his licence plate is spattered with mud and half hidden behind his bumper, which is falling off at one end, as you'll remember.'

'Can you email me the clip?'

'Already did. It should be with you by now.'

'Let me check.' He opened his email and there it was. It was only a few seconds long, dark and grainy, but Quinn was surely right that it was Warne's van, even though he couldn't make out the front plate. It was the right model with the same empty roof rack, the same scrape down its side, and its front bumper hanging loose in the same way too, as if it had hit a wall. He gave a grunt. 'This makes me look like a right tit, you realise?'

'Sorry, sir. I was only trying to help.'

'Don't apologise. It's a good thing. Just not too often.'

'No, sir. And I did try to tell you earlier.'

'Yes. Yes, you did.' He played the clip again, wondering where Warne had been, to be coming home that late. Logic would suggest a dinner party or maybe a secret lover, except that he hadn't eaten, drunk or had sex for at least several hours before his death. 'Are there other cameras you could check?' he asked. 'Up towards Sleaford, say?'

'To find out where he'd been?'

'Or even narrow it down a bit. If he didn't pass a camera, that would be helpful too. And maybe look for his outward journey, if you have time. When he set off. Whether his van was already banged up.'

'I'm off out in a minute,' she said. 'Then I've got the boys to pick up from school. Would first thing tomorrow do?'

'That's fine. And, may I say, excellent work. You'd make a top detective.'

Quinn laughed. 'Me a detective. I'd like to see that.'

'I'm serious. You've shown observation, intelligence, resourcefulness and a willingness to make me look like an arse. All qualities my superiors value highly.'

'Thank you, sir.' She sounded stunned yet wary, so that he couldn't help but worry that she'd read too much into his earlier glance at her ring finger. 'But I love what I do now. My family all lives around here.' Then she added pointedly: 'My husband's family too.'

'Good to hear. Good to hear.' He felt like shit suddenly. 'I mean I wasn't… All I'd be doing is having a word in an ear. No more than that.'

'Yes, sir. I know. Thank you.'

He finished the call then stood there clutching his phone, angry with himself, at how clumsy he'd become around women. But maybe it simply meant he was finally getting his appetite back. He could only hope.

He replayed the traffic cam clip again and again, trying to make out the driver's face or its licence plate. But the poor resolution, the dazzle of oncoming headlights and the broken bumper made it impossible. Yet surely it was Warne, which meant his jigsaw puzzle had been given a right good shaking. He returned to the rocking chair and closed his eyes once more, then began the engrossing task of fitting its pieces back to a different pattern.

EIGHTEEN

Anna had no way of knowing whether her room was indeed the best the hotel had to offer, but she could easily believe it. It was freshly painted in lavender, apricot and white, and it had a cast-iron fireplace, a pair of crystal chandeliers, and a four-poster bed with a firm, springy mattress. Its en suite was plush and sparkling clean, its TV large and wall-mounted, and its fridge and kettle tray were both generously stocked. Its double windows offered fine views too, over the gardens down to the seawall and the Wash beyond. And by pressing her cheek against the glass, she could even see the tiled roof of Uncle Dun's barn.

The room also had a good-sized oak writing desk and a comfortable black leather swivel chair. She linked her phone and laptop to the hotel's Wi-Fi then caught up with her email before carrying on the dispiriting task of calling the people in her uncle's address book to let them know about his death. She was still at it when Oliver came knocking. 'The hunger beat me,' he confessed, holding up a large brown paper bag. 'And they aren't doing food downstairs, so I had to pop out. You have a choice. Cheese and pickle or egg mayonnaise. I like them both equally myself, so it's entirely up to you.'

'Oh,' she said. 'That's brilliant. Then the egg mayo please.'

'Outstanding,' he said, delving into his bag for her sandwich and a napkin. 'I was lying through my teeth. Nothing against egg mayonnaise, mind, but there's only one true king.'

He checked his watch. 'I was planning to take a stroll after. I don't suppose I could coax you into joining me, could I? Cajole you, even? I could go as high as a wheedle, if you really push me. I'm not proud.'

'I'd love to,' said Anna, gesturing vaguely at the desk. 'But honestly...'

'Another time, then. Another time.' But he made no move to leave. 'A confession before I go, though. Your egg mayonnaise wasn't an entirely selfless act. I have a favour to ask. A quid for my quo, so to speak. A tit for my tat. I'll quite understand if you say no, but please don't get offended. Because if I'm to ask it at all, I really need to ask it now.'

'This sounds awfully mysterious.'

'Not really, no. It's just, I've cancelled my crew for tomorrow, as you know. But I'm going to spend the night here anyway. The room's already paid for, so why not? And frankly I've got a problem I need to fix, and doing so will likely be easier here than in Lincoln. A gap has opened up in my programme, you see, where your uncle used to be. I mean he wasn't the whole thing, of course. But he had an important and distinctive voice, so obviously he'll need replacing.'

'Yes,' said Anna, puzzled. 'Obviously.'

'You're okay with that, then? I wouldn't want you thinking me callous, approaching other people so quickly.'

'Of course not. The show must go on.'

'Good. Good. Glad to hear it.' He paused a moment and dropped his eyes, making it clear that all this so far had been mere throat-clearing. 'Such a shame about your uncle, though. A shame as well as a tragedy, I mean. He had a real quality. Authenticity, I guess you'd call it. Or authority, maybe. But the kind you get from living a subject rather than just studying it, if you know what I mean?'

'I know exactly,' she said. 'And yes, you're absolutely right.'

'I knew he'd be TV gold the moment I met him. Between you and me, it's the one talent I truly do have. Spotting people the camera will love.'

'Must be useful.'

'Yes,' he said. 'Yes, it is.'

It took her a moment to realise what he was getting at. Then she burst out laughing. 'You can't be serious,' she said.

'Why ever not?'

'I'm no replacement for Uncle Dun, believe me. He knew infinitely more about King John and the Fens than I ever will.'

'That's not what he thought.' He screwed up his face into an unexpectedly accurate imitation of Uncle Dun, and adopted his fenland growl too. 'You'd best ask young Anna that. She's the 'storian o the family.' His impersonation was both absurdly over the top yet so evocative that tears sprang to her eyes. Oliver winced when he noticed, he touched her arm. 'I'm such an idiot,' he said. 'It's just, he was so proud of you, he truly was.'

'Even so,' she said. 'I'd be no good.'

'That's not what the camera will say. Trust me on this. When I approached you that day at Bolingbroke Castle, sure I fancied you. Why wouldn't I have done? But, honestly, making good TV means too much to me to let that cloud my judgement. I simply have a good instinct for who the camera will like and who it won't. It's not just looks. It's personality, excitement, passion. That old biddy and Mr Twitch knew their stuff, sure, but they had all the voltage of roadkill hedgehogs. Whereas you're going to light up the screen.'

'No, I'm not,' said Anna firmly. 'Because I'm not doing it.'

'Come on. At least think about it. Academia's such a bear pit, surely a BBC credit would do wonders for your career.'

That stopped her. He was absolutely right. More than that, she sensed suddenly that it might be just the lifeline she needed to pull her out of her slump. Yet instantly the usual reaction arrived. She was a failure, a fraud, a disappointment, an imposter. She had nothing new to contribute. To do such a programme would be a lie. She'd be found out and denounced, and it would be no more than she deserved. 'I don't know,' she said feebly.

'Of course not. You'll need this afternoon to think about

it before saying yes. So how about dinner tonight? An egg mayonnaise sandwich only goes so far, after all, and there's this fantastic trattoria I know in Holbeach. But I can't go there alone, can I? People will start calling me Olly No Mates. It'd be death to my career. So how about I book us a table for eight o'clock, say? On me, of course. Let me take another crack at talking you onto my programme, I can even put it on expenses.'

'That sounds great,' said Anna. 'But right now...'

'Sure,' he said. 'I'll leave you to it.'

NINETEEN

Elias's search of the farmhouse took him the rest of the afternoon, yet all he found of interest was a sack of muddy potatoes that made him realise just how hungry he was. He wouldn't be leaving for a while yet, and Anna Warne had said they could help themselves, so he scrubbed clean the largest one he could find then stabbed it with a skewer and popped it in the oven to bake while he wrote up his day's report.

When he judged there was no longer the slightest chance that Scene of Crime would return tonight, he called Frank Mason to let him know about the vault beneath the barn floor, though not yet about the butyric acid beneath the fields. He claimed he'd just discovered it and downplayed it as far as he could, making clear that it was empty and without obvious sign of recent use; and anyway he had to go home now, so he'd secured it again, but would be back first thing in the morning to show him and his team then.

Mason had some news for Elias too. Back on Monday, after Dunstan Warne had been found, he'd had his van taken up to Nettleham on a flatbed truck for a full forensic examination. That was now complete. Like the farmhouse, it had been locked up and with its keys in Dunstan Warne's pocket, so they'd not expected much; but they had found a camera drone in the back with a couple of hundred photos on its drive. Would he like to see them? He would. The photos arrived in three separate lots a minute or so later. Elias unzipped them and scrolled through them. They were undated, which was irritating, and most were of Warne Farm. But the most recent set were of harvested fields, some trees and a stretch of cobbled lane that he didn't recognise at all.

He completed his report, again without mentioning the butyric acid, and posted it to the case file. Then he braced himself to make a more testing call. Murder investigations were run by his own Major Crimes Unit, but the smuggling angle meant he'd been instructed to keep the Serious and Organised Crime Unit informed too, despite their having kept him in the dark about their recent raids. Worse, he had Jay Patterson as his liaison, a man passed over for promotion so many times that he'd come to treasure his bitterness.

Patterson laughed when Elias told him about the vault. 'How the hell did you miss that?' he scoffed.

'You never told us to look,' said Elias, rubbing the nape of his neck.

'Why would we? Are we psychic?'

'You knew it was smugglers. You knew it was a farm on the coast. Didn't you even think about that Norfolk silo business?'

'Oh,' said Patterson, taken aback. 'You think it's the same crew?'

'Maybe. But more likely they stole the idea. Because I'm thinking it was your Lincoln friends.'

'What?' He was on alert suddenly. 'Why?'

'It's only a hunch so far. Thing is, though, I have a kind of eye-witness.'

'An eye-witness?'

'A kind of eye-witness.'

'Okay. Stay there.' He put Elias on hold. A minute passed before he came back on. 'You were telling me you have an eye-witness,' he said, the echo on the line suggesting they were on speaker.

'A kind of eye-witness,' sighed Elias. 'They were in the house last night when they heard a noise and went to investigate. They found two men in the barn. They were wearing balaclavas, so mugshots won't help. But they were right up close at one point, and they had very distinctive physiques. So I was thinking maybe your surveillance footage...'

A new voice now. Raymond Hollis, Patterson's ambitious new boss. 'These guys don't know what we've got on them. I mean to keep it that way.'

'You wouldn't have to give them any names. It could be the break you need.'

Silence fell. He was put on hold again as they discussed it between themselves. 'They'd have to come here,' said Hollis, after a minute or so. 'I'm not letting any footage out, not after last month.'

'Okay, I'll ask. Just wanted to make sure it was feasible first.'

'It's feasible,' said Hollis. 'Call us when you know.'

TWENTY

On a sunny September afternoon some thirty-odd years ago, León de Bruin's grandfather Ronnie had gone for a ride on his old boneshaker, only to be clipped by a delivery van. The fall had shattered his right hip, leaving him in a wheelchair for months, unable to manage the five apartments he'd owned and rented out around Skegness, and which had provided him with his income.

By a happy coincidence, de Bruin had just left school and had been in search of work. It had suited them both, therefore, for him to take over the day-to-day running of the business. Ronnie had been a cheerful and kind-hearted man. He'd valued the good opinion of his tenants and so had been understanding of arrears, swift to undertake repairs and generous in returning deposits. Not de Bruin. His years of being bullied at school had drained him of compassion. He'd welcomed his power to squeeze those tenants dry. What was more, his grandfather had soon discovered that he liked the extra income, now that he didn't have to face his tenants personally.

The hip had duly healed, but the partnership had continued, with Ronnie giving de Bruin ten percent of the business on his twenty-first birthday, in recognition of his efforts, along with an option to buy the rest in the event of his death. Tragically, that had happened less than a month afterwards, with Ronnie breaking his neck when falling down his stairs. The timing had been such that de Bruin might have had awkward questions to answer had he not been on a rare holiday in Corfu at the time.

Ronnie had left everything to be shared equally between his two daughters, de Bruin's mum Alice and his aunt Diane. Neither of them were worldly, so they'd gladly accepted de Bruin's offer to handle everything. A friendly solicitor had helped him undervalue the apartments, allowing him to get them on the cheap. He'd mortgaged them to the hilt in order to buy three more, then had ploughed his rental income back into the market. Within twelve years, he'd acquired a portfolio of nearly a hundred properties this way, making himself a paper millionaire many times over.

He'd thought himself set for life.

The global financial crisis had put an end to that. House values had crashed, plunging him underwater just as mass redundancies had meant his tenants couldn't make their rent. Eviction had been no use. There'd been no one to take their places, and no buyers for his properties. He'd duly fallen behind on his payments. His banks had lost patience and had started to foreclose. Just like that, he'd been facing ruin.

In the good times, he'd used a local biker gang to scare out deadbeat tenants. But their main business had always been drugs. Two of them had approached him one evening with a proposition. Their previous supplier had done a bunk with all their money, leaving them with neither funds nor product. They'd found a potential replacement, but they were demanding cash upfront, and they didn't have any left. Would he be interested in staking them for half the profit? They'd been a hapless lot, in dire need of the kind of organisation de Bruin could bring, but too lazy and ill-disciplined to be trusted. It had been a chance to save his empire, however. He'd somehow scraped together enough cash for that first buy, only for the new supplier – perhaps inevitably – to turn out to be an undercover detective with the East Midlands Special Operations Unit. The gods had been smiling on him for once, however, for the detective had proved almost comically corrupt. For a large yet acceptable cut, they'd not only put him in touch with an authentic Dutch supplier, they'd advised him on the best ways to bring the product in. They'd also been alerting him to investigations and raids ever since, and had even helped take down rival gangs on his behalf, allowing him and his biker friends to expand across the county.

The cash had started flooding in, astonishing great waves of it that had put his more honest endeavours to shame. He'd kept it going, therefore, even after the property market had recovered and he'd become rich again in his own right. It had seemed safe enough, after all, what with the pipeline now running itself, and his source still in place, feeding him information in virtual real time via a secure Dark Web address that he normally checked maybe once a day, but which he'd been visiting compulsively since learning of Dunstan Warne's murder.

It was the first thing he did on returning home that evening. Several new documents had been posted, including a witness statement by Anna Warne. He saved that as a treat for later, and started instead with Elias's latest case report. It was a jolt to read that Oliver Merchant had been at the farm. There were few people in this world who de Bruin disliked more. But it seemed to be a genuine coincidence, so he put it from his mind. More worrying, by far, was that Elias had discovered the vault beneath the barn.

He sat there brooding. He and Andrei had cleared the place out and scrubbed it with bleach. They'd double checked it last night too, so he was confident there was nothing there to put Elias on his trail. It was unfortunate, certainly, but he was used to dealing with the police, thanks to his grandfather's untimely death and the woes his more troublesome tenants kept suffering. They'd not pinned anything on him yet, and they wouldn't this time either.

He pushed himself to his feet, went over to his drinks cabinet. He chunked a couple of cubes from his ice maker into a crystal tumbler, less for their chill than for the pleasant crackle they made when he glugged his favourite Laphroaig over them. He took a small sip then set the tumbler down on a coaster before settling back into his armchair. Then he opened Anna Warne's witness statement, trying not to let himself get too excited by the possibility of photographs.

TWENTY-ONE

The Holbeach trattoria proved the perfect tonic for Anna's spirits, colourful, warm and packed with boisterous young families and cheerful couples out for fun rather than romance. Oliver was clearly a favourite guest. Their hostess Mirabella shrieked with delight when she saw him arrive, then rushed to the kitchen to fetch her husband Paolo so that the pair of them could envelop him in a hug. They cooed approvingly over Anna too, mistaking her for Oliver's new girlfriend, scolding him affectionately for not having settled down earlier with a charming young woman like this.

Mirabella had reserved them a corner table in an effort to minimise the gawking. Not that it worked. The turned heads and excited whispering made it clear to Anna that Oliver was far more of a celebrity around here than she'd realised. A heavily tattooed woman with mauve lipstick prodded her shy young daughter over to their table for a picture that Anna took for her on her phone. Then Mirabella brought them a complimentary bottle of chianti and talked them through the specials, waving some off as unworthy of their attention, while warmly recommending others. And everything on the house, of course. 'What the hell?' murmured Anna, once they were alone again. 'Are you their long lost son?'

Oliver laughed. 'I did a piece on them a couple of years back. They were going bust at the time. Then suddenly they were it.'

'Such power!'

'Meh. I only bought a crew. The rest was them. All that warmth and friendliness and love of food. The camera gobbled them up, just as I'd known it would.'

'Ah. Your gift.'

'Mock me all you like. I was right.' His eyes slid sideways. His expression grew solemn. His train of thought was obvious even before he raised his glass. 'To your uncle,' he said.

'Yes. To Dun.' She took a sip. The chianti was dark and coarse and delicious. 'But how did you talk him into it? In a million years, I'd never have imagined him agreeing to do TV. Anyway, since when have documentaries been your line?'

'They aren't, really,' admitted Oliver. 'They're kind of an accident. Like my whole career, if I'm honest. I seem to stumble dazed from one rake to the next.'

'How do you mean?'

'The whole TV business, for a start. I was painfully shy as a kid. I'd never have got into it if my mum hadn't pushed me. She's an actor, you see. My dad too. They actually met playing Beatrice and Benedick in *Much Ado*.'

'How very sweet!'

'I know. Sickening, isn't it? They never quite reached the top, but they still make a living out of it. You'd recognise their faces, I'd guess, but probably not their names. So anyway Mum was doing some commercials for a bank at the time, and the kid playing her son got the mumps at the last minute, so she pushed me forward instead. I hated it. I felt so self-conscious. But I must have done okay because I got offered more parts off the back of it. Likeable nerd stuff, mostly. Slap an oversized pair of glasses on me and muss up my hair, I can do perplexed as well as the best of them.'

'Cute but baffled. I can see that.'

'Exactly. I was a natural at bafflement. I can't imagine why. I grew out of that, of course, but somehow I got cast as a stroppy teen on a soap, which was great, at least until my TV dad demanded too large a pay rise and the writers killed off our whole family in a car crash.'

'Bastards.'

'Scum of the world, writers,' agreed Oliver. 'But thank god one of the producers took pity on me and found me a gig on children's TV. Me and this lovely girl Ellie went around farms and factories and fire stations and the like, to see if we might want to do it when we grew up. God, no. That's the trouble with TV. It spoils you for proper work. But I aged out of that too, only to land a job here, mostly doing bits of feel-good colour at the end of regional news bulletins. You know the kind of thing. You were almost in one once. And I've got a knack for it, though I say so myself. I'm upbeat. I know when to smile, when to frown, how to laugh at myself. I can even squeeze out a tear or two if you say something really mean. But my real gift is for getting the best out of the people I'm with, even ones you'd expect to run a mile.'

'Ah. Uncle Dun.'

'Yeah. So I've got this mate who commissions documentaries for the BBC. I pitch him from time to time, because I've learned not to rely on my current gig, and you never know. Anyway, this new biography of King John came out a few months back. I hosted a Q&A with the author when she was in Lincoln. Obviously, the baggage train came up. It gave me the idea for a series on famous lost British treasures. Excalibur; Loch Arkaig; Llywelyn's coronet; the Graff diamonds. My mate liked it enough to commission the King John one as a pilot. No budget, of course, so I had to write it myself. Wisbech Library has a special collection on it, as I'm sure you know. That's where I found your uncle's book. Authoritative, quirky, packed with fun local stories and weird bits of arcane knowledge. It was perfect.'

'Except for his conclusion, I expect,' said Anna. 'About the baggage train not being here.'

'Well, yes,' grinned Oliver. 'There is that. Though...'

'Though?'

'I mean did he *really* believe that? Sure, that's what his head said. But his heart? I'd say he was conflicted at best. Which was great, because I needed a sceptic to explain why the baggage train had never been found; but I didn't want them going in too hard or it'd have taken the piss out of the whole thing. And, honestly, once your uncle got talking, he was like a dog hearing his lead jangle. His eyes gleamed. He literally quivered.'

Anna laughed. Metal detectors had been a craze when Dun had been a boy. He'd begged one for his seventh birthday, then had set off to find the crown jewels, promising to be back with them in time for tea. And while that childish optimism had been battered by decades of failure, it had never entirely gone away. 'That sounds like him,' she admitted.

'I know, right? Anyway, his address was in the book. It was only fifteen minutes away. So I thought, why not? I found him in the barn, cleaning the carburettor on his tractor. I explained who I was and how much I'd enjoyed his book; but also that I was out of my depth and needed help.'

'Ah,' said Anna. 'That old standby.'

'Yeah,' agreed Oliver. 'Nothing like throwing yourself on someone's mercy.' Their main courses arrived: fettucini for her, gnocchi for Oliver, each with aromas to make the mouth water. Anna leaned back for parmesan and pepper then picked up her fork and set to, while Oliver continued with his tale. 'Anyway, he brewed us up a pot of tea and started talking. I keep a video camera in my car, just in case, so after a minute or two I asked him if I could get it to have a record, because I'm genuinely terrible at taking notes. He soon forgot it was even there, as people do. He talked for hours. There was so much that never even made it into his book. So I went home afterwards and made a cut of the best bits and emailed it back to him, along with my thanks and the tentative suggestion that maybe I could come back later with a crew and do it properly. I knew it would hook him. People don't write and put out a book unless there's something they want to say. What I didn't expect was how caught up in it he'd get. He kept calling me with new ideas. Which was great and all, but this was an hour on the Beeb, if we got lucky, not Season One on Netflix.'

'He'd taken all his old books off his shelves,' said Anna. 'They're stacked up around his desk.'

'Yep. My fault. Apologies.'

'You made his last days fun. I couldn't be more grateful.'

'I guess.' He toyed with his gnocchi for a few moments, then looked back up. 'So are you a sceptic too? About the crown jewels, I mean?'

'Pretty much,' said Anna. 'I mean that book was all my uncle's work, but it came out of the time we spent together, the places we visited, the conversations we had, the questions I asked. Because there's this amazing paradox at the heart of the story, as I'm sure you already know.'

'Never assume I know anything.'

'But you've read my uncle's book.'

'I've read lots of books. It's weird. You read one and you think you know it all. Then you read some more and you realise you know jack. So tell me about this paradox of yours.'

'It's simple,' she told him. 'History and archaeology usually work hand in hand together to tell us about the past. The history in this case couldn't be much clearer. The crown jewels were in the baggage train when it got bogged down halfway across the Wash, and then were swallowed by the incoming tide. But the archaeology says no, not so fast. Archaeology says, where the hell is it, then?'

TWENTY-TWO

De Bruin read Anna Warne's statement three times, along with the extra paragraphs appended by DI Elias. When he was done, he closed his laptop and set it down gently beside his chair. He knocked back the last of his Laphroaig then went upstairs to the master bedroom. He stripped down to his powder blue Armani boxer shorts and stood in front of his full-length smoked-glass mirror, turning this way and that to admire his physique. He'd always been stick-thin, but it hadn't been so noticeable until around his fifteenth birthday, when for some unaccountable reason he'd sprouted straight upwards yet had barely filled out at all. He'd come to appreciate his leanness over the years, even though keeping the weight off had proved an increasing challenge. But then he'd never shied from hard work, at least not when it was in pursuit of—

Cadaverous.

He closed his eyes and waited for the moment to pass.

Carmen Trent had told everyone about his humiliation beneath the oak tree. Of course she had. His bullies had used it gleefully to make his life hell. They'd taken to surrounding him and throwing him to the floor, calling him foul names, taunting him and kicking him while he'd lain there curled up and defenceless. The hatred he'd felt for them had, perversely, been the making of him. Until then, he'd tried ingratiation. Afterwards, he'd cared only about getting even. Except for with Carmen Trent. He'd hated her as much or more as any of them, but he'd still lusted for her and worshipped her too, the different emotions mixing into a single bewildering brew.

His mother had loved those old black-and-white romantic comedies. He'd taken to watching them with her in those dark days, drawing comfort from the way the handsome brash hero was always slapped down by the haughty beauty in the first reel, because you knew then already how it was going to end, that the two of them would—

Repellent.

His cheeks blazed. Suddenly all he could see in the mirror was his thirteen-year-old self in all his grotesque ugliness. The old rage flooded back through him. He welcomed it like a lost friend, for it was rage that had made him rich, enabling him to fix the things he'd most hated about himself. Elocution and deportment lessons. A trainer to build up muscle. His teeth straightened, his lips plumped, his nose shortened, his ears pinned back, his—

Creepy.

… his jaw reshaped, his cheekbones sharpened. Top-end tailors and hairdressers, expensive creams and lotions, classic cars, a change of name from the vacuous nobody Len Brown to the aristocratic León Alessandro de Bruin. A string of increasingly attractive girlfriends had followed, drawn by his success, each helping him bury a little deeper his self-loathing and traumatic history. Yet buried though it was, it was still very much there, giving rise to his more shameful lusts. He'd hoped these would vanish altogether as he'd aged. If anything, they'd grown stronger. Or perhaps more accurate to say that the ebbing of his more conventional appetites had left only the twisted driftwood behind, so that he couldn't be aroused much anymore by the sight of a naked woman, however beautiful. It was only their horror, disdain and disgust that truly excited him. Being scorned, belittled and found repellent – it made him seethe even as it took him in its thrall. And it had to be raw and real, straight from the heart rather than the wallet. He'd twice tried the ersatz offerings of high-priced London dominatrices; both had left him utterly unmoved. Safe words, for crying out loud! They made a mockery of the whole thing. Yet somehow a young woman trapped in her bedroom and fearing for her life could—

Nosferatu.

A pleasurable hot wave coursed through him. He saw her face. His hand drifted to his groin and the first proper stirrings he'd felt in weeks. He was overcome by the need to see her again, by the need to break her spirit and make her his, just as he'd done with his wife Samantha.

According to Elias's report, she'd moved next door to the King John Hotel. She'd likely be there now. He knew full well that going there to see her would be madness, yet he couldn't help himself. Or, rather, he had no wish to help himself. He felt alive in a way he hadn't felt for years, in a way that he'd feared he'd never feel again. And what kind of man would he be to turn his back on such an opportunity, just because it carried a little risk?

It was sure to get cold tonight. He put on some winter clothes and headed for the cars.

TWENTY-THREE

Elias's potato was perfectly baked, its skin crisp and a little blackened, its flesh soft enough to mash with a fork. He ground some pepper onto it then ate it with a small can of cold baked beans. There was a stack of blankets in an upstairs cupboard. He carried two of the heavier ones out to his Leaf, in whose boot he kept a small emergency overnight bag for such situations. He took his toothbrush inside to do his teeth, then filled a bottle with drinking water and nabbed the last few biscuits while he was at it. Then he locked up the farmhouse and set off.

The squad car was still at the end of the drive. He thanked the officers for their help, told them they could call it a day, but asked them to arrange another car for the morning. He watched them out of sight then headed off in the other direction. There was a lay-by a mile or so up the road. He pulled into it, doused his headlights, turned off his engine then sat there in the darkness, giving his eyes a chance to adjust.

Ten or maybe even fifteen years ago, a gang of 'Ndrangheta Mafiosi operating out of Amsterdam had used an abandoned Norfolk grain silo right by the coast as a stash house for dropping off shipments of cocaine and other drugs for collection by their English counterparts. To make sure they never walked into a trap, they'd monitored the place for police activity with hidden cameras in and around the silo and the farmhouse. Elias suspected something similar had happened here, as it would explain why they'd believed the place empty last night, what with Anna having no car of her own. If so, and he got insanely lucky, there was even an outside chance of recovering footage of Warne's murder – or at least of the murderer arriving or leaving. But he couldn't yet look for their cameras, not without tipping them off. He didn't want them tipped off. He wanted them believing that not only would the farmhouse be empty and unwatched tonight, but that a Scene of Crime team would be conducting a full search of the vault first thing in the morning, making tonight their last chance.

There was a mole inside Nettleham HQ. Elias was sure of it. There'd simply been too many botched operations over the years. Too many missed arrests and empty stash houses. Too many confidential informants intimidated, beaten or even found dead. His friend and former boss Colin Vaughn had been equally sure of it, which was why he'd started his own private investigation, only to get framed for it himself. Elias had known Vaughn too well to believe him guilty, despite the evidence produced against him at his trial. He'd testified in his defence, therefore, even while knowing that it would taint him and damage his career.

After Vaughn's conviction, Elias had been put under intense pressure to transfer out. He'd resisted on the perfectly true grounds that this was where his kids were. But what he hadn't told anyone was that he'd also promised Vaughn he'd uncover the real mole for him, and clear his name. He'd failed utterly so far. But tonight, at last, he sensed he had a real chance.

Ten minutes had now passed. His night vision was as good as it was going to get. He started the Leaf back up but kept its headlights off, then crept back along the lane by the clouded thin moonlight to the field across from Warne Farm. He reversed into it, turned off his engine, pushed his seat as far back as it would go. He took off his shoes, covered himself with the blankets and generally made himself comfortable.

Then he settled down to watch.

TWENTY-FOUR

Anna's long day finally got the better of her. She tried to fight off a yawn, but it proved too strong for her, so she had to hide it behind her hand instead. Oliver took it as their cue to go, leaving a generous tip in lieu of the bill they weren't allowed to pay. They hugged Mirabella goodnight then went to thank Paolo too, finding him outside the kitchen door, smoking a cigarette in furtive short sharp drags, as though he were fourteen again, squeezing in a tab behind the bike shed in the break between lessons.

'So this paradox of yours,' prompted Oliver, as they pulled out of the car park and set off back for the hotel.

'Well, yes,' said Anna. A party of drunk young men were walking down the street, arms around each others' shoulders, bellowing out some kind of football chant. 'The history says one thing. The archaeology says another. And they both have strong cases. I mean it's not just the writings of Ralph of Coggeshall and Roger of Wendover that tell us the crown jewels were lost in the Wash. There are other pointers too.'

'Such as?'

'Okay. For one, John was certainly a cruel and vicious king, but no one can complain about his record keeping. We have receipts for everything he took from his various treasuries in the year before he died, and which he was carting around the country with him. It's genuinely astonishing. *At least* two royal crowns. *At least* two golden sceptres. A ceremonial sword that had supposedly belonged to Tristram of Tristram and Isolde fame, whose broken tip had led to it being known as the Sword of Mercy. Then there were all the robes and other finery for his coronation: Fur-lined cloaks and tunics of samite and dark purple. Embroidered shoes and gem-studded leather belts. And it wasn't just regalia either. He had cartloads of gold and silver goblets, of bowls, basins, plates and platters. Great chests of brooches, necklaces, pendants and other jewellery, including four rings given to him by the pope, set respectively with a sapphire, an emerald, a topaz and a garnet. Then there were all the religious artefacts they carried into battle to secure God's favour. Gold crosses, candelabras, phylacteries, shrines. Sacred relics kept in caskets encrusted with precious stones.'

'That's some memory you have.'

'I was a sixteen-year-old girl stuck in the middle of nowhere, thinking it might be buried beneath my house. What else do you think I dreamed of? But here's the point. Not a single item from that list has ever been seen since, despite the very detailed descriptions we have. That's doubly so for the crown jewels, of course, because they played such a crucial role in coronations, helping to make them sacred. Yet none of those pieces appeared at the crowning of Henry III, even though that took place just a few weeks later. And there was a completely different set at the coronation after that. So, yes, they clearly vanished. The only real question is where.'

'And...?'

'Well, quite. That's the point. If a whole baggage train really had been lost in the Wash, surely *some* trace of it would have turned up by now.' It was bizarre how little had resurfaced from that era. You'd expect a fair amount simply by coincidence. The region had hardly been crowded, but it hadn't been empty either. There'd been ports like Lynn along its coast, and monasteries at places like Ramsey, Ely and Thorney, all connected by a network of roads and crossing places. 'It's not as if the environment is too toxic. Silt and peat are actually excellent at preserving artefacts. And people have put real resources into the search too. An American foundation spent millions on it back in the nineteen thirties. Multinationals have conducted extensive geological surveys in preparation for building their new plants. Archaeological departments and institutes have been coming here for decades to test their new techniques and equipment. And it's mostly arable farmland, of course, which means that the fields get ploughed up year after year, which brings out all the nighthawks with their metal detectors and...' But then she frowned and tailed off.

'And...?' prompted Oliver.

Anna shook her head. 'Nothing.' But the thought wouldn't leave her. 'Don't you think it's a bit weird that Uncle Dun was found buried like that? Sure, he'd just deep ploughed that field for sugar beet or whatever, so it would have been a lot easier to dig there than elsewhere. But it would still have taken a fair old time, right? And they could have been spotted at any moment. Surely safer to pop him in their boot and take him off elsewhere to bury.'

'Maybe they didn't have a car. Maybe they panicked. What's your alternative?'

'That the hole was already there, of course. Dug by a detectorist in search of the crown jewels.'

Oliver gave a grunt. 'The police must have considered that.'

'I doubt it. You saw Elias earlier. He barely even knew who King John was.' She took out her mobile to call him, only to realise to her surprise that it was almost eleven o'clock. Morning would do fine. She put her phone away again, rested back her head and closed her eyes.

'Hey,' said Oliver, reaching over to tap her arm. 'You can't go to sleep just yet. Not before you tell me whether the history or the archaeology is right.'

'I honestly don't know,' she said. 'The whole thing's like a vanishing trick – except where did it all vanish to? Uncle Dun used to joke that it's what Robin Hood stole to give to the poor.'

Oliver squinted sideways at her. 'He never told me that.'

'He wouldn't have. Like I say, it was a joke. Not fit for his book, and certainly not for the BBC. Though, to be fair, there really was an outlaw Robert Hod at the time. Robert was essentially the same name as Robin, and Hod was an alternative spelling of Hood. We also have a separate record for an outlaw called Robert of Wetherby, who may well have been the same man, only designated by where he came from rather than by his surname. John's son Henry III had the Sheriff of Nottingham hunt him down and then hanged, which is very unusual, as kings didn't typically concern themselves with individual outlaws. But if word had got around that he'd been the big brain behind the hijacking of his father's baggage train...'

'Doesn't sound that crazy to me.'

'I know. But it doesn't really hold up. There were a few outlaws living in the Wash. All the fish and birdlife made it good for foraging, and the sheriffs tended to leave them be, because the place was so rife with malaria, plague, dysentery and the rest. But it couldn't have supported large groups like the Merry Men. Even if it had, they still wouldn't have had the numbers to overcome an escort and hijack a baggage train two miles long. You'd have needed several hundred skilled warriors for that, armed with excellent inside information, not a bunch of starving, rheumatic misfits.'

'Then...?'

'How many times must I say it? I don't know. No one does. If you forced me to take a position, I'd guess that a cart or two got stuck in the mud, blocking the ones behind even as the tide turned and came rushing in. Then it would have been everyone for themselves, taking whatever they had with them, because the war looked lost by then and John was the kind of king who'd have hung the ones that did show up to work off his rage at the rest.'

'That's how your uncle saw it too.'

'I know. We talked about it a lot. It's not as if a fenland farmer and a sixteen-year-old Manchester girl have a huge range of shared interests. History was it. And it was fun. For us both, I think. Uncle Dun had been brooding on it for years, but he'd never really had anyone to talk to about it. And you know how setting out your case gets you to see the weaknesses in it, so that you have to rethink it and make it stronger? So he found it helpful too, I hope. But then of course I headed off to university and he put it in his book instead.'

The hotel was locked up by the time they made it back. Anna tapped in the key-code. The reception lights were dimmed and there was no one behind the desk, just a sign inviting them to ring the bell if they needed service. They went upstairs together. Oliver's room was to the left; Anna's to the right. 'Thank you,' she told him. 'That was fun.'

'No need to sound quite so surprised.'

'Damn it,' she said. 'I thought I'd hidden it better than that.'

'Mind if I see you to your room?'

Anna gave him a wry look. 'I think I'll be safe from here.'

'I'll bet you thought that last night too.'

It was meant as a joke, a way to prolong their time together. But suddenly those men from last night were in her mind again, the way the tall one had twirled his screwdriver in her face. She didn't protest, therefore, when Oliver walked her to her door, or even when he went in first, checking her bathroom, wardrobe and beneath her bed. 'Ah, well,' he said, getting sheepishly to his feet. 'Better safe than sorry.'

'Yes,' she said. 'Thanks.'

He returned to the doorway where she was still standing. Its narrowness forced them together, so that they almost touched. He stopped in front of her, his proximity disturbing. When she'd called him old that day at Bolingbroke Castle, it had been less a comment on his age than on the gap between them, given that she'd been just nineteen at the time, and him in his late twenties. But that gap didn't seem so large anymore, not least because her abduction by Harry Kidd had left her feeling old and soiled. In truth, Oliver was an attractive man, with gorgeous pale blue eyes, a good-humoured mouth and a strong jaw that glittered with evening stubble. She'd shut down that part of her life so completely that it had been two years since she'd even kissed a man, and the sudden physical longing she felt for him was powerful enough that she had to turn away her face.

He smiled gently, as if realising her confusion. He put a hand on her shoulder and pecked her chastely on her cheek. 'Oh well,' he said. 'Goodnight, I guess.'

'Yes,' she said, stepping inside the sanctuary of her room and making to close the door. 'Goodnight.'

TWENTY-FIVE

For the second morning in a row, Anna woke with a start. But there was no banging door to blame this time. No howling storm. It was an idea instead, prompted in part by yesterday's check-in, but even more so by last night's conversation with Oliver. She threw back her duvet and sat up, half expecting it to fade away into nothingness under closer scrutiny, as night-time inspirations so often did.

Not this one.

It was too early to call Elias, and, besides, his manner yesterday still rankled. Her curiosity wouldn't wait, however. She washed and dressed, went downstairs. Breakfast wasn't yet open, though she could hear the jangle of cutlery. She pinged the reception bell then apologised to Priya for the ungodly hour as she came padding out of a back room in slippers, oversized blue pyjamas and a white dressing gown. She looked bewildered when Anna told her what she wanted, but shrugged it off and led her to a storeroom containing bikes, trowels, spades and metal detectors, then invited her to take her pick. She chose a trowel and the simplest-looking of the detectors, then asked how much.

'No charge,' said Priya, with her charming warm smile. 'Our honoured guest, remember?'

Oliver gave a muffled groan when Anna knocked on his door. She called out warning then went on in. He was lying face down on his pillow, his arms thrown up above his head like he was doing the fifty-metre fly. 'I need you,' she told him.

He turned bleary eyes upon her. 'Where was this attitude last night?'

'Downstairs, quick as you can. Bring your camera.'

He pushed himself up onto an elbow, his curiosity piqued. 'Whatever for?'

'Come down and find out.'

Breakfast had now opened. She helped herself to a banana, toast and coffee. Oliver appeared a few minutes later in baggy black jeans and a navy guernsey, his green canvas camera bag slung over his shoulder. She went to meet him at the door. 'Follow me,' she said.

'How come you get breakfast and I don't?'

'Don't worry. We won't be long.'

It was still dark outside, though dawn was lifting like a slow grey curtain away to the east. Anna took out her phone for its torch, but it proved such little help that she put it away again. They jumped the drainage ditch then forced their way through a gap in her uncle's hawthorn hedge, taking a few scratches and getting spattered by morning dew. Patches of pale thin mist lingered like lazy ghosts in the hollows all the way up to the seawall. The grass verges were still squelchy from the storm. Her old trainers quickly grew wet and cold.

Anna had hated it here when she'd first arrived. It was so flat and bleak and featureless. So chill and grey and open. Nowhere did windswept quite like this stretch of the south Lincolnshire coast, particularly when the weather was coming in off the Arctic. After Manchester, it had seemed an alien, friendless and lifeless world, miles from anyone or anything remotely interesting.

Uncle Dun had let her grieve a while, but eventually he'd grown so exasperated by her sullen refusal to help out that he'd grabbed her by her wrist one freezing evening and dragged her out with him on his nightly round, ignoring her teenage screeching as he'd named the various crops he'd be cultivating that year, describing their virtues, vices, needs and idiosyncrasies, their life-cycles, treatments and likely future market values.

He'd done the same the following morning and evening too, interspersing his lectures with questions designed to see how much she'd taken in. Her tantrums had done no good. There'd been no one around to hear. She'd taken to sulky silence instead. He'd dragged her out the next day too, changing his questions slightly, testing not just her memory but also her ability to reason. She'd been too proud to give answers out loud, of course, but she hadn't been able to stop herself from working them out in her mind, and it had given her a thrill whenever she'd got one right.

The rounds had become routine. The exercise had put colour in her cheeks, muscle in her legs. Winter had thawed into a gorgeous spring. The farming year had got underway in earnest. Weekends and holidays meant gruelling long days in the fields which had left her tanned, sore and exhausted, her hands calloused, her feet so blistered it had pained her even to walk. Yet there'd been rewards too.

He'd taught her how to drive in his old van and then had trained her on his tractor, his ditch digger and various other bits of machinery. The seasonal workers had arrived for the harvest. Many of them had already known one another, and there'd been a great spirit of camaraderie. Best of all, she'd got to see the fields bloom with crops that she herself had helped to sow and care for. It had been a wondrous sensation, provoking strange new feelings of motherhood inside her, so that sometimes – despite her exhaustion – she'd slip out on her own before breakfast or after dark, and wander proudly among her fields. So it had been that, some eighteen months after arriving, she'd woken one Saturday morning filled with unexpected joy at the prospect of a whole weekend on the farm, and she'd realised she'd come to love it.

'Woah,' said Oliver, when he saw the ribbons of police tape fluttering ahead. 'Isn't that where your uncle…?'

'Yes,' said Anna. She turned on the metal detector as she

walked, sweeping it this way and that, just to get a feel for it.

'Is that where we're going?'

'Yes.'

'But... won't that be, I don't know, tampering with evidence or something?'

Anna laughed. 'The police are finished with it. Besides, that's what your camera's for. To prove I didn't do anything dodgy.'

'Making me an accessory. Nice.'

'Go have breakfast then, if you must. But you'll miss the highlight of your documentary.'

'How do you mean?'

'Turn on your camera and find out.'

He sighed but complied, holding it out at arm's length to film himself first. 'I'm only doing this under protest,' he said, 'and to create a record that otherwise wouldn't have been made.'

'Coward,' said Anna.

'Damn right. You don't have to deal with these people for work.'

It had grown distinctly lighter by now. The silhouettes of the house and barn were black against the dawn. A mound of rich brown earth lay beside the pit. She ran the detector over it. Nothing. She got down onto her knees. The ground was cold and wet and muddy. The pit was maybe four feet across and almost as deep. Uncle Dun had been found curled up in the foetal position at its foot, his skull cleaved in two by a single massive blow. She put a hand on the ground to support herself then reached the detector down with the other. Almost at once, it began to screech. It happened so quickly, indeed, that she suspected some kind of malfunction. But it fell silent when she raised it back up a little, then screeched again when she lowered it once more.

'My god,' muttered Oliver. 'What's down there?'

'Not a clue.'

'Then how did you know to look?'

'I told you last night. It made no sense, someone digging a pit to bury my uncle. It would have taken too long. And surely they'd have stopped to think about what they were going to do with the van once they were done. The only way it made sense was if the pit was already dug. I mean, can't you see it? Some nighthawk out with their metal detector and spade. They have to do it in the dark, of course, or they'd be certain to be seen. They get a signal on their detector and start digging. But Uncle Dun catches them at it and comes to confront them.'

'Only they get the better of him,' murmured Oliver. 'They kill him and bury him in their pit.'

'Exactly. Clearly they panicked, or they'd have checked for his keys first. So maybe they abandoned their treasure hunt too. In which case whatever they were digging for will still be here.'

'Any idea who they were?'

'No. That's for Elias to find out.'

'You're going to call him?'

'In a moment,' said Anna. She clambered down into the pit, taking with her a small landslide of the loose wet soil that made Lincolnshire so fertile. A team of university geologists had once taken core samples from various fields around here. They'd drilled down through thirty feet of silt before finally hitting a layer of sand and seashells, with bedrock deeper still. Back in 1947, just a few miles from here, five World War II landing craft had been swallowed whole during a bad flood. One had since been recovered, but the other four were still missing. That was why it was just about possible to believe John's treasure was here, despite the lack of finds; because thirty feet of silt could swallow a baggage train whole and keep it beyond the reach of even the most sophisticated remote-sensing devices. 'Uncle Dun had been searching these fields all his life,' she said, digging with her trowel. 'He never found all that much. But maybe his detector was just too old. Some of the latest models can see far deeper. They can distinguish between metals too, so you won't waste time on can-pulls and nails and bottle tops. You only dig this deep for something really worth the effort.'

'A precious metal of some kind?'

'That would be my guess,' said Anna. She sifted the silt through her fingers before tossing it aside. She'd barely been at it a minute before she found a shard from a broken pot of some kind, followed almost instantly by a second shard, and then, a little deeper, by a first metallic glint. Her heart gave a thump. She crouched for a closer look. A round thin greenish object the size of her thumbnail. She cleared its face of silt then leaned back for Oliver to film.

'Jesus,' he muttered, squatting down low. 'What is it?'

She picked it up carefully between her fingertips, turned it around to inspect both faces. 'A silver penny.'

'What date? Tell me it's John. Please tell me it's John.'

She brushed away the rest of the soil. It was tarnished, but not too badly. The pot must have spared it from any worse, only for it to be shattered by her uncle's deep-ploughing, making the silver easier for the metal detector to pick up. Yet the morning was still so gloomy that she had to hold it at an angle to see. 'See this?' she asked, indicating the lettering around its face. 'It reads Henricus Rex. That's for Henry II, as it happens. John's father.'

'Bollocks,' said Oliver.

'Not so fast,' said Anna. 'This will seem weird, but all early Plantagenet coins were stamped this same way. Even after Richard took the throne, and then John after him. And of course John was succeeded by his son Henry III, and the world made sense again.'

'Like not changing your clocks until summertime comes back around?'

'Exactly,' said Anna. 'So you can't tell who was king just from that. You have to look at the portrait, which *did* change with each king. John was the only one of them to have himself shown in three-quarter profile. The others were all face on.'

'And? Don't tease me like this.'

'It's John.' She grinned up at him in delight. 'We may just have found the first trace of his lost treasure.'

TWENTY-SIX

Elias was brushing his teeth in the field across from Warne Farm when his mobile rang. It was still so early that he suffered a spike of panic that something had happened to the twins – but then he saw it was Anna Warne and calmed down again. 'What?' he asked. He listened in increasing disbelief as she told him about her morning. He rinsed out his mouth, pulled on a fresh shirt then drove across the lane to find her crouched down in her uncle's burial pit while being filmed by Merchant. 'What the hell?' he said furiously, slamming his door and marching up to them. 'This is a crime scene. Your uncle was murdered here. Is this any way to honour him?'

'Yes,' said Anna. She stood up and held up her left hand to show him three shards from an ancient small pot and five small coins, two of them stuck fast together by their tarnishing. 'I just found these here. They may help catch whoever killed him. And you idiots missed them.'

Elias stared at the coins in shock. 'That's no excuse for contaminating the scene,' he said weakly.

'Contaminating the scene!' she scoffed. 'You were done with it. You know you were. These would never have been found if I hadn't thought to come looking.'

Her phrasing caught his ear. 'You *thought* to come looking?'

Anna nodded. 'I realised something at dinner with Oliver last night. Why bother burying my uncle without moving the van? A pit this deep would have taken ages to dig. Surely in that time they'd have checked for keys. So the only way it made sense was if the pit was already dug. And who else would have dug it in the middle of the night except a treasure hunter? It was obviously possible that my uncle had surprised them before they'd recovered whatever it was they'd been digging for, so I borrowed a metal detector and came to look.'

Elias was still furious, but he was also conscious of Merchant's camera upon him. 'What are they?' he asked grudgingly.

'King John silver pennies. And the detector's still screeching, so there's obviously more down there. But I figured it was time to let you know.'

'That's something.' He fetched a pair of evidence bags for her to tip the shards and the coins into. 'You still should have called me first.'

'And have you kick me off my own property again?'

'Oh. So that's it, is it? You're miffed.' He turned to Merchant. 'Her I can understand. She doesn't know better. You damned well should.'

'I didn't tell him where we were going,' said Anna. 'He tried to stop me when he realised, but I went ahead anyway. His choice was to film or not to film. You should be thanking him.'

Elias glowered a few moments longer, but then he sighed and let it go. 'Do you get a lot of treasure hunters around here?'

'Yes. Particularly at this time of year, with the fields just ploughed. Though it's hard to know exactly how many. Some leave pits behind, but presumably others go away empty-handed, or cover their traces better. It drove my uncle nuts, particularly the ones from the hotel. You could tell them by their tracks. But what could he do? He was already running a whole farm by himself. He could hardly sit up nights as well.'

'Are you saying this was someone from the hotel?'

'Not necessarily. There are plenty of places around here where people can park and walk on in. But sure, if any of their guests checked out unexpectedly first thing last Monday morning, that might be a place to start.'

TWENTY-SEVEN

The morning was rapidly growing brighter. A little traffic began passing by as people set off for work. Maria Quinn and another constable arrived in a squad car, pulling up on the drive behind Elias's Leaf. Elias excused himself to go talk to them, then came back over. 'My colleagues will take you back to the hotel now,' he told Oliver.

'I'm fine here, thanks,' Oliver replied.

'I'll take your camera too.'

'You and whose army?'

'For god's sake,' said Anna irritably. 'Email him a copy of your footage. It's what I brought you along for.'

'Come on, Anna,' pleaded Oliver. 'It's gold dust for my doc. What if it leaks?'

'We don't leak,' said Elias.

'Sure!' scoffed Oliver.

'Then send it to my personal account. I give you my word no one else will see it without your express permission. If it gets out, you'll know exactly who to blame.'

'Damn right, I will.' But it was a concession.

Anna made to follow him to the squad car, but Elias touched her on her arm. 'Can you spare me a few minutes?' he asked. 'I need your help with something up at the house. I can run you back to the hotel myself afterwards.'

She handed Oliver the trowel and metal detector to return, climbed into the Leaf. 'So those coins of yours,' said Elias, waiting for the squad car to leave before reversing back out and heading up to the farmhouse. 'Just pennies, yeah? Nothing larger?'

'Pennies were all they had back then, apart from a few gold bezants brought back from the crusades. Shillings and the rest only came in later.'

'Oh,' he said, abashed, as though he should have known. 'And they're part of this lost baggage train, are they?'

'Maybe. I think they're from the 1206 coinage, which would fit. And they show roughly the right amount of wear and tear.'

'But…?'

Anna nodded. 'Every penny back then was stamped with the name of the man who struck it. That way, if they mixed too much lead in with the silver, they'd literally be stamping their name upon their crime. It was the only way of keeping track, because there were so many different mints. The biggest by far were in London and Canterbury, but there were plenty of others around the regions, including one in Lynn.'

'And these are from there, I'm assuming,' said Elias, pulling up by the barn. 'But why's that a problem?'

'It isn't, necessarily. John had just come from Lynn, where he'd collected fines and taxes and gifts. So he'd certainly have had *some* Lynn pennies. But he'd also been travelling around the country, collecting money from all kinds of different places, so frankly you'd expect a mix. On the other hand, if a local merchant lost their cache while crossing the marshes, or a householder stashed their hoard because the war was getting too close…'

'Ah. Shame.'

'Telling me. Honest to god, it'd double the farm's value overnight if it really is John's.'

Elias fetched a flat-headed screwdriver from the workshop then led the way inside the barn. A little morning light seeped through the slats and around the edges of the doors, but it was still gloomy enough for torches. Elias went directly to the oil tank. 'Any idea when your uncle put this in?'

'The summer before last, I think,' said Anna. 'The old one started leaking. Why?'

For answer, Elias lay down on his side to prise the plastic casing off the base with his screwdriver, then release a pair of catches inside. He stood back up, put his shoulder to its other end and slid it along a pair of rails to expose a hatch in the floor that he lifted up and set to one side. Anna stared down the shaft in shock. 'What the hell?' she muttered.

'You didn't know?'

'Of course I didn't know. You think I wouldn't have said?'

'Maybe you wanted to protect your uncle.'

'Then I'd hardly have told you that this was where those men were searching, would I?'

'A nice professional job,' Elias told her. 'Would have taken a crew at least three days to dig it out, brick up the sides, cover it up and install the tank. At least. More like a week. So tell me this: Was your uncle the kind of man not to notice his barn floor being torn up by jackhammers then covered with a brand new fuel tank?'

'Do you have to be quite such an arse, Detective?' said Anna. 'This is my uncle you're talking about.'

'There was a similar case in Norfolk a few years back,' he told her. 'It was what prompted me to look. The farmer there used seasonal workers during harvest. Like your uncle, yeah?'

'Everyone does. It's that or let your crops rot.'

'Yes. Anyway, this farmer, he made a deal with his gangmaster for super-cheap labour. The workers were illegal, of course. If they got caught, they'd all be for it. But the gangmaster told him not to worry. He'd fit an abandoned grain silo with a hidden chamber where they could all hide if anyone came looking.'

'Oh. You think that's what happened here?'

'You tell me. You knew the man.'

Anna gave a helpless shrug. 'I guess it makes as much sense as anything.'

'This farmer, he lived by himself too, and bang up against the coast. Just like your uncle. Anyway, he soon found out that the bit about hiding workers was bullshit. They used it for smuggling instead. That way, there was no one moment of handover when both sides could be caught. The first lot would stash their product and go home. Then the second lot would come to move it on. Unfortunately, this Norfolk farmer was in too deep by the time he realised this. Plus they slipped him a few hundred quid every now and then to make sure he looked the other way. Assuming the same happened here, your uncle was their dupe. It's the smugglers I want, before they ruin someone else's life. Unfortunately, we have nothing on them.' He turned to look at her, his arms folded. 'Nothing but you.'

'*Me?*'

'You saw them up close. You heard them talk.'

'At night,' protested Anna. 'With their faces covered.'

'People aren't just their faces, though, are they? They have builds, postures, movements, accents. My colleagues in Serious and Organised Crime have some surveillance footage you could look at.'

'But there must be hundreds of suspects. How am I supposed to pick out two?'

'There won't be anything like that many, not with the descriptions you've already given us. Especially as we already have a fair idea of the people behind it.'

'You do? How come?'

Elias hesitated. 'There's something I haven't told you yet,' he said eventually. 'But you need to promise me it goes no further. Not even to your TV friend.'

'You've got him wrong. He wouldn't do anything to harm the investigation.'

'Maybe not. I still need your word.'

'Fine,' she sighed. 'You have it.'

'Good. Thank you. Then it's too dark for you to see, but there's graffiti on the walls down there. It wasn't just drugs being trafficked.'

Anna looked sourly at him. 'So some people wanted a better life. Big deal.'

'You misunderstand. I'm pretty sure that the foreign end of this operation smuggled in a family group about six weeks ago. The locals were supposed to collect them, only they got delayed. By the time anyone arrived to let them out, at least one of them had suffocated.'

'Oh Christ,' said Anna.

'At least one. Probably more. So they felt compelled to kill the others too, to make sure they didn't talk. There's spatter on the walls, you see. They tried to scrub it off, but they didn't do a great job, probably because they had the more pressing problem of what to do with the bodies. They could hardly leave them here. Far too many people knew about this place, any one of whom could have traded it for a lighter sentence. But getting rid of them wasn't so simple either. Dump them in the river or the Wash, they might bob up or be spotted at low tide. And who'd want to drive around Lincolnshire with half a dozen corpses in their boot? Especially as there was a more obvious solution literally staring them in the face.' He gestured at the old ditch digger. 'All they needed was a night to themselves and a spot on the farm that would never get ploughed up.'

'Those footprints between the fields,' murmured Anna.

'Yes.'

'That's what you fetched that stake for yesterday. You used it to probe for bodies.'

'Yes.'

'And?'

'I think so, yes.'

'I don't understand. Where are all your people, then?'

'On their way.'

'On their way?' she said angrily. 'But you knew this yesterday. The place should be crawling with...' Then she realised. 'That would have tipped the killers off. You didn't want them tipped off. You wanted them thinking it was safe to come back again last night. That's why you kicked me out yesterday. You needed the house empty. It's how you got here so quickly this morning too, and why you haven't shaved, and why you're in yesterday's clothes. You spent the night watching.'

'It seemed worth a shot.'

'You're mad. Those men would have killed you.'

'I can look after myself,' he assured her. 'And we've got nothing else to go on. Nothing but you.'

'I don't know,' she said unhappily. 'You didn't see them.'

'I understand. Truly. But still.'

Anna gazed down the shaft, which Elias had deliberately left open. There was something horrible about its darkness. 'You think my uncle knew? That people died down there, I mean?'

'I'm pretty sure he was away the night they moved them.'

'He was never away.'

'I found a ticket to a West End musical from around that time in his desk, along with a hotel receipt. I'll bet that was the smugglers telling him to make himself scarce.' He paused a moment, then added: 'But people change too, you know. Would it surprise you to learn that we've got his van on a traffic cam at three in the morning on the night he died, coming back from up Sleaford way?'

'Three in the morning?' said Anna, bewildered. 'He was never out that late. Where had he been?'

'I was hoping you'd tell me.'

'I mean he used to buy farming supplies from a dealer up there, but not at that time of...' Then she realised. 'Is that how it happened? He spotted his killer as he arrived home.'

'That's how I see it, yes. He catches your treasure hunter in his headlights when he turns in up his drive. He gets out to give them a piece of his mind. Only they smack him with their spade instead and bury him in their pit, forgetting about his keys until it's too late. We find him. It makes the news. Our smuggler friends freak out. Your uncle's murder has nothing to do with them, but what if we find their vault? What if we find the bodies? Because what particularly spooks them is that they lost something here. Something that could link them to their crimes. So they wait for us to leave and then come look. Only you surprise them in the barn.'

Anna nodded. 'You really think you know who these people are?'

'There's this gang in Lincoln that runs most of the county's drugs. My colleagues in Serious and Organised Crime raided them about six weeks ago, which is exactly when this went down, meaning they were all under arrest or in hiding when they should have been letting these poor sods out.'

'Six weeks ago?' She gave a grimace. 'That was just before my uncle asked the neighbours if they'd be interested in buying this place from him.'

'Too many ghosts,' murmured Elias.

'He knew, then.' Her expression hardened. 'This footage of yours. How do I look at it? Can I do it here?'

'Ah. No. That's the thing. Smuggling is handled by Serious and Organised Crime, like I say. They're very protective of their material. You'd have to go to Nettleham.'

'Nettleham?'

'Our HQ. About five minutes drive north of Lincoln. But I can at least offer you a carrot.'

'I don't much care for carrots.'

'You'll like this one, I think. We had your uncle's van taken up there for a full examination. It's done now. It's waiting to be collected. You could pick up some of your uncle's other effects too, the ones we don't need any more. His bank cards, for example. You'll want those for starting probate.'

'Is this a tit for tat? I get his stuff if I look at your footage?'

'No. You get it anyway. I'm just saying, two birds, one stone.'

'Three birds,' she said. Then she noticed his look of puzzlement and added: 'My uncle's at the Lincoln coroners. They told me I could go visit to say goodbye, if I wanted. So yes, okay, I'll do it.'

'Great. You're a star. I'll let the guys know. Give me a few hours, I could even drive you up there myself? Or I can have you taken to the railway station?'

'No need. Oliver's heading back up there this morning. If he hasn't left already.'

'Then why not check to make sure, and I'll run you back to the hotel.'

TWENTY-EIGHT

Anna texted Oliver about a lift. He sent back a pair of happy-faced emojis and a thumbs up. The Scene of Crime team arrived before they could set off, however. Elias begged a few minutes to show them the new sites he needed investigating, so Anna went inside the house. The silver pennies had assured her of a starring role in Oliver's documentary whether she wanted it or not, and only cowardice was now stopping her from seizing the opportunity. But she'd forgotten so much about the Fens and John's crown jewels that she needed a refresher.

She took a cardboard box from the pantry through to her uncle's study. The books she was after were mostly already out on the floor. She chose eight of them, including a copy of her uncle's own book, then checked through the papers on his desk, quickly becoming absorbed by the articles and maps, as well as by the old excavation reports he had out for places like Byard's Leap and Temple Bruer.

Intriguingly, she found among them a letter from an address in Swineshead, the small Lincolnshire town in which King John had spent the night after losing his baggage train. And while the abbey he'd stayed at had been torn down centuries ago, a single relic from it had survived in private hands: a statue supposedly of a monk called Brother Simon, accused by some of having laced King John's cider with poison he'd harvested from the skin of a toad. It was pure folklore, of course. Toad venom produced completely different symptoms, and John had anyway already been sick with the dysentery that killed him before arriving at the abbey. Yet the story had gained enough traction for Caxton to publish it in a pamphlet and for Shakespeare to put it in a play.

Uncle Dun had naturally hankered to see this statue, and so had written twice to its owners many years ago. He'd never even heard back from them, however, and he'd been too proud to ask a third time. Yet, presumably prompted by Oliver's documentary, he'd given it another shot, and had received a charming reply from the new owner inviting him to drop by whenever he so wished.

'Ready?'

Anna looked up. Elias was in the doorway, hands stuffed in pockets. 'Sure,' she said. She gathered up her uncle's papers and added them to her box, then lugged it out to the car.

'The vault, the bodies,' said Elias, as they pulled away. 'It goes no further, right?'

'I already gave you my word.'

'I know. I'm just saying. Your mate Oliver has a gift for making people open up. A scoop like this could win him his old job back.'

She turned to gaze at him. 'What do you mean, win it back? Did he lose it?'

'You didn't know? Sorry, I just assumed. It caused a major stink.'

'Not up in York, it didn't. What happened?'

'Okay, so your mate used to front our local consumer rights show. You know the kind of thing, I'm sure. Shoddy extensions, botched surgeries, pensioners cheated of their savings. He'd go confront the baddies on camera, seek justice for the little guy. He pissed off a lot of nasty people that way, but small-fry, you know, not big enough to kick back.' A farmer was tilling the field beside the lane, the breeze blowing the churned up mud and dirt like bushfire smoke across their path. 'Then he moved up a couple of leagues, by taking on our county's most notorious slumlord. His apartments are just soul destroying. Infested with rats and roaches, broken boilers, peeling wallpaper, leaking ceilings, rising damp, every horror you can name. Squeezes his tenants ruthlessly too. And heaven help anyone who tries to challenge him. You wouldn't believe how many end up in hospital. Or worse.'

'Christ. Why doesn't someone do something?'

'Your mate tried, to be fair. But the man's too rich and well connected. His father-in-law isn't just a hereditary peer, he's also a former government minister who sits on all the boards around here, and is mates with everyone who matters. Word is he gets paid a small fortune to run interference.'

'And he got Oliver fired?'

'So I heard. For sure the programme got binned. And your mate was out on his ear shortly afterwards.'

They reached the hotel, pulled into an empty bay. Anna collected her box of books from the back then thanked Elias for the lift, only for him to come inside with her. 'Forgotten already, have you?' he asked, amused. 'Your tip about guests checking out first thing on Monday morning?'

'Oh hell. Don't tell them that was me.'

'You borrowed their metal detector at some ungodly hour. I reckon they'll work it out.'

She went upstairs to dump her books on her bed, then knocked on Oliver's door. He was on the phone, discussing plans for some filming he'd arranged for Newark Castle tomorrow morning. He beckoned her in while he finished up. 'So what did Elias want?' he asked.

'Just a question about the barn. You sure you're okay giving me a lift? I kind of ambushed you.'

'Of course. A pleasure, a joy, a treat. Oh, and I've something fun to show you.' He went to his desk, revived his laptop. Anna was already on its screen, standing in the pit holding that first silver penny. The light was gloomy, her hair was tousled and she had smuts of dirt on her nose and forehead, yet her face was aglow from the early morning cool and the thrill of discovery. He set the clip playing and she began talking about ancient coinage not just with excitement, but with a confidence and fluency that frankly amazed her.

'Wow,' she muttered. 'I'm not that bad, am I?'

'Wait till I've fixed the lighting,' he grinned. 'Honest to god, you'll be a star.'

'As if,' she said, reflexively. Yet she couldn't take her eyes off it.

TWENTY-NINE

León de Bruin prided himself on being up early. The best time of day, he always said. Not this morning, though. He lay in bed long after he'd woken, arms wrapped around a pillow to give himself comfort. He'd forgotten the downside of being smitten by a woman, these passages of lassitude and even despair between the moments of euphoria.

When finally he dragged himself downstairs, Samantha was at the kitchen table helping Melanie with a colouring book. 'You were out late,' she said, in that tone of hers. He placed a kiss upon his daughter's crown. 'Morning, scrumptious,' he said.

'I'm drawing,' she said.

'Where did you get to?' asked Samantha.

'Skegness,' said de Bruin. It was at least partially true. Two hours he'd sat in the corner of the King John Hotel's car-park, waiting to see Anna Warne, fully aware of how ridiculous and reckless he was being, yet unable to leave. *One minute more*, he'd kept telling himself. *One minute more*. Then finally she'd appeared, back from a night out with Oliver Merchant. Watching them go inside together had been bad enough, but nothing compared to the lights coming on in an upstairs room, Merchant walking by the window then Anna drawing the curtains. Jealousy was like being gutted by the world's sharpest knife. And with Merchant of all people! The yearning to make him suffer almost overwhelmed him. He should have hated

Anna for it too, yet perversely he'd only longed for her all the more. 'One of my tenants had a problem.'

'I wish you'd let me know. I get worried.'

'It was an emergency. I had no choice.' He rented out one of his nicer Skegness houses to a husband and wife team called the Kents, who ran a series of pop-up brothels along the coast. An Armenian brunette on his last visit had had something of Anna Warne about her, not just in her looks but in her defiance too. But he'd arrived to find her spirit broken by drugs, and she'd merely disgusted him instead.

'Isn't that what you have managers for?'

'Everyone deserves the odd night off.'

He took his coffee through to his study to check for updates on the Dark Web. His source had just posted an urgent message. Elias hadn't only discovered the vault, it seemed. He'd also found what appeared to be human remains buried between two fields.

De Bruin felt nauseous. He and Andrei had only gone to Warne Farm that awful night on a mission of mercy, what with everyone else under arrest or in hiding. They'd opened the vault to a haunting silence and a dreadful smell. Andrei had wanted to close the place back up and get out of there, but de Bruin had insisted on making sure. He'd actually had his hand on the woman's forehead when suddenly she'd gasped and sat up, giving him the shock of his life. She'd looked around for a moment or two, dazed by lack of air. Then she'd seen her family lying dead around her, and had simply gone berserk. No other word would do. She'd hurled herself at him, clawing at his eyes, leaving him no choice but to use his screwdriver on her, blood spurting over his face and hands and clothes, splashing the walls and floor and other bodies, until finally she'd subsided into unconsciousness and he'd lain spent upon her.

Worse still was that her little girl had then revived as well, picking up where her mum had left off, sobbing and shrieking until he'd clamped a hand over her mouth to quieten her, squeezing her throat with his other until she too had succumbed. She'd only been a year or two older than Melanie. Sometimes, at odd moments since, he'd feel again the wetness of her saliva upon his palm, and have to wipe it off on his trousers. But what choice had he had? What choice? Anyone else would have done the same, wouldn't they? Anyone at all.

THIRTY

Elias presented himself at hotel reception to be greeted by a plump, forty-something Indian woman with a charming warm smile that turned noticeably cooler when he produced his warrant card and explained that he was investigating Dunstan Warne's murder. Then it turned cold when he asked if they'd had any detectorists staying last weekend, or whether any of their guests had checked out unexpectedly early on Monday morning. She didn't answer directly, but rather called her boss Penny Scott, who instructed her in an imperious voice not to say another word until she arrived.

Elias used the time to do his customary study of the receptionist. She had a paperback copy of Jane Eyre on her desk, borrowed from the local library, to judge from its protective cover and its reservation slip bookmark, which gave her name as Kapur, Priya. She was wearing a navy jacket with gold piping that was both too snug across the shoulders and too long in the sleeve, suggesting it was inherited, and she sat with her feet tucked beneath her and with her back commendably straight. Her lips and fingernails were painted an identical bright shade of crimson and – despite numerous rings, bangles, pendants and other items of jewellery – her ring finger was conspicuously bare. She noticed him looking and pursed her lips. He picked up a brochure for Frampton Marsh and wondered again what the hell was wrong with him.

Footsteps crunched gravel outside. The door opened and Penny Scott arrived like a compact whirlwind, her husband trailing haplessly behind her like a plastic bag caught in its tug. She looked to be in her mid-fifties, tall, thin, blonde and attractive, but with a brittleness that was emphasised rather than mitigated by her expensive clothes and heels, by her painted long nails, her lashes and whitened teeth. 'So you're this detective, are you?' she said, marching up to him. 'We already told your people all we know.'

'And we're grateful, believe me,' said Elias. 'But a new line of inquiry has opened up. We think you may be able to help us with it.'

'And? Are we supposed to guess?'

'The detective was asking whether we had any detectorists staying last weekend,' piped up Priya.

'Detectorists?' asked Penny Scott.

'Yes,' said Elias. 'Detectorists.'

'I thought you were after smugglers.'

'We were. Now we're looking at detectorists too.'

She gazed at him a second or two, then turned to Priya. 'You were on duty, weren't you? Did we have any detectorists staying?'

'No,' said Priya.

'There you go, Detective. No.'

'Who did you have staying?'

Priya glanced at Penny Scott. Penny Scott nodded reluctantly for her to go ahead. 'Most of our guests were here for a wedding,' she told him. 'Those ones all checked out some time on Sunday. Only five stayed that night. Mr Inwood is one of our regulars. He works all hours on an environmental project. He only comes in to sleep and have breakfast. I've never seen him with a metal detector, and he's certainly never hired one of ours. Anyway, he hurt his ankle a couple of weeks ago, and he's still on crutches. Otherwise, it was only the Grahams and the Gwynns, both here on our weekend package. I don't think they knew each other before, but they spent a lot of time together. They're all quite elderly and frail, so I can't imagine they had anything to do with it. They did all check out early on Monday morning, though. But then they would, wouldn't they?'

'You were here that night?'

'On duty, yes,' said Priya. 'Not at the desk. I have a room in the back. If anyone needs me, they ring the bell.'

'Did anyone ring it that night?'

'No.'

'What if a guest is out late? How do they get back in?'

'They have keys and the code for the door.'

'Is there a log of when it's used?'

'No. It's just a lock.'

'How about your metal detectors? Could someone take one without you knowing?'

'I suppose. We keep the key behind the desk. But the storeroom's next to me, and I think I'd have heard.' Her eyes flickered to Gregory Scott as she said this, however, and then she flushed slightly, as though realising she'd made a mistake.

Elias turned to look at him, half hidden behind his wife. He looked to be about her age, but where she was still gamely fighting time, he'd happily given in. Overweight, with thinning grey hair and an uneven shave, wearing a crumpled blue blazer over his peach polo shirt and a pair of tight red jeans that seemed to squeeze all the fat up from his thighs into his midriff instead. His complexion suggested he liked it out of doors, and there was plenty of power in those meaty arms, easily enough to cleave a skull in two. 'How about you, sir?' he asked. 'Would you happen to be a detectorist yourself?'

'What's that supposed to mean?' demanded Scott.

'Which part of the question do you find confusing, sir?'

'Why do you want to know? Are you accusing me of something?'

'We found a number of coins beneath where Mr Warne was buried. It seems possible that someone was digging for them when Mr Warne spotted them and came to challenge them.'

Penny Scott stared aghast at him. 'Are you saying he was killed by a detectorist?'

'I'm saying it's a line of inquiry. Well, sir? Are you one yourself?'

He tugged a finger inside the collar of his polo shirt. 'Not as such, no.'

'Not as such?'

'I used to be. I haven't been out in ages.'

'What kind of ages? Days? Weeks? Months?'

'More like years.' But his voice betrayed him, as did the pleading look he threw his wife. 'I'm sorry not to be more specific. It's not like I keep a diary.'

'But you do own a metal detector?'

'Everyone does around here. It's our local pastime.'

'What make is yours? What model?'

'I haven't the faintest idea.'

'How much did it cost, then?'

'Be reasonable, Detective. It was years ago.'

'Roughly, then. A hundred pounds? A thousand? More? Less?'

'I'd say about a thousand. Perhaps a hair more. I'm a wealthy man, Detective. I don't like second best.'

'Very well. So you own a top-of-the-range metal detector. Have you ever taken it out onto Warne Farm?'

'Absolutely not. Mr Warne was quite clear that his fields were out of bounds.'

'What about last Monday morning? Were you up and about early, by any chance?'

'I was not. I slept like a log.' But again that plaintive glance at his wife.

Elias turned to her. She'd frozen stiff, save for a tremble in her jaw. 'Can you confirm that, ma'am?'

A marked hesitation. An angry glance at her husband. But then: 'Yes. I can.'

'You share a bedroom, then?'

'I happen to be a *very* light sleeper. I wake at the *slightest* noise.'

'If you slept through a noise, how would you even know?'

She gave a blink, like one of his old opponents caught with a jab. 'It's not just the noise. We have intruder lights too. They'd wake Rip Van Winkle.'

'Ah,' said Elias. 'Then that settles it.' He turned back to Priya. 'Do you rent out spades as well as metal detectors?'

'Yes.'

'Good. Then we'll be taking them away for examination. I assume that's okay?'

'Examination?' protested Penny Scott. 'Whatever for?'

'For blood,' Elias told her. 'For hair. For fingerprints. To clear your guests of suspicion. That's what you want, I imagine. To clear them of suspicion?' He gave her the chance to reply. She didn't take it. 'Where are they?' he asked Priya. She took a key from the rack, led him to the storeroom. He photographed everything in place then locked it and pocketed the key. 'No one goes in there until my people have been,' he told her, before turning to Gregory Scott. 'Do you own a spade too, sir?'

'This is an outrage,' he said.

'An outrage to ask if you own a spade?'

'An outrage to imply I had anything to do with Mr Warne's death.'

'I'm looking to exclude you, sir. Do you not think you should be excluded?'

'Of course I should.'

'Good. Then if you could show me…'

'If you insist. But this whole thing's a farce.' His defiance fell flat, however. He looked trapped and guilty as they filed out of the hotel.

There were CCTV cameras on the roof and in the car-park, noted Elias. He texted Quinn as they walked to come review last Sunday night's footage. Then he called Frank Mason to have him send a team to collect the spades and metal detectors.

The hotel and the Scotts' converted barn were screened off

from one another by a high conifer hedge. To get from one to the other, they had to walk out of the hotel car park to the shared drive, then take the other fork. An automated gate had a postbox and a buzzer on it, along with a gap down its side for anyone on foot. Gregory Scott was still leading the way, but his shoulders slumped ever more heavily as he trudged with gallows slowness. If ever Elias had seen guilt, he was seeing it now.

An open-faced garden shed was set at an angle from the barn. The three of them went inside together. A huge green sit-on mower took up much of its interior, while a pair of rakes, a fork, a hoe, some shears and other such garden implements hung neatly from hooks on the right-hand wall. They all had Dewit's trademark ash handles, and looked to be of the same model and vintage too, as if the Scotts had ordered the complete set on first moving in. Yet Elias could see no sign of a spade, only of a gap where a spade might fit.

'Well?' he asked.

Scott turned and spread his hands. 'I don't understand it,' he said. 'It's gone.'

THIRTY-ONE

It was time to leave. Anna lugged her bags and box of books down to reception, where to her surprise she found WPC Maria Quinn reviewing CCTV footage on the hotel computer while Priya watched unhappily. 'It was you who found those coins, wasn't it?' said Priya, almost accusingly, when Anna handed back her key. 'That's what you borrowed the detector for.'

'I had a hunch, that's all.'

'That horrible detective thinks it was Mr Scott,' she said, loudly enough for Quinn to hear. 'I know he does. It's crazy. He's a good man. He wouldn't hurt a fly.'

The BMW's boot was already full of Oliver's stuff, so Anna stowed her things on his back seat instead. 'You've certainly stirred things up,' he murmured.

'I know. I feel terrible.'

'Hey. If he did it, he did it.'

'Sure. But they'll never comp me another room, will they?'

He laughed as he belted himself in. 'Speaking of which, where are you going to stay tonight?'

'York, I think. I'll head up there once I've got the van. Then back down tomorrow to see my uncle's solicitor.'

'That's nuts,' he said. 'Stay at my place. And no, before you get all hoity-toity, my spare room has a sturdy lock on its door – not to mention a lovely view of the cathedral. And all I ask in return is that you tell me about Newark Castle.

I'm interviewing some fearsome custodian woman there tomorrow morning. I should at least do *some* prep.'

'I honestly don't know that much myself. Other than it's where King John died.'

'Damn it. That's the one bit I already knew.'

They headed west, along winding back roads tightly flanked by deep drainage ditches, mantraps that often caught drunk or careless drivers. A bower of trees was carpeted golden with autumn leaves that they set swirling in their wake. A pair of piebald horses in winter rugs grazed contentedly in a paddock next to an ancient barn with a colourfully patched roof, reminding her of how hand-to-mouth life as a small farmer could be, despite the richness of this soil. An idyllic life in some ways, but it bred toughness and self-reliance too.

They reached the A17 at Fleet Hargate, crossed the Welland on the Fosdyke Bridge. The rigging of the shipyard yachts clacked and jangled in the breeze. Oliver was good behind the wheel, relaxed, assured and courteous to other drivers. Throw in two nights of broken sleep, a pleasantly warm car and Lincolnshire's famously flat straight roads, and it wasn't long before Anna's eyelids began to droop. But then a road sign snapped her awake again.

'Not my driving, I hope?' said Oliver.

'No.' She was silent a few moments, then said: 'Elias told me something this morning. He told me that my uncle was caught on a traffic camera driving back home along this road in the early hours right before he was killed. He asked if I knew who he might have been visiting so late. I didn't have a clue. Dun was the least social person you could imagine. But there is *one* possibility.' She pointed at the outskirts of a small town to their right. 'Because that's Swineshead there. Where John stayed the night after losing his baggage train.'

'Wasn't the abbey pulled down?'

'It was, yes. Ages ago. But a statue survived. It's of a monk called Brother Simon, the one who supposedly poisoned King John. Uncle Dun wrote to its owner after your visit, asking if he could go see it. And the guy said yes.'

'You think that's where he was that night?'

'I think it may have been. And he seemed friendly enough, so how about we go ask? If we have time, that is?'

'Sure. You know where he lives?'

She reached in back for his letter, plugged his address into her map app. They had to cut back through the town, a mix of family homes and retirement bungalows that offered little trace of its rich history. They found the house. A long drive led them between unkempt lawns and an orchard of fallen fruit and drunken wasps to an Edwardian mansion covered by thick ropes of ivy that had burrowed deep into its paintwork. It had a shabby conservatory to one side and a large low extension to the other, whose sloped roof was given over entirely to solar panelling.

The bell made a melodious chime. Anna took a step back. A door banged inside and a man cursed loudly, as though he'd stubbed his toe. Bolts were drawn and the front door opened to reveal a portly, red-faced man in his early sixties with ink-stained hands, a bushy beard and a pair of gold-rimmed glasses pushed up over his unruly grey-brown hair. Despite the seasonal chill, he was dressed in khaki shorts, a gaudy Hawaiian shirt with the buttons done up wrong, and a pair of mismatched flip-flops. He beamed gladly at the pair of them, as though they were an early Christmas present some kindly neighbour had left upon his mat. 'Yes,' he said, phrasing it less as a question so much as wholehearted agreement to anything they might ask.

'I'm sorry to turn up out of the blue like this,' said Anna, set at ease by his obvious geniality. 'But I was wondering whether my uncle might possibly have come to see you the other night.'

The man brought down his glasses, the better to peer at her. 'He might have done,' he acknowledged. 'He might very well have done. An extraordinary number of people do come to see me, for some unfathomable reason. That said, I'd find it easier to answer your question one way or the other if I had even the slightest idea of who either you or your uncle are.'

'Oh,' said Anna. 'Yes. Forgive me. My name's Anna Warne. I believe my uncle Dunstan wrote to you about—'

'Dunstan Warne. Of course.' His face fell instantly. 'I only just heard the news. I'm so terribly, terribly sorry.' He held the door wide open for them. 'Come in, come in, and I'll tell you all I know.'

THIRTY-TWO

Elias had witnessed too many protestations of innocence over the years to worry overmuch about the words themselves. He'd learned to study tone instead, to watch hands and faces. And so he found himself intrigued by the way Gregory Scott kept turning to his wife, as though she were the one he most needed to convince. She knew something, Elias was sure of it. What was more, he was fearful that she'd tell. 'And your metal detector?' he asked, when finally Scott was done. 'Or has that vanished too?'

'I can't see how,' said Scott unhappily. 'I saw it just the other day, I know I did.' He led the way inside their home, to a closet beneath the stairs. 'There!' he said. He was about to pull it out when Elias asked him to step back. A metal detector was indeed leaning against the wall: a Minelab CTX 3030, with its own monitor and headphones, and with a hooded battery lamp on the floor beside it. What was more, a vacuum cleaner, an ironing board and a pair of brooms were all stored behind it – a curious arrangement for something so rarely used.

Elias photographed it with his phone. 'You've not taken it out in years, you say?'

Scott looked utterly deflated. He must have realised how thin his story sounded. 'We've obviously moved it around a few times. To get at other stuff.'

'Does it store data?'

'I beg your pardon?'

'A top of the range piece of kit like that, I'd assume it logs all your searches. Date, time, GPS location, things like that.'

Scott closed his eyes as the quicksand sucked him ever deeper. 'I never set it up that way.'

'Then why spend so much on it?'

'Because it saw deeper underground than any of the others.'

'Is that so?' He called Scene of Crime to have them come here first, before the hotel. They waited in uncomfortable silence until they arrived. Elias showed them the closet and gave them the keys to the hotel storeroom too, then left them to it and returned to his Leaf to write up his notes while everything was still fresh in his mind. That done, he muted his phone, pushed back his seat and closed his eyes to think.

Gregory Scott was clearly now the prime suspect in the murder of Dunstan Warne. It wasn't just his demeanour and missing spade. The man himself had admitted his interest in King John's lost baggage train. And while metal detecting was indeed a common enough hobby, most practitioners didn't own state-of-the-art machines capable of seeing further underground than other models. Nor had they been offered the chance to buy the farm next door.

How tempting it must have been for him to check out those fields while considering whether or not to bid. By night, of course, and wearing headphones to dampen any eureka shriek, and using a hooded lamp to see by, degrading his night vision enough not to notice Warne's van until it was almost upon him. And then? Easy to imagine Warne getting out to confront him. Easy, too, to imagine Scott being so terrified of exposure and disgrace that he'd turned his spade sideways and wielded it like an axe, killing Warne on the spot. Panic would then have replaced fear, causing him to do the obvious rather than the strategic things, burying Warne's body in the hole he'd already dug before thinking to recover his keys.

Dawn would already have been breaking. The first dribble of morning traffic. So he'd fled while he still could, taking his spade with him, lest it give him away. Now what? A bleach bath would get rid of the blood and hair and brain, but what innocent person bleaches their spade? Better to dump it altogether then try to replace it before anyone noticed. But driving off with it at such an early hour would have drawn attention, and maybe left traces in his boot. So he'd have sought another solution.

Elias opened his eyes again. He gazed out over the hotel gardens down to the high earthen bank that separated the land here from open sea. Except that it *wasn't* open sea on the other side, of course, but rather acres of salt marsh inundated by each high tide, only to reappear again at the ebb. And it occurred to him suddenly that maybe their previous search hadn't found the murder weapon simply because it had been conducted at the wrong time of day. So he checked the tables on his phone, and found that the next low tide was in just forty minutes.

Elias's ex-wife Julie had been brought up on the north Lincolnshire coast, where her parents still lived. Whenever they'd gone visiting, their constant bickering had driven her nuts. She'd therefore bought him a pair of field glasses one birthday, to pack him off with her birdwatcher dad so that she and her mum could spend some quality time alone together. To his surprise, he'd come to enjoy it, less for the birds themselves than for the stakeout thrill. Until, at last, her dad had confessed that birdwatching was how he got to go out for a pint or two without getting moaned at. So they'd mostly gone pubbing after that. But he still had his field glasses in the boot.

He fetched them now, along with a pack of latex gloves and his towel. He made his way through the hotel gardens to the seawall, then up the flight of stone steps to the footpath upon its top. It was a popular local walk that continued on past Warne Farm before turning sharply inland to run alongside the River Nene. A small crowd had gathered at the boundary between the two properties. He went to check it out. Police tape had been strung up across the path and a privacy tent had been erected in the gap between the fields where those bootprints had been. They'd clearly found what he'd feared. The only surprise was that Mason hadn't called to let him know. Except, of course, he'd muted his phone. He checked it now and found a pair of messages from him, the first about forty-one additional silver pennies they'd recovered from Dunstan Warne's burial site, the second alerting him to the discovery of a mass grave.

Trevor Wharton had called too. Because of course he had. Mason would have alerted him at once to the new bodies, and he'd have seized upon them as his ticket out of Grimsby. Yet Elias was on the verge of nailing Warne's killer, and he'd be damned if he'd let Wharton simply swoop in to steal the credit. He turned his phone completely off, therefore, then showed his warrant card to the onlookers and asked them to disperse, which they did with surprising good grace.

Murder had that effect on people.

He waited till they were gone then turned to face the sea and scanned a strip of the salt marsh through his field glasses, taking it nice and slow, determined not to miss a thing.

THIRTY-THREE

It was hard now for Penny Scott to remember, but she'd been very much in love with her husband when planning the barn conversion. That was why she'd had the east-facing wall of the master bedroom fitted with a single sheet of smoked glass, that they might snuggle together on lazy weekend mornings, to watch the sun rise over the Wash.

Her romantic visions hadn't lasted long, however. Embarrassingly, she simply hadn't realised how early it grew light during the summer. Nor had she anticipated the violent electric storms that sometimes bombarded this coast like a fleet of warships, or the high winds that kept triggering their intruder lights, no matter how they adjusted their sensitivity. But she'd been too proud to admit her mistake by having curtains or shutters fitted.

Gregory had finally had enough of it some years before. He'd left for the spare bedroom on a particularly filthy night, never to return. And she'd slept so much better herself, freed from his snoring and clumsy overtures, that she'd left the glass wall as it was, lest he take it as an invitation to return. And it really did offer a magnificent view of the seawall and the Wash beyond, which was why they were standing there now, watching Detective Elias as he scanned the salt marsh through a pair of field glasses.

'Well?' she asked. 'Will he find it?'

'Find what?'

'Don't be an arse, Gregory. Your spade, of course.'

'How would I know?' he said. 'Ask whoever stole it.'

'Stole it!' she scoffed. 'What kind of imbecile do you take me for?'

'You don't believe me?' he said, looking hurt.

'Of course I don't fucking believe you. You already lied about going out at all. Why would I believe you this time? Especially now they've found coins beneath his body. He was killed by a detectorist. Nothing else makes sense.' She sighed miserably. 'Talk to me, Gregory. Tell me how it happened.'

'I haven't the first idea, I assure you. I wasn't there.'

'But you were!' she protested. 'That's exactly where you were, with your metal detector and your mysteriously vanished spade.'

'Someone must have stolen—'

'Stop it!' she cried. 'Just stop it, please! I *hate* being treated like a fool. Be straight with me and I'll stand by you, I promise I will. You're my husband, I took a vow. But one more lie and I swear to god I'll march over there right now and tell that detective everything.'

'You don't mean that.'

'I *do* mean it,' she said. 'I can't stand this any longer. I want the truth, right now. The *full* truth. I don't care how bad it is. I just need to know.'

He sat heavily on the side of the bed, buried his face in his hands. He stayed that way for so long that she began to fear he'd never answer. But finally he looked up again. 'I didn't mean to do it,' he murmured, so softly she barely heard him. 'You have to believe me.'

'Oh god,' she said.

'He came out of nowhere. He was crazy. He was literally crazy. You should have seen him. Yelling and shouting and threatening me with all sorts. I thought he was going to kill me, I swear I did. He tried to wrest my spade off me. He'd have killed me with it. It was written on his face.'

'So you hit him?'

'Only with the flat bit. To stun him. To bring him to his senses. But it must have twisted in my hands. Then suddenly I was looking down at him…' He shook his head helplessly. 'I'm sorry. I'm so sorry.'

'Sorry!' she scoffed. But the fight went out of her too. She groaned and sat beside him, still staring out at Elias on the seawall. 'I don't believe this. My husband a murderer. What will people say?'

'They won't say anything,' he said softly, taking and pressing her hand. 'Not if they don't find out.'

She removed her hand from his. 'But they *will* find out, won't they? That bloody detective. He knows, I know he does. He'll find your spade, won't he? Because you threw it in the sea, didn't you, just as he suspects?'

'What else was I to do with it?'

'Will he find it?'

'I don't know. I don't think so.'

'You don't think so?'

'It was dark. I was in a panic. But I threw it pretty far.'

'He knows it's there,' she said grimly. 'He'll keep looking until he finds it.'

'Then what do we do?'

'*We*? *We*?'

'You gave me your word.'

'I gave you my word that I wouldn't volunteer anything,' she told him. 'And I won't. But if he finds your spade…'

'Yes? If he finds it, what?'

'You're not taking me down with you,' she told him flatly. 'I'm sorry, but you're not.' She looked out the window to the seawall again, at Elias in his dark clothes framed by the greyness of the Wash, the splash of white towel over his shoulder. 'So you'd better hope that you threw it further and deeper than he can search.'

THIRTY-FOUR

'My name's Royston Flynn, by the way,' said their host, as he led Anna and Oliver along a gloomy corridor lined with dusty prints of Pre-Raphaelite beauties to a large warm kitchen with framed maps on the wall, an electric Aga, racks of Le Creuset cookware and patterned crockery on an antique dresser. 'But do please call me Royston. Or Roy, if you absolutely must, though I'd greatly prefer it if you didn't. And charmed to meet you both, of course.' A huge, hand-drawn schematic took up most of the pine table, its four corners pinned down by jars of marmalade, jam and honey. He removed these and it furled up into a cylinder of its own accord, to be dumped upon the rattan sofa. 'Your uncle spoke warmly of a brilliant historian niece. Would that be you?'

'I think it must be, as I'm his only niece,' said Anna. 'But I'm barely a historian at all, let alone a brilliant one. I'm still working on my PhD.'

'Well, he was terribly proud of you. You must be heartbroken.'

'I am. Yes.'

He nodded and turned to Oliver. 'Are you family too? I'm afraid he didn't mention a nephew.'

'No,' said Oliver. 'My name's Oliver Merchant. I'm working on a documentary about—'

'Oh that's *you*, is it?' Royston gazed delightedly at him. 'A

TV star! A real live TV star in my humble home.'

'Hardly a star,' said Oliver.

'That's not what dear Dunstan thought. He was terribly excited. Me, I'm not much for TV, or doubtless I'd be pestering you for an autograph. I'm more a radio man myself. It gives me all the company I need.'

'And you don't really have the time for it, I suppose,' suggested Anna, 'what with all these unfathomable people constantly dropping in.'

'Exactly! Exactly! Though in my darker moments I sometimes fear that that has less to do with my personal attractions than with the scope and liberality of my cellar. Speaking of which, perhaps a glass of the blushful Hippocrene in memory of your poor uncle?'

'Oh,' said Anna. 'A bit too early for me, thanks.'

'I wasn't thinking of you, my dear young lady,' said Royston severely. 'You don't think I'd waste my best Richebourg on a mere student, do you? Come back once you've defended your thesis and we can talk. But perhaps your television friend…?'

'No,' said Anna firmly. 'He's driving.'

'You poor young man,' said Royston. 'A terrible thing, a woman with scruples. Very well. The corkscrew shall wait.' He pulled out a chair for himself, invited them to sit. 'So, then. Ask me what you will.'

'Please don't take this the wrong way,' said Anna, 'but we're still trying to work out my uncle's movements last Sunday night. He was caught on a traffic camera, you see, a little way south of here. And when we were driving past just now, I remembered your letter.'

'And you think he may have been here that night? No, I'm afraid not. It was well over a week ago. Closer to a fortnight, I'd say, though everything rather blurs these days, for some unaccountable reason. And it was early afternoon, not evening. Though he did stay long enough for us to polish off a bottle of that Richebourg you so rudely spurned. I say us, though your uncle barely touched his glass, as I recall. Perhaps our conversation was to blame.'

'Why? What on earth did you talk about?'

'Poisons, my dear,' said Royston with relish. '*Medieval* poisons. *Shakespearian* poisons. How a villainous monk might murder a king with venom harvested from pricking the skin of a toad.'

'But that's just folklore, isn't it?' asked Anna. 'John was already sick when he arrived here.'

'Perhaps,' admitted Royston. 'Though would a man suffering from dysentery really have ridden south to Wisbech on an errand he could easily have delegated? Our only source for his being ill is Ralph of Coggeshall, remember, and he littered his journal with bright green children and other fantastical guff. More to the point, he was a Cistercian, just like the monks at the abbey here.'

'But surely that would make his information more reliable,' frowned Oliver.

'It would certainly make his *sources* better,' said Royston. 'But it would also have given them far more reason to lie. John's son was still only a boy when he came to the throne, but he was a young man by the time Ralph was writing. A young man with fond memories of his father. So of course the Cistercians would have wanted to blame his death on a Lynn banquet. Any hint of their own culpability might have doomed the entire order. And our only other contemporary source says nothing at all about John being sick. Nor about poison either, to be fair. He blamed his sickness on our excellent Lincolnshire cider. As if! The idea refutes itself. Anyway, why shouldn't he have been poisoned? The country was on fire, his barons were in open revolt, and pretty much everyone hated him. If that isn't enough, local tradition offers two additional motives, including that Brother Simon acted to save the virtue of the abbot's sister, a nun called Judith, who'd caught John's eye.'

'And the other?'

'That John was so furious about losing his baggage train that he declared a brutal new tax on bread.'

'So many different motives,' murmured Anna. 'Doesn't that suggest guesswork?'

Royston cackled delightedly. 'That's just what your uncle said. But there is a way to reconcile them. John had just come south after relieving the first siege of Lincoln Castle. He likely spent a night at the abbey, for there were precious few other estates on his route that were large and well-provisioned enough to accommodate his army.'

'So?'

'So he was notorious for raping the wives and daughters of the men around him. It delighted him to cause them pain. Imagine this, then. On his first stay here, Judith catches his eye. Not merely a nun, but the abbot's sister too! How very delicious! Lynn won't wait, but he can't shake her from his head. So when Lincoln is besieged again, and he needs to head back north…'

'He insists on stopping here,' said Anna, completing the thought, 'where he learns of his lost baggage train and declares his tax on bread.'

'Would a monk really risk his immortal soul for a penny on a loaf?' asked Oliver.

'It was more than that, from what they say. Enough to cause widespread misery and wreck the abbey's finances too. Besides…' He turned back to Anna with a mischievous smile. 'It's time you saw my famous statue.' He sprang to his feet and led them back the way they'd come, past the front door then through a plush drawing room out into the extension, where the statue stood in a marble alcove. Except it wasn't a statue at all, Anna now saw, but rather a tomb effigy that had been stood upright. It had lost its legs at some point, leaving only the weathered grey trunk, arms and head of a middle-aged man. Yet that was enough for her to turn to Royston in surprise. '*This*?' she asked. '*This* is Brother Simon?'

'So the legend goes.'

'But he's not a Cistercian,' she protested, taking in his chain mail, sword and shield. 'He's barely a monk at all.'

'Then what is he?' asked Oliver.
'He's a knight,' said Anna. 'A Knight Templar.'

THIRTY-FIVE

There was a single slash of watercolour blue low on the eastern horizon as Elias started his survey of the salt marsh, but it quickly vanished. The afternoon grew blustery and weighty with rain. He could see grey sweeps of it far out at sea, but drawing ever closer. He didn't let this rush him, however, but rather made his way methodically along the seawall, stopping every twenty paces or so to scan another strip, until he'd drawn level with the King John Hotel, and then had passed beyond it.

At high tide, these marshes were an archipelago of disconnected islands. But at low tide, like now, they were more like badly waterlogged fields. They were thronged with birdlife too, what with the autumn migration underway. A pair of little egrets pecked the mud in search of lunch. A lapwing flew in joyous whorls and swoops. A bad-tempered oyster catcher kept shooing some mischievous sand warblers from its patch, only for others to sneak up from behind. There were avocets too, and plovers, and a harrier. But not what he was after.

The tide turned and began coming in. He was beginning to lose heart when at last he caught a glint of silver, though he lost it again almost immediately, and before he could fix its position. He waited patiently and it reappeared briefly from the backwash before vanishing once more. The waves were coming faster now, lapping ever higher. It would soon be gone until the next ebb, if it wasn't dragged out to sea to be lost forever. He marked the spot in his mind and, without taking his eyes off it, removed his jacket and sat down on the bank to take off his shoes, socks and trousers. He opened a pack of latex gloves, lightly powdered to make them easier to pull on, then made his way down the seawall to the water's edge, stepping sideways on the slippery steep wet grass to avoid an undignified tumble.

He tested the temperature with a toe. It was so cold it made him shiver. He reached a foot out anyway, set it down on the marshy ground, resting more and more weight upon it, plugging up to his shin in the soft mud, unnerving him enough that he threw his weight backwards in order to pull it out again. He stood up and stared back out. The tide was coming in quickly, in shallow, foamy waves. He'd lost his fix on the silvery glint. There'd been no sign of it in at least a minute. It was now or never.

He stepped boldly out onto the marsh, sinking up to his calves until the firmer ground beneath enabled him to pull himself free before he stuck. It was a weird sensation, like walking on a particularly yielding mattress, only with his ankles being tugged at by slimy ropes of samphire and sea grass. But once he'd gone a certain distance, the vegetation grew lusher and the ground somehow firmer, allowing him to make brisker progress, scattering birds as he went, until he reached the approximate spot he'd marked in his mind. But there was nothing there.

The waves were growing larger, crashing against his shins, tugging him with their backwash. He had to flail his arms to keep his balance. Hoots of laughter reached him from behind. A new crowd had gathered on the seawall, including two teenagers on mountain bikes. He felt ridiculous, a grown man in his shirt and boxer shorts, flapping his arms like he was trying to—

There!

A glint of brushed steel beneath the surface, covered a moment later by the foamy, turbid water. But he had it now. A spade, all right, its ash shaft part buried in the marshy ground. If any traces had survived all this time, they'd most likely be on its handle or its blade, so he grabbed it by the midpoint of its shaft. Water spilled from it as he lifted it from its muddy sheath, splashing cold against his legs. He held it up and turned it to check its branding, even though he already knew.

And, yes. It was a Dewit.

THIRTY-SIX

Royston Flynn gazed at Anna with proud delight. 'Excellent, my dear. Even faster than your uncle.'

Oliver shook his head. 'I don't get it,' he said. 'Why would a Cistercian abbey have a statue of a Templar knight?'

'It's not as surprising as you might think,' said Royston. 'The two orders were extremely close, constantly in and out of each others' properties. You might even say that the Templars were the Cistercian's military wing. Monks of a sort, yes, but warrior monks, with the emphasis very much on the warrior bit. Not just allowed to kill, but positively encouraged. It was their *raison d'être*. Going on crusade earned them dispensation for their sins, however grave. Slit a man's throat and you could still be saved, so long as you took the cross.'

'Not a king's throat,' said Anna. Even unpopular ones like John had been considered sacred, making their murder a grievous and shocking sin. 'That would have required approval from the very top. But the Pope was backing John to the hilt, while the head of the Templars in England was Aymeric de St Maur, who wasn't just one of John's closest advisors, he was literally bankrolling his war. Why would either want him dead?'

'I'm not saying the theory's perfect. Merely plausible.'

'Is it, though?' asked Anna. 'Wouldn't toad venom have caused completely different symptoms.'

Royston raised his eyebrows. 'Quite correct, my dear.' He

turned again to Oliver. 'It's called bufotoxin, which sounds terribly scientific until you realise it's just Latin for toad poison. A dangerous dose would make you convulse and vomit and gasp for breath. But should you survive a nasty first few hours, you'd likely recover fine. Which was very unlike the dysentery that killed John, which took several days of severe abdominal pain, bloody diarrhoea and dehydration.'

'Well, then,' said Anna.

'Yes. Not skin of toad, I grant. But there is one poison that fits perfectly. Arsenic.'

'Arsenic?' frowned Oliver. 'Was that even around back then?'

'Oh yes, for sure,' nodded Royston. 'Hippocrates wrote about it. Nero murdered his stepbrother Britannicus with it. It dropped out of sight for a while, it's true, but it had certainly been rediscovered by John's time. Take King Baldwin III of Jerusalem, for example. He succumbed to dysentery some fifty years before John's time. Suspicion fell on his doctor, who'd been giving him strange tablets. They fed one to a dog, which promptly died.'

'Not a great look for the defence,' admitted Anna.

'Quite. Arsenic can't be proven, not without his remains to test. But if not arsenic, then a substance with identical effects, which essentially amounts to the same thing. Tasteless, odourless, colourless, soluble and producing the exact same symptoms as a very common and often lethal condition. What more could an assassin ask? The king of poisons and the poison of kings, as we English called it, though the French gave it a typically pithier name. *Poudre de succession.* Inheritance powder. Hah!' He slid Anna a sly look. 'Odd, don't you think, for it to have earned such a fearsome reputation despite no English or French king ever having been killed with it?'

'What are you getting at?'

'Come, my dear. You must know the ditty: "Treason never prospers. What's the reason? Because if it prospers, none dare call it treason." Think of all those Anglo-Saxons toppling over so soon after their coronations. And is it really plausible that so many twelfth-century English kings went out the same way?'

'That's pretty circumstantial.'

'Of course, of course. After all this time, how could it be anything else? But it's not just the manner of their deaths, it's the context. Has a king ever died quite so conveniently as Stephen, for example? Or Young King Henry. I'd put my house upon him being poisoned. One of my houses, anyway. One wouldn't want to leave oneself entirely homeless. The poor lad was only twenty-eight, and in rude health. But he and his mates would insist on trying to knock off his dad. What was the poor man to do? Your uncle agreed with me on that, for what it's worth. In fact, I'm pretty sure he knew more about it than he let on.'

'How so?'

'Alas, he didn't share. But he suddenly had this look in his eye. He got to his feet and made his excuses. I asked him what was up. He said there was something he needed to check, and that he'd let me know. But of course...'

'Arsenic, eh,' said Oliver. 'You seem to know an awful lot about it, if you don't mind me saying.'

Royston laughed good-naturedly. 'You're righter than you know. I grew up in Plymouth, you see, just a few streets from where a woman known as the Dark Angel once lived. She murdered a good two dozen people with it, including three husbands and several of her own children, god rest their souls. Unluckily for her, the first reliable test for arsenic was then developed, and that was that. Being kids, naturally enough, we told each other stories about her to spook ourselves. Then, for my sins, I patented a process using arsenic to manufacture semiconductors. The Americans offered me an obscene amount of money for my company, along with assurances they'd keep me on as boss. Only they fired me the first moment they could, to replace me with a marketing executive from Wichita.' He spread his hands. 'So here you find me, enjoying a short sabbatical while I consider my next move.'

'I'm so sorry,' said Anna. 'This all just happened?'

'Nine years ago, come December.' He paused a moment to contemplate the flight of time, but quickly cheered up again, and rubbed his hands together. 'Anyway. That Richebourg you've been pestering me for. It's hardly going to uncork itself, is it?'

THIRTY-SEVEN

Elias turned slowly on the muddy bed of the salt marsh and began his careful trudge back to shore, holding the spade out like a tightrope pole for balance. His feet were frozen by now. He couldn't feel his toes. His movements became increasingly jerky and clumsy. The small crowd on the embankment footpath held up their phones to film his return. The mockery had stopped, replaced by sober silence. They all knew about Dunstan Warne's murder. They all guessed the meaning of the spade.

He reached the foot of the embankment and sat down, holding the spade up in one hand while scooping water with the other to rinse off the worst of the mud. People gave him room as he climbed back up to the top. They asked questions in respectful tones. He ignored them. He wiped himself down with his towel then slung it over his shoulder before picking up the rest of his things and setting off for Warne Farm, stepping over the string of police tape while still holding the spade out ahead of him. It would take a miracle to glean anything useful from it, but you never knew.

His arm was getting tired. He shouted for someone to come meet him. It was Mason who did so. 'This what I think?' he asked, taking the spade carefully from him.

'It's the neighbour's,' said Elias, shaking out his arm and shoulder. 'He threw it out on the salt marsh.' He dried his legs off properly, pulled his clothes back on. 'Looks like you've been busy too,' he said, nodding at the privacy tent, against which a white coroner's van was now backed up, its rear doors open.

'Want to see?' asked Mason.

He made Elias put on booties and a cap before going inside. A pit had been sunk in the ground, exposing a tattered sky-blue tarpaulin peeled back to reveal several bodies: an elderly, grey-haired woman; a man and woman of indeterminate age; and a teenage boy and a pair of young girls. Middle Eastern, to judge from their looks and clothing. No watches or jewellery that he could see, perhaps stripped for profit or to prevent them from being found by a metal detector. 'How?' he asked.

'We think suffocation for the older woman, the man, the boy and one of the girls. But the mum was stabbed multiple times with a screwdriver or something similar. And we think the second girl was strangled.'

A swell of anger, like a humpback bridge. Elias waited for it to pass. 'You've told Wharton?'

'Already on his way. Didn't you get my messages?'

'No signal.'

'That's weird. Mine's working great.'

'Guess I should change provider.' He nodded and left them to it, discarding his cap and booties before setting off back for the hotel. With the spade now recovered, it was time to go after Scott. The only question was whether he could crack him before Wharton arrived to take the case and credit too.

THIRTY-EIGHT

Royston insisted on them staying for a cold lunch, during which Anna persuaded him to email Elias about her uncle's visit, while Oliver won permission to return with a crew to film him and his statue both. Rarely had Anna met anyone quite so eager to please. Yet, for some reason, it left her feeling sad. 'What a lovely man,' said Oliver, as they set back off for Lincoln. 'Though what was all that business about arsenic and twelfth-century kings?'

'It's nothing,' said Anna, raiding Oliver's glove compartment for a fresh tube of extra strong mints, to clear the lingering taste of Royston's hummus from her mouth. 'Dysentery was rife back then. They fertilised their fields with raw human waste, for goodness sake. And kings were just as vulnerable as anyone else, what with all the travelling and feasting they did.'

'Nice way of avoiding my question,' said Oliver, pulling up at the junction with the A17. 'How many are we talking?'

'Twelfth-century English kings? Who died from what might plausibly have been arsenic poisoning?' She ran briskly through them in her mind, gave a little grimace. 'All of them.'

'*All* of them?'

'It's not as bad as it sounds. There were only six.'

'Since when does six out of six constitute an "only"?' He beckoned for a mint for himself, popped it in his mouth. 'Did people want them dead?'

'They were kings. Of course people wanted them dead.'

'Come on. You know what I mean.'

'Fine,' she said. 'First up is Henry I. He took over from William Rufus, who himself died in dodgy circumstances. He managed to stay on the throne for the first thirty-five years of the century, despite multiple attempts to kill him, including by one of his own daughters. But it was dysentery that got him in the end, supposedly from eating too many eels. A surfeit of lampreys, in the famous phrase.'

'Arsenic poisoning number one.'

'Dysentery death number one,' corrected Anna. 'Anyway, there was a major dispute over the succession, between Henry's nephew Stephen and his daughter Matilda – not the one who'd tried to kill him. They spent fifteen years fighting over it before finally agreeing a truce under which Stephen got to rule for life, after which he'd be succeeded by Matilda's eldest son.'

'Don't tell me. Stephen promptly contracted dysentery and died.'

'It took about a year, but yes, pretty much. That put Matilda's eldest son on the throne. Henry II, first of the Plantagenets. He was so desperate to avoid another war of succession that he made his eldest son co-regent when he was still only a teenager. Confusingly, the son was named Henry too, so people took to calling them Old King Henry and Young King Henry. The Old King kept all the power, though, and the Young King grew so frustrated by this that he rebelled. His dad defeated him easily enough, and forgave him too. But he kept him even further from power than before, so that he spent the next few years travelling around the continent with his best mate William Marshal, beating up the flower of European nobility at tournaments.'

'William Marshal? He's your thesis guy, yes?'

'Yes. Exactly.' It had been the dawn of the chivalric age, and tournaments had been the great new entertainment. They might have been designed with Marshal in mind, not just a skilled horseman and warrior, but a virtual giant too, at least for the era, well over six foot tall, and broad and powerful to match. His exploits and his charisma had made him a celebrity, feted in courts across Europe. 'But the Young King eventually got bored of the life, and rebelled a second time.'

'I'm going to take a wild guess here. He got the squits and died.'

'Yes.'

'So the Old King murdered his own son?'

'This is Royston's theory, not mine,' sighed Anna. 'But it's fair to say that he had a genuine problem. His son was king too, remember, which made him sacred. Trying and executing him for treason would have been profoundly shocking, while imprisoning him wouldn't really have solved his problem, for his son had too many powerful friends who'd have loved to see him on the throne. So his death was certainly convenient. Not that the Old King could have done it himself. He was on the other side of France at the time. But he was the one who got rid of Thomas Beckett by wondering aloud why no one would rid him of his turbulent priest, so it's hardly unthinkable that he asked the same about his son, and some ambitious knight took him up on it.'

'Like who?'

Anna slid him a look. 'It was over eight hundred years ago. How the hell would I know?'

'Fair enough. So that's Henry, Stephen and the Young King. You owe me three more.'

'Okay. The Young King's death made Richard Lionheart heir presumptive. Unhappily for his dad, he was every bit as impatient as his brother had been, only a far better soldier. He allied with the King of France, went to war and won. Which gave him the same headache his dad had had. He could hardly imprison or execute him, so it was a stroke of luck for him when he died almost immediately from stomach troubles.'

'Making Richard king. But wasn't he killed by a crossbow?'

'He was *wounded* by a crossbow. But not that seriously. He

died because of complications that there shouldn't really have been.' Medieval Europeans had been far better about hygiene than most people thought. They'd kept their homes and towns proudly clean. They'd washed regularly, and with soap. They'd known the importance of dressing wounds properly too. William Marshal himself was testament to this, when taken captive as a young knight after being badly wounded in the leg. According to his own account, he'd likely have died had a kindly woman not taken pity on him, smuggling fresh linen into his cell in a hollowed out loaf of bread. 'So there's always been a suspicion that he was poisoned by the bolt itself or by one of his doctors. The French actually tested his remains for arsenic. It was inconclusive, but still.'

'The fact that they tested them at all…'

'Exactly. And then of course Richard was succeeded by John, who you already know about. Making six.'

'You can really test for arsenic after all this time?' frowned Oliver. 'What about the others? Could they be tested too?'

'John, for sure,' said Anna. 'He's still buried in Worcester Cathedral.' They'd opened his tomb back in the eighteenth century, expecting to find it empty, only to be startled by the skeleton inside, dressed in modest clothes and with so few kingly goods that it had been taken as further confirmation of his lost baggage train. 'They keep his thumb on display in their archives. Though good luck persuading the bishop.'

'You'd be surprised what people will agree to when you stick a camera in their face,' said Oliver. 'And the others?'

'Henry II is in Fontevraud, I think. And the Young King is definitely in Rouen. I guess you could always ask. But Stephen's grave was dug up a while back, and there was nothing there. And Reading Abbey is just a ruin now, so you'll never be able to prove Henry I either.'

'Or disprove it.'

'What kind of attitude is that?' laughed Anna.

Oliver shrugged. 'The kind that gets TV programmes made,' he said.

THIRTY-NINE

The afternoon was growing windy and dark. Elias turned up his jacket collar as he hurried back along the seawall then down the steps and up the garden path to the hotel. He returned his towel and field glasses to his car then went into reception, where he found Maria Quinn still reviewing CCTV footage on the monitor. 'Anything good for me?' he asked.

Quinn turned the screen for him to see. It showed the car park, weakly lit by a pair of lamps on the hotel roof. She touched a dark strip at its far end with her fingertip. 'See this. It's the hedge on the far side of the shared drive. At twelve twenty-five last Sunday night, it lights up a little. I thought at first it was a passing car, except it stays still and lasts for a whole minute.'

'The Scotts' intruder lights,' murmured Elias.

'Yes,' said Quinn. 'They come on again in the morning too, though that's even harder to see, because it's already getting light. But it's the same full minute.'

'What time was that?'

'Six twenty-eight. Six hours and three minutes later.'

'A man could get plenty done in six hours and three minutes,' observed Elias. He thought a moment, then asked: 'Do the lights come on often? Could they have been triggered by the wind, for example?'

'That's what I'm checking now. Nothing on Monday night,

but they came on four times during the big storm, and once again last night too. But really I'd need more time.'

Elias checked his watch. Time was what they didn't have, what with Wharton already on his way. 'Leave it,' he said. 'We need to go see the Scotts.' He briefed her on Scott's spade as they walked, how he'd found it in the salt marsh. 'The wife's the key,' he told her. 'She knows the truth, I'm sure of it. If we can somehow get her to flip...'

It was Penny Scott herself who answered the door. Her face fell when she saw Quinn in her uniform, bringing home how official this was turning. 'Was there something else, Detective?' she asked.

'I have good news,' Elias told her. 'I've found your husband's spade.'

'Oh,' she said, striving to sound surprised, but failing badly. 'That's wonderful. Where?'

'Out on the salt marsh. Whoever stole it must have thrown it out there, for some reason. Can you think why?'

'How could I? You should ask them.'

'Perhaps your husband might have an idea?'

'He didn't even know it was missing.'

'Even so.'

They gazed at each other for several moments. Penny Scott broke first and looked away. 'He's in the drawing room,' she said. They followed her through into a large, bright, sparsely-furnished space, designed to impress rather than to put at ease. Gregory Scott was seated at one end of a long black leather sofa, sipping scented tea from a white porcelain cup. He'd shaved since their earlier encounter. He'd also changed into a fresh white cotton shirt, a charcoal suit and a pair of polished brogues. Courtroom clothes. Yet he feigned surprise to see them all the same, though even less convincingly than his wife. 'Detective,' he said, setting down his cup and saucer on the smoked glass coffee table. 'What now?'

'I was telling your wife that we have good news. We've found your spade.'

'Oh,' said Scott. 'Excellent. Thank you. Where was it?'

Elias didn't reply for a moment or two, except to smile. 'Out on the salt marsh.'

'How bizarre.' He looked pleadingly up at his wife then patted the cushion beside him for her to join him on the sofa. 'I wonder how it got there.'

Elias settled into the armchair across the coffee table from them both. 'I was hoping you'd tell us.'

'I didn't even know it was missing.'

'We believe it was likely used to murder Dunstan Warne. So any help you can give…'

'I've been straining my mind, Detective, believe me. All I can say for sure is that I haven't used it myself in ages. It could have been gone for weeks.'

'That great big gap on your shed wall. And you didn't notice?'

'Gardening season is over. I've hardly been out.'

'Your lawns are neatly mowed.'

'That was at least a week ago.'

'And was the spade there then?'

'I certainly didn't notice it missing. But I can't say more than that.'

'Fair enough. You went out at twelve twenty-five on the night of the murder, then came back in again six hours later. Can you tell us where you were?'

Scott stared at him aghast. 'Went out? What are you talking about?'

'You were caught on the hotel CCTV.'

'I… No.' He frowned for several moments, then shook his head more confidently. 'That's not possible.'

'Your intruder lights came on.'

Relief washed over him. 'Oh, those damned things. They come on all the time.'

'Except they don't, do they?' said Elias. He nodded at Quinn, standing against the wall. 'My colleague has checked half a dozen other nights. Your lights didn't come on even once.'

'So? It could have been anything. A rabbit. A deer.'

'A rabbit,' mocked Elias. He turned to Mrs Scott. 'Is that what you think too? You think it was a rabbit?'

'I expect it was something like that.'

'Did you see it yourself, this rabbit?'

'I was asleep.'

'Even though the lights would wake Rip Van Winkle?' He turned to Quinn. 'How long did they stay on?'

'One minute,' she replied. 'One full minute.'

'A full minute!' repeated Elias. 'The lights blazing for a full minute. Twice. Yet you slept through it both times, you who never sleep through anything!'

Her cheeks blazed. She looked furious. 'So I was mistaken. Is that a crime now?'

'If you slept through them, what makes you so sure it was a rabbit?'

'The rabbit is your interpretation of events, not mine. My husband says that he didn't go out that night, and I believe him.'

'That's good,' said Quinn, companionably. 'That you trust your husband, I mean.' She came over to perch on the armrest of the sofa beside Penny Scott. 'Think how scary it would be otherwise! Living with a man who'd already killed once and who you could send to jail for life if you ever changed your mind and decided to talk. Honest to god, I'd never sleep again. Every time a floorboard creaked. Every time he was behind me on the stairs.'

A whole play unfolded in front of Elias in the next few moments, even though not a word was said. There was Maria Quinn, her throat and cheeks flushed with the thrill of the hunt. There was Gregory Scott, stiff as a shop dummy, gazing desperately at his wife, trying telepathically to remind her of her vows. But most of all there was Penny Scott herself, the way her lips pursed and her pupils flickered as she calculated the paths open to her: to stand by her man in a loveless marriage, or to seize this opportunity to rid herself of him while getting to keep the house and money. She turned to look once more at him. He gave her a beseeching little shake of his head. But the way her lip curled showed Elias that her decision was already made. She shifted away from him along the sofa, then turned back to Elias. 'You're right,' she said. 'Gregory *did* go out that night. I saw him leave and then I saw him come back in again. Six hours later, just as you said. He confessed the whole horrible story to me only a few minutes ago. And now I'm ready to tell you.'

FORTY

There was nowhere to park directly outside the coroner's office, so Oliver dropped Anna off then went looking for a spot. She gave her name at reception. A tall stooped black man in a loose white coat and half-moon glasses came out to meet her. His hands were rough and badly chapped, though a little greasy with cleansing gel. He introduced himself as Simon Parker and led her to a pair of faux-leather crimson armchairs in the corner so that they could talk in private.

An inquest into her uncle's death had been opened, he told her, as was compulsory in such cases. Unfortunately, there was a backlog at the moment, as there always seemed to be these days, and it would be many weeks before it was heard. He leaned forward as he spoke, resting his elbows on his knees so that he could keep his voice discreetly low. She kept catching whiffs of disinfectant, and something uglier underneath. In the meantime, he went on, he'd completed her uncle's postmortem and submitted his report, though it would need clearance by the investigating officer before his body could be released for burial or cremation. He wasn't able to issue a full death certificate yet either, though he'd already submitted an interim one to the registrar. He'd give her a copy before she left, which she'd need to close his bank accounts and start probate.

He talked slowly and kept glancing up at the wall clock over her left shoulder, clearly stalling while her uncle was made ready. It gave Oliver enough time to arrive. He stayed near the door, offering her the choice. She beckoned him over and introduced him to Parker, who checked the clock a final time then invited them to follow. They made their way down a flight of stairs to a basement that smelled pungently of bleach, then along a passage into a brightly lit, white-tiled room with a brushed steel table at its heart, upon which Uncle Dun was lying with a white sheet up to his throat and a black rubber skullcap over his crown. His face was badly lopsided, even so, as if he'd suffered a stroke. Yet otherwise he was much as Anna remembered, if paler and less well shaven.

Her eyes moistened as she gazed down at him. She remembered his kindness. The inescapable physical truth of his death felt crushing upon her shoulders, yet at the same time she had the most perverse urge to laugh, as though life itself were all some incomprehensible practical joke. Oliver put a comforting hand upon her back. It released something stuck inside her, and the tears finally arrived. She buried her face against his chest until she'd managed to compose herself again. Now the anger came, pulsing hot waves of it that burned away any last reservations about her visit to Serious and Organised Crime. She wanted people caught. She wanted them punished.

Silence in the car as they drove north through Lincoln. Oliver, to his great credit, left her alone with her thoughts. The twin spires of the cathedral came briefly into view. She even caught a glimpse of the town's storied castle, the one that had played such an outsize role in the events around King John's death. For while the surrounding town had fallen to the rebels, the castle itself had stayed steadfastly loyal, thanks to the valiant leadership of the remarkable Lady Nicola de la Haye. Not only had she seen off the two sieges of 1216, she'd held on well into the next year too, until William Marshal – now serving as regent to John's young son Henry III – had managed to muster...

Anna frowned and shifted a little in her seat, then looked

back over her shoulder. But the castle was long gone. She couldn't even see the cathedral spires any more.

'What is it?' asked Oliver.

'Nothing,' she said. But she couldn't shake the thought. 'You know how Royston said Uncle Dun suddenly got up to leave, as if he'd had some kind of idea about how Young King Henry died?'

'Sure. Why?'

Anna hesitated again. It felt doubly disloyal, to her uncle and William Marshal both. Yet she could hardly stop now. 'Remember how Old King Henry had his son crowned when he was still just a teenager? Well, he was young enough that his father thought he needed a mentor, but he wanted one who was close enough to him in age that he could be his friend too. William Marshal got the nod. They became virtually inseparable for years, until a rumour started circulating about Marshal and the Young King's wife.'

'He was boinking the queen?' laughed Oliver. 'Good lad.'

'He *may* have been boinking the queen. No one knows for sure. He certainly denied it furiously. But the Young King kicked him out anyway. This was before he launched his second uprising, which went badly, as you know. So badly that he sent his chamberlain off to find Marshal and beg him to come back, because Marshal was far and away his best soldier. And Marshal agreed, but only after going to see the Old King first, to ask his permission.'

Oliver threw her a look. 'He asked permission to go to war against him?'

'I know it sounds bizarre, but it was a matter of honour, which Marshal took seriously. The Old King had originally appointed him, after all, so he owed him a duty. And maybe even more than that. We know for a fact that the Old King had at least one spy in his son's camp, because he was caught sending him a message. What if Marshal was another? What if that's why the Old King agreed to his return? Not to support his son's uprising, but to end it? Because the Young King fell sick and died almost immediately after Marshal's return.'

'You're saying he poisoned him? On the Old King's orders?'

'No. I'm saying I'll bet it's what Uncle Dun thought. He was always far more cynical about Marshal than me. It's certainly true that his shows of chivalry and loyalty tended to coincide with his self-interest. Then there's what happened next, of course.'

'Of course,' said Oliver. 'Because my PhD is on the Plantagenets too.'

'Sorry,' said Anna. 'Marshal left almost immediately on crusade. Apparently the Young King begged him to do so on his deathbed, to fulfil a vow that he himself wasn't going to be able to honour. Maybe so. But crusade was also how men like Marshal absolved themselves of terrible sins. And, when he came back home again, the Old King not only forgave him for his part in his son's uprising, he awarded him estates and titles too.'

'The workman is worthy of his wage,' grinned Oliver. 'Looks like your thesis is going to need one hell of a rewrite.'

Anna smiled wryly. 'Just as well I haven't got to that bit yet.'

FORTY-ONE

Elias was walking Gregory Scott to his Leaf when Trevor Wharton came speeding up the hotel drive in a convoy of three Range Rovers. The man had impeccable timing. Even Elias had to give him that. He leapt out of the middle car and marched up to him with a warpath glint in his eye. 'Your phone's off,' he said accusingly.

Elias gazed coolly at him. Wharton was a striking looking man, tall, lean and tanned, with large dark eyes, a strong nose and a powerful jaw, and with that trick that Elias had never even tried to master, of being able to emerge from a two hour car journey still immaculately turned out. Elias had known him for six years, and had got on well with him for the first four of those, when they'd both been on the fast track together. But Wharton had raced ahead since then, while Elias had stalled and fallen back. That was when he'd discovered that what he'd thought was friendship had actually merely been manoeuvring for advantage. 'Is it?' he frowned, taking it from his pocket to check. 'Oh. Yes. So it is.'

'So it is!' mimicked Wharton, his breath misting in the gathering cold. 'You did it on purpose.'

'You're absolutely right,' admitted Elias, putting his hand on Gregory Scott's arm. 'I didn't want to be disturbed while arresting the murderer of Dunstan Warne.'

Wharton gave a snort. '*This*?' he said, looking Scott disdainfully up and down. '*This* is the murderer of Dunstan

Warne?'

'I demand to speak to my lawyer,' declared Scott. 'I refuse to say another word until I've spoken to my lawyer.'

'He keeps telling me how he won't say another word,' said Elias cheerfully. 'He won't shut up about it. But he should have thought of that before spilling to his wife, because she just told us everything.'

'His wife?' asked Wharton. 'Where is she?'

Elias nodded back at the barn. 'WPC Quinn is with her, taking her statement.'

Wharton gestured to two of his men, who set off for the barn. Then he took Scott by his other arm. 'Very well. We'll take it from here.'

'No need,' said Elias, still holding Scott. 'We're doing fine all by ourselves, as you can see. And you've still got Grimsby to deal with, haven't you? Unless you've already managed to eradicate the scourge of knife crime there once and for all, in which case kudos.'

Wharton flushed. 'That's enough,' he said.

'Enough for what?'

'Enough for you to be off the case. You can't be trusted any more.'

'*I* can't be trusted?' retorted Elias.

'You knew about the vault in the barn hours before you notified Mason,' said Wharton. 'Don't even try to deny it. There were timestamps on your photographs. And one of Mason's men saw you yesterday, out where those bodies were found, probing the ground with a metal stake. Yet no mention of *that* in your report. So I have to ask myself: why were you buying time? I have to ask myself: who were you buying it for?'

'Fuck you,' said Elias.

'Your former boss was a crook,' said Wharton happily. 'He's in prison right now for tipping off a dangerous drugs gang to our investigations, in order to feed his gambling habit. You worked alongside him for years yet somehow never noticed. Then last month this same drugs gang was warned at the last minute about our raids, making it clear we still have a problem. Everyone told me not to trust you. I was foolish enough not to listen. That was a serious mistake on my part. But it ends now. Go back to Nettleham. Wait for me there. You're off all casework until further notice.'

'But you can't—'

'I can,' said Wharton. 'I just did.' He pulled Scott towards him by the arm. 'Now go.'

FORTY-TWO

Lincolnshire Police's Nettleham HQ turned out to be a long, low, dark building of brick and smoked glass, a layer cake of chocolate and caramel. 'You want me to wait?' asked Oliver, pulling up by its front steps.

Anna shook her head as she got out. 'I could be hours, for all I know,' she said, grabbing her laptop bag. 'And I'll be picking up my uncle's van afterwards, if all goes well. But I can't be lugging my books and all this other stuff around in there, so if I could leave it with you, then swing by later...?'

'Of course. Just text me when you're setting off. I'll make sure I'm there to meet you.' He jotted down his address for her on a scrap of paper. 'And call with any problems, okay? I'm literally five minutes away.'

She went inside, gave her name. A Detective Sergeant Yvette Coombs came down to meet her. She had spiky short fair hair and arched eyebrows that gave her a permanent expression of startled affront, as though someone unexpected had just insulted her. But she couldn't have been more helpful. She arranged a visitor's pass then led Anna up to her unit, stopping at a machine along the way to get them each some scalding tea-coloured water in plastic cups so flimsy that she burned her fingers and slopped it over her hand.

Coombs dragged over a spare chair from an empty desk for her to sit on, then expressed sympathy for her loss before fetching a grey plastic tub of the effects taken from her uncle's van or person that were no longer needed for the investigation, each in its own transparent evidence bag. Anna went slowly through them as she packed them away, experiencing bittersweet pangs of memory and loss. There were his gold-rimmed driving glasses, its left arm held on by a snip of fuse wire. There was his ancient Timex watch, its cheap strap in dire need of replacing for the umpteenth time. His old black leather wallet was in there too, its contents bagged separately but clipped together: his bankcards, driving licence, library card, a pair of ten-pound notes and even his old wedding ring, kept in his wallet rather than on his finger, perhaps to avoid painful questions about his wife. Most poignant of all, two passport-booth photographs of him and Anna with their cheeks pressed together, taken years ago on the Skegness seafront on one of their rare days out, the other two of which she kept in a desk drawer in York.

'Elias said I should take you to see Jay Patterson,' said Coombs, once Anna had packed it all away in her laptop bag, and signed the receipt.

There was a woman-to-woman note in her voice that caught Anna's ear. 'Is there something I should know?'

Coombs hesitated. 'He's a bit of an acquired taste, is all. They do tend to be, over there, if I'm honest. Too much time spent undercover, watching villains living it large on the Costas. It messes with your mind.'

Serious and Organised Crime lay at the far end of a long corridor with a beige carpet worn through in places to the underlay. Jay Patterson looked to be in his mid to late fifties, with unkempt long hair, narrow shoulders and a paunch that lay upon his lap like a dozing pet. He saw them making their way towards him and hurriedly did up his zip, trouser button and belt before standing up to greet them. Then he waited for Coombs to leave again before directing Anna to a pair of moulded black plastic chairs set against the wall. He told her he'd only be a moment, but five minutes passed before he turned round again. 'You have ID?' he asked.

'I beg your pardon?'

'This is confidential intelligence we're about to show you. We need to know you're who you say you are.'

She offered him her driving licence. He held the photograph up beside her face, then handed it back without a word and set off along the passage without telling her whether to follow him or not. She chose to follow. A cleaning lady pulled her cart out of their way and dropped her eyes, as women the world over did with pests and bullies. He showed her to an interview room with more of the same moulded black plastic chairs on either side of an old pine table in which names and dates and other graffiti had been gouged. 'Wait here,' he said, then left.

The room was unheated. Anna paced around it and hugged herself to keep warm. And perhaps it was this chill as much as anything, but she couldn't help but feel that something about all this was badly wrong.

FORTY-THREE

It hadn't been diamond bracelets that had won Samantha for León de Bruin. It hadn't been pearl necklaces or Armani bags or teas in the Ritz. She'd had so many handsome and wealthy admirers that she'd barely even noticed him. Her favourite at that time had been an up-and-coming actor a year or two her junior, tall, arrogant and quite ludicrously beautiful. He'd had little money, though, so he'd used de Bruin's infatuation with Samantha to his own ends, inviting him along to expensive restaurants and fashionable nightclubs so that he could pick up the tab, while either ignoring him completely or mocking him for it.

De Bruin was a proud man. He'd seethed at this treatment, but he'd been too afraid of Samantha's displeasure to stand up for himself. Then one night, back in Lincolnshire, a pair of his biker friends had come to see him, worried about how he'd been letting things slip. He'd confessed a little to them. They'd guessed the rest. Two nights later, Samantha and her young actor friend had been heading out for the night from her Pimlico apartment when they'd been set upon by three men in black leathers and motorbike helmets. She'd watched in horror as they'd beaten him to the ground then had kicked him where he lay, breaking his hand and disfiguring that beautiful face. 'Don't you ever fuck with my mate again,' one of them had told him, when they were done. 'You neither, love.'

She'd noticed him after that.

The latest news from Warne Farm was up on de Bruin's screen. The Scene of Crime team had found that poor family, thanks to Elias having been alerted to footprints in the mud. Who else but Anna would have noticed those? Worse still, she was planning to visit the county's Serious and Organised Crime unit this afternoon in an effort to identify him and Andrei from their library of photographs and footage. In short, she was doing everything in her power to bring him down. He should have hated her for this, yet all he felt was longing.

Diamonds wouldn't make Anna Warne like him. Nor money, nor shows of violence. She seemed neither avaricious nor vain, and she believed he'd killed her uncle. Worse, if they should ever meet again, she might even recognise him, and he wasn't yet *that* crazy. But he found himself possessed of a terrible restlessness all the same, a compulsion to be near her that was intensified rather than lessened by the risk involved. Even thinking about being in Nettleham while she was there made his heart pump harder, filling him with that dry-mouthed anticipation junkies must feel on contemplating their first score after rehab.

And he knew he was going to do it.

Andrei was in the garage, washing the wheels of the Lamborghini Huracan with soapy hot water. It wasn't his job. De Bruin had a man for that. Cars simply filled the hole in his heart where others kept their families or pets. During his interview, indeed, he'd asked more questions about de Bruin's fleet than about his duties. He stood up when he saw de Bruin approaching. Suds dripped off his hand to form a soapy pool on the concrete floor. 'Are we going out?' he asked.

De Bruin had made no plan. He simply needed to be in Nettleham. Andrei was indifferent to human weakness, yet he still felt ashamed to admit this to him. 'That girl from the farmhouse the other night,' he said. 'She's trying to identify us from police surveillance footage.'

Andrei looked unmoved. 'Are we on police surveillance footage?'

'No.'

'Then what's the problem? She never even saw our faces.'

'We have distinctive builds. She noticed our accents too. They might get lucky.'

'You want her killed?'

Even after all this time, Andrei's bluntness could take de Bruin aback. 'No,' he said. 'It would only make things worse.'

'We could have your biker friends do it.'

'No. I don't want her hurt. Not unless we have no choice.'

'Then…?'

'I don't know.' But he had to give him more than that. 'She's going to collect her uncle's van while she's there. I thought maybe to follow her. So that we know where she is, should we need to act.'

Andrei nodded. 'I'll get a tracker.'

'You have one?'

'Of course.' He tossed his sponge into the bucket then wiped his forearms and hands off on his towel before heading up to his rooms to fetch it.

They took the Ford Discovery for its anonymity and tinted windows. Neither of them had visited Nettleham Police HQ before. It was hardly a place to put them at their ease. It was dusk when they set off, but night by the time they arrived, the lamps in the huge car park glowing a sulphurous yellow. They took a spot away from the CCTV cameras, but with a good view of the station's front steps and main entrance. It began to drizzle, misting up the windscreen and blurring their view. A steady stream of officers and support staff emerged to set off home, wrapped warm against the weather.

'Stay here,' said de Bruin, turning up his jacket collar and getting out.

The pound ran along one side of the car park, but it was sealed off from it by an unbroken tall wire fence. A sign directed visitors to its main entrance on a residential street around its other side. He put up his hand to shield his eyes from the rain as he peered through the mesh. And there it was, backed up against a wall, a white transit van with a loose front bumper and a scratch down its side.

'Well?' grunted Andrei, when de Bruin returned to the Discovery.

'Still there.'

'So what now?'

De Bruin scratched his cheek. There were far too many police around to risk scaling the fence to fit the tracker. But he wasn't ready to give up either. 'We wait,' he said.

Neither man was much for small talk, so de Bruin took out his phone. It was a very special and very expensive device. Press its power button for less than five seconds and it operated as a perfectly normal Samsung Galaxy, albeit one that needed both the correct thumbprint and a six-digit code to get past its lock screen. Get the code wrong twice in a row and it would be wiped and reset. Ditto if anyone tried to open it, or if they pressed the power button for longer than ten seconds. But press it for between five and ten seconds twice in a row and it turned into a very different device, opening a specialist application called C-Cure that disabled its camera, microphone and GPS, then used a Tor browser and end-to-end encryption to route messages, conversations and other traffic through multiple servers in distinct jurisdictions, making it virtually impossible to trace.

He used it now to check the Dark Web for new documents. There was only one: a receipt for certain items belonging to Dunstan Warne that had been returned to his niece. He was glancing idly through it when he sat up electrified and showed it to Andrei.

'Bastard,' muttered Andrei. 'All this time.'

'All this time,' agreed de Bruin.

No question now of hanging back. His sense of self-preservation had finally kicked in. They couldn't do anything here, not with all these cameras and police around. But Anna was due to collect her van from the pound, whose main entrance was on a different street. And he could see no reason not to go wait for her there.

FORTY-FOUR

It was another ten minutes before Patterson returned, bringing with him a laptop and a second man who came straight up to her and introduced himself as Raymond Hollis, and who was everything Patterson was not. Tall, good-looking, athletic, energetic, with a warm smile and shrewd brown eyes. His moustache and goatee were well trimmed, he had a gap between his upper front teeth and a gold band in his left ear. If she'd seen him out at a pub, or more likely in a wine bar, she'd have taken him for a salesman or maybe an advertising executive. A successful one, too, for he was expensively if casually dressed, with an Anonimo Nautilo watch and a gorgeous soft black leather jacket with tiny droplets of rain still on its shoulders, making it clear that he'd just come back from somewhere, so that Anna couldn't help suspect that he was the real reason Patterson had been making her wait – for though he looked at least ten years the younger, it was instantly clear who was in charge.

He invited her to sit then placed his own chair at an angle to her, the better to watch her without being watched in return. 'So this is all pretty unorthodox,' he said. 'Trying to ID people whose faces you never even saw.' He spoke brightly, as if to put her at her ease, yet she could sense his mind at work. 'But my colleague DI Elias tells us that your two intruders from the other night may be linked to a group we're very interested in, so it would be dumb of us not to try, right?'

'I know why I'm here,' said Anna.

His smile grew broader. His eyes went the other way. 'Not that it's a formal process,' he said. 'Nothing that could be used in court, I mean. Not when you didn't see their faces. It's just, it might give us a helpful steer.'

'I'm not an idiot. Can we get on with it?'

Hollis forced a chuckle. 'No nonsense, eh? Fair enough. Obviously, photos of faces won't be much use, so what I had Jay here do, I had him check our files for full-length shots of men who broadly fit your descriptions. That is to say, for a white male aged between forty and sixty, about six foot two or three, and strikingly thin. And also for a second white male, this one aged between twenty-five and forty, around five foot ten and very bulky. If any of these men ring a bell, we have footage of some of them too. But there's little point looking at that if it's obviously not them. Make sense?'

'Yes.'

'Good. Then let's start with the first guy, because we've only got three plausible candidates.' Patterson took this as his cue to bring up the first picture on his laptop, a fair-haired man in black leathers standing outside a pub, chatting to a red-headed woman, also in leathers, but with her back to the camera. The man was certainly tall and thin, but he himself was all wrong: too young, loose-limbed, gangling and good-humoured in a way her intruder simply hadn't been. Anna shook her head. 'I mean I only saw him for a few seconds,' she said. 'And I was terrified.'

'It's okay,' Hollis assured her. 'We all realise this is a long shot.' He gestured at Patterson for a new photo. Meaner this time. Darker of complexion and of countenance, staring belligerently at the camera, clearly aware he was being filmed. Another biker, to judge from the black helmet with red flashes in his left hand, and from the motorbike behind. Too young again, though. Too broad. She shook her head once more. The third was even easier to dismiss, thanks to his beer belly.

'Oh, well,' said Hollis. 'Let's try your second guy.'

Patterson opened a different folder on his laptop, pulled up a new photo. It showed the upper body of a shaven-headed man in a black T-shirt, his arms muscled and tattooed, standing on the pavement outside a bookies. Big, yes, but not even close to big enough. He showed her the next, then eight more. Medium height and stocky seemed to be the build of choice among Lincolnshire's bikers. But none had the sheer immensity of the man from her bedroom.

'I'm sorry,' she said finally. 'I've wasted your time.'

'Ruling people out is almost as valuable as ruling them in.'

'Sure it is,' she said.

Patterson gave a snort of laughter, perhaps enjoying the way she'd put Hollis down. 'Just to be clear, love,' he said, 'are you saying it's definitely not any of these men? Or only that you can't be sure?'

'I was petrified, like I say. That could have made them look bigger, I guess. But I'm pretty sure.' She turned back to Hollis. 'Do any of them have accents?'

He raised an eyebrow. 'Accents?'

'The big guy sounded foreign. The tall guy sounded posh.'

'You never told me that,' said Hollis to Patterson.

'I didn't know it,' retorted Patterson. 'Elias never said.'

'They only spoke a couple of words each,' said Anna, feeling an obscure urge to defend Elias. 'And I might have been imagining it anyway. They might even have been putting it on.'

'You don't think...' murmured Patterson.

'No,' said Hollis. 'No, I don't.'

'Shouldn't we at least ask? I mean I've got those new photos.'

Hollis gave him a glare. The two men might be colleagues, but Anna got the strongest sense that they didn't much like or trust one another. 'Wait here,' Hollis told her. He picked up the laptop and left, beckoning for Patterson to follow. The door had a small glass viewing window. She could see Patterson's mulish expression through it, while, out of sight, Hollis scolded him in a voice so low that she only caught the odd word.

A minute passed. Hollis poked his head back in. 'Sorry about this,' he said, with his bright false smile. 'You couldn't give us five, could you?' He didn't wait for her to reply but closed the door instead. Anna paced around the room again. She was genuinely cold by now. She kept breaking into shivers. The two men finally came back in. Patterson went to stand in the corner with his arms folded, his eyes on Hollis rather than on her. For his part, Hollis sat back down beside her with what he doubtless intended as a reassuring smile. Yet the more he smiled, the less comfortable she felt. 'Okay,' he said. 'It's possible that you'll recognise one of the two men I'm about to show you. It would cause us no end of grief if he learned he was under surveillance, so I need your word it goes no further.'

'Fine,' said Anna.

Hollis opened the laptop back up. 'It won't be him, mind,' he said, with another glance at Patterson. 'He's too careful for that. But we might as well make sure.' He tapped a key. A new photograph appeared, of two men in suits outside an office building, about to get into a gold Mercedes S-Class. The first – short, balding, fat and frightened – clearly wasn't the one she was supposed to be looking at. That was the man behind: Slavic of features, with a face carved from granite, dressed in a bright white silk shirt and a sharply-tailored black suit, yet clearly a bruiser of some kind, not just from his immensity and multitude of scars, but from the way his eyes were fixed on the other man's back, as if expecting him to make a break for it, as if *wanting* him to, just for the sport of catching him and making him pay. But what really got to her was the way he carried himself, his torso so bulky that it pushed his arms out from his body in a way that was so instantly familiar that she flinched and drew in a breath.

'Jesus,' muttered Hollis. 'It's him? You're sure?'

Anna nodded uncertainly. 'I mean I never saw his face. But otherwise…'

'Okay,' said Hollis. 'Fair enough. How about this one?' He

tapped a key and a new picture appeared, of the same gold Mercedes S-Class, only parked inside a huge open building of some kind, perhaps an aircraft hangar, with the two men from the first photograph standing with their backs to the camera while they talked to a tall, thin man in a gorgeous charcoal grey suit with a cream silk handkerchief neatly folded in his breast pocket, standing in front of a silver Rolls Royce.

Anna was about to ask for a closer look when Hollis anticipated her, zooming in on his face and shoulders. A peculiar-looking man, not handsome so much as aristocratic. Or, to be more precise, a casting department's idea of how an English aristocrat from between the wars should look. Thin to the point of gauntness, with pronounced cheekbones, a Roman nose and weirdly full lips curled into a permanent sneer. His hair was of such a glistening blackness that it had to be dyed, and he had a peculiar posture too, his chin upraised in order that he might look down his nose at the others, and his chest puffed out like some populist politician taking the podium at a rally. And suddenly she was back in her bedroom, facing a man who meant her ill. 'It's him,' she said flatly.

'How sure are you?' asked Hollis. 'We can't afford mistakes. Not on this.'

Anna hesitated. How certain could she be when she'd only seen two or three pieces from the full jigsaw of his face? 'I mean I wouldn't like to swear to it in court,' she said. 'But I'm more confident than I ever expected to be. Far, far more. Who is he? Who are they both?'

'I can't tell you that.'

'Why not?'

'I told you. This is an ongoing investigation. A highly sensitive one. If word gets out…' He glanced up at Patterson once more, still standing there with his arms folded, gazing at Hollis with an expression she found hard to decipher. 'Honestly, we can't afford even a whisper. Not right now. And it's for your own safety as much as anything, believe me.'

'My safety? Are you trying to spook me?'

'Yes, frankly. I'm trying to make sure you don't say a word. Not to anyone. Not even to Elias.'

'But he's leading the case,' protested Anna.

'Not any more, he isn't,' said Hollis. 'He got taken off it this afternoon. I'm surprised you haven't heard.' And there was the faintest flicker in his eye, which might just have been satisfaction or even relief, but which might also have been merely the poor lighting, or even her imagination hard at work.

FORTY-FIVE

A kink in Elias's character compelled him, when feeling low, to push himself lower still. He thus ignored Wharton's order to return directly to Nettleham HQ and left the A17 at Heckington instead, cutting cross country to a florist he knew in Walcott before continuing on through Dunston to St Mary's Church.

Elias had become a father much younger than he'd intended. Neither he nor Julie had planned it, they'd just been careless. He'd been silently furious with her, all the same, as though only she had been to blame. He'd felt trapped for those next few months, increasingly filled with dread. Then Marcus had arrived in the early hours of a winter morning, and it had decked him faster and for longer than any uppercut had ever done. It had felt as though a new colour had been added to the world, or more accurately a new dimension – as if he'd seen the world only in 2D until that moment, but now could see its depth.

It had been for Marcus's sake that he'd set aside his fading dreams of boxing glory to concentrate on his career in the police instead. It had been for him and the twins, when they'd arrived some eighteen months later, that he and Julie had bought a near-derelict cottage a few miles up the road from here, even though he'd known what brutal hard work restoration would be, on top of his regular job. He'd wanted it brutal. He'd wanted to build empires with his bare hands.

It was dark by the time Elias arrived, but the old church was spotlit from beneath, making it plenty bright enough to see by. He turned off his phone out of respect for the dead, then knelt by his son's graveside to lay his flowers against his headstone. He could feel the wetness of the grass through his trousers. It pleased him that he'd have to wash them later. All penance welcome here. Some weeds had been tugged up by their roots and set in a small heap to one side, and there were fresh lilies in a weathered crystal vase whose sides were splashed with watery mud. Julie had clearly been by, though she hated it here in the rain, for it gave her nightmares to think of his coffin filling with water, of Marcus battering his little fists against the wood as he drowned all over again.

Nearly four years had now passed, yet Elias hadn't healed. It wasn't just grief. A bone had lodged in his throat, forever choking him. After it had happened, he and Julie had gone to counselling. She'd taken his hands in hers and looked into his eyes to tell him that she forgave him. A lie, of course. Bitterness had been her way of keeping Marcus alive. Elias, too, had said what had been expected of him: That sometimes terrible things happened despite our best efforts; that consequences could be out of proportion to failings; that if this had happened to a friend, he'd have felt desperately sorry for them, but he wouldn't have blamed them. All of which was abstractly true, but none of which helped the slightest bit. He'd let his beloved son die. Everything else was bollocks.

Eighteen months he'd worked on the cottage. But finally it had been ready. The garden had still been a mess, of course, but that could wait. There was only the sitting room to finish off, where they'd been storing their new furniture beneath dust sheets. He'd been putting up the last of the masking tape when Julie had arrived, wanting him to look after Marcus while she took the twins shopping. No worries. He was a joy to look after. Give him a book or some toys to play with, he could entertain himself for hours. He even enjoyed helping decorate, though five minutes of that usually took fifty to put right.

Decorating mostly bored Elias, but he did enjoy a roller. That smell of paint, the satisfying sticky noise, the speed of transformation. He finished the first coat and stood back. It looked amazing. He'd had reservations about Julie's choice of lilac, but he should never have doubted her. He turned to Marcus to share the moment. All parents must know that humpback sensation when their kid isn't where they should be. That plunge of heart, that swell of terror. Usually it's over in a blink, the little rascal popping up from behind the sofa, delighted at the trauma they've caused. Not this time.

The door was closed but the sash window was raised a little for ventilation, and Elias had left his paint pots beneath it, almost like a set of steps. And there was a lilac smudge on the sill that he knew he hadn't left himself. It made him feel quite ill. He lifted the window all the way and yelled for his son. Nothing. He climbed out, feeling so dizzy he feared he might fall over. The cottage was at the end of a private track that led to a lane with so little traffic that people drove recklessly fast along it. Elias ran to it now. Thank Christ, no sign of Marcus. Wherever he was, he surely couldn't have done himself any—

That was when Elias remembered the old swimming pool.

He sprinted back up to the cottage and across the overgrown lawn. There were metal stakes around the pool, and bundles of wire mesh with which to fence it off before Julie and the children moved in; but his eagerness to get the house finished had taken precedence. He told himself that Marcus must be somewhere else. Fate couldn't be that cruel. He slowed as it came into view, approaching it from the deep end. He felt hollow inside. He pledged his soul for a reprieve.

The walls were grey cement, cracked and bulging. The bottom was covered by leaves and dirty brown water. Elias was almost at its edge before he saw the leg of Marcus's blue dungarees and then a sleeve of his red jersey. He must have fallen from almost exactly where Elias was now. He was lying on his front, his face in the water. The floor was so slick with vegetation that Elias's feet slid from under him when he jumped down. He cracked his head sickeningly hard against the side, but managed to hold onto consciousness by an effort of pure will.

He picked Marcus up in both arms and staggered up the pool's sloped floor to the shallow end, where he laid him on his back. His skin was pale and blue. A gash in his forehead was leaking blood, and more was coming out of his ear too, along with a fine white froth from his nostrils. Yet he looked so at peace that it was impossible to believe anything serious was taking place.

Elias had learned emergency first aid in the police. He checked for breathing and a pulse, couldn't find either. He put his arms around Marcus's waist, as he'd been taught, then made a fist of his right hand and pressed his thumb below his ribcage and gave it an upward thrust, sending water gushing from his mouth and nostrils, leaving his face covered by slick trails of pinkish foam and mucous. He laid him on his back again, pinched his nostrils, breathed into his mouth, gave him chest compressions. He still couldn't find a pulse, but he was so panicked he couldn't have found his own. He needed help. Professional help. A doctor, a paramedic, an ambulance.

He picked Marcus up again and raced to the house where he gave him another round of CPR. It was the most gruelling thing he'd ever done, pressing that hard on his beloved son's chest as his skin somehow turned both white and blue. His eyelids were closed. Elias lifted one with his thumb. His eye was upturned, pale and watery. The telephone hadn't been connected yet, his mobile had no signal. The nearest hospital was in Lincoln, a good ten minutes away, but what choice did he have? He gave Marcus another round of CPR on his back seat then sped off, tooting traffic out of his way, overtaking on blind corners.

The hospital entrance was on the other side of the road. A silver Bentley was approaching sedately down the other lane. Elias flashed his lights in warning but the arsehole only accelerated. He cut across him anyway, his car jumping as its rear was clipped, blaring his horn non-stop for attention as he raced up the approach, nurses and visitors jumping out of his way as he screeched to a stop outside the front doors.

He must have looked a sight in his wildness and distress, his clothes sodden and covered with blood and paint. But they knew what they were doing. They put Marcus on a trolley while one doctor asked precise questions and another searched for vital signs and shouted orders. Assured, brisk, calm. They'd done this a hundred times, it gave him confidence and hope. His legs gave way beneath him. A nurse helped him to a chair. He tried to explain how Marcus must have been alive when he'd found him because he'd still been bleeding. Her expression told him that that wasn't much of a straw to clutch at. The shock kicked in. He began to shiver. He took out his phone to call Julie without the first idea what to say. A door opened behind him and the nurse looked up and he read the news on her face, and he really didn't remember much else after that.

In the graveyard, Elias heard the squeaking of the gate, then excited laughter. A boy and a girl appeared, arms around each others' waists. They stopped when they saw him kneeling by that tiny headstone. They winced in sympathy. He pushed himself back to his feet then dried his eyes and gave them the most encouraging smile that he could find as he turned and headed past them for the gate.

Because life rolled on. It was what it did.

FORTY-SIX

It was blustery, cold and dark by the time Anna left Nettleham Police HQ. She hugged her jacket tight around herself as she set off for the pound, following the directions the desk officer had given her. It began, almost inevitably, to drizzle, scattering diamonds in the car headlights and making the flagstones glisten. She upped her pace as the rain fell ever harder, turning into such a violent squall that she ran the final stretch, splashing past a school outside which the last few parents were waiting in their cars for their children.

The pound's main gate was only a little further on, but she arrived to find it padlocked and its Hours of Opening sign telling her it had closed fifteen minutes ago. She stood there seething at Patterson and Hollis for having wasted so much of her time, and at the desk officer for not bothering to warn her. But there was nothing for it now.

She took shelter beneath a bus stop a little way down the road. She didn't want to throw herself on Oliver's mercy, not without at least trying for a taxi. But it was the afternoon rush, and the first two companies she called were booked solid. She was about to try a third when a black SUV with tinted windows parked a little way up the hill from her began to roll slowly out of its spot on the slope, yet without turning on its engine or its lights.

Anna had no memory of her abduction by Harry Kidd.

He'd coshed her hard enough that everything between leaving work and waking up in his boot was a blank. And Kidd himself had never spoken of it either, hanging himself in his stairwell before even being charged, and making no mention of it in the note he'd left behind, so self-pitying that it had burned itself into Anna's memory. *Forgive me,* he'd written. *I saw you in the library and you were so beautiful. I couldn't stop thinking about you.* But they'd found his cosh beneath his floorboards with her blood and hair still on it, and hundreds of photographs of her on his phone and computer from his months of stalking, including dozens between work and home, suggesting he'd been plotting her kidnap for weeks.

Little wonder, then, that she'd become so exquisitely sensitive to cars, particularly in deserted places and at night. The ones outside the school had been fine. Their engines and their lights had been on, advertising themselves to their kids. But the black SUV wasn't like that, all dark and silent despite the cold and gloom, yet with the silhouettes of two people just visible inside. Her heart began to race. She looked back up the road at the school. The last of the waiting cars had just picked up their child and now was heading off the other way, depriving her of both their headlights and their witness, leaving the road empty all the way down to a late night grocers at its foot.

The black SUV's engine and lights suddenly sprang on. It accelerated towards her down the hill. And at once Anna found herself back in the forest of her nightmares, being chased by a man who meant her ill. Panic instantly consumed her. She turned and simply fled.

FORTY-SEVEN

Elias waited until he was out of the churchyard before turning his phone back on. It rang almost instantly. Maria Quinn. 'There you are,' she said, in the kind of breathy whisper that suggested there were others nearby who she didn't want listening in. 'I was getting worried.'

'No need,' he told her. 'What's up?'

'That wretched man. I can't believe what he's doing. Stealing credit for your arrest of Gregory Scott like that!'

'*Our* arrest. And what are you talking about?'

'Wharton. Claiming he had to come down from Grimsby to salvage the investigation.'

Elias laughed. 'He really said salvage?'

'He's saying it now, at his bloody press conference. Aren't you listening?'

'I'd rather hammer nails into my kneecaps.'

'I can't believe you're taking it so calmly.'

'Yeah, well,' he said. 'There are worse things in this world.' An awkward silence followed. She clearly knew his story. 'Was that it?' he asked. 'Or was there anything else?'

'I've been taken off the case too,' she said. 'I'm back at the station. But it's been quiet enough here that I gave those traffic cams another shot. I know it doesn't much matter any more, but I do hate a loose end.'

'Me too. And?'

'I checked them last Sunday afternoon, like you suggested.

I found Mr Warne heading up towards Sleaford in his van at a few minutes after three. It's definitely him, you can see him and his plates. But his front bumper's fine, there's no scratch down his side, and there's a ladder on his roof rack too.'

'A ladder? Are you sure?'

'Am I sure there's a ladder on his roof rack?' she retorted. 'Just how bad at this do you think I am?'

Elias laughed. 'Fair enough. Go on.'

'I've traced him as far as Sleaford, but then he vanishes. Until the early hours, at least, when I've got him coming back. But there are loads of other traffic cams around there, thanks to all those nice straight roads that our boy racers do so love to speed on. I've drawn a kind of net from the cameras he *didn't* pass. You'll see what I mean. I've already sent it over.' He found it in his email and opened the attachment, a screenshot of a roadmap with the traffic cameras marked by an X, drawing a jagged triangle around Warne's possible destinations, from Sleaford up to Lincoln and across to Newark. 'Nice work,' he said. 'Have you given this to Wharton and his team?'

'Why would they care? They've got their man.'

'Do it anyway. If they get irritated, tell them I told you to. Otherwise, just take the credit.' He stared at the map. 'Any chance you'd be up for another job? It'd have to be off the books, though, what with both of us being off the case. Would that be a problem?'

'No.'

'Okay. Great. Thank you. Warne had a drone in the back of his van with a bunch of photographs on it. Most are old, and of his farm, but the latest set are from somewhere else, and were taken recently, to judge from the state of the fields.'

'You think that's where he was that day? And you want me to see if I can't locate it?'

'You did say you hated loose ends.'

'I did, yes. Send them over.'

'You're a star. Oh, and obviously start with the area inside your map.'

'Yes,' said Quinn. 'Obviously.'

'Oi,' he said.

'Oi yourself.'

He grinned as he finished the call, feeling unexpectedly cheerful, all things considered. He sent Quinn the photos and received acknowledgement, along with a screenshot from a traffic camera showing Warne's van heading north, exactly as Quinn had described, undamaged and with an extensible aluminium ladder on its roof. He checked through his other emails and found a message from a man called Royston Flynn, setting out in commendable detail a visit Dunstan Warne had paid him some twelve days before and explaining that Anna Warne had suggested he let him know. He thanked him by return then rang Anna to thank her too, and also to make sure she'd heard the news about Gregory Scott. Her phone was busy, however, so he left it for later and set off for Lincoln, searching through the local stations on his radio for one carrying Wharton's press conference live.

FORTY-EIGHT

Anna made it inside the grocers a moment before the black SUV with tinted windows caught up with her. She watched through the glass door as it drove on by, stopping at the bottom of the hill to turn left and then vanish out of view. Probably nothing, then, but it still left her with her heart pounding and her nerve shaken enough to give up on taxis and call Oliver for a lift instead.

She ate a bar of milk chocolate while she waited. He pulled up outside just ten minutes later in a spray of rainwater and with a loud double toot. She thanked the woman behind the till for letting her stay inside then hurried out into the rain, apologising to Oliver both for her wetness and for calling him out at all.

'Don't be daft,' he said. 'It's a naughty night to swim in, as my dad always puts it. How did everything go?'

'I've had better afternoons.'

'Is that all I'm getting?'

'Yes.'

'So what about tonight? You can't seriously still be thinking of York.'

'Don't worry. I'll find a hotel.'

'A hotel!' he protested. 'Come on. I hoovered the spare bedroom for you, *and* I changed the damned sheets. All on the off chance, too. Me! Changing sheets! On the off chance! You wouldn't let that crazy hard work go to waste, would you?'

'I wouldn't want to impose.'

'You wouldn't be imposing. You'd be giving me a treat. Especially as you'll be buying me dinner in exchange.'

'Okay, that's fair. Though I'll need a shower and a change of clothes first.'

'Damn right. I'm not having you sneezing all over my lobster. Lincoln's top restaurant does have its standards, you know.'

'In your dreams,' she told him. 'You're scoring a kebab.'

Oliver lived in a converted coach-house in a cul-de-sac by the cathedral. It had an archway entrance leading into a cobbled courtyard with five parking bays, one for each of the four apartments, and the fifth for guests and deliveries. She grabbed her bags and hurried inside then up to his first floor flat, compact yet beautifully finished, with deep pile maroon carpeting and elegant modern furniture. 'So I guess TV pays okay,' she said.

'I wish,' he said. 'The salaries are a joke. But the world is full of people who'll pay even complete nonentities like me to speak at their dinners and cut their ribbons. Bizarre, but there it is. Anyway, you should see my mortgage.' He showed her the bathroom and the spare bed. It had a lock on its door, just as promised, and a fine view of the cathedral's spires. 'I've got to pop out for a bit,' he said, checking his watch. 'And you'll be wanting that shower. How about we meet back here at eight?'

The shower was hot and delicious, spraying her from every angle. She stayed in until her fingers pruned. For the first time in forever, she felt like making the most of herself. She used Oliver's dryer on her hair then tamed it with a clip. As ever, these days, she'd packed for practicality rather than glamour, but she did what she could with what she had, ironing a blouse then tightening her belt a notch to give herself a waist. She found an old makeup kit rattling around the bottom of her bag, and was glossing her lips in the bathroom mirror when Elias called from his car, at least to judge by the background noises. 'So how did your afternoon go?' he asked.

'Fine,' she told him. 'Except that the pound closed before I got there.'

'Why didn't you call me?' he said. 'I could have had you met.'

'Never occurred to me. Anyway, it's fine. Oliver picked me up. I'll collect the van in the morning.'

'You're staying with him tonight, then?'

Anna hesitated, taken aback by the unexpected slight catch in Elias's voice. 'He's got a lovely little guest bedroom,' she told him, though she wasn't entirely sure why. 'It has an amazing view of the cathedral.'

'Is that so?'

'I'm staring up at it now. Oh, and I'm glad you called. We met this guy called Royston Flynn earlier.'

Yes,' said Elias. 'He emailed. That's actually why I called, to say thanks.'

'No worries. Though your friends in Serious and Organised Crime tell me you're off the case? Is that true?'

'It was those bodies you helped us find. They've turned the story national. National stories need major figures, not humble DIs like me.'

'I'm sorry.'

'It happens. And at least we got your uncle's killer first.'

'You did?' she said, amazed. 'Who?'

'Shit. Sorry. I assumed you'd have heard by now. It's been all over the news. Let's just say your tip about the hotel paid off.'

'One of their guests?'

'Not exactly. But close.'

'Oh Christ,' she said. 'Of course! Gregory Scott.'

'Why of course?'

'We bumped into his wife yesterday, when we were checking in. You should have seen how relieved she was when I told her about the intruders. I should have known then that she feared he'd done it. At least... It was him, right?'

'Your uncle caught him digging in that field, just like we thought. He's going to be claiming self-defence, apparently, but I think he'll find it hard.'

'He's confessed? Already?'

'To his wife, who told us. Plus I found his spade out on the salt marsh.'

'On the salt marsh? What an idiot.'

'Panic. It messes with your mind.'

'Thank you,' she said. Her earlier visit to the coroner came rushing back, the sight of her uncle laid out upon the brushed steel table, his lopsided face and the rubber cap over his scalp. 'I can't tell you how much that means.'

'Forget it. It's my job. Speaking of which: Any joy IDing your two intruders?'

'Oh. Your colleagues told me not to say.'

'My god,' he said. 'You got them, didn't you? Who?'

Anna hesitated. But it had been clear to her that Hollis and Patterson hadn't fully trusted one another. Why then should she? Yet she did now trust Elias, she realised to her surprise, and not because he'd found her uncle's killer so much as because he'd chosen to spend last night sitting in his car across from Warne Farm's drive. 'They didn't say. And I never saw their faces, remember? So I can't be certain.'

'And yet you are, aren't you?'

'Yes.'

'What can you tell me?'

She took a deep breath, came to her decision. 'For a start, they said I might recognise one of them. I didn't, but they obviously have some kind of public profile. They showed me two photos. The first was of the weightlifter. He looked Slavic, with a shaved head and lots of scars. He was outside an office building, escorting a man I didn't recognise out to a gold Mercedes. The poor guy looked terrified. The second shot was of those same two men inside an aircraft hangar talking to the tall thin posh one who was standing with his back to a silver Rolls Royce.'

'An aircraft hangar?' asked Elias.

'Not a proper airport one. It was too rundown. A private

airfield, I'd guess.'

'Jesus,' muttered Elias.

'Why? Does that mean something?'

'Maybe. Can I come see you?'

'I thought you were off the case?'

'Even so. Please. I'm almost in Lincoln now. I can be with you in ten minutes.'

'Okay. Do you know where…?' Then she stopped herself, belatedly remembering Oliver's affair with his wife.

'Yes,' he said dryly. 'I know where… Ten minutes. I'll call you when I arrive.'

FORTY-NINE

Elias was as good as his word, calling from downstairs before Anna had even finished getting ready. The rain had stopped, she was glad to see. Better yet, the downpour had cleared the air, turning it into a pleasant autumn evening. Elias was already out of his car, holding an open laptop in his left hand. 'Before I forget,' he said, 'we found another forty-one of those silver pennies. All from Lynn, as best the guys can tell, except for two from London and one from Canterbury.'

The way he phrased it turned it almost into a question, but Anna only shook her head. 'What do you want me to say?'

'I thought you'd be interested, mostly,' he told her. 'But does it change your thinking at all? About it being a private cache rather than part of the baggage train?'

'Not really. People did move around.' Despite the heavy taxes and constant wars, England had largely prospered under the Plantagenets. Better roads, stone bridges and iron-sheathed cartwheels had led to a boom in trade, with new fairs and markets springing up everywhere, and town charters creating a sturdy middle class. 'You'd expect a private hoard to include *some* pennies from elsewhere. It's the proportion that matters.'

'Okay, good. That's what I thought.' He set his laptop on his bonnet and tapped a key. 'Now, then. Your two intruders.' He turned his screen to show her a photograph of a man and a woman standing beside a Rolls Royce Silver Shadow, its rear door being held open for them by a formidably-built man in a chauffeur's uniform. The woman was a classically beautiful thirty-something brunette in a gorgeous white and gold dress and a playful, wide-brimmed hat. Her hand was resting lightly on the arm of a tall, thin man in his late forties, wearing a cravat and a pearl grey swallowtail coat, and holding a top hat in his left hand, the pair of them clearly off to some fun yet prestigious event – Royal Ascot, say, or a royal garden party, or an awards ceremony. The man was leaning slightly towards the woman, as if to whisper in her ear, revealing just a hint of baldness in his glistening black hair. As for the chauffeur, he was a powerfully built Slavic man with a badly scarred face. 'It's the same two men your colleagues showed me,' she told him. 'How did you know? Who are they?'

'The driver's Andrei Lubov. Ex-Russian army, I believe, and now a high-priced bodyguard. The tall one is the slumlord I told you about yesterday, the one who got your friend Merchant fired. He goes by León Alessandro de Bruin these days, though he used to be plain Len Brown as a lad. Only there were so many stories about what a bastard he was to his tenants that it got to be bad for business. So he took a leaf out of that Brighton guy's book and upscaled his name. Len Brown might scam you, but surely not León Alessandro de Bruin. Then he set his Rottweiler lawyers on anyone who badmouthed him in the media or online. My colleagues were right. You need to keep this to yourself. He's a genuinely evil bastard. If he found out you could finger him...'

'Oh, that's just great,' said Anna. 'But I don't understand. Why would a man that rich get his hands so dirty?'

'We've known for ages that he had some kind of relationship with this gang. They've beaten up too many of his tenants for it to be coincidence. But obviously the ties go deeper than we thought. In fact...'

'In fact?'

'This gang, they used to be small time. A bit of dealing, a

bit of violence, the odd robbery. Then about ten or twelve years ago, they suddenly got their act together. Now they pretty much run drugs across the whole county.'

'You think that was him?'

'It would explain a lot. The rest of the gang was in custody, in hiding or under surveillance, and someone had to go let those poor bastards out. Maybe he and Lubov were the only ones left. They killed them, then returned the next week to bury them. Except they lost something while they were at it, and had to go back for it themselves the other night. Because they could hardly tell anyone else where to look, could they? Not without revealing where they'd put the bodies.'

'So what now?' asked Anna.

'That's not up to me. I'm off it, as you know. But I will say that with people like this, your case better be watertight or they'll wriggle. So be patient. It might take time.'

'Got it. Was that everything?'

'Except for your uncle's van. How about I give you a lift up to the pound in the morning? That way, I can deal with any problems that might come up.'

'That would be great, thanks.' She hesitated, then added: 'It's quite spooky up there at night. There was a car that gave me the creeps.'

'How do you mean?'

'It was pelting down. I took cover at a bus stop. This black SUV came rolling out of its spot with its lights and engine off. There was something about it. I ran into a late night grocers at the foot of the hill. Then it just drove off, so I figured it was nothing. But now that you've told me about this de Bruin character...' She saw movement in the archway and fell silent. But it was only Oliver, hanging back to give her and Elias space.

He stepped forward on being noticed. 'You're not talking about León de Bruin, are you?' he asked. 'He really tried to snatch you at the pound?'

'There was a car, that's all,' said Anna. 'I don't see how he could have known I'd be there.'

'Because Nettleham leaks like a fucking sieve,' said Oliver, with a glare at Elias. 'Everyone knows it.'

'Is that right?' asked Anna.

Elias nodded reluctantly. 'Yes.'

'Christ,' said Anna. 'How worried should I be?'

'I doubt he'll try anything here,' said Elias. 'Too many people. But you should be careful all the same. Call me at the first sniff of trouble. I mean it: the first sniff. I don't care what time it is. I'll be straight over.' He checked his watch. 'That should hold us for tonight. I'll work out something better in the morning, I promise. Speaking of which, the pound opens at nine. How about I pick you up here at a quarter to?' He waited for her to nod, then he bid them both goodnight before getting back into his Leaf, pulling an adroit three-point turn and heading off.

FIFTY

A few blades of grass and some patches of moss were growing in the gaps between the cobbles in the coach-house courtyard. 'León de fucking Bruin,' muttered Oliver, scraping them out angrily with the heel of his shoe. 'Of all the damn people.'

'Is he really that bad?' asked Anna.

He looked around, almost as if fearful of being overheard. 'Let's go inside,' he said. Anna followed him upstairs. He double locked his front door, which unsettled her further, as did the way he went straight to the kitchen for a bottle of red. 'Okay,' he said, pouring them each a glass, handing her one. 'Did Elias tell you I had a run-in with him?'

'He said you tried to make an exposé of him, but that it got stopped.'

Oliver nodded grimly. 'I'd actually met him a few times at events over the years. I liked him, would you believe? He can be charming when he puts his mind to it. And his wife's just scrumptious. It's impossible to imagine her being mixed up with anything really nasty. So when my producer suggested we do a programme on him, I thought he was joking. I mean he's one of the county's largest landlords, so of course his tenants are going to grumble. It's the nature of the relationship. But then I talked to some of them, and wow. None of them would go on the record. They were all too scared. And with good reason. He seems to get off on wrecking lives.'

'Did he... did he do that to you?'

Oliver grimaced. 'He got me fired, if that's what you mean. But I was planning to leave anyway, to do my documentaries, so all he really achieved was to get me a decent payoff. But he wasn't to know that.'

'It was definitely him?'

'His commiserations card arrived the morning before they told me.'

'What a bastard.'

'Yeah. But I got off lightly, compared to some. He's left me alone since, presumably because I still have some clout around here. But if you want to give yourself nightmares, there's a support group for tenants who tried to stand up to him. You wouldn't believe their stories, how vindictive he can be. It's like a point of honour with him, to make sure the other guy comes off worse. He sues people for fun, then keeps at it long after anyone rational would stop. He has people stalked, harassed and beaten, some so badly they're hospitalised or even crippled. And of course he's clever enough that nothing can ever be traced back to him. Several of the group's members had breakdowns. One woman tried to kill herself. Another succeeded. I can show you if you like.'

'God, no,' said Anna.

'Good call. Then how about we get something to eat? Though maybe we should order in, all things considered? I could even cook, if you're feeling reckless, though wars have been fought over lesser insults than my bolognese.'

'No,' said Anna firmly. 'We're going out. I hate the idea of cowering.'

'We'll stick to Bailgate,' said Oliver. 'We'll be safe enough there.'

She put on her jacket, slung her bag over her shoulder. Bailgate was barely a minute's walk away, and thronged with people taking advantage of the pleasant evening to do some early Christmas shopping. Several did double takes or nudged each other when Oliver walked by. 'So this is what it's like to be famous,' murmured Anna.

'You'll find out for yourself, soon enough.'

His favourite chippie was near the top of Steep Hill, the other side of Westgate. The cobblestone road was still so slick from the earlier rain that Anna's feet simply went from beneath her at one point, and she'd have taken a fearful tumble had Oliver not grabbed her by her arm, which she rubbed a little ruefully after he let her go again. 'Sorry,' he said.

'Don't be. Better than the alternative.' She clung to him and shuffled in comical little baby steps to the gritted pavement, where they joined the queue for the chippie. She bought them vast portions of haddock and chips that they ate with their fingers on a damp bench in the square between cathedral and castle, while a bearded busker outside the Magna Carta pub tempted fate with an upbeat rendition of *Have You Ever Seen The Rain*.

Anna couldn't finish her portion. She gave the rest to Oliver then sat back and looked around, filled not just with the contentment of a full stomach but with a potent sense of history too. This small patch of cobbled ground had witnessed one of England's most consequential – if largely forgotten – battles. It had taken place some seven months after King John's death, with William Marshal now regent. He'd done what he could to reunite the country, lowering taxes, offering reconciliation to those who wanted it, and reissuing Magna Carta in the name of the boy king Henry III. Yet the French and the remaining rebel barons had still controlled London and great swathes of southern and eastern England. Far from backing down, they reinforced over the winter to lay siege to the strategic castles at Dover and right here in Lincoln.

King John had gone to great lengths to avoid open battle. Marshal, by contrast, had sought it. He raised the largest army he could muster then led them here himself, despite being almost seventy years old and in the certainty of being outnumbered. The direct approach would have meant an uphill assault, so they circled around instead, to come in from the north. The rebels and the French stayed inside the town, trusting to its high walls and sturdy gates. They left one gate unguarded, however, believing it too blocked by masonry to be capable of breach. But Marshal thought otherwise.

A diversionary attack provided cover for its clearance, then he led the main assault himself, charging into the city on his warhorse, meeting the rebel forces right here on Westgate. The battle had been in the balance until one of Marshal's men had thrust his sword through the French commander's visor, killing him instantly. Dismay had spread among the rebels, who broke and fled, allowing Marshal and his men to chase them down Steep Hill, using the very slope Anna had just slipped on to turn advantage into victory, and victory into rout.

'Bloody hell, that was good,' said Oliver, scrunching up the various wrappers and lobbing them expertly into a nearby bin. 'Time for an ice cream.'

'Are you nuts? It's freezing.'

'Yeah. I guess it is a bit.' He got up then offered her his hand to help her to her feet. The contact was brief and entirely natural, yet it still gave her a tingle. He bumped his shoulder playfully against hers. She bumped him back. They smiled at one another, and for the first time in years—

A cry of anger and dismay. The roar of a motorbike. Anna turned to see a huge bearded man in ripped blue jeans and a zipped-up leather jacket speeding towards her on a fat red and black motorbike, its licence plate covered by masking tape. His visor was half raised, so that Anna could see a squashed portion of his face, his narrowed eyes, his flared nostrils and weathered cheeks, the flecks of grey in his chestnut beard. He had a pillion passenger too, but so much smaller than himself that Anna could only see his arms, as though the pair of them formed some grotesque, malignant spider. This second man was holding several bags of different styles and colours, including the pink one he'd clearly just snatched from the woman who'd cried out. They veered by Anna at the last moment, slowing just enough for the passenger to grab her bag from off her shoulder too. Then they were gone with it before she even properly realised it was under threat.

FIFTY-ONE

One of the few benefits of Elias's Nissan Leaf was that he had to recharge it at least twice a week. And seeing as his nearest charger was in the local McDonald's car park, it gave him the perfect excuse to dine guilt-free on a burger, fries and a milkshake. He sat at the window to keep an eye on it, just in case, because there'd been a spate of thefts around here recently, and though he could do with some new wheels, he didn't need the hassle. It badly needed a wash too, spattered with mud from all those rural lanes, but he couldn't face it tonight. Maybe in the morning, before collecting Anna.

He chomped down the last of his burger a little too hurriedly and paid for it with that unpleasant stretched feeling in his throat and chest all the way home. Parking near his bedsit was a nightmare. He normally didn't even bother trying, but rather used a cul-de-sac some fifteen minutes walk away, which was well lit and always had a few free places. But he'd promised to get to Anna quickly should she need him, so he circled round and round his block until finally a spot opened up.

He collected his post on his way in. The usual mix of bills and junk mail. The lift was still out of order so he trudged upstairs to his top-floor bedsit. Its shabbiness depressed him even on good days, but he hated it more than ever right now, after his earlier visit to Merchant's plush coach-house conversion, the sour memories it had inevitably provoked.

You learned to think a certain way when you became a detective. Everything had meaning. This wasn't always helpful. Another man, to take one example, would have been glad to see his wife emerging from the desperate misery of Marcus's death, taking trouble over her appearance again, buying new outfits, trying out different hairstyles, visiting the gym. Another man would have thought himself forgiven when she'd started being kind to him again, and tolerant of his flaws.

Elias wasn't that man, however. Suspicion was his default state. He'd taken to ringing home at odd hours, or going there unannounced, catching her that way in a series of flat-out lies. And, rather than subtly letting her know, or giving her more time and space to work through her anger and her grief, he'd bought himself a surveillance device instead. It was barely the size of a book of matches, yet it came equipped with GPS and a 4G SIM, all powered by a coin battery, enabling him to track her in her car and listen in to any phone calls she made from it. That was how he'd found out about her affair – and with Merchant, of all people. It had made him so furious that he'd followed her to his place one afternoon to confront the pair of them, managing to lose his dignity, his wife and his family in the space of five incandescent minutes.

Yes. Sometimes it was better not to know. Yet turning a blind eye wasn't in his nature.

Anna Warne had washed and brushed her hair, then had put on perfume, eyeliner and lip-gloss. She'd been wearing a pair of gold hoop earrings and a silver bracelet, neither of which he'd seen before, and she'd tightened her belt a notch too. All for Merchant's benefit as well, seeing as she'd be spending the night with him, for all her talk of spare bedrooms.

Observation was only one aspect of detective work. Another was deduction. It was hardly a mystery that an attractive young woman like Anna would seek to make the most of herself. The puzzle was why she hadn't done so until now; why, indeed, she'd almost gone out of her way to make herself appear shapeless and plain. Elias had come across the phenomenon before, and there was usually a good reason for it, so that he couldn't help but wonder whether that applied here too.

He felt bad about googling her. It felt like stalking. Yet he did it anyway, only to be defeated by the commonness of her name. He added Dunstan and then Lincolnshire to his search, but without success. Then he remembered how frosty she'd turned when he'd asked about her switch to York for her PhD, so he added Nottingham to his search, and there it was. He even remembered the incident now. Her abduction had been major news for a while. What he hadn't realised was that Harry Kidd had stalked her for months beforehand, or that she'd gone to the police about him on three separate occasions – only to be called up by one of the officers she'd spoken to, and asked out on a date.

That glance he'd given her ring finger that first day. No wonder she'd looked so sickened. He felt nauseous about it himself now, not least because he'd been toying with the idea of asking her for a coffee himself once this was all over. He had no great romantic aspirations. She was out of his weight class, and that was fine, though it would pain him grievously if she ended up with Merchant. But the simple truth was that he was lonely and that he longed for the companionship of a smart, attractive woman. The simple truth was that there was something about Anna that called out to him. He'd have liked her for a friend.

No chance of that now. He'd rather burn. And look at this place anyway. It was a pit. It was humiliating enough having to bring the twins here. And not just because it was awful in itself, although it was. It was because he no longer even tried to make the best of it. He'd let himself go, that was the fact of it. He'd let himself go because he was the kind of man who needed someone in his life to make an effort for. And he had no one like that left.

But that stopped now.

He filled a black bag with old takeaway cartons, beer cans and the rest, then cleared his sink of dirty plates and mugs. He fetched his hoover from the closet and ran it over his threadbare old carpet, for all the good it did. Then he pulled on rubber gloves and filled a bucket with soapy hot water and set about scrubbing every surface he could find, until they were as clean as he could get them.

FIFTY-TWO

The two bikers were away before Anna could react. Fortunately, Oliver was faster. He sprinted after the bike then simply leapt for her shoulder bag, grabbing it and almost jerking the pillion passenger from his seat, but instead tumbling to the ground himself and being dragged a short distance along the cobbles like a hapless waterskier until one of the bag's buckles broke, turning its strap into a snake that slithered through the man's grasp. He yelled out and the biker screeched to a halt and skewed around, as if intending to come back; but too many people were now converging to risk it, so he turned ahead once more and roared away.

Anna helped Oliver to his feet. He grimaced as he checked his left hand. Blood welled up from a pair of scratches to pool in his palm and then drip from there onto the wet cobbles, splashing in little scarlet coronets. A middle-aged couple came to ask if they needed help or witnesses. Oliver thanked them but assured them he was fine. 'That was amazing,' said Anna, fishing a pack of tissues from her bag and handing him a couple. 'I'd be lost without my stuff.'

Oliver pressed tissues against his palm. Spots of blood blotted through the thin paper almost at once. 'Can we get out of here?' he asked. 'I don't want a circus.'

'Sure,' she said. 'Is there a clinic or something nearby?'

That made him laugh. 'Don't be absurd. I only need a plaster. I've got some in my first aid kit.'

'If you're sure,' she said doubtfully.

'I'm sure,' he said. 'Though you should call your detective mate. He needs to know about this.'

'They were just bag thieves.'

'I don't care.'

'He was up all last night. I'll tell him in the morning.'

He shook his head at her, but let it go. They set off for his place, only for his knee to start hurting him badly enough that he began to limp. She put her arm around him and they hobbled awkwardly on. She helped him upstairs and through to his kitchen where she rinsed his hand with cold water, then made him sit at the table so that he could stretch out his sore leg. His first aid kit was beneath the sink. She swabbed his hand with cotton wool, plucked out specks of grit with tweezers, disinfected his cuts and covered them with antiseptic cream, gauze and a little cotton wool, all held in place by long strips of tape. 'Okay,' she said, when she was done. 'Now let's have a look at your knee.'

'It's fine,' he said. 'I just won't try to land any triple axles for a week or two.'

'Probably wise. Then you're good to go.'

'What about my lollipop?'

'Lollipops are for brave boys. I saw you wincing.'

'Hey!' he protested. 'And after I saved your bag too!'

'It was brilliant, what you did,' she told him seriously. 'Thank you.'

'My pleasure.' He pushed himself to his feet then hobbled across the kitchen for the bottle of red he'd opened earlier, only to find himself hampered by his bandaged hand. She did the honours, therefore, finding a pair of fresh glasses for them to take through to the sitting room. He patted the sofa beside him. She took an armchair instead. Conversation turned personal. Oliver made her laugh with wild stories about being the child of touring actors, then listened sympathetically as she told him about watching her mother die and moving in with Uncle Dun.

They finished the first bottle. She fetched a second. This time, when he patted the cushion, she settled in beside him. They talked some more, about all manner of things. He touched the back of her hand with a fingertip, traced a feathery figure of eight. She told herself to move her hand away, yet somehow it stayed. He covered it fully with his own. She turned hers around to let their fingers interlace. They stared down at them together for a few moments, then up into each others' eyes.

Of all the injuries Harry Kidd had done Anna, the one that had taken longest to heal was probably her newfound fear of men. She liked men. She missed them. She longed to trust them. She simply hadn't been able. Not until now, at least, sitting on Oliver's sofa, gazing into his eyes. *Two crazy days together*, she told herself. *That's all this was.* But so what? She longed for companionship again, for those delicious moments of connection, for the simple joy of being desired and held.

Irritatingly, however, Elias came suddenly to her mind – specifically, Oliver's affair with his wife. Because Elias liked her too, she was sure of it. It wasn't just the catch in his voice earlier, it was the way he'd blinked when he'd noticed her makeup, her brushed hair and tightened belt. And though she owed him nothing in that regard, and indeed was a little annoyed by his interest, she found that she didn't want to cause him pain either, certainly not on the night he'd caught her uncle's killer – especially as she'd be seeing him again first thing in the morning, when he came to take her to the pound. Because he was far too sharp and dialled in to her not to be able to tell. 'It's getting late,' she said, letting go of Oliver's hand, pushing herself to her feet. 'It's been a brute of a day.'

Oliver stood with her, a show of old-fashioned courtesy. 'You know where everything is?'

'Yes,' she said. 'Thanks.'

'Do I at least get a goodnight hug?'

She put her arms around him, rested her head against his shoulder. It felt so good she clasped him a little tighter. He ran a hand over her hair then kissed her gently on her cheek. When she didn't move away, he kissed her there a second time before moving to her mouth. She let him for a moment, enjoying the taste and feel of his lips, the press of his tongue, the scratch of his evening stubble. But she pulled back before she could get carried away. 'I really need my sleep,' she said.

'If it's sleep you're after,' he said, 'you'd be far better off in my bed. It's a million times more comfortable.'

Anna couldn't help but smile. 'Is that the best you've got?'

'We wouldn't need to do anything. Just hold each other is all.'

'Sure,' she said.

'I mean it. There's nothing like waking up alongside a beautiful woman. Best feeling in the world. You should try it yourself sometime. I'm serious. You really should. I'd sit in the corner, quiet as a mouse. You'd hardly even know I was there.'

She laughed and took a step back, grateful he'd made it so easy. 'Good night, Oliver,' she said. 'Sleep well.'

'Fat chance now,' he said ruefully. 'But I'll do my best.'

FIFTY-THREE

Oliver's hand healed overnight as well as could be hoped. Anna cleaned and dressed his cuts again at the kitchen table, bandaging them as lightly as possible to be unobtrusive during filming. They breakfasted companionably on yoghurt, toast and coffee until Elias rang from downstairs. He looked cheerful and well rested, though he'd clearly been up a while, for his Leaf was gleaming from a car wash, its tyres still wetly black. She went back upstairs for her belongings, which Oliver helped her carry down and stow. He put his arm around her waist and gave her a big warm kiss on her cheek. Then he told her he'd see her later and set off in his BMW.

'You're seeing him later?' asked Elias, with that same catch in his voice, too faint to object to, yet there nevertheless. 'I thought you'd be back off up to York?'

'I'm booked in with Uncle Dun's solicitor this afternoon,' she told him, annoyed both with Oliver for his pointless needling of Elias, and with Elias, for letting himself be needled. 'That leaves me time to kill. Oliver's filming at Newark Castle, so I thought I'd kill it there. Then back home tonight, van willing.'

They headed out along Eastgate to the Nettleham road, sitting in tedious queues at each of the roundabouts, which at least gave Anna the opportunity to tell Elias about last night's attempted bag snatch. 'For god's sake!' he protested. 'You were supposed to call me.'

'It was nothing. You were beat.'

'Even so.'

'It wasn't like they hurt me. They only wanted another bag for their collection. It was coincidence, that's all.'

'Maybe so. You've still got to tell me.'

'What do you think I'm doing now?'

Elias laughed, he couldn't help himself. 'Okay, fine,' he said, throwing up his hands in exasperation. 'You win.'

Anna smiled, surprised to discover how much she'd come to like him. 'So how's your day looking?'

'Bit grim. I'm due the mother of all bollockings.'

'Whatever for? You caught my uncle's killer.'

'Don't worry about it. Office politics.'

'If you'd like me to speak up for you…?'

'Hell, no. But thanks.'

They reached Nettleham, passed police HQ, arrived at the pound. Elias settled the paperwork with the duty officer while Anna checked out the van. Despite its age and cranky handling, it was a useful beast, rugged yet still nimble enough to reach the hardest places on the farm, and with plenty of room for equipment in its rear, which her uncle had changed around depending on the tasks at hand. The ladder was missing from its roof rack, but otherwise it was fuller than she'd ever seen. His hedge-cutters were inside, along with the petrol-driven augur he'd used to drill fencepost holes along the lane, some noise cancelling headphones, safety gloves, goggles and disposable breathing masks.

His portable toolkit was there, some telescopic tree loppers, a coil of orange nylon rope, a torch and a pack of spare batteries. A pair of ragged old bath towels stuffed into a large plastic bag were damp to the touch and almost black with grime. There were two timber planks and a handsaw with pale flecks of sawdust in its teeth, which was very unlike Uncle Dun, a stickler for cleaning and oiling his tools after use. His drone was in there too, along with its remote control. 'I bought it for his birthday a few years back,' she told Elias, when he arrived with a receipt for her to sign. 'Second hand, of course. I couldn't afford a new one. But still brilliant for finding lost baggage trains beneath your fields.'

'I wish you'd got him one with GPS,' said Elias. 'Then we'd know where he went that day.'

'He used it last Sunday?'

'We think so, yes. But his photos are all of plain flat fields.'

'This *is* Lincolnshire,' she pointed out.

'And don't I know it.' He took back the signed receipt, consulted his watch. 'Look, I really need to head off. Music to face, and all that. Unless there's anything else?'

'No. That's great. And thanks for everything.'

'No worries.' He stood there a few moments longer. 'And please. I know you hate asking for help…'

'Sure,' she said.

'Come on. At least pretend.'

'Okay. I'll call. I promise.' Aware she might not see him again, she wanted to make some extra show of gratitude for all he'd done for her, but she dithered so long over it that he nodded and returned to his Leaf and left.

She fixed the van's front bumper with gorilla tape, then mended the buckle on her bag with it too. She still didn't trust it to hold much weight, however, so she transferred most of its contents to her overnight bag, while pocketing her uncle's wallet so that she didn't forget to take it in to show his solicitor. She still had time before filming started at Newark, so she downloaded her uncle's drone photos onto her laptop. But Elias was right: save for a wedge-shaped copse, a pair of scarlet oaks and a short stretch of cobbled lane, the latest set could have been taken anywhere. There was, however, enough overlap between them for her to crop them and assemble them into a single composite image. But still she didn't recognise it, and then she was out of time.

The van was a cranky beast to drive any distance, with soft brakes, temperamental electrics, poor visibility and bad enough fumes that she lowered her window to let some fresh air in, despite the October chill. Then it began to rain, so she raised it back up again. The dual carriageway south to Newark was ugly yet evocative – for Anna, at least – passing as it did through the Templars' ancient heartlands of Byard's Leap and Temple Bruer, of Willoughton, Aslackby, Eagle, East Mere and South Witham, huge properties endowed by wealthy barons seeking to avoid the hellfire that their lives had often so deserved.

The Templars had acquired many thousands of acres of prime Lincolnshire land this way, then had worked them with free labour, thanks to the order's vows of poverty. They'd been excused most tolls and taxes too, by virtue of their sacred mission and their closeness to power, and they'd been highly entrepreneurial as well, introducing windmills, setting up their own smelting works, creating a pioneering banking network and owning whole fleets of trading ships.

They'd thus become a money-making machine, and not all of it had gone to fund the crusades. Numerous European regimes had depended on Templar loans, an arrangement that had suited everyone until Philip III of France had found a different method of payback, accusing them of satanism, sodomy and all kinds of heretical practices as an excuse to destroy the order and confiscate their wealth. But that had still been a century away while John had been on the throne, and he'd borrowed as much from them as anyone, courtesy of his advisor Aymeric de St Maur, head of the Knights Templar in England, and William Marshal's closest friend.

Something about this thought made Anna frown. She drifted from her lane. A lorry coming up behind blasted her with its horn. The shock made her slow right down and move over almost onto the hard shoulder, allowing the traffic behind to overtake – all except for a white Tesla several cars back that slowed with her, to stay the same distance behind, putting her instantly on her guard. She stamped her foot down and accelerated away as fast as the old van allowed, watching closely in her mirrors to see if the Tesla would speed up with her. But it held the same slow pace until it vanished from her view.

FIFTY-FOUR

Elias grabbed his usual cup of morning filth from the coffee machine on his way up to his desk. He turned on his computer to check out the latest from Warne Farm, only to discover that his case file access had been revoked. He sat there seething. He had paperwork to catch up on, but he was too riled up for that. Besides, he'd promised Anna he'd protect her from León de Bruin, and his expenses would hardly help with that.

He still had internet access, at least. He used it to google de Bruin. There were pages of photographs of him, mostly with his wife. In fact, he soon realised, it was Samantha that the photographers were really after, thanks to her beauty, her wild youth and titled father.

It was instructive to see how de Bruin behaved around her. In the earliest shots, from the time of their marriage, he'd gazed upon her with besotted pride that turned to open jealousy whenever she talked to another man. More recently, however, he'd simply looked bored.

One such photograph at a society bash showed her with England's latest rugby sensation, her eyes sparkling with laughter and her hand upon his wrist, while de Bruin hid his sneer behind a champagne flute. And Elias could see exactly why he'd given Anna the horror movie shivers.

She wouldn't call him, though, whatever trouble she was in. She'd think she could handle it herself until it was too late. Even then, she'd go to Merchant first. This shouldn't have got beneath his skin, and yet it did. He scrolled through more pictures of the de Bruins. At the races. On the red carpet. But he kept returning to that one with the rugby player at the society bash. It piqued him enough that he traced it back to its publication, from which he learned that it had been taken at Samantha's parents' fortieth wedding anniversary, just five weeks ago.

Wharton's PA called. He let her go to voicemail. Wharton wanted him upstairs now. Similar summons arrived moments later by text and email. But he knew he'd only say something stupid and make matters worse, so he grabbed his jacket and headed out instead. Now what? He was determined to do what he could to protect Anna. But how? He could go see de Bruin himself, to let him know she was under his protection. But the man had had countless brushes with the law over the years, and still his tenants kept getting attacked and beaten.

He needed something more.

The tracker he'd used to catch his wife with Merchant was back at his bedsit. He went to fetch it now. It needed a new coin battery but then it worked fine. Planting it on de Bruin or in his house would be breaching all kinds of protocols, of course, and would be the end of his career if he were caught, but his prospects were rock bottom anyway, and he found he cared more about keeping Anna safe. If he could spook the man into a mistake, then listen in, it would be worth it.

De Bruin lived in a large, walled estate some twenty minutes south of Lincoln. Its heavy steel gate was topped by spikes, a pair of CCTV cameras and an intercom placed so awkwardly that Elias had to get out to reach its buzzer. From what he'd heard about the man, he'd very likely designed it that way, to put visitors at a disadvantage.

A woman with an aristocratic drawl answered and asked his business. He held his warrant card up for the camera and told her he wanted to speak to Mr de Bruin. She asked him why. He told her it was private. Five seconds passed. He heard the clunk of a lock and the gate trundled open. He drove along a freshly-laid tarmac drive through old woods to a stunning Tudor mansion of exposed timbers, herringbone brickwork and twisting chimneys. A gardener was cutting elegant patterns in the front lawns with a sit on mower. Another was pruning roses in the beds. And a man up a ladder was cleaning out gutters.

The front door opened before Elias even rang the bell. Lady Samantha de Bruin, every bit as lovely in the flesh as in her photographs, if not so obviously glamorous. Her hair was up in an imperfect bun, so that wisps of it fell forward over her cheek. She had a tiny diamond stud in her left nostril, a pair of plain gold hoop earrings, and her only makeup was some pale pink lipstick and a little eyeliner. Her tattered peach sweater was several sizes too large for her, so that it hung like a miniskirt around her thighs, and she'd pushed its sleeves up over her elbows as if about to do the washing up, though her various rings, bracelets and Cartier watch suggested otherwise. She had her daughter Melanie with her too, dressed as a fairy princess and with a silver wand in her hand that she tapped rather gingerly against Elias's knee before stepping back with an apprehensive look, as if expecting him to turn into a toad. 'Good morning, ma'am,' he said. 'I was hoping to see your husband.'

'He left after breakfast,' she said.

Elias nodded. She could easily have told him that over the intercom, meaning she was curious about the purpose of his visit. Perhaps that explained why she'd brought her daughter with her, so that he wouldn't say anything too shocking. Or perhaps she merely knew – better than he had – not to leave a young child alone and unsupervised. 'Do you know where he went?' he asked.

'One of his properties, I'd imagine.' She rested her left hand on her daughter's crown and stroked her with her thumb, to reassure her that all was well. 'He likes to give his tenants the personal touch.'

'Yes,' said Elias. 'So I've heard. Did he say when he'd be back?'

'No.'

'Do you have a number for him?'

'I'm his wife. Of course I have a number for him.'

'But you're not going to give it to me.'

'I can see why they made you detective, Detective. But if you'd care to leave me yours, and tell me what it's about…'

He took a card from his wallet, handed it to her. 'Perhaps you've been following events at Warne Farm,' he said.

Her thumb froze on her daughter's hair, drawing his attention back to her hand. With a jolt, he finally realised why that photograph from her parents' anniversary bash had put its hook in him.

'Warne Farm?' she said. 'What on earth could my husband have to do with that?'

He gave her a level look. No one could be married to de Bruin for as long as she had without getting to know the kind of man he was – however beautiful and blue-blooded they might be. 'That's what I'm hoping to establish, ma'am. Tell me, though. Did he take his black SUV this morning? The one with the tinted windows?'

Samantha de Bruin gazed coolly at him. 'I think that's enough, Detective,' she said. 'Have a wonderful morning.'

'You too,' he said. He winked at her daughter then returned to his car, forcing himself not to hurry, despite his eagerness for another look at that photograph. Despite, too, his growing anxiety that the real reason de Bruin had left so early that morning had been to get to the pound before Anna could collect her van.

FIFTY-FIVE

It was instantly apparent to de Bruin, from the manner in which Anna Warne sped away, spewing black smoke from her exhaust, that she'd at the very least spotted their Tesla in her rear-view, and wanted to see if they'd give chase.

'Hold back,' he told Andrei.

'I know,' Andrei replied.

'I'm just saying.'

'Do I tell you how to manage your apartments?'

De Bruin looked at him in surprise. The man wasn't given to backchat, or indeed to any chat at all. But he let it go, just as Andrei let Anna Warne go, letting her pull well out of sight before picking up pace again. They had no need to tail her closely, after all, for they still had the tracker Andrei had planted on her van in the small hours, which showed her progress on their dashboard monitor.

They were approaching Newark when Samantha rang, sounding shaken. Elias had just been by, asking questions about Warne Farm. 'Warne Farm?' he said, feigning bewilderment. 'What the hell was he asking about that for?'

'Why don't you tell me?'

'It's nothing to do with me, my dear, I swear it on my life. The man is just stirring trouble, that's all.'

'Are you sure?'

'Of course I'm sure. Perhaps a word with your father? Have him ask his friend the Chief Constable why he's allowing his detectives to pester his daughter.'

'He knows about us and Warne Farm?' asked Andrei, when he'd ended the call. 'How?'

'I don't know.'

'You think the girl made us?'

'No. I'd have heard from my source.'

'Sure. If it was in their interest.'

De Bruin didn't reply, but it was something to consider. His source had betrayed his badge without a qualm. He'd betray de Bruin just as swiftly. And while prison in itself didn't exactly frighten him, he found himself offended by the prospect of being deprived of everything he'd worked so hard to achieve. Several years ago, he'd therefore spent a small fortune on a second identity as an expatriate Canadian businessman called Patrick Browne, in whose name he'd bought a charming villa overlooking Saint Lucia's Donnery Bay, and had lodged sufficient funds in Cypriot, Panamanian and British Virgin Islands accounts to live handsomely for life. But that was a last resort. Lincolnshire was home. His empire was here. His power and status. His wife and beloved daughter.

He checked the dashboard monitor again. Anna Warne crossed the River Trent on the Great North Road then headed past Newark Castle into the town centre, where her signal abruptly vanished. The explanation for this became clear when they reached the spot themselves, for it proved to be the entrance ramp to a supermarket's underground car park, up which Anna herself now came striding even as they drove by, though fortunately she was too busy pulling up her hood against the drizzle to spot them. And she had no bag upon her shoulder, he noted, perhaps because his biker friends had broken its buckle in last night's failed snatch.

He watched over his shoulder as she headed off towards the castle. They found a place to turn then headed down the ramp into the car park. Two workmen were digging up a section of floor with a jackhammer, making a terrible din and filling the air with dust. They drove a circuit of the place before spotting Anna's van in a far corner, perhaps chosen out of guilt for using the supermarket's car park without intending to shop there.

De Bruin made to get out but Andrei grabbed his wrist. 'No,' he said, pointing up at a CCTV camera.

'I need that bag,' de Bruin told him irritably.

'Yes. But not like this.'

They headed back out, found a place to park on a side street further on. They pulled on waterproofs, baseball caps, scarves and gloves then made their way back on foot. The jackhammer was still thundering away, providing them with cover. De Bruin stood guard while Andrei slipped down the gap between van and wall. Locks were one of his skills. This one took him no time at all. Anna's bag was on the passenger seat. He passed it back to de Bruin. Its broken buckle was crudely mended with black tape, but all it contained was a slimline laptop. Either she'd taken her uncle's wallet with her, or it was somewhere else inside the van.

They climbed in through its passenger door, clambering between the seats to get into the back, packed not just with farm equipment, but with an overnight case and a box of books too. Then they set about their search without a word. No word was needed, after all, for Andrei was the one person in the world who knew what they were after.

And, more to the point, why.

FIFTY-SIX

Newark Castle was less a castle these days than a monumental wall that ran along the ridge between the River Trent and the small but pretty public gardens on its other side, whose lush lawns, flowerbeds and bandstand were screened off from the main road by a thick line of trees. Anna had only visited it once before, when she and Uncle Dun had brought a picnic here on a bright summer's day before harvest had kicked off in earnest. But all she could remember was drinking too much white wine and falling asleep on a grassy bank.

The weather today could hardly have been more different, what with the cold and the drizzle, yet the place was still buzzing. A coachload or two of schoolchildren in weatherproofs were shrieking in competitive delight as they hunted for clues in some kind of Civil War treasure hunt. Anna weaved between them in search of Oliver and his crew. The path down to the river had been roped off for filming. That had to be it. She turned off her mobile in case they were already at it, then slipped beneath the rope and peeked around the wall.

It was indeed them. Even better, they were clearly on a break. Two young men she took to be Oliver's cameraman and sound engineer were standing beneath a golf umbrella by the river wall, discussing how best to bring into shot a colourful canal boat moored against the far bank, while Oliver was taking shelter beneath a blue canvas canopy while chatting away with a stout, grey-haired woman in a green macintosh, a flat tweed cap and a long rainbow scarf.

He saw Anna and beckoned her over. 'Bloody rain,' he said cheerfully, when she joined them. 'The forecast keeps telling it to stop. But it will not listen.' He introduced her to his companion, Newark Castle's custodian and historian Philippa Underhill. 'We were just talking Brother Simon,' he said, with a twinkle in his eye. 'You'll never guess who they say he was round here.'

'How do you mean?'

'They say he was Friar Tuck,' said Oliver. 'And that the reason he poisoned King John was in revenge for his having murdered Maid Marian.'

'It's only a piece of colour for our tour parties,' said Philippa, a touch embarrassed. 'They do so love their Robin Hood. But it's nonsense, I'm afraid. Mendicant orders like the friars didn't even exist yet in King John's time. And Maid Marian was a much later addition to the canon. So even if there were any truth to the larger Robin Hood legend, which frankly I doubt—'

'Don't say such things!' protested Oliver. 'Certainly not on camera.' He turned to Anna for support. 'Weren't you telling me there really was an outlaw Robin Hood?'

'I said there may have been,' said Anna. 'It still wouldn't make the stories true. Many are classic folklore, dating from well before his time. And the genuine exploits among them were mostly carried out by people like Roger Godberd and Willikin of the—' She broke off as half a dozen or so schoolchildren came racing around the side of the castle, screeching in excitement as they searched for planted clues, closely followed by a mortified young teacher apologising profusely as she brought them to heel and then shepherded them away.

'You were saying?' prompted Oliver.

Anna shook her head, feeling a little dazed. The world had just shifted on her, like an optical illusion that switched suddenly from one image to another, and then you couldn't understand how you hadn't seen it before. 'We've been thinking about it all wrong,' she muttered, to herself as much as Oliver.

'Thinking about what all wrong?'

'Nothing,' said Anna, for it was too huge just to blurt out. Too huge and too dismaying. 'I need to check something in the van, that's all. Give me ten minutes. I'll be straight back.' She touched his elbow in apology then set off before he could ask the question she could see already on his lips, hurrying back up the path to the road then along the pavement to the supermarket, her distraction such that she bumped first into a woman pushing a blue pram, then an elderly couple hunched beneath an old black umbrella being tugged this way and that by gusts of wind.

She told herself to focus, but it was hard. Her mind was in turmoil. King John's failing war against the French, the loss of his baggage train, Brother Simon and his arsenic, Robin Hood and his Merry men, the regency of William Marshal and the silver pennies beneath her uncle's body – all those distinct pieces now fitting together to form a completely different picture – and fitting so sweetly, too, that it surely had to be the truth. Only one question remained. The question of *where*. Yet Anna suspected she knew that too, or at least where the answer lay: in those photos on her uncle's drone, and in the papers she'd taken from his desk, boxed up in the back of the van.

The workmen were still at it when she arrived back in the car park, their jackhammer sending shivers through her feet and filling the air with galaxies of dust that got into her eyes and mouth, so that she put up her hand to clear her throat into it. She threw an irritable glance over her shoulder as she unlocked the van's rear doors and pulled them open, only to freeze at what she saw. For two men were on their knees inside, their faces hidden by their caps and scarves, yet instantly recognisable all the same.

She turned to run but the weightlifter was too fast. He grabbed her wrist then pulled her violently towards him. She banged her knee painfully against the back bumper as he dragged her inside. Then he threw her to the van floor and clamped a hand over her mouth before anyone could hear her scream.

FIFTY-SEVEN

Priya Kapur had lived a quiet life, never once knowingly breaking the law, or even coming close. She was the last kind of person to need a solicitor, let alone a criminal one. But she needed one this morning. For the first time since joining the King John Hotel, therefore, and despite the indignant protests of Penny Scott, she took one of the many days holiday she had owing, then packed her best kurta and a pashmina into a small backpack before cycling the three miles into Long Sutton on a boneshaker borrowed from the hotel stock.

She padlocked the bike to a stand in the pub car park then caught the Number 50 bus into Wisbech, where she changed into her kurta and pashmina in the shopping arcade toilets before making her way to the offices of the town's largest solicitor, whose name and address she'd found online earlier that morning.

It took ten minutes of pacing up and down outside before duty finally overpowered shame. She went inside. An elderly man was shouting at the receptionist about a decision the local council had made against him, while the poor young woman tried her best to explain that it had nothing to do either with her or even with the firm. Priya waited until he'd stormed off, then went up to the desk where she expressed solidarity with a sympathetic smile. Then, in a soft voice, fearful of being overheard, she gave a hint of her situation.

The solicitor's office had been buzzing all morning with the latest news out of Warne Farm. The moment the receptionist realised that it was this that had brought Priya there, she called the firm's senior criminal law partner to let him know. He appeared a minute or so later, a tall, thin, querulous-looking man called Basil Young who led Priya back to his office then invited her to tell him all. But she only managed to blush and stammer and twist her hands.

A minute passed. He rolled his eyes and checked his watch. She'd have fled right then had it not been for the large framed photograph on his desk of his wife and four children hugging a golden Labrador, which made her think there must be kindness in there somewhere. Yet still the words wouldn't come. She sat in anguish for another half minute or so before finally giving up, getting back to her feet and apologising for wasting his time.

Basil Young had been practising criminal law for nearly forty years. In that time, he'd come across every imaginable kind of human frailty. His eyes narrowed shrewdly. His expression softened. 'Don't leave,' he said gently. 'Not just yet. There's someone I'd very much like you to meet.'

FIFTY-EIGHT

The fight was lost before Anna even realised she was in it, Andrei grabbing her by her hair to slam her head against the van's metal floor, stunning her for long enough for de Bruin to close the van's rear doors and then take over, pinning her shoulders to the floor with his knees and gagging her with his hand. Andrei meanwhile wrested the van's keys from her weakened grip then clambered over the seats into the front. He reversed out of their bay and headed for the exit, turning right onto the main road and accelerating away. 'Where now?' he asked, over his shoulder.

'Just drive,' said de Bruin. His scarf had fallen away during the struggle, revealing his face flushed with a strange excitement. He pressed his hand unnecessarily hard down upon her mouth, his teeth clamped together from the effort, as much to hurt her as to keep her quiet. 'Where is it?' he demanded.

Anna shook her head, bewildered. He ran his free hand all over her in a crude mockery of a pat-down, squeezing her breasts and feeling between her legs before trying the various pockets on her winter jacket. He ignored her house keys but took out her phone, powering it down before tossing it to Andrei when he stopped at a set of lights, for him to throw out the window. Then he continued his search of her pockets until finally he found her uncle's wallet with its contents still clipped together in their evidence bags. His eyes lit up.

He separated one of these out from the rest then lifted it to his mouth to tear it free with his teeth. The plastic ripped, however, and the gold wedding ring inside fell to the floor and rolled away.

The look on his face told Anna the truth. Not her uncle's after all, but de Bruin's own. Presumably, to justify all this craziness, with his and his wife's initials inscribed around the inside, along with the date of their wedding and perhaps even traces of blood and DNA from the bodies between the fields. Uncle Dun must have found it and kept it as a hold. No wonder de Bruin had stalked her outside the pound last night. No wonder his biker friends had come for her bag.

All this passed through Anna's head in a blink even as de Bruin lunged for it. His eagerness was his undoing. His knee slipped from her shoulder, tipping him off balance and releasing Anna's arm for a moment, enabling her to grab the ring herself before he could recover. Yet what to do with it? There was nowhere to hide it or throw it that he wouldn't retrieve it instantly. So she popped it in her mouth instead, and swallowed.

De Bruin's snarl turned terrifying, his skin flushing bright red and his lips drawn all the way back over his teeth. He meant to kill her, she could read it on his face. Perhaps he might have done so, too, had he not needed his ring back first – for how would he explain it being found in her stomach? He pinched her nostrils together, punched her in the stomach to make her gasp for air, then tried to thrust two of his gloved forefingers down her throat to make her vomit. She bit down hard instead. He yelped and snatched back his hand, then clutched it around her throat and began to squeeze, only to be struck suddenly by an idea so delightful that his fury left him in an instant, leaving him looking almost gleeful instead. 'Call Victor,' he shouted out to Andrei.

'And tell him what?' grunted Andrei.

'To get the Twin Otter ready. We're going on a flight.'

FIFTY-NINE

After leaving the de Bruin's estate, Elias drove around for a minute or so until he found a suitable farm track to pull in to. He switched off his engine then took another look at the gallery of photographs he'd checked out earlier. His memory had served him well. León de Bruin was wearing a gold wedding ring in all but one of them – the one taken at his in-law's anniversary bash, where he'd had instead a band of paler skin where the ring should have been. Because of course you'd put on rubber gloves to move dead bodies and scrub the walls. And how easy to pull your ring off when you removed them again, and have it drop unnoticed to the floor.

He couldn't risk the Nettleham switchboard, so he called Yvette Coombs on her mobile instead. 'Where the hell are you?' she whispered. 'Wharton's going crazy. He wants your blood.'

'Don't worry about it,' he told her. 'Can you check something for me?'

'Of course. What?'

'Dunstan Warne's wedding ring. Is there any kind of inscription on it?'

'I don't have it any more,' she told him, puzzled. 'I gave it back to Anna Warne last night. I thought that's what you wanted.'

'Hell,' muttered Elias. 'Yes. It was. Sorry.' He pinched the bridge of his nose. 'Did you tell anyone?'

'No. Why would I?' But then she added: 'It was on the

receipt, though, which I posted to the case file.'

'What time was that? Can you remember?'

'Not exactly, no. But it was straight after I took her to see Jay. Four, four-thirty, something like that. Why? What's going on? You want me to ask her for it back?'

'No. It's fine. I'll do it.' He ended the call then sat there for a while, thinking it through. A lost wedding ring would explain why de Bruin and Andrei had gone to the farm the other night, and why they'd lurked outside the pound yesterday evening, and the bikers' failed bag-snatch too. And de Bruin was unlikely to stop there. He'd want that ring back before anyone realised its significance. Which meant Anna was in serious danger still. He called to warn her, but her phone was off. He left a message then tried Merchant instead. His phone was off too. He told himself not to worry. They were filming this morning, so of course their phones would be off. And at Newark Castle, too, which was only twenty minutes away, so that he could easily go there now himself to take back the ring.

He drove a little faster than was prudent on the narrow, twisty lanes. He reached the A17. Traffic was heavy in both directions, yet he took every opportunity to overtake, for all the good it did. He was so focused on the road ahead that it was only after passing a white van headed in the other direction that he became properly conscious of it. Its front bumper had been held on with black tape, he was sure of it. And its driver had had a scarf over his chin and a baseball cap tugged down over his eyes.

He glanced over his shoulder. The van was already well down the road. But it certainly looked similar to Dunstan Warne's, and it had the same empty roof rack too. He dithered a moment but felt too uneasy just to let it go. He braked to turn. His indecision had cost him, however, as another flurry of oncoming traffic arrived to baulk him, while his sudden slowing caused everyone behind him to come to a screeching sharp halt, letting him know their displeasure with their horns.

He held his warrant card out the window in a forlorn attempt to appease them, then swung around into the next gap to race back the way he'd come, catching occasional glimpses of the white van ahead, thanks to the openness of the terrain. The van turned right down a side road. He saw it flickering through gaps in a hedgerow. Then he approached the turn himself, and saw its signpost, and realised with a sickening lurch where it was most likely headed, and maybe even why. So he called Yvette Coombs once more and told her he needed backup at Fenton Airfield now.

SIXTY

Basil Young led Priya Kapur along a passage with a flickering ceiling light and a worn beige carpet. 'I very much want you to meet my colleague Ursula Yates,' he told her, turning around every pace or two for her to see his face, as though she were hard of hearing. 'She works mostly in family and contract law these days, but she also has an extraordinary gift for crime.' He gave a dry chuckle to make sure she realised that this was just his little joke, then stopped outside an unmarked door and listened for a moment. There was only silence from within, so he knocked gently and then opened it, revealing a formidable grey-haired woman sitting on the other side of a long conference table of polished oak, a pair of fat law books open while she made notes with a red pen on a brief of some kind. She was wearing large, thick tortoiseshell glasses that both magnified and blurred her dark brown eyes. 'Basil?' she said, as though she were his disapproving aunt, and had caught him in some mischief.

Young touched Priya on her elbow before she could flee. 'Ursula,' he said, 'I'd like you to meet Ms Priya Kapur. Ms Kapur works at the King John Hotel. That's right, isn't it, Priya?' he asked, though only, she suspected, to force her to find her tongue.

'Yes,' said Priya. Then, when she saw Ursula Yates's continued puzzlement, she added: 'It's the property next door to Warne Farm.'

'Ah,' said Yates, half rising to her feet. 'I see.'

'Ms Kapur has some important information to share about the dreadful recent events there,' said Young. 'However, thanks to the... delicate and personal nature of this information, I believe she'll find it easier to share it with another woman rather than with a man.' He turned back to Priya. 'Isn't that so, Priya?'

'Yes,' said Priya gratefully.

He nodded, pleased with himself. Then he touched her elbow one final time in encouragement or support before leaving again, closing the door firmly behind him.

Ursula clearly realised her skittishness, for she hurried around the table to take Priya by her arm and lead her to the pair of green velvet armchairs in the corner. 'Sit with me a moment,' she said. 'Take your time. Tell me what you know.'

It still didn't come easily. But Priya had no choice now. Hesitantly, with her eyes fixed upon the floor and her cheeks flushing almost purple, with numerous backtracks, pauses and qualifications, she explained herself, her situation and what she knew. Ursula listened patiently until she was done, then commended her for coming forward. She asked a few follow-up questions to clarify one or two small points, then buzzed her assistant to have her reschedule her appointments for the next three hours. That done, she led Priya out the back way to a private car park where she kept a silver Audi A3, in which she drove them the short distance to Wisbech Police Station. Then, holding Priya lightly by the arm once more, she made her way up to the desk and demanded in her most imperious voice to speak to WPC Maria Quinn.

SIXTY-ONE

The road to Fenton Airfield was a narrow and winding single track lane with passing places every hundred yards or so, whose pitted surface was made even harder to navigate by the shadows cast upon it by the broken hedgerow it was flanked by. Elias raced along it far faster than was prudent, his foot hovering over the brake. Just as well, for he came around one bend to find a tractor nosing out of a field ahead. He tooted a plea for it to let him by, but it was already too late and he had to slam his brakes on hard.

The tractor came lumbering out, hauling an open container of sweet potatoes clumped with mud that jumped like Mexican beans at every pothole. There was no chance to overtake, yet Elias kept pulling out anyway, if only to put pressure on the driver. He flashed his lights and held his warrant card out the window, and finally it pulled into the side with just enough room for him to squeeze by, the hedgerow raking down his side. He waved thanks and sped on.

He hadn't seen the white van for at least three minutes, but thankfully Fenton Airfield now appeared to his right, the other side of a sagging wire fence. It looked huge. No wonder de Bruin had coveted it. A pair of light aircraft were parked on the grass in front of a line of three corrugated iron hangars, beyond which the old grey concrete runway lay at an angle, ending near a line of trees that served as a screen between it and the neighbouring property. No sign of the van, though.

He was beginning to think he'd got it wrong when suddenly it came racing around the front of the hangars, then vanished into the middle one. And it was Warne's, no question. He could see the scratch down its side.

Elias sped on to a junction at the end of the lane. He turned sharp right and then right again, passing between a pair of crooked wooden gateposts into the airfield itself, then along an old track in terrible disrepair. A white Twin Otter with pale blue trim and an open hatch in its side came taxiing into view, trundling to the short end of the runway before turning in preparation for take-off. He'd never reach it in time if he stuck to the track and had to circle all the way around the hangars, so he muttered a prayer for his Leaf and cut across the grass instead.

The ground was horrendously uneven. He bounded all over the place, spitting stones up against his undercarriage. But he made it to the strip even as the Twin Otter began its take-off run, screeching to a halt in front of it, blocking its path. He jumped out and held his warrant card up for the pilot to see, waved at him to stop. The engines lost their thunder. The plane drifted to a halt. He thought, for a moment, that it was over. Then de Bruin appeared over the pilot's shoulder and shouted in his ear. The pilot shook his head. De Bruin tried to drag him from his seat. The pilot shook him off. De Bruin vanished then returned with a small red fire extinguisher that he crashed down on the back of the pilot's head before pulling him from his seat and taking his place.

The propellers roared once more. The Twin Otter swung out onto the grass. Elias had to duck beneath its wing as it circled around his Leaf before regaining the strip on its far side. He ran after it, not altogether believing his eyes. Surely even de Bruin would have to accept reality. But then he caught a glimpse through its open hatch of Anna lying on the cabin floor with tape over her mouth while Andrei bound her arms and legs to a chunk of broken masonry. And suddenly their recklessness made sense.

He sprinted after them, stumbling in his haste before flinging himself at the steel platform step behind and beneath the starboard wing, grabbing it with both hands and being dragged along for a terrifying second or two before he successfully hauled himself up onto it. Again he assumed that that would be that, that the plane would stop. Again he was wrong. The Twin Otter sped ever faster down the strip, juddering and bouncing so violently that it was all Elias could do to cling on.

He grabbed the wing strut for support then rose awkwardly to his feet, even as Andrei finished binding Anna to the masonry and came to stand in the hatchway, blocking Elias from the cabin and holding a stun gun up in warning, which seemed somewhat redundant considering the size of the man. An Olympic weightlifter, Anna had called him, and it described him perfectly, with his massive limbs and torso, his tree-trunk neck and the look of stolid concentration on his face.

The plane was pelting along now, the air buffeting Elias and flapping his jacket into chaotic wings. The detour around his car meant they were close to the end of the runway before reaching take-off velocity. He feared for a moment they wouldn't make it over the trees, but they lifted so sharply that he had to adjust his feet to keep his balance. He had a crazy urge to leap before it was too late, but then the ground fell away beneath them dizzyingly fast.

They reached a first few wisps of broken cloud, cold and wet on his fingers, reducing the fields and villages below to occasional glimpses. They wouldn't be turning back now. De Bruin was committed to this madness. Andrei was still blocking the hatchway. Just looking at him left Elias feeling weak and helpless, as had happened once or twice in the ring when he'd caught his opponent with his best shots without hurting them at all. No way could he match him, let alone defeat him. Indeed, all the man had to do was come down onto the platform step with his stun gun and it would soon be over. Yet he stayed inside the cabin instead, throwing baffled glances down at the ground beneath, until Elias finally realised that the man was simply scared of heights.

An impasse followed. They each considered their next move. It was Andrei who decided first. He switched his stun gun to the hand already anchoring him to the hatchway frame, then crouched and reached behind him for Anna, all without taking his eyes off Elias. He dragged her by her ankle towards him, the masonry scraping over the cabin floor. He positioned her so that she was balanced on the hatchway rim, then put his foot upon her back, ready to push her forwards out of the cabin to tumble down onto the platform step and fall from there to her certain death. Then he grinned at Elias, challenging him to act.

Elias felt sick. He didn't stand a chance against the man. But Anna was gazing pleadingly at him and so he couldn't do nothing either. It wasn't in his nature. He adjusted his grip on the wing strut then edged closer to Andrei. He set his feet and flicked out a jab at his face. Andrei swayed back out of range then reached his chin tauntingly forward to offer Elias another shot. He threw a second jab. Andrei snatched at his wrist, but Elias was too quick.

Andrei rocked Anna a little closed to the edge with his foot. She yelled into the tape over her mouth, yet it wasn't the yell of terror Elias would have expected, but rather one of determination and exhortation. At the same time, she was working her hands back and forth in a frantic effort to free them. She might even manage it, too, for in his hurry Andrei had done a shoddy job, and she almost had one hand free already. Elias had no idea what she meant to do with it, but there was such purpose on her face that it gave him heart. His job was to buy her time. He flicked out another jab, catching Andrei on his cheek. The man only grinned, goading him into trying again. Elias's fingers were growing icy from the altitude, but he reset his grip once more anyway then edged closer and threw yet another punch.

But this time Andrei was too quick for him, and he got

caught.

SIXTY-TWO

It was quite true what Maria Quinn had told Elias. She did hate a loose end. When her lunch hour arrived, therefore, she didn't take her usual walk around the park to get some exercise and some sunlight, but rather bought herself a chicken salad sandwich from across the road to eat at her desk while browsing Google Earth for a stretch of cobbled lane beside a pair of scarlet oaks, by far the most distinctive landmark in Dunstan Warne's drone photos.

She'd only been at it a few minutes when Tom rang from the front desk. 'Ursula Yates for you,' he said in a puzzled low voice.

'Yates?' said Quinn, equally nonplussed. The woman was a civil rather than a criminal lawyer, and senior enough not to have to deal with humble WPCs.

'She has a lady with her,' added Tom. 'An Indian lady. From the King John Hotel.'

'Ah,' said Quinn. 'Okay. I'll be straight out.'

She found Priya Kapur and Ursula Yates by the cork board, pretending interest in the notices. Priya looked very different today, having exchanged her hotel jacket and skirt for an ivory kurta and an embroidered peach pashmina with which she'd covered her hair and head, yet which still couldn't quite hide the torment in her expression, as though she'd rather be anywhere else on earth. Quinn put on her friendliest smile as she went to greet them both and ask what this was about.

'Not here,' murmured Priya, so softly that Quinn almost had to lip-read. 'Is there not somewhere more private?'

'Of course,' said Quinn. The interview rooms were all free, yet she took the end one anyway, to make quite sure they wouldn't be overheard. The room was small and bare, designed for interrogations, so she rearranged the chairs in a circle to make it less confrontational. 'So Priya?' she asked, with another encouraging smile. 'How can I help you?'

Priya looked miserably down at the floor. Some kind of confession was coming, Quinn was sure of it. Yet her expression and the way she was twisting her hands spoke of shame rather than guilt. And, just like that, Quinn realised why Priya had wanted a woman solicitor to accompany her here, rather than one of the firm's male criminal lawyers; and also why she'd asked to speak to Quinn specifically, rather than any of the more senior officers on the Warne Farm investigation. And with a thrill of what she recognised to be utterly inappropriate excitement, she guessed exactly what Priya was about to tell her, and how it was going to throw Dunstan Warne's murder investigation back into complete chaos.

SIXTY-THREE

Andrei's grip was crushing, as though someone had parked a truck upon Elias's wrist. He cried out and let go of the wing strut as Andrei jerked him towards the open hatchway and within range of his stun gun. He brought it down to bear and was about to jolt him with it when he paused and looked irritably down at Anna, who'd finally managed to free her right hand. She grabbed her keyring from her pocket and brought its fob to her mouth, clamping it between her teeth to pull the rubber cap off a box-cutter blade that she then thrust straight upwards into the fork between Andrei's legs. He gave a grunt of shock and pain. She stabbed again, and this time dragged the blade down his inner thigh in search of an artery. Blood spurted, staining his trousers dark. He swatted her hand away. The keyring went flying out the hatchway. Then he reached his stun gun down for her face, its nodes spitting blue.

It was Elias's chance. He threw his shoulder at Andrei's arm. It was like trying to tackle a lamppost, yet he managed to deflect the gun so that it brushed Andrei's own calf for a moment, giving him enough of a jolt that he let go of Elias altogether and dropped the stun gun to the cabin floor. He recovered almost immediately, however. He swung his arm backhanded across Elias's face, catching him on his cheek with the force of a sailboat boom, sending him staggering back along the platform, from which he'd have fallen for sure had he not thrown out a hand to catch Andrei by his sleeve and so save himself.

Andrei was still off balance from the stun gun. The sudden tug now dragged him from the cabin too. Worse, he misjudged where to place his foot on the platform step, so that his ankle turned beneath him. He went lurching sideways, flapping his arms to save himself. But it was no good, he reached and then passed his tipping point, only to twist around in the air with surprising agility and catch Elias by the knee as he went, his hand sliding down his calf to his ankle, clutching it so tightly that he pulled him off the platform step with him, forcing Elias to grab it with both hands before the pair of them fell to their deaths, leaving them swinging from it like some bizarre trapeze act, while also giving the Twin Otter such a jolt that it banked sharply to its right, forcing de Bruin to take corrective action.

The platform step was cold and slick with cloud, and Andrei was so heavy that it was all Elias could do to cling on. Indeed, his grip on it kept slipping, little by little, even as he tried to kick Andrei off. But Andrei grabbed his other leg too, then began climbing him like a pole.

The Twin Otter had stabilised enough for de Bruin to leave the cockpit and come back into the cabin. He saw the stun gun lying on the floor and made straight for it. But Anna finally freed her legs from the gorilla tape and she dived to reach it first. De Bruin tried to wrest it from her. She gave him a squirt with it instead. He grunted and fell hard, hitting his mouth against the edge of the bench as he went. She pressed the gun to his throat for several seconds as he lay there, putting him completely out of the fight before hurrying to the hatchway. Then, without a moment's hesitation, she stepped out onto the platform.

Andrei had by now clambered all the way up onto Elias's back. His left arm was around his chest and his right hand was upon his shoulder. Anna knelt down on the step. She reached the stun gun for his face. He tried to draw away but she stretched out after him and touched it against his cheek. It was only for a moment, but the shock still robbed his arms of their Samson strength. With a dull grunt of surprise, he let go of Elias and began to fall in slow balletic rolls until suddenly he recovered, howling and clawing at the air as if he could still somehow save himself. But then he was swallowed by a cloud and was gone.

Elias was utterly spent. It was all he could do to cling on. Anna grabbed him by his arm and then his belt to help haul him back to safety. He lay on the step for a few moments, breathing hard as he regathered his strength. But then the Twin Otter began to bank once more under their combined weight. They scrambled back into the cabin, on whose floor de Bruin was still lying, unconscious from the stun gun. 'Can you fly?' asked Elias.

'No,' said Anna. 'Can you?'

'Sure,' he said. He had to lean against the growing camber as they made their way to the cockpit, stepping over de Bruin's pilot, the back of his head sticky with blood from an ugly-looking gash. He slipped into the pilot's seat while Anna sat copilot. He stared in dismay at the Twin Otter's complex array. His experience of flying was a single lesson on an adventure weekend the best part of ten years ago, in a much smaller aircraft that hadn't been about to tip into a dive. But he had to try something. He took the stick in both hands and began to draw it towards him when a man spoke softly from behind.

'No,' he murmured.

Elias looked around. De Bruin's pilot was still lying on the cabin floor but looking at him with a pleading face. He tried to push himself up onto an elbow and say something else, but he couldn't manage it. The plane tipped further, filling Elias with a dizzy, heady sensation, with the certainty that they were about to stall. Maybe he could have worked out how to save them in time, but time was exactly what they didn't have. He came to a decision. He hurried back to take the pilot beneath his arms and lift him bodily into his seat. But he just sat there with blood leaking down his forehead into his glazed eyes. 'Talk to me,' said Elias desperately. But the man just shook his head.

The Twin Otter finally stalled. There was a moment of floating lightness and then they began to dive and spin at the same time, slowly at first, yet still enough to send Elias tumbling onto Anna in the copilot's seat. He cried out in fear and threw his arms around her, he couldn't help himself. She hugged him back every bit as fiercely, muttering prayers into his ear as they hurtled out of control, glimpses between the clouds of the sea beneath, its rippled surface drawing ever nearer as rays of thin afternoon sunlight glinted off the huge white blades of a wind turbine away to their left.

The way they rolled made Elias nauseous. He couldn't have taken the controls even had he wanted. But it seemed to have the opposite effect on the pilot, slapping him from his stupor at last. He took hold of the stick. The Twin Otter spun even harder for a moment but then somehow straightened out. They were still in their dive, however. It was pull up now or hit the sea and die. Yet the pilot pushed the stick forward instead, steepening their angle of descent, plunging them at the sea below, which now completely filled their view. This couldn't be right, it couldn't be. The man had chosen death over disgrace and prison. And it was too late to do anything about it.

Elias cried out again. He clutched Anna to him and buried his face in her neck. But now the pilot finally pulled the stick towards him, and the Twin Otter instantly responded, so that Elias belatedly realised he'd simply been getting traction back into the wings, like steering into a skid on an icy road. And finally their nose began to lift and they pulled up out of their dive to skim bare metres above the water, passing so close to a gorgeous blue-and-gold pleasure yacht that he could see the breeze rippling in its sails and the open mouths of the crew in their orange life-jackets as they gaped at the Twin Otter, not entirely sure what it was that they'd just witnessed.

SIXTY-FOUR

De Bruin slowly recovered consciousness from his stun gunning, yet he remained in a highly disoriented state, fuzzily aware of things happening around him but unable to make sense of them. He was lying face down on the cabin floor, twitching involuntarily from time to time, his groin damp with what felt like his own urine, while blood and drool leaked from the side of his mouth.

Elias and Warne came to stand beside him. He could see their shoes and hear them talking, but it might as well have been in another language. His hands were taken and pinned behind his back. He heard the Velcro rip of gorilla tape being pulled from its roll, then his wrists were bound so tightly together with it that his fingers began to tingle. Elias heaved him up onto the bench across from the hatchway and strapped him in with a belt. The moment he was let go, however, he slumped helplessly forward, though it put such stress upon his spine that the pain finally roused him and he sat up as best he could and rested his head back against the cabin wall.

Bubbles of blood kept blowing out of his left nostril to burst in a spatter of ticklish flecks on his upper lip. He longed to wipe them away, but couldn't. His mouth was so sore that he must have hit it when he'd fallen, though he had no memory of doing so. He'd bitten his tongue too, while his gum and lower lip were puffed and aching, as when the dentist's anaesthetic is wearing off. Then there was the cold wet chafing of his trousers against his thighs, taking him back to one of the more humiliating moments of his childhood, lying curled up in a ball on the changing room floor while his classmates gathered around him to taunt him for pissing himself, which he'd only done in the first place out of terror of another of their beatings. The memory stirred in him an old hatred, an old defiance. He squared his shoulders and sat up straighter. He wasn't that pathetic, whiny creature Len Brown any more, he told himself. He was León Alessandro de Bruin, a man of stature, wealth and influence.

He turned his head left, defying the crick in his neck. Victor was at the controls, his hair badly matted with blood, but clearly recovered from his earlier blow. Anna Warne was on the bench seat behind him while Elias was sitting copilot, making calls on the cockpit radio, bragging about having de Bruin in custody and about to talk, the triumphalism in his voice only fuelling de Bruin's determination to say nothing. He looked the other way. There was no sign of Andrei. He must have fallen. At once, he started fashioning strategies to blame him for everything.

The coast came into view below, from Skegness up to Ingoldmells and the pale blur of Chapel St Leónards. He owned properties in all three. Then came Croft, site of one of his earliest solo projects, converting a pair of rundown semis into six starter apartments. All he'd ever done was provide people with places to live, yet they'd still try to make him out a monster.

Elias came back from the cockpit. He gazed down at de Bruin with his forehead creased, as though de Bruin was an oversized sofa that needed taking up a spiral staircase. He'd found a bottle of water somewhere. He uncapped it then held it for de Bruin to drink. His pride told him to refuse, but the sticky dryness of his mouth overruled it. He swilled the first mouthful around and spat it out sideways, then nodded for another, which he swallowed gratefully.

Elias plucked the silk handkerchief from de Bruin's breast

pocket. He moistened it then dabbed away the worst of the blood from de Bruin's lips and chin with surprising gentleness before stuffing it back again. He stood up, recapped the water, took out his phone to film. 'Mr de Bruin,' he said, enunciating loudly and clearly over the roar of the twin propellers, 'I am arresting you on suspicion of murder, kidnapping and attempted murder. You do not have to say anything, but it may harm your defence if you do not mention when questioned something which you later rely on in court. Anything you do say may be given in evidence. You have now been officially cautioned. Do you understand?'

'I want my lawyer,' said de Bruin – or would have, at least, had his tongue and mouth been working properly.

'You kidnapped a woman and tied her to a block of masonry to dump her into the sea,' said Elias. 'You knocked your pilot out with a fire extinguisher in full view of a police officer. Then you took off with that same police officer clinging to your wing. Cooperation is your only chance, and even that's not much.'

'Lawyer,' said de Bruin.

'You have exactly one thing of value to me. The name of the mole inside Lincolnshire police. Tell me who it is and—'

'Lawyer.'

'...undertake to testify against them, and I promise you that—'

'Lawyer.'

Elias shrugged and gave up. 'Suit yourself,' he said, putting his phone back in his pocket. 'But this lawyer of yours had better work for Merlin, Potter & Houdini, or you're done.'

SIXTY-FIVE

Anna shifted her legs aside to allow Elias past her and back into the copilot's seat. Every few moments, she'd remember that she'd just killed a man. His name had been Andrei Lubov. She'd put a stun gun to his cheek despite knowing it would send him to his death. The enormity of this act was astonishing to her, yet not so astonishing as how fine she felt about it, despite the nightmares she sensed ahead.

Her ears began to ache. They'd begun their descent into Fenton Airfield. They dropped low enough for Elias's phone to pick up a signal and ring. He snorted in amusement when he saw who it was, turned to offer it to Anna. 'It's Oliver,' he told her. 'I imagine it's you he's really after.'

'About bloody time,' cried Oliver, when she answered, but before she could say a word. 'I've been calling and calling. Have you found her yet?'

'It's not Elias,' she told him. 'It's me.'

'Thank Christ,' he said, with touching relief. 'Are you okay? Where did you get to? I've been going crazy. And why the hell are you using Elias's phone?'

'I'm fine,' Anna assured him. 'Everything's fine. I lost my own phone, is all. Elias lent me his.'

'Thank Christ,' he said again. 'I've been imagining all kinds of horrors.'

'Yes, well,' she said.

'Yes, well?'

She gave him a précis of events since leaving Newark Castle, from how she'd surprised de Bruin and Andrei in the back of her van through to their current return to Fenton Airfield. He listened in stunned silence. 'I don't believe it,' he managed at last. 'Are you okay? I mean... Jesus.'

'I'm fine,' she assured him. 'Though I could use a lift. I've lost all my keys.'

'You want me to come pick you up?'

'Could you?'

'Of course, of course. Anything. My god. Sorry, I'm still all scrambled up. Fenton Airfield you said, yes?'

'You know it?'

'I'll find it. I'll set off now. I'll be as quick as I can. Oh, and I hope it goes without saying that if you need a place to stay again tonight...'

'Thanks,' she said. 'I might, at that.'

'We'll probably be needing your van for evidence anyway,' Elias told her, when she handed him back his phone. 'As well as another statement.'

'No worries. I'm an old hand now.'

'And for god's sake don't worry about that man. You saved my life.'

'Only after you saved mine first. Leaping up onto the step like that. You must be nuts.'

'Yeah, well. I never thought they'd still take off. And then it was too late.'

'That's not what my statement will say. I'm going to get you medals.'

Fenton Airfield came into view ahead, angled slightly for the breeze. Elias's Leaf had been towed from the runway, which was lined by an astonishing number of police cars, ambulances and fire engines. There were so many, indeed, that it made her think they were in greater jeopardy than she'd realised. She looked again at their pilot Victor. For all his calmness, skill and experience, he was clearly still badly dazed from the blow he'd taken, and the gash in his scalp was bleeding so freely that he had to wipe his forehead every few seconds to keep it from his eyes.

She belted herself in. She placed her hands on her knees and pressed her feet against the floor to brace herself. They passed over the southern end of the airfield. It seemed to her that they were coming in too high. They lurched downwards and hit the strip so hard that they bounced back up again before touching down a second time. Their brakes shrieked. The cabin filled with fumes. They slowed to taxiing speed before coming to a gentle stop some thirty feet shy of the trees. And the way Victor leaned back in his seat, closed his eyes and let out his breath told her everything about how close they'd all just come.

SIXTY-SIX

There was a moment, as the Twin Otter came to a stop, when de Bruin was possessed by a wild urge to release himself somehow from his seatbelt and make a run for it. Then everything went crazy. Six police officers in body armour and glass-visored helmets came storming into the cabin with handguns drawn, yelling at everyone to stay where they were and to raise their hands above their heads – which presented quite a problem to de Bruin, what with his wrists still taped together behind his back. But thankfully they realised the plane was free of threat and everything quickly calmed.

The squad leader went to the hatch to give the all clear to someone out of view, then stepped aside to allow them aboard. Trevor Wharton. He took a moment to assess the scene. 'This man needs urgent medical help,' Elias told him, putting his hand on Victor's shoulder. 'But keep an eye on him. He's one of them.'

'Thank you,' said Wharton coolly. 'I'll be making the decisions from now on.' But then he undermined himself by nodding at his squad leader.

'He's the one you really want,' said Elias, pointing at de Bruin. 'Be careful with him, though. He's dangerous.'

Wharton smiled thinly. 'I think we can manage.'

'I'm just saying—'

'You'd be well advised not to say anything further,'

Wharton told him. 'A man just died up there, as I understand it. That means an automatic referral to the Independent Office for Police Conduct, as you must very well know. And while you were under suspension too. What the hell's got into you? Running out of HQ this morning after I asked to see you. And going to see Lady Samantha de Bruin, of all people! Don't you know who her father is? I've had the Chief Constable chewing me out all morning.' He shook his head. 'How could you be so stupid? If you've undermined our case—'

'Your case!' scoffed Elias. 'You had no case.'

'You've no idea what we have,' snapped Wharton. 'For the very good reason that we can't trust you any more.'

'Sure,' said Elias. 'I'm the problem.'

'Finally he sees it!' mocked Wharton. 'Yes, you are. I'm having you taken back to Nettleham to wait for me there, before you can make the situation even worse.' He turned to his squad leader and gestured at de Bruin. They unstrapped him and hoisted him to his feet with his wrists still bound behind his back. They helped him down from the Twin Otter and over to a waiting paddy wagon, its sliding side door already open. Half its rear was taken up by a steel-barred prisoner cage. They unlocked it and made to put him inside. The indignity was such that de Bruin fought against it, but the policemen were far too strong. They locked him in there then left. He sat on a cold steel bench consoling himself with dark thoughts of revenge. He wasn't alone long. Trevor Wharton soon stepped up inside, followed by one of his armed officers who slid the panel door closed behind him, leaving the three of them in there alone.

Wharton unlocked the cage and came inside. He sat on the bench across from de Bruin then nodded at his officer who banged the end wall as a signal to the driver to set off. They bumped across uneven ground before reaching the relative smoothness of the airstrip. Wharton leaned forward, elbows on his knees. 'So what the fuck happened up there?' he asked quietly.

'You think I'll tell you that?' retorted de Bruin, flickering a warning glance at the armed officer outside the cage.

'Don't worry about Anton,' said Wharton. 'He's one of us.'

'One of us?'

'Yes. One of us.'

'Fine,' said de Bruin, turning to offer Wharton his taped wrists. 'Then get this shit off me.'

'Forget it,' said Wharton. 'You brought that on yourself. Now answer me. What the fuck happened up there? How much did you tell Elias?'

'I told him nothing.'

'That's not what he said over the radio.'

'Then he was lying.'

Wharton shook his head. 'What the hell's got into you? Going back to the farm the other night. Abducting the Warne woman. Have you gone mad?'

'I needed my ring back.'

'Then tell me, for god's sake. I'd have found a way. It's what I do.'

'Good. Then find me a way out of this.'

'Too late,' said Wharton. 'You've gone too far. Jesus. Even if you'd managed to… I don't even want to know what you had planned for that poor woman. But taking off with a policeman on your fucking wing. How did you think that was going to work out?'

'I have resources.'

'Plastic surgery?' scoffed Wharton. 'A false passport? A new name?'

'Like I say, I have resources. Including the head of Lincolnshire's Special Operations Unit in my back pocket.'

'In your dreams. I'll do what I can, but I can't work miracles.'

'You'd better start praying, then. Unless you want the cell next door.'

'Don't be an idiot. You need me on the outside.'

'What for, if you won't help? I'll be better off making a

deal. How much do you think they'll offer me for the name of their mole? For receipts for all the payments I've made into your Cayman account over the years, the one you bought your lovely Tenerife villa with? Talk about stupidity! And then there's Colin Vaughn, serving time for your crimes. I bet that will go down well. So find a way. Undermine your investigating team. Taint the evidence. Scare off the witnesses. Pin it all on Andrei. I'll leave the how up to you. Just get it done, or I talk.'

They glared at each other across the cage until a noise like ripping paper startled them both. De Bruin looked around to see that Anton had undone his Velcro holster strap to draw his handgun. Now he fed its barrel through the bars of the cage. 'The prisoner managed to free his hands without us realising,' he said to Wharton, while aiming at de Bruin's face. 'He threw himself at you while you were conducting an interview. I had no choice but to shoot.'

Wharton gazed coolly at de Bruin, calculating whether or not they could make it work. Then he nodded. 'Do it,' he said.

SIXTY-SEVEN

Anna waited until de Bruin had been escorted off the Twin Otter, then made her own way down with Elias, only to be greeted by Hollis and Patterson, the two Serious and Organised Crime detectives from yesterday afternoon. 'We've been ordered to take you back to Nettleham,' Hollis told Elias, with an apologetic shrug.

'He saved my life,' protested Anna. 'I'd be dead if not for him.'

'It's fine,' Elias assured her. 'Everything's going to be fine.'

'I don't care. They can't treat you like—'

'It's fine,' he said again. 'I'll call you later, okay?'

'How?' she asked plaintively. 'They threw my phone out the window.'

'Then I'll call Merchant, if I must. But right now you need to get yourself looked at.' He touched his forehead. 'You've got a cut.'

She watched unhappily as he was put into the back of a squad car, bracketed by Hollis and Patterson, as though he were some kind of criminal. She wanted to do more for him, but she didn't know how, so she stood there feeling foolish instead, until an earnest young paramedic touched her arm and led her to his ambulance. He checked her for concussion then cleaned and dressed her cuts before releasing her to a constable who'd been waiting patiently to take her statement. He had a beak nose and a smudge of blue ink on his lips from sucking his ballpoint pen, and he jotted notes in a pad while also recording everything on his phone, as though he didn't altogether trust the technology. She was telling him how she'd returned to her van to find de Bruin and Andrei inside when she realised she had a job to do. Unpleasant, yes, but less so now than later. She excused herself and walked off a little way, then knelt on the grass and put fingers down her throat until she'd vomited up de Bruin's wedding ring along with her breakfast sludge. She wiped it off and offered it to the policeman who gave a dainty little grimace as he opened up an evidence bag for her to drop it into.

There was still no sign of Oliver, but then the police had sealed off the entire airfield, except to let vehicles out. No one seemed interested in her any more, so she walked back up the airstrip to the central hangar where her van was still parked, its rear doors wide open, presumably waiting for Scene of Crime. Her laptop was still in there, as were her overnight bag and box of books. Ask permission, she'd likely be refused, so she marched boldly in as if she'd been authorised, and took everything she needed before anyone thought to stop her.

Oliver was indeed at the airfield entrance, gamely trying to blag his way past the four policemen on duty there, who were having none of it. He waved wildly when he saw her. She slipped between a pair of squad cars then set down her belongings and took him in a hug that she hadn't realised she'd needed quite so badly until she was already in it, clutching him hard and burying her face into his neck. A minute passed. She felt better. 'Thanks for coming,' she said, letting go of him and taking a step back.

'Of course. What did you think?'

'Can we get out of here?'

He nodded down the lane at his BMW pulled up on a grassy verge. 'Merchant Taxis at your service,' he said. 'Where does madam fancy?'

'How about your place?' she asked.

He grinned and slung her bags over his shoulder, picked up

her box of books. 'I was hoping you'd say that.'

SIXTY-EIGHT

In the back of the paddy wagon, de Bruin stared at Anton's handgun more in disbelief than in fear or horror. Its muzzle looked impossibly big. It seemed to occupy the whole world. His wrists were still bound behind him but he'd have been frozen anyway, his limbs drained of strength. It was impossible, but he was about to die. He, León Alessandro de Bruin, was about to die. And, just like that, the protective shell of the persona he'd spent years building shattered and fell away, leaving him as little Len Brown once more, blubbing with fear and self-pity on the changing room floor.

A sudden ugly wailing noise outside, so unexpected that it made them all jump. It took de Bruin a moment to recognise it as a siren. *Two* sirens, rather, slightly out of kilter with each other. The paddy wagon braked and pulled off the road, bumping to a halt across rutted mud. Wharton looked questioningly at Anton. Anton shook his head. Wharton gestured for him to put away his gun then turned to de Bruin. 'Not a word,' he warned him. 'No one would believe it anyway, so why even try?' He left the cage and locked it behind him then slid open the panel door to find out what was going on.

A pair of squad cars had pulled up ahead and behind, their blue lights fluttering. Car doors opened and then slammed shut again. A number of police officers in plain clothes and uniform appeared, Elias among them.

'What the hell's going on?' demanded Wharton, in his

most imperious voice.

'You're under arrest,' Elias told him.

'*Me* under arrest? *Me?* Have you lost your mind?'

A plain clothes officer stepped up into the paddy wagon. He had on a pair of latex gloves, de Bruin noticed, and he took the keys to the cage from Wharton's shocked grip even as he pushed by him. He unlocked the door then walked straight up to de Bruin. 'Breast pocket, yes?' he asked, glancing around.

'Beneath his handkerchief,' said Elias.

The officer carefully pulled out de Bruin's silk handkerchief then dipped his fingers back in for a small black electronic device. De Bruin stared sickly at it. Elias must have planted it there when replacing his handkerchief earlier after mopping the blood from his face. The bastard had set him up. The bastard had saved his life.

The plain clothes officer left the cage. Still standing outside, Elias held up his phone for all to see. He tapped its screen and at once Anton's voice rang out. 'The prisoner managed to free his hands without us realising,' he said. 'He threw himself at you while you were conducting an interview. I had no choice but to shoot.'

'Do it,' said Wharton.

Elias stopped the recording then gazed up at Trevor Wharton with a savage grin. 'My friend is in jail because of you, you treacherous piece of shit. My god, I'm going to enjoy testifying at your trial.'

SIXTY-NINE

They were halfway to Lincoln before Anna remembered her appointment with Uncle Dun's solicitor. No way could she make it now, even had she wanted to, which she didn't. She borrowed Oliver's phone to find the number of his office online, then called to let him know. 'That was you on that plane?' he asked in amazement, once she'd explained why. 'I was just watching it on the news.'

'Yes, well,' she told him dryly. 'I was just watching it live.'

They rescheduled for next week. She gave Oliver back his phone. Inevitably, a reaction set in. She felt utterly drained. 'Mind if I close my eyes a minute?'

'The week you've had, you deserve a month.'

'Wouldn't that be lovely?' She pushed back her seat and rested back her head, but it was no good, she had too much adrenaline still knocking around her system. She sighed and sat up again. 'So did it ever stop?' she asked.

'Did what ever stop?'

'The rain. To get your filming done.'

'Oh, that.' He gave a laugh. 'God. Talk about lifetimes ago. But yes. All safely in the can. Though…'

'Though?'

'Philippa was great, but I was a mess. I kept thinking about you.'

'How very sweet.'

'Well yeah, I guess, up to a point. But I didn't even know

you were in trouble then. It was more the way you ran off.' He squinted sideways at her. 'You looked as though you'd had some kind of breakthrough.'

Anna nodded. Events since had driven it from her mind, but now it all came back. 'I did, kind of.'

'And?'

She hesitated, but she felt the need to tell someone. 'It's quite complicated,' she warned him. 'There are lots of different bits to it. But let's start by assuming that King John really was murdered, just like Royston said. It's hardly unthinkable, what with so many people wanting him dead. But kings were sacred, even ones as vile as John. They were appointed by god, not man, which meant that assassination was beyond the pale. So you'd have needed to do it in such a way that no one realised, not even John himself.'

'Hence the poison.'

'Hence the poison,' agreed Anna. 'Which of course was why John took such stringent precautions against it. He had a whole team of stewards to secure his personal supplies of food and drink. His meals were prepared by his own cooks before being sampled by his own tasters to make sure they were safe. And these people went everywhere with him – except, of course, to Swineshead Abbey, because they'd been lost in the Wash along with the rest of the baggage train.'

Oliver nodded. 'Enabling Brother Simon to seize his chance.'

'But that's part of what I realised. What if Brother Simon *wasn't* seizing his chance? Or, more precisely, what if that chance had been deliberately engineered for him? We've always assumed that the loss of the baggage train and John's death were essentially unrelated, except by time and place. But what if that's wrong? What if they were both part of a single overarching plot?'

'I don't follow.'

'Think about it. You want to poison the king, but you can't, because he's got all these stewards, cooks and tasters with him.

Wouldn't your necessary first step, then, be to separate him from those people, but in a way that wouldn't put him on his guard?'

Oliver looked sceptically at her. 'Are you saying that someone had the baggage train swallowed by the Wash just to poison John?'

'Not swallowed by it, no. It was too valuable for that. But hijacked, sure. Why not?'

'Because you told me yourself it would have been impossible.'

'Impossible for some random outlaw like Robin Hood with a few dozen men and no inside information, yes. But not for one of John's top advisors, particularly one with enough influence to persuade him to split his army from his supplies. Especially if he also happened to lead a powerful order of battle-hardened knights loyal to him personally rather than to the king. An order, don't forget, that John's assassin also supposedly belonged to.'

'You mean that St Maur guy, I assume,' said Oliver. 'The one who led the Templars in England. But wasn't he John's good friend?'

'Kings like John don't really have good friends,' said Anna. 'They have courtiers skilled at navigating dangerous seas. And St Maur had better reason than most to resent John. He and Marshal had negotiated Magna Carta on his behalf in perfect good faith, yet John reneged on it so quickly that it had obviously been his plan all along, humiliating them both in the process. More to the point, St Maur had lent John extraordinary sums of Templar money. That would have been fine had he been winning the war, but he was losing it instead. The rebel barons and the French were never going to repay John's debts, so all that money was about to be lost forever. Yet John had baggage carts filled with treasure taken from his various castles, but which he refused to offer up as security, claiming he needed it to pay his mercenaries. Now put yourself in St Maur's shoes. Your order's on the verge of ruin thanks to your bad loans. What wouldn't you do to get your money back?'

'You really think that's how it happened?'

'I do, yes. Because all that's not even the most exciting part.'

'Then what the hell is?'

'All that stolen booty, what's left of it, at least. I'm pretty sure I know where it is.'

SEVENTY

Elias allowed himself the satisfaction of watching Wharton being handcuffed, cautioned and driven away. He'd have ridden along with him, except that his Leaf was still at the airfield, so he begged a lift back there from one of the many squad cars that had now turned up, and set off. His phone was ringing almost non-stop by now, what with word of Wharton's downfall spreading fast. It seemed the man had been universally disliked. Odd, then, how few of those calling to congratulate him had spoken up when it might have mattered.

He arrived back at the airfield to find Frank Mason and his team loading the van onto a flatbed. 'Just heard about Wharton,' said Mason, a touch sheepishly. 'Hell of a thing. How did you know it was him?'

'I didn't,' said Elias.

'Everyone's saying you did.

'Then they're wrong. I just told everyone I thought it might be that de Bruin was under arrest and about to talk. I figured that the person who fought hardest to take him off me was likely it.'

'I was one of the people you told,' said Mason gloomily.

'Yes.'

'You really thought it might have been me?'

'Yes. Though mostly I needed to get word to Wharton. I could hardly call him myself, could I? He'd have realised immediately it was a trap. But I knew you'd call him the moment we were done, and tell him everything.'

Mason flushed. 'I guess I deserved that.'

'Yes. You did.'

'Ah well.' He gave a shrug, consigning it all to history. 'Any idea who'll be taking over at Warne Farm?'

'Not a clue. Why?'

'My guys turned up something this morning, is all. I told Wharton and his team, but obviously that's all moot now. And I guess you're as likely to get it as anyone. You'll find it interesting anyway, that's for sure. Though it may seem a bit flat, after the day you've had.'

'Jesus, mate. Enough tuning the guitar already. Play the damned song.'

'Sorry. Yes. Sorry. It's just, you'll never guess what we found on some of those silver pennies we dug up.'

'Do I have to throttle you?'

'Okay, yeah, fair enough. So, anyway, we found fingerprints on them.'

'Fingerprints?' said Elias. But then he realised. 'Oh. No. It's nothing. They're Anna Warne's. She handled a few before I got there.'

'You think we're idiots? Those were bagged separately. These were on the ones my guys found. And they were wearing gloves, believe me. Whatever else you may think of me, I don't tolerate that kind of sloppiness. Anyway, we have all their prints on file. Yours too, for that matter. First thing I checked. No. These belonged to someone else. What's more, I already know who. Because I had this crazy, crazy thought. And guess what…?'

'Just tell me, for god's sake.'

'Very well,' grinned Mason. 'They belonged to Dunstan Warne.'

SEVENTY-ONE

Rain started to fall in a thin mist as Anna and Oliver made their way north towards Lincoln, just heavily enough to stir the BMW's wipers from their slumber. 'You know where King John's treasure is?' frowned Oliver, pulling up at a crossroads to let a blue removals truck pass by. 'Are you saying it's not beneath your uncle's fields?'

'I am, yes,' said Anna.

'So those silver pennies weren't part of it?'

'No. They were.'

He shook his head as he pulled away again. 'You've lost me completely. Talk to me like I'm four.'

'It was those schoolkids running around Newark Castle that gave me the idea,' she told him. 'Because they weren't looking for real Civil War treasure, were they? They were looking for clues that had been planted there for them to find. It set me wondering. We've all been assuming that Uncle Dun returned home last Sunday night to find Gregory Scott digging a hole in his field. But what if it was the other way around? What if Scott surprised my uncle? And what if he was digging that hole not to *find* those coins, but to *bury* them instead?'

'But…' Oliver fell silent as he thought it through. 'You're saying your uncle found those pennies elsewhere? Then brought them home to plant?'

'It was all the research he'd been doing for your programme, I expect,' nodded Anna. 'Rereading his old books and pamphlets, talking arsenic and Brother Simon with Royston. It told him where to look. So he drove over there last Sunday. He took a bunch of photographs with his drone and spotted something that led him to those coins. Now what? It had all happened too quickly for him to get permission from the landowner. Under English law, that would have meant he got nothing. In fact, he'd have been guilty of trespass and theft. How unfair would that have seemed, after all his work? Yet there was still a way for him to profit.'

'By taking the coins home,' murmured Oliver. 'By planting them in his field.'

'Exactly. That way, when he "discovered" them again, not only would he be entitled to their full value, he'd virtually double the value of the farm – especially if he found them while you were there filming. Can you imagine the excitement that would have generated?'

'And you know where this was?'

'I think so, yes,' said Anna. 'If I'm right about the other part, at least. Because St Maur wouldn't just have needed a small army to hijack the baggage train, he'd have needed a place to stash it too. And wouldn't it have solved both those problems if there'd been a major Templar property nearby manned by hundreds of well-trained knights loyal to him rather than to the king?'

'And?'

'We passed the turning for a place called Temple Bruer about five minutes back. It's where the Templars trained for the crusades. It was also *by far* the richest Templar property outside London – even though no one's ever been able to work out why.'

'And you think this is why? King John's treasure?'

'It would explain it, wouldn't it?'

'What about all those coins being from the Lynn mint?' frowned Oliver. 'You said that sounded like a private cache.'

'I did, yes,' admitted Anna. 'But now I think I was wrong. Or, at least, that there's a different possible explanation. Let's say you're the boss of Temple Bruer. There's a brutal civil war going on, but you're too busy training knights for the crusades to care much about that. Then one day the leader of your order sends word that a baggage train stuffed with Templar gold is about to set off across the Wash, and charging you with taking as many men as you'll need to seize it. It all goes swimmingly. You bring your booty home. But it's not over yet. One careless mistake and you'll all be for it. That holds true even after John dies. His son Henry III is still young, sure, but he's quite capable of taking revenge if you're foolish enough to start tongues wagging by splashing inordinate numbers of Lynn pennies around. And it's hardly an imposition. You have barrels of the damned things from other mints. So it becomes second nature, when taking out a handful to spend, to toss the Lynn ones back.'

'Until there are only Lynn ones left? And then they got lost somehow, until your uncle found them again?' He considered this a few moments, then nodded. 'You're sure this was at Temple Bruer?'

'I'm sure it's our best prospect. Because there's one other thing. Uncle Dun had various excavation reports out on his desk, including one from Temple Bruer back in the 1830s. It was led by this colourful local vicar who claimed to have found a string of underground chambers between it and the next village along, a place called Wellingore. He also claimed to have found evidence of child sacrifice and live burials, so everyone wrote him off as an anti-Templar crank, especially as nothing remotely like that has ever been found since. But what if it *wasn't* all bullshit? What if he really did find some kind of underground network?'

'And you think that's where those pennies are from?'

'I think it's only fifteen minutes away,' she said, fully energised once more. 'So how about we go look?'

SEVENTY-TWO

Elias turned off his radio as he headed north for Lincoln, too drained for anything but silence. The blurred headlights of oncoming cars in the drizzle threatened to bring on a headache. He drove largely on autopilot, brooding on the revelation that Dunstan Warne's fingerprints had been found on the silver pennies – or, more exactly, on the implication that he'd been planting them at the time of his murder, rather than Gregory Scott having been digging them up, hard though that was to reconcile with that man's confession. He'd have to tell Anna, of course, tarnishing her memories of her uncle and diminishing the value of the farm. Yet what got to him most was the silver pennies themselves, and where they'd come from.

He pulled off the road into a lay-by, ran a search on his phone. A handful from the 1206 coinage were available from dealers and on eBay, but all were from Canterbury or London, with not a trace of anything from Lynn or indeed from any of the other regional mints. Buying over forty of them would have been nigh on impossible, even had Warne had tens of thousands of pounds to spare. And there'd been no trace at the farm of the equipment he'd have needed to strike those coins himself. Anyway, such a forgery would surely have been discovered on their first proper examination, as Dunstan Warne must have known. Besides, there was a far simpler explanation. The man had been obsessed with John's lost baggage train, particularly since Merchant had first made contact. Was it really so implausible that he'd worked out where it had ended up, that he'd found a part of it and brought it home to bury? If so, then surely that was where he'd been last Sunday.

'My god!' said Maria Quinn excitedly, when he called her. 'People here are saying the maddest stuff. They're saying that you and Anna Warne were up on that plane. They're saying that Wharton's under arrest.'

'All true,' he told her. 'And plenty else besides. I'll tell you everything when we have a moment. But right now I need to know if you've had any joy with those drone photos.'

'Sorry, no. I got called away on that Priya Kapur business.'

'What Priya Kapur business?'

'You didn't get my message?'

'Honestly, I've got about two thousand of the damned things. It'll take me a week to go through them. Why? What's happened?'

'Okay. Well, you remember Priya Kapur, yes? The receptionist from the King John Hotel.'

'Bloody hell, Quinn. It was only yesterday afternoon. I'm not that old yet, am I?'

Quinn laughed. 'Sorry. Okay. Well, she came in to the station a bit earlier to make a statement. She brought her own lawyer and everything.'

'And? What did she have to say?'

'Only that Gregory Scott didn't murder Dunstan Warne. Only that he couldn't possibly have done. Because he spent the whole of that Sunday night in bed with her.'

SEVENTY-THREE

For all its once fabulous wealth, the single surviving trace of Temple Bruer was a three-storey limestone tower with a rusted weathercock on its turret, which sat at the end of a private road between a small enclave of modern housing and a tumbledown stone barn with a wired-off chicken run. Anna and Oliver were its only visitors. They parked by the chicken run then went through a latched wooden gate and up a short flight of steps to a heavy door that creaked open to reveal a large gloomy chamber with slit windows, graffiti-scrawled walls and a strange buzzing noise that sounded like faulty wiring until Anna looked up to see that the ceiling was turned almost black by an astonishing swarm of flies.

A narrow spiral stairway led upwards to a similar-sized chamber above. 'There's something I don't get,' said Oliver, as they searched for they knew not what. 'Let's say you're right. Let's say that St Maur got worried about having lent too much Templar money to King John, and so decided to hijack the baggage train to get it back. That's how you see it, right?'

'Broadly, yes.'

'Then why still kill John? He'd already pulled off his heist. Going after the king meant taking a huge additional risk even though he'd already got what he wanted.'

Anna frowned. It was a valid question. 'Maybe he was scared John would work out what he'd done,' she said. 'Or maybe he'd just had enough of the man.' But neither answer satisfied her. She went to stand at one of the windows to gaze out over the patchwork of fields, some tilled, others still coated with their harvest stubble. Oliver came to stand beside her, close enough that their arms brushed. She pulled reflexively away before remembering everything he'd done for her, and also what it was like to have a man in her life, a man she liked and found attractive, so she let it fall back again. He waited a moment then took her hand in his, and it was as warm and sweet as honeyed toast.

The sun was setting behind them and to their left, stretching the tower's shadow out like a finger across the fields towards an ancient copse. Those weren't the trees that grabbed Anna's attention, however. That was rather the pair of stately oaks whose foliage blazed scarlet in the day's dying rays. She explained their significance to Oliver. They went back down to the BMW. The sealed road ended at the tower, but a badly rutted farm track continued onwards. They bumped along it between open fields to a cobbled lane, surely putting beyond doubt that this was where Uncle Dun had come with his drone. They pulled up by the oaks, got out. Anna opened her laptop on the bonnet to show Oliver the composite she'd made from her uncle's photos. He came to stand behind her, clasping his arms lightly around her waist, resting his chin upon her shoulder. 'What are we looking for?' he asked.

'Anything unnatural.'

He tilted the screen further backwards, reducing the reflected glow of sunset. They studied the image in silence for a minute or so, until Oliver reached out to trace his fingertip diagonally across the screen. 'How about this?' he asked. Anna leaned closer and squinted to make it out. Yes, he was right. There *was* something there – a faint line of dots and dashes that ran like ancient Morse between Temple Bruer and Wellingore, crossing multiple fields, hedgerows, paths, even a small wood.

'Your vicar's underground network?' he asked.

'What Uncle Dun saw, at least.'

The line ran almost the full breadth of the screen. He might have dug down at any point along it. Except that these fields were almost as exposed as Warne Farm's, meaning that he'd surely have had to wait until after dark. Even then, on a moonlit night, he might easily have been spotted by anyone out walking their dog or returning home late from a drink with their neighbours. Except that that wasn't completely true, for the broken line passed at one point beneath the old copse, and he could have dug there to his heart's content.

They got back in the BMW and drove on a little way. The sun had fallen behind the western trees, making it gloomy enough for headlights. There was a small walled-off area next to the copse for hikers and picnickers to leave their cars. They parked in it and got out. 'Have a look at this,' said Oliver. Anna went around to see. The gatepost had clearly been struck by a vehicle, for several bricks had been dislodged. And recently too, to judge by the paleness of the exposed grey mortar. 'I'll bet this was your uncle.'

'He was too good a driver.'

'Even if he was overexcited by the silver pennies he'd just found? Even if he had his headlights off for fear of being seen?' He didn't wait for her reply, but rather went around to the boot of his BMW for his video camera. 'To prove we behaved,' he said, when he saw her disapproval. 'Just like yesterday morning.'

'We weren't trespassing yesterday morning,' she pointed out. But she let it go, not least because it was dark enough that they'd need the light from its lamp. In fact, she rather wished she had some light of her own. 'You don't have a spare torch, by any chance?' she asked.

'Only the one on my phone.'

'Thanks,' she said. 'That would be great.'

'Ah,' he said. 'That wasn't quite what I...' But then he laughed and handed it over. She tapped on its torch and led the way into the copse, hoping for the kind of open woodland that pleasant afternoon strolls are made of. It wasn't like that at all, however, with only a thin animal track wending between the tangled thickets, creepers, nettles, ivy and brambles. She had to high step her way through them with her forearms up, yet still she got stung and scratched and snagged by thorns, from which she had to keep stopping to pluck herself free.

The sun had fully set by now, and the canopy of trees blocked out what little ambient light remained. Inevitably, it stirred memories of her abduction, crashing through woodland that in places had been almost as thick and tangled as this, the dried leaves and dead branches crunching treacherously beneath her feet, making it easy for Harry Kidd to follow her. He'd been the faster too, catching her slowly yet remorselessly, until in the end she'd had no choice but to throw herself to the ground and roll beneath a bush, drawing up her legs, tucking her hands beneath her stomach and burying her face in the earth lest their pallor give her away. Rustling and heavy breathing and a flash of light as Kidd shone a torch right over her before moving on, then having to listen to him as he hunted both closer and further away.

She'd lain there for hours, terrified that he'd been lingering nearby, waiting for her to stir. First light had finally arrived, not only enabling her to see a little, but also to be seen. It had been the most terrifying time of all, her nerves so frayed that she'd imagined him behind every tree. She'd been disoriented too, with no idea which way to go. Then she'd heard sporadic traffic and had crept towards it, reaching a back lane with occasional vehicles passing by, any one of which might have been him still out looking.

She'd waited for enough light to see the drivers' faces. When a young woman in a blue Mini had approached, Anna had run out to wave her down. Her name had been Sophie Prior. She'd been wonderful. She'd driven her straight to the nearest police station to report her ordeal, and had stayed with her all morning, until Uncle Dun had arrived to take her home. They'd become friends for a while, until the stress of living in

Nottingham had become too much and Anna had moved to York in the hope of starting over. Yet she'd taken her trauma with her, slowly reducing her to a huddled mess upon her sofa, a shell of what she'd once been, without friends, pleasures or prospects – at least until Oliver and his documentary had offered her a path back. She glanced gratefully around. He grinned and gave her a wink, buoyant with adventure.

They drew roughly level with the broken line from the photographs. It appeared the same as all the rest, thick with nettles and brambles, and no obvious sign of Uncle Dun ever having been there.

'What now?' asked Oliver.

'We look,' she said.

SEVENTY-FOUR

Jubilant shouting and the blaring of horns forced Elias into silence as a convoy of wedding cars drove by, festooned with ribbons and shaving foam, while the happy couple waved from a back seat. He waited until they'd all passed by then double checked with Maria Quinn to make sure he'd correctly understood what she was telling him. 'Gregory Scott spent last Sunday night in bed with Priya Kapur?' he said. 'Are you telling me they were lovers?'

'There's no getting by you today,' said Quinn.

'The whole night, yes? He didn't slip out, not even for a bit?'

'That's what she said, yes. She says she's prepared to testify under oath that he arrived a little after midnight and stayed until some time after six, though she can't be more accurate than that. She says they were both awake the whole time too, talking as well as the other stuff, because they didn't get so many chances to be together that they could afford to waste them. And he didn't leave at any point, except once to go to the loo.'

'Then what did he need his metal detector for?' asked Elias plaintively, only to realise the answer for himself. 'Don't tell me. He can't leave home at night without triggering the intruder lights and waking the wife. So he spins her a line about going to search Warne Farm for King John's gold, meaning he has to take his metal detector with him as a kind of cover. But the moment he's out of sight it's off to the hotel instead.'

'It's like you were there watching.'

'Why didn't he tell us this yesterday?'

'Because it would have meant confessing the affair to his wife. She has a fearsome temper, according to Priya. You should have seen how scared she was at the thought of what she'll do when she finds out. Plus her own family is very strict. She thinks they might disown her for sleeping with a married man. So he kept silent to buy her time. Rather noble of him, really.'

'You believe her, then?'

'Yes,' said Quinn. 'Yes, I do. And not just because of how hard she found it to squeeze it all out of herself. She brought evidence too. Love notes he'd written her over the past couple of months. Text messages they'd exchanged, including one from earlier that Sunday afternoon telling her he hoped to be over at around midnight; and another from Monday morning, all kisses and love hearts.'

'But he confessed,' protested Elias. 'I get that he needed a cover story for his wife, but why tell her he'd killed Warne? Why not simply deny he'd been anywhere near him?'

'This is partly guesswork, but I'm pretty sure it's right. When I took Penny Scott's statement, she told me how she'd seen Gregory go out that Sunday night, yet she'd still managed to convince herself that it was smugglers who'd killed Warne. That wasn't possible any more, not after you told her about those silver pennies, so she confronted him about it when they got back home, and threatened to tell us everything unless he came clean, in which case she promised to stand by him. And what could he do? Tell her the truth, he'd give Priya away. Keep quiet, it would come out anyway. His one chance of keeping it secret was to admit to killing Warne in self-defence, then hoping she kept her word.'

'And his spade? Why throw it out onto the salt marsh?'

'Are we sure he did?'

'He said he did.'

'Yes, but for the same reason. They were upstairs together watching you search the salt marsh through your field glasses. She asked him whether you were going to find it. And what could he say? His answer had to work whether you found it or not. So he said he'd thrown it out there, yes, but no, he didn't think you'd find it.'

'Is this still you guessing?'

'Yes. But it works, doesn't it?'

'Except how the hell did his spade get out there, then?'

'That's for a detective to discover,' she told him. 'Not a humble WPC.'

'Don't give me that. You're loving this, aren't you?'

'Yes,' she said simply. 'I am.'

Elias laughed. 'Good,' he said. 'My offer still stands.'

'I'd have to speak to Tim and the boys.'

'Of course. Just don't take too long. I have some clout at the minute, thanks to that Wharton business, but no doubt I'll screw it up again soon. Meantime, you should know that we found Warne's fingerprints all over those silver pennies. Seems like he was planting them when he was killed, rather than Gregory Scott digging them up.'

'Christ,' she said.

'Quite. Which certainly tends to support Priya's claim of Scott's innocence. But I still need to know where Dunstan Warne took those photos. Because that's likely where the coins came from.'

'Then get off the phone,' she told him. 'I'll call you when I have it.'

SEVENTY-FIVE

In the near total darkness, relieved only by Anna's modest torchlight and the lamp on Oliver's video camera, they'd never have found it had they not actively been looking, so cunningly had Uncle Dun hidden it. But, after a minute or two of struggling with the brambles and other thickets, Anna's eye was caught by a tangle of thorns between a blackberry bush and a bed of nettles that looked too twisted and bunched up to be quite natural, as though it had been uprooted elsewhere then stuffed into the gap. She made mittens of her sleeves to pinch its branches between her fingers and then pull. It came far enough to encourage her to take a firmer grip then drag it all the way aside. Yet it only revealed the same packed earth, twigs and leaf litter as she could see elsewhere.

She got down onto her hands and knees for a closer look, while Oliver stood above her with his camera on his shoulder, both to film her and to give her light. She dug her fingers into the soil, which proved to be cold, damp and unexpectedly brittle, as if broken up only to be stamped back down again. She scraped away maybe three or four inches of it before encountering something more solid, a first glimpse of what proved to be a pair of short pine planks sawn from the timber in the back of the van.

She cleared them both of earth then worked her fingers beneath the nearer of the two. It was still so firmly plugged that she had to lean backwards and lift with her legs, only for it to give in such a rush that she went tumbling onto her backside. Its partner came more easily, exposing the top of a shaft not much broader than her shoulders, and against whose wall her uncle had fixed his aluminium ladder with orange rope and steel pegs.

Oliver stood on its lip and shone down his lamp, its powerful beam lighting up a mound of earth and broken brickwork far below. An underground chamber of some kind, whose ceiling – some ten or twelve feet beneath them – had presumably collapsed beneath her uncle's assault. There was no way he could have dug that deep with a spade, meaning he must surely have used his augur instead, despite the din it would have made. Nor could he have done it in a single visit. He must have come here multiple times, photographing the fields on his first visit, then choosing this spot to dig before returning with the necessary equipment packed into the back of his van. 'Enough,' she said. 'We need to report this now.'

'Of course,' said Oliver. 'But come on! Surely a quick look first. In and out. Thirty seconds. Just to make certain it's what we think.'

'What else could it be?' asked Anna. Yet she couldn't deny the tug. 'You'll have to stay up here,' she told him. 'In case anything goes wrong.'

'Nothing will go wrong.'

'No. Because you'll be up here to make sure.' She sat on the edge of the shaft then turned onto her side to feel for a rung with her foot, gradually increasing her weight upon it until she was confident it would hold. Yet it still gave such a wobble when she committed herself to it that she had to claw at the earth to save herself.

Oliver had to fight back his laughter. 'Maybe I should do it,' he said.

'In your dreams,' said Anna.

'I'm only thinking of your safety.'

'You're only thinking of your documentary.'

His teeth flashed. 'Can't blame a man for trying.'

She tucked the phone into her waistband to give herself some light while leaving her hands free. Then she began her descent, feeling out each rung with her foot, slowly delivering herself into the gut of this monstrous serpent. The soil had that rich and pungent wet earth smell, and looked to be kept from collapsing in on itself only by the chaotic mesh of yellow roots that her uncle had sliced through with his augur. The shaft grew narrower and narrower. Her breathing echoed unnervingly loudly back at her and she could feel the thumping of her heart. But then she reached the point beneath which it had collapsed, and it immediately opened up wide. She paused to shine her torch around. Its feeble beam was little match for the huge space in which she now found herself, yet it was still strong enough to make out a colonnaded hallway with an arched ceiling supported by two rows of fat pillars, creating aisles either side of a taller central spine. An ambulatory, perhaps, around which Knights Templar would have walked in quiet contemplation or in murmured conversation.

She completed her descent, stepped off the bottom rung onto the mound of fallen moist dark earth in which a number of limestone blocks were mixed, each the size of a farmhouse loaf and trapezoid of shape, the better to fit together to form the vaulted ceiling. She bedded the ladder's feet a little more securely into the earth then looked around once more. The walls on either side bulged alarmingly from the pressure of the surrounding land, but thankfully were buttressed by sturdy ribs every few paces, each one sculpted with gargoyles both beautiful and grotesque. This place would have been built during the first great flowering of cathedral architecture, of course, from which it had doubtless borrowed techniques and designs. It looked as though it would have been well lit back then, for she could see the rusted traces of iron beckets on the walls, as well as several niches at chest height in which a few clay oil lamps still remained.

A soft, discordant tapping caught her ear. It took her

several moments to work out that it was water dripping at different tempos from various fissures in the ceiling, which presumably was why the floor was gently cambered, to channel such leaks into the gutters that ran alongside either wall, to be drained from there into cisterns or maybe the earth beneath. The moisture meant that the carpet of dirt and earth had taken beautiful impressions of her uncle's footprints, and had held them almost perfectly since his visit. On one side, they led away along the central spine before returning down the left-hand aisle. On the other, by contrast, there were too many to make sense of, as though he'd been back and forth at least half a dozen times. The latter, then, looked the more promising; but the former seemed easier to rule out, so that was where she headed first, filming as she went.

Her shoes and socks grew damp, giving her the graveyard chills. A cobweb caught in her face and throat and hair. She brushed it away then checked herself for spiders. The darkness began to play upon her nerves. The ancient stone creaked like an old house, and she kept sensing movement out of the corners of her eyes, absurd though she knew that to be. She felt twelve again, spooked by the ghosts in the local woods when moonlight had played upon the trees.

She reached the end of the ambulatory. An arched doorway would have led into the next chamber along, or perhaps to a flight of stairs, except that it had been bricked up centuries ago. She was taking photographs of it when a bloom of light behind her gave her a start. But it was only Oliver, of course, approaching with his camera on his shoulder, its lamplight bright in her eyes. 'You promised,' she said.

'Come on,' he said. 'That poxy phone isn't up to a job like this. And how else will you prove you behaved?'

'People will trust me,' she said.

'People will trust footage.'

She scowled, but he had a point. And his lamp was a comfort in this profound and ancient darkness. 'Fine,' she said, leading back the way they'd come. 'Then follow me.'

SEVENTY-SIX

The road split ahead, offering Elias a choice between Nettleham HQ and home. Both filled him with such profound dismay, however, that in the end he opted for a third. If Priya Kapur's testimony held up, it would seem to clear Gregory Scott of Dunstan Warne's murder, and lead to his likely release without charge. And Anna deserved to be told this in person rather than learning it from the news.

Merchant wasn't home, however. Nor was his car in its spot. He tried Anna's mobile, in case she'd managed to retrieve it somehow, but got only voicemail. Same with Merchant. They were probably out for a drink or a bite to eat. Or maybe he'd taken her to see her uncle's solicitor. There were all kinds of possibilities.

He was in no great rush to get anywhere so he parked in Merchant's spot and left a note beneath his wiper for them to call him. Then he wandered down to Westgate and Lincoln Cathedral, as good a place for contemplation as a man could wish for.

Evensong was underway. He could hear the singing from outside. He turned his phone to vibrate before going in, then took a pew at the back. His wife had been a believer, and had insisted on bringing the kids up that way too, so that at one time he'd come here often. But then their son had died, and he'd stopped. He closed his eyes, bowed his head and rested his chin upon his clasped hands, for all the world in prayer, but in truth still brooding on the case – though perhaps that was prayer too, after a fashion.

Priya Kapur might well be flat-out lying about Gregory Scott having spent the night with her, of course. People would do that for the ones they loved. More likely, though, she was shading the truth a little, perhaps about what time he'd left. If he'd headed off at five-thirty, say, he could have heard or seen something in Warne's fields that had prompted him to investigate. If so, he might have caught Warne digging his hole to plant his silver pennies. Except that the pennies would already have been planted by then, covered by several inches of silt. So why kill him?

The organist and choir started on a new hymn, flooding the great space with their gorgeous music. *I will lift up mine eyes* they sang, prompting Elias to do just that, gazing up at the stained glass windows for which the cathedral was so justly famous. He was too far away to make out their detail. They simply gleamed with colour instead, as though handfuls of rubies, sapphires, emeralds and other such gemstones had been tossed haphazardly into a set of bowls. And only then did he realise what should have been obvious: those forty-six silver pennies might not have been all that Warne had brought home to plant. He might have had hundreds more. And not just coins, indeed, but other kinds of treasure too, intending to bury it at various spots around his fields, so that he might rediscover it at appropriate intervals. A knapsack full of that would most certainly have been worth killing for.

Elias could almost picture the scene, indeed, with Scott gazing down at it all in disbelief, demanding to know where it had come from, while Warne told him angrily to get off his land. Easy to imagine them coming to blows, a pair of medieval knights hammering at each other with their spades, until Scott had caught Warne with his killing blow, leaving him little choice but to bury him and flee.

His phone buzzed in his pocket. It was Quinn. He hurried back outside before answering, surprised by the new chill of the night air.

'Hey,' he said, hugging his jacket tight around himself. 'What's up?'

'I've found your fields,' she told him. 'At least I've found fields of roughly the right shape alongside a pair of oaks and a cobbled lane. But please understand that the satellite photos I'm comparing them to were taken in the summer and from a different angle too. Everything looks a bit off, so I can't be one hundred percent—'

'I get it,' said Elias. 'It's hard. Where?'

'Yes, that's the other thing. It's between a village called Wellingore and a place called Temple Bruer. We took the boys there for a picnic a couple of years back. It used to be this great big Templar estate, so they say. And that was Mr Warne's kind of history, wasn't it?'

'Yes, it was,' said Elias. 'Brilliant work. Thanks.' Temple Bruer. Dunstan Warne had had some kind of pamphlet or paper about it on his desk, which Anna had boxed up and taken away with her. What was more, he'd driven right by it barely an hour ago, on returning to Lincoln from Fenton Airfield, following exactly the same route that Anna and Oliver would most likely have taken themselves. Was it possible, then, that she'd realised its significance, and that that was where she and Merchant were right now? She had all the information she'd have needed, and she was most certainly sharp enough. He briefly considered sending a car to look, except that it could embarrass her or even get her into trouble. Yet he could hardly stand by while they trampled over a site of potential material importance in the investigation of her uncle's murder.

He hurried back to his car and set off south.

SEVENTY-SEVEN

The ladder glittered silver in their lamplight as Anna and Oliver returned towards it, as if to indicate the way out they really ought to take. But neither was in any mood for retreat now that they were down here, so they clambered back over the mound of fallen earth and rubble without a word, then continued onwards to the far end of the ambulatory, from which a narrow stone staircase led down, its steps so steep and badly rutted that they had to turn sideways to focus on their footing – which perhaps explained why Anna was already at the bottom before she noticed that this section wasn't built from limestone blocks, as was the ambulatory above, but rather had been hewn out of bedrock.

Oliver arrived behind her with his better light. They set off along a passage. It kinked right after a few paces, taking them down a flight of three shallow steps into a chamber with unfinished walls, so that it looked more like a cave or grotto than a burial vault. Yet a burial vault was what it unquestionably was, with three raised tombs on either side of its central aisle, each topped by the effigy of a Knight Templar.

Five of these were neatly groomed and dressed in chainmail, with solemn or even beatific expressions on their faces, and their hands pressed together in prayer. But the sixth was very different. He had unkempt long hair and a huge beard that lay like a bib over his chest, as well as a fat scar that ran from his hairline down to his right eye. He was missing most of his right ear too, though that might simply have been an accident, or the passage of time. He looked to be well into his fifties, or even older, yet he had a Templar shield strapped to his left arm and was drawing his longsword from its scabbard with his right hand. His legs were similarly captured in motion, his left sinking into the tomb beneath him, while his right was raised as if striding into battle, so that their lamplight brought him to a kind of life, causing Anna to put a sympathetic hand upon his arm. But the stone was rough and cold and still, and the spell was broken.

Another short flight of steps led up to a second crypt, dedicated to a single Templar grandee. His tomb and effigy were to their left, but it was the wall to their right that caught the eye, for the stone had first been smoothed flat and then sculpted in relief into a battle scene that commemorated what presumably had been the great moment of the man's life, leading a mounted charge against the infidel.

A third chamber followed, this one more like a morgue, with columns of loculi cut into its walls, and crude yet evocative portraits painted on the plaster seals. Several of these had fallen away over the centuries, exposing the skeletons within, their broken grins and dully glowing skulls patched with dessicated hair, and their leg bones folded up beneath their jaws to fit into the cramped, boxlike spaces.

A labyrinth of more such crypts followed, all linked by short passages and flights of steps set at odd angles to one another, sometimes splitting off only to rejoin again further along, or turning into dead ends from which they had to retreat. Anna was beginning to think that this necropolis was all there was when they passed through a narrow opening into a longer passage that ended in a fan of steps down into a large domed chamber whose floor was submerged beneath a foot or so of water, at least to judge from how high it reached up the legs of the four granite tables that were set in a diamond pattern at its centre, and the stone blocks on either side of them on which wooden planks would presumably once have rested, to turn them into benches. There were three other doorways too, one at each point of the compass, though the mouth of the one directly across from them was completely blocked by earth and broken brickwork that spewed well out into the chamber, suggesting that whatever lay beyond had collapsed in the distant past, allowing all this rainwater to seep through its imperfect filter ever since, and gather here.

There were tall marble niches in each of the walls too, though the statues they presumably had once housed were long gone, leaving only their empty shells behind, casting ghostly reflections on the water's surface, which was flat as a silvered mirror, save only for a few tiny ripples provoked by skippers and other insects.

Anna sat down on the steps to remove her shoes and socks. Oliver likewise. She dipped in her toes. It was cool rather than cold. She rolled her trousers up above her knees to test its depth, her foot pale and shimmering as a fish as it sank some six or seven inches through crystal clear water before hitting the sludge beneath and stirring up an ugly dark cloud.

The doorway to their left looked the more inviting. She waded over to it, setting off waves that threw rippling bands of lamplight onto the walls. It led to a long corridor with partly flooded storerooms on either side, some with crude shelving cut into their walls, but all empty save for a few earthenware vessels of various shapes and vastly different sizes, but all broken or at least badly cracked, making it ever clearer that this place had been deliberately abandoned, with everything of value removed.

The passage sloped gently upwards. Soon they were out of the water. Anna stopped to brush dry her legs. The floor here was worn almost smooth by ancient feet, yet it still felt as scratchy as fine sandpaper on her bare soles. There was enough dust on it, too, to see the tracks Uncle Dun had left. It touched her disproportionately to see the little dabs left by his toes.

They reached a pair of armouries, still sparsely stocked with broken swords, rotted shields and the concentric rings of rusted iron hoops left behind by a wooden barrel that presumably had once contained arrows, to judge from what remained – not only barbed arrowheads but others like tiny baskets designed to be stuffed with pitch and set alight before being fired at haystacks or thatched roofs. Helmets too, a pair of greaves, even a suit of chain-mail, all long-since rusted into uselessness, though that couldn't disguise the wretched state they'd been in anyway – mend-and-make-do equipment just about good enough for practice, but not for the crusades.

The passage grew narrower and lower, until first Oliver and then even Anna had to watch their heads. A relief, then, to reach the final storeroom. She shone in her torch, expecting to find it as empty as the others – and so it was, after a fashion, save for a broken pot or two, including a number of shards that looked very much like the ones she'd dug up with the silver pennies. It was smaller as well – the same breadth and height as its predecessors, but barely half as deep. Yet the explanation for that was instantly apparent, and it stopped her dead; for its far wall wasn't hewn out of the bedrock, as were the others, but built instead from stone blocks that had been plastered over and smeared with grime. Time had since done what time will do, cracking the plaster badly enough that clumps had fallen away to reveal the brickwork behind. And Uncle Dun had clearly spotted this for himself, for he'd knocked a hole in the wall at around chest height, plenty large enough for a man his size to have clambered through.

She felt light-headed as she made her way towards it, torn between shame for what her uncle had done and excitement at what he'd discovered. For where else could those silver pennies have come from? Yet she still wasn't prepared for what she found, the floor of this secret chamber packed tight with baskets and caskets, with bowls and chests, each filled to the brim with treasures of one kind or another, all in fine condition too, kept so by their hermetic seal, and thus glittering, gleaming and sparkling in their twin beams, which themselves were given extra potency by the pair of huge silver platters leaned up against the facing wall, each large enough to hold a haunch of beef, and still bright enough to act like tarnished mirrors.

There were two half-tubs of rotted oak directly beneath the hole. The first contained a high mound of silver pennies, hollowed like a quarried mountain at its peak, thanks to the fistfuls Uncle Dun had taken home to plant – far more than the forty-six so far recovered. But it was the second tub that shocked her, not only because it was filled with ancient brooches, buckles, rings and clasps, but because it too had clearly been plundered. And where the hell had all that gone?

'Jesus,' muttered Oliver, clearly asking himself the same question. 'You think your uncle buried it already?'

'No,' said Anna. 'I'd have noticed.'

'But if he took the trouble to cover his—'

'You can't just dig up a tilled field without leaving traces. Certainly not in the middle of the night.'

'Then?'

'How about this?' she said, while running her torch across the floor, which at least relieved her of one concern, for there was no sign that Uncle Dun had ever made it through his hole. 'He has it all lying on the ground next to him, planning to bury it next. Only that's when Gregory Scott comes across him.'

'So he killed him out of greed,' said Oliver. 'Bang goes his claim of self defence.' He shook his head, struggling to take it in. 'I don't get it, though. What even is this place? Why go to all the trouble and risk of hijacking John's baggage train only to wall it up again?'

'I don't suppose they meant it to be forever,' said Anna. 'But obviously I got it wrong earlier. They didn't weed out the Lynn coins as they took them out to spend. They did it all upfront. I mean look at this stuff. What does it have in common?'

'Apart from being priceless, you mean?'

'Yes. Apart from that.'

'Come on, Anna,' he sighed. 'Just tell me.'

'It's that it's *identifiable*. The Lynn pennies we already know about. But look at these brooches and buckles. Animals and birds, flowers and geometric patterns. Trust me, anyone who'd seen them before and who had even a half-decent eye would have recognised them at once.'

'And the silverware? The goblets?'

'Stamped with a royal crest, I'll bet. King John and his army were only a day's ride away. For all anyone here knew, he might have got wind of what they'd done and been already on his way. So they'd have needed to get rid of the evidence fast. They might even have prepared this place ahead of time. It wasn't as though they'd have been needing this stuff anytime soon. They'd have had cartloads of coins and bullion and other anonymous loot that they could safely add to their general stores. But not this. This would see them hanged. They didn't have time to cut it up or melt it down either, so they had to separate it out and wall it up until it was safe again.'

'Which it was within days,' pointed out Oliver. 'After John died.'

'Yes, but only to be succeeded by his son. A son who'd loved him dearly. Better safe than sorry, right? Wait until the dust had fully settled. Henry was a Plantagenet, after all, and only a boy. Some ambitious cousin was sure to knock him off in a month or two. But he lived fifty more years, during which time Temple Bruer would have filled with idealistic young knights who'd have felt great loyalty to their new king, and who'd have been horrified to learn that their order had been party to his father's murder.'

'That's an awful lot of daisies for a single chain,' said Oliver. 'And if you're right, where are the crown jewels? The sceptres? The Sword of Mercy?'

Anna didn't answer, struck by a different curiosity. She reached across to raise Oliver's camera so that its lamp lit up the facing wall, and yes, there was indeed a mural on it. She'd missed it before, partly because it was half hidden behind the two silver platters, but also because its colours had faded over the years, and because it was naturally dark and shadowy anyway, being of a night-time scene, as attested by the crescent moon in its top right corner. But it was easy enough to make out, now that Oliver's lamplight was upon it. Its main subjects were two men wearing hooded capes over chain-mail coifs and coats, seated together upon a chestnut warhorse with a white blaze. They were depicted in three-quarter profile, as if headed off over Anna's left shoulder, while a line of other mounted knights trailed along behind, riding escort to a baggage train.

'My god,' muttered Oliver. 'They painted their own confession.'

'Their own homage, more like,' said Anna. 'They'd all have been for the gallows anyway had this place ever been found. So why not celebrate it where they could?'

'A whole damned baggage train. You'd think those two up front could afford a horse each.'

'It's a symbol,' she told him. Two men on a single horse had been depicted on Templar seal stones, pottery and everything else. All kinds of ingenious explanations had been offered for this, including that it had been to honour the poverty of their two founders, or to represent their dual roles as warriors and monks, or their refusal to leave fallen comrades behind on the battlefield. But no one knew for sure.

The two knights in the motif were typically depicted in profile, charging the enemy with a lance and a shield apiece. Yet its use here couldn't be an accident. No. It was meant as a tribute to these two particular men. What was more, Anna knew who they were. The man sitting behind had to be Aymeric de St Maur, head of the Knights Templar in England. She was confident of that, even though she didn't recognise him, because she *did* recognise the man in front, the evident leader of this extraordinary expedition, for his long thin face, his aristocratic nose and chevron moustache were virtually identical to those on his tomb effigy in London's Temple Church.

It was William Marshal, St Maur's closest friend and the

hero of her thesis.

SEVENTY-EIGHT

Traffic was rush hour heavy as Elias headed back south out of Lincoln towards Temple Bruer, but he had so much on his mind that for once he was content to let the cars around him set his pace. He tuned his radio to an oldies station then tried to assemble the various facts of Dunstan Warne's murder into a coherent picture. But he invariably had a piece or two left over that he couldn't get to fit. He gave a defeated sigh as he approached Navenby, then turned his radio down to call Quinn yet once more. 'You must be sick of me by now,' he said.

'I'm still hiding it okay, though, aren't I?'

'You are, you are,' he assured her. 'But this Warne business is driving me nuts. Mind if I think out loud?'

'Go for it.'

'Okay,' he said. 'Let's start with this. Maybe Priya was lying about what time Scott left. Say he went at five-thirty instead of a quarter past six, and he saw Warne digging in his field on his way home.'

'It would have been dark still.'

'I know. I know. But perhaps he had a lamp or something. Allow me a bit of rope here. Anyway, he hurries over to investigate and he finds Warne planting his silver pennies. Maybe he has a bagful of other goodies too, and the greed is too much for him. He kills Warne, buries him, grabs his loot and legs it. So my first question is this: what happened to Warne's spade? He must have had one to dig his hole, right? Yet we didn't find it with his body, even though it would have been easy enough to bury it with him. So Scott must have taken it, yes? But then why not dump it in the salt marsh with his own? Or hang it up in his shed, in place of his own? Who'd have noticed? Come to that, why toss his own spade out in the salt marsh at all? He'd lived there fifteen years. He must have known it could be spotted at low tide. Surely better to wrap it in a bunch of bin bags and dump it in a lake somewhere. And that's before we get to the intruder lights. Because didn't you tell me they were difficult to see in the morning, as it was already getting light?'

'Yes. So?'

'You'll know that coast better than me. Say you wanted to dump a spade out in the salt marsh, but it's starting to get light. What are your chances of wading out thirty metres or so, dumping it and making it back again, all without being spotted? By someone out for a jog, say, or walking their dog before setting off for work?'

'Oh,' said Quinn. 'I see what you mean. Those seawalls get busy early. And you can see for miles once it starts getting light.'

'Exactly. It would have been a crazy risk, even for someone in a panic. Surely you'd wait for night instead, when you could be certain of not being seen. Except the intruder lights would have come on if he'd done that, which they didn't, not until the storm, at least, which was hardly the kind of weather you'd want to wade out onto the salt marsh in, and which could easily have triggered them all by itself.'

'So Priya was telling the truth. Like I said.'

'That's how it looks. Except how then did Scott's spade get out there? And what happened to Warne's?' He'd arrived outside Temple Bruer while they'd been talking. There was no sign of Merchant's BMW, but he pulled to a stop anyway, switched off his engine. 'You could just about construct a scenario whereby someone else borrowed Scott's spade to go treasure hunting. They surprised Warne and used it to kill him and then dumped it. But who? I doubt Penny Scott has the strength for a blow like that. And who else? One of those old couples from the hotel? The environmentalist with the broken ankle? I mean come on. So maybe the spade *wasn't* used to murder Warne, but was thrown out there to make Scott look guilty. Now I *can* see the wife doing that, especially if she'd found out about her hubby's affair. A sweet bit of revenge while getting to keep the house and all the money. Except if the intruder lights clear the husband, they surely clear her too.'

'It's a puzzler,' agreed Quinn.

'A puzzler? Is that the best you've got?'

'Like you're doing so much better.'

'True enough,' he sighed. 'But keep thinking. Call me if you come up with anything.'

He grabbed his torch and went to explore. The tower was dark and empty and quiet, save for someone in a neighbouring house pumping out some early Taylor Swift. He went upstairs to make sure, though without much expectation. Dunstan Warne had photographed fields, not buildings. He stood at a window and stared out towards Wellingore. Lights twinkled from a house or two, but that was it. Yet Warne had found a cache of ancient treasure somewhere in that darkness, Elias was sure of it, and all his instincts were telling him that Anna and Merchant were out there right now, searching for the spot.

SEVENTY-NINE

Anna waited for Oliver to film his fill of the treasure chamber, then they headed back the way they'd come. Their duty to report this place was clearer now than ever, yet there was still at least one more section to explore, and curiosity so trumped responsibility that they waded across the flooded hall to it without exchanging so much as a word.

A short passage opened up into what had clearly once been a chapel, with a high vaulted ceiling and rows of pillars carved with demons and angels, and stone benches either side of a central aisle oriented to face a large dais a bare few inches above the water. A long white marble table stood at the front of this dais, making it easy to imagine some Templar notable celebrating mass or calling a meeting to order. But it was the wall behind it that stunned Anna, covered as it was by a mural of such bright fresh colours that it was instantly obvious how the towels she'd found bagged up in the back of Uncle Dun's van had got so wet and filthy.

Oliver gave a coughing kind of grunt, as though someone had punched him lightly in the gut. He waded past her, splashing up the aisle, turning his camera this way and that as he went. Anna hurried after him. A flight of steps took them up onto the dais. Oliver stood back a little way, the better to pan across the whole wall, but she went straight up to it. Though no art historian, even she could tell at a glance that it was a fresco, a technique popular in ancient Egypt and Greece before falling out of fashion, only to be revived in medieval Italy and then spread across Europe by returning crusader knights.

The vividness of colour alone would have suggested as much, painted on while the plaster was still wet, allowing the pigments to soak right in. Equally revealing was the greyness of the backdrop sky, for blue had been the one pigment that wet plaster hadn't absorbed well, and so had tended to fade over the decades. But the biggest tell by far was that fresco artists had only had eight hours or so before the plaster set too hard, at which point they'd had to stop for the day, returning the following morning to cut away the unused areas and start afresh.

The seams between these different panels – *giornatas* as they were known, from the Italian for a day's work – tended to crack over the centuries. And as the artist would typically concentrate on completing a single element of the larger painting each day, this had the incidental effect of putting a kind of aura or halo around the key figures, exactly as had happened here with the mural's central subject, a boy in splendid purple robes with a gold circlet on his head, seated upon a throne so much too large for him that his legs were left dangling several inches above the floor.

Who else but Henry III, and at his coronation too? That had taken place inside Gloucester Cathedral, of course, but he was shown here in the great outdoors, the artist taking full advantage of their licence to fill the background with the towns and villages of this green and pleasant land, as well as with cheering crowds of nobles and commoners alike. A work of historic importance, then, yet turned into a masterpiece by the boy's expression, overwhelmed by the magnificence of the occasion, yet determined to make his late father proud.

A man was standing a little behind and to the side of the throne, his head respectfully bowed as if not wanting to be noticed. The artist had portrayed him as a vigorous if grizzled middle-aged warrior, his hand resting loosely upon the pommel of his sheathed sword. William Marshal again, serving as regent to the boy king, and thus England's *de facto* ruler. He too had a telling expression on his face: not of triumph at his ascension but rather of solemn awareness of his responsibility, leading a bankrupt country still at war with itself.

It was no great surprise to find Henry honoured here, for kings were always liable to drop in unannounced on tours of their realm, but it was a puzzle to see Marshal so prominently feted. He'd become a Knight Templar on his deathbed, true, inducted by Aymeric de St Maur himself, but he hadn't yet been one at the time of Henry's coronation. Though in a sense he had been, for he'd pledged himself to the order many decades before, while in the holy land on crusade – a crusade he'd only ever gone on because of the vow he'd made to Young King Henry as he'd lain dying.

So many vows. So much sudden death. 'I think I have the answer to your question,' murmured Anna, turning around to Oliver.

'What question?' he asked.

'About why St Maur still had John killed even after pulling off his heist.'

Oliver turned his camera on her, its lamp so bright that it made her squint. 'And?'

'It was never about the treasure. It was always about killing John. And St Maur wasn't even the man behind it. He was just another member of the cast. An important one, yes, but still. The baggage train was his pay-off.'

'Then who was behind it?'

Anna nodded at the fresco, at the man standing beside the throne. 'Him,' she said. 'William Marshal.'

Oliver gazed sceptically at her. 'History's greatest knight? England's chivalric hero? A common assassin?'

'Hardly a common one. And it's not *that* unthinkable, is it? We know for a fact that he'd been involved in at least one royal murder before.'

'You mean Young King Henry's?'

'No, actually. I'm talking about Arthur of Brittany.' But Oliver looked so blank that she knew she'd have to elaborate. 'Arthur was the son of Geoffrey, another of John's older brothers to die young. He probably had the strongest claim to succeed Richard Lionheart to the throne. It was just that John moved faster. Arthur didn't give up, though. He won the backing of the French and went to war, only he got unlucky and was captured. John held him in Rouen while he and his closest advisors agonised over what to do, because killing a king was such a no-no, even for John. Yet they killed him anyway.'

'And Marshal was part of it?'

'He never spoke of it, but yes. We can place him there from other sources.'

'So much for his famous gallantry.'

'There was a lot at stake, to be fair.'

'And that makes it okay, does it? You can kill a king if the prize is big enough?'

'I'm not just talking money and power. There was a war going on. Killing Arthur would have looked like a way to end it at a stroke, and bring peace to…' But then she fell silent.

'Bring peace to…?' prompted Oliver.

'Nothing,' she said. But Oliver kept his camera on her face, and she felt compelled to continue. 'It's just, there's a bit of a pattern with Marshal. I've been *aware* of it forever, everyone has. It's part of what made him such a legend. But I've only just *noticed* it, if you get the difference, even though it happened again and again and again.'

'Go on.'

'Okay. It's that every time Marshal served a king, that king died. What's more, their death proved to be Marshal's stepping stone to a bigger and better job under their successor – even though those kings and their successors had pretty much all been literally at war with one another.'

Oliver shook his head. 'I don't get it.'

'Maybe it would be easiest if I went through them. Arthur of Brittany you already know about. And Young King Henry we discussed yesterday. Remember how I said the Old King rewarded Marshal handsomely after his return from the crusades? Well, he invited him to join his court too. He became very good friends with the new heir presumptive Richard Lionheart while he was there. But then Richard rebelled against his father too, only more successfully than his brother had done. The two sides met outside Le Mans. Richard won. The Old King had to flee the field. Marshal famously dropped back to buy him time to escape, while Richard himself led the pursuit. He and Marshal actually met right there on the battlefield. The two great champions of English knighthood. Marshal used to boast afterwards that he was the only person ever to best Richard in single combat. He could have killed him, he claimed, but he drove his lance through his horse instead. Richard used to seethe at the story, but he never denied it. Yet we only have their word for it that it happened that way. What if there was no fight? What if they talked instead? Marshal was a pragmatist. He knew the Old King was lost, and that prolonging the war would only cause needless suffering. There was an obvious deal to be struck.'

'And?'

'The Old King fell sick and died directly afterwards. And Richard made a great show of forgiving Marshal and praising his loyalty to his father. He even agreed his marriage to a fabulously rich young ward of the crown called Isabel de Clare, turning him overnight into one of the wealthiest and most powerful barons in the realm.'

'You're saying it was a pay-off?'

'It has the ring of one, doesn't it? Rich wards were hugely valuable to a king. They didn't just give them away. Certainly not to someone who'd just humiliated them in single combat. Yet Richard gave her to Marshal. And then when Richard died unexpectedly from his crossbow wound, it was the same pattern again. John rewarded Marshal handsomely and made him his right hand, only to die himself of possible arsenic poisoning too, allowing Marshal to reach the highest step of all.' She nodded at the fresco. 'Regent to an overwhelmed young boy, England's effective king. Not bad for the younger son of a middle-ranking noble.'

'And his reputation for chivalry? For loyalty?'

'He'd hardly be the first villain in history with a talent for PR. But it would also depend on what he was most loyal to – his king or his country. The Young King's death prevented a civil war, while the Old King's ended one, as did Arthur of Brittany's. As for Richard, England had bankrupted itself to pay his ransom after he'd been captured returning from the crusades. Yet did he care? No. It was straight off campaigning again, extorting ruinous taxes that the country couldn't afford. Marshal would have had every reason to hope that John would make a better king. It didn't work out that way, of course, but how was he to know? Then came John, who Marshal had plenty of reason to hate, despite his public show of loyalty. He'd humiliated him by reneging on Magna Carta. He'd kept his son hostage for years to ensure his good behaviour, and he'd threatened his estates and family too. But more than any of that, we were at war, and we were losing. Worse, we were *running*. The French and the rebel barons had seized half the country, yet John was still scurrying from them like a frightened mouse. Marshal was a warrior. He'd made his bones fighting in tournaments all across Europe. How was he supposed to respect a man who wouldn't fight, not even to save his crown? And it's not as if we need to speculate on what he'd have done in John's shoes. We know. Because he marched on Lincoln the first chance he got.'

'Even so,' said Oliver. 'All these kings dropping dead around him. Someone would have noticed. Someone would have said something.'

'Would they? Marshal wasn't just physically intimidating, he was by all accounts extraordinarily charismatic too, and a huge celebrity from all his tournament victories. Men like that don't get accused of murder. They get sucked up to and flattered instead. You'll know far better than me how you can literally get away with murder when you're famous.'

'I wish,' said Oliver, with a light laugh. Except that his laugh wasn't light. It sounded forced instead, causing her to look curiously at him. 'What?' he asked. But his stiffness had now reached his posture and his expression too, making her realise suddenly how little she truly knew of him, and how very alone with him she was down here. How very alone and how very vulnerable. And suddenly the internal alarm that had been making a wasteland of her life ever since her abduction by Harry Kidd began shrieking at its loudest volume yet, sending a shudder rippling straight through her.

She didn't know how, or why, or even what.

She simply knew.

EIGHTY

Elias made his way back down from Temple Bruer's tower and out to his car. The road that had brought him here quickly degraded into a farm track. He made his way carefully along it until he reached a cobbled lane. A pair of scarlet oaks appeared in his headlights. A little further on, they glinted off the rear reflectors of a white convertible with a black soft-top in a walled-off parking area. He pulled in beside it and yes, it was Merchant's BMW. He'd seen enough of it these past few days to recognise it on sight, after all. First at Warne Farm, then at the King John Hotel and again last night outside his...

The King John Hotel, he thought suddenly. *Oliver Merchant had spent the night before last at the King John Hotel.* That was to say, he'd been there the night before Scott's spade had been found on the salt marsh, and right after his dinner out with Anna at which she'd first suggested that maybe her uncle had been killed by a treasure hunter rather than smugglers, an idea that had been virtually certain to transform their investigation, and thus to require a new suspect. He'd checked in to the hotel with Anna too, and so would have witnessed Penny Scott's relief at news of the intruders, suggesting she'd had reason to believe her husband guilty, thus making him the perfect person to frame.

Why then had Merchant come to Warne Farm at all? Surely safer to lie low. Except that lying low hadn't been a possibility, not with his interview booked with Dunstan Warne, and having spoken to him all those times on the phone. They'd have got round to him eventually, so better to do it on his own terms, when braced for the challenge and ready to make light of Elias's request for alibi witnesses, which he hadn't followed up on anyway, believing the case already solved.

'You again!' said Quinn cheerfully, when he called her back once more. 'We need to be a bit careful, or Dan'll start getting worried.'

'That hotel CCTV,' said Elias. 'Didn't you tell me that the intruder lights came on again the night after the storm?'

'Yes. Once. Why?'

'Can you remember what time? Or, better yet, were Merchant and Anna back from dinner by then?'

'Yes. They'd been back about an hour. Why?'

'Okay. Okay. I need you to run another search of your traffic cams, if you can bear it?'

'Sure. What am I to look for?'

'A white BMW with a black soft-top heading away from Warne Farm early last Monday morning.'

'Christ!' said Quinn. 'You think it was Merchant.'

'Yes,' he said. Then he added balefully: 'And Anna's with him now.'

EIGHTY-ONE

Anna gazed at Oliver in dismay. Gregory Scott had confessed to murdering Uncle Dun. Elias had told her so himself. How then could Oliver be guilty? She had no answer to that, yet he was involved somehow, she was certain of it, perhaps as Scott's partner or simply by having stumbled across the scene. 'We should probably get back,' she said, doing her best to keep her voice flat. 'We need to let people know about this place.'

Oliver lowered his camera to his side, its up-lighting making a devil of his face. Then he raised it back up again and pointed it at her eyes, making her blink and raise her forearm. He gazed at her for several moments. She could sense his mind at work, wondering what she knew and how to play it. He put on a disconcertingly bright smile that she'd likely have found charming a minute ago, but which now merely chilled her. All those years of childhood acting, equipping him with the skills he needed to pull off this monstrous deception. He held out his hand. 'Could I have my phone back a moment, please?' he said. 'There's something I need to check.'

'What?' she asked.

'It's private.' He stretched his hand out further. 'Please.'

It was Anna's turn to think. Should she disappear, his phone's triangulation data would bring the police to this general area, even if its GPS was off. But give it back to him and he could maroon her down here and lay false trails elsewhere, making it far harder for her ever to be found. 'It's the only light I have,' she said.

'I'll only be a sec. I'll give it straight back.'

She shook her head. 'Sorry,' she said.

'Sorry?'

'Sorry.'

A moment of stillness before Oliver gave the strangest and most unnerving snort, a combination of frustration, rage and laughter. Before she could move, he shot out a hand to grab her wrist and tug her towards him. She did the only thing she could, jabbing her other hand up at his precious camera, knocking it from his shoulder. He gave a cry and tried to save it. It slipped through his grasp and hit the floor anyway, extinguishing its lamp and plunging them into a darkness relieved only by the weakening light from her torch and the lamp's firefly afterglow. But they were enough between them to give her a terrifying glimpse of his face, of murder written plain upon it. Then she turned off her torch and the firefly died and the darkness was complete.

She jumped backwards before he could grab her again, banging the marble tabletop with her hip. She scrambled across it then dropped down the other side. She felt for the edge of the dais with her foot, then leapt into the water, landing with a huge splash that threw out a faintly luminous foam in front of her. She stumbled but quickly found her feet and waded towards the aisle. But she got her angles wrong and hit a bench instead. She shuffled along it to the aisle then risked a look back. Oliver had given up trying to fix his lamp and was using the camera's digital display screen instead, its moonlight glow just about bright enough for her to see him by, though thankfully not for him to see her. Not that that was such a help, for he could of course still hear her as she waded away from him up the aisle, and anyway there was only the one plausible route out of here. She turned her torch back on but kept a finger over it to keep it mostly hidden, while giving herself brief blinks of light to orient herself and stop herself from crashing into walls. She made it out of the chapel in this way, and back into the domed hall, intent only on beating Oliver to the ladder. If she could climb it and pull it up after herself, she'd be safe.

She followed the wall around to the fan of steps up into the crypts. She was halfway up them when Oliver arrived in the chamber behind her, his display screen illuminating her wake. He came marching across on an interception course, throwing up great foamy washes with each stride. But still she beat him into the labyrinth of Templar dead, guiding herself by memory as much as with her torch. There should be a short flight of steps to her right. She gave herself another blink of light to see it by, then hurried along a short passage before allowing herself another blink. But Oliver was closing fast. It wasn't just his footsteps she could hear, it was his heavy breathing too. No way would she beat him to the ladder, at least not with enough time to—

A clatter behind her, a yelp of pain. 'You *bitch*,' he bellowed. 'Come *back*.'

His words undid her. Or not his words alone, but rather the combination of words and voice, cutting through the haze that had fogged her since her abduction on that awful Nottinghamshire night, fleeing through pitch black woods from a man calling her a bitch and demanding she come back. Not Harry Kidd after all, but Oliver Merchant, his darkness voice imprinted forever upon her mind. And finally she saw him as the narcissistic monster he truly was, not as the charming, self-deprecating TV presenter he affected to be.

No longer could she doubt that he'd stalked Elias's wife in that supermarket, wrecking his marriage in revenge for Elias having humiliated him in front of his crew by challenging him to a fight that he'd chickened out of. It transformed their own previous encounter at Bolingbroke Castle too, when she'd twice made people laugh in his face. His unhinged need to get his own back had driven him to snatch her off that Nottingham street, while letting the blame fall upon the hapless Harry Kidd. *Forgive me,* that poor man had written. *I saw you in the library and you were so beautiful. I couldn't stop thinking about you.* Not a suicide note at all, but rather an apology for his stalking, perhaps coaxed out of him by Oliver himself, visiting him under the protection of his TV fame, only to hang him in his stairwell. But his stung pride had needed yet more salve, so he'd used her uncle's book to inveigle his way back into their lives and try again.

What joy *that* must have given him! What *power!*

The shock of it left her disoriented. She forgot about the steps down into the final crypt. She planted her foot only to find nothing there, spilling heavily onto the floor below, throwing out her hands to brace her fall, ripping open her palm and sending such a jolt through her shoulder that she feared for a moment she'd dislocated or even broken it. She was pushing herself back up when she heard Oliver close behind and she looked around to see the pale glow of his arrival. She did the only thing she could, covering her torch even as she rolled out of the aisle between a pair of the raised tombs. Her clothes and hair were dark but her skin was pale, so, as on that other night, she turned her back and averted her face then drew her legs up to her chest and clasped her arms around them.

He came down the steps a moment later, his discordant footsteps suggesting he was limping, and muttering darkly to himself, though too incoherently for Anna to make out. Her back was turned so that she couldn't see him directly, only gauge his position from the faint sundial shadow cast by his display screen. He passed so close behind her that she was sure he'd see her – but he was in too great a hurry, or perhaps his night vision was simply too degraded, for he strode on by, still muttering, out of the crypt then up the steps to the ambulatory and her uncle's ladder.

She turned around as his light dimmed, listened to the fading echo of his footsteps. Her heart slowed from its dangerous hammering. She felt nauseous. She let out a breath she hadn't even realised she'd been holding then stretched her legs back out in front of her. Her ankle throbbed. She must have turned it when she'd fallen. She rose unsteadily to her feet anyway, her movements clumsy and confused, as when woken too abruptly at night. She had to force herself to think. Oliver would soon realise that she hadn't made it up the ladder and out, meaning that she was still trapped down here with him. He'd make sure that she hadn't hidden at the far end of the ambulatory, then he'd come hunting.

A high-pitched squeaking noise. It baffled her for a moment until she realised it was two different sections of her uncle's ladder scraping against one another. Either Oliver had climbed out and was pulling it up after himself, or he was pushing it up from beneath to put it out of her reach, while making sure that he himself could still grab it back down. But which? She held her breath as she waited for the answer. Then she heard his footsteps again and knew.

His intent was obvious. He'd come back this way, chamber by chamber, corralling her into an ever smaller space. And then what? Perhaps he'd simply kill her and lay false trails elsewhere. Smarter, though, to make her death look like an accident. Brain her with a brick, sling her over his shoulder, carry her up the ladder then drop her back down onto her head before calling the emergency services and putting on the performance of his life.

'I'm sorry about your uncle,' he shouted suddenly, his voice echoing through the chambers, loud yet incongruously calm, an effort to communicate rather than scare. 'Truly I am. I liked the guy. But he asked for it, you know. He tried to cheat me.' His words got under Anna's skin, almost provoking her into retort, even though she knew that was what he wanted. 'He'd worked out about this place,' continued Oliver, once he realised he needed to toss more chum into the water. 'I could tell it from his voice when we spoke last Sunday. All excited, but trying not to show it.' Light flared suddenly. He'd fixed his lamp. She hurried the other way, up into the grandee's vault, her ankle paining her with each step. 'He'd never have found it without me. It was *my* discovery as much as his. We were partners, for Christ's sake. Yet still he tried to cheat me.' His voice hardened as he remembered this betrayal. 'Sorry, mate. No one does that. Not gonna happen. I drove halfway across the fucking country to make that clear to him. He wasn't even home. Your uncle, the famous hermit. That was when I knew for sure. I sat there half the fucking night until I had to leave for my Ludlow Castle interview. Only his van was right there as I headed out, parked by that damned field. And there he was too, standing beside his pit with his spade and a bagful of fucking jewels. You should have heard him trying to justify himself. Pathetic.'

In the chamber of loculi, Anna shone her torch into the cramped tombs with broken seals, to see if she might hide inside one. But the spaces were tiny and the grinning skulls and bleached bones so unnerved her that she carried on instead.

'I bet you think you're innocent in all this, don't you?' he called out. 'Like hell. You brought it on yourself. Your uncle would still be alive if you hadn't been such a bitch that day at Bolingbroke. Think about *that* for a moment.' He fell silent to let her respond. She glared back through the darkness. 'One lunch, for fuck's sake! One sodding lunch and none of this would have happened. Your uncle would still be with us. But nooooo. You had to make fun of me instead. Pretend I was some kind of cradle-snatcher. Saying I had a face like an arse. Don't you realise how hurtful that was?'

Despite his feigned indignation, Anna could sense the relish beneath. All she'd done was give him an excuse to inflict the horrors his heart had yearned for. She reached the fan of steps down into the flooded chamber. There was nowhere to hide here either, not knee deep in water as it was, and with the slightest ripple likely to give her away. The chapel would be no better. By default, then, she headed for the storerooms, though those too offered precious little cover.

'And poor Harry Kidd,' shouted Oliver, switching tack.

'Such a nice, sweet, gentle guy. You'd have liked him if you'd met him, honest you would. So he had a crush on you, and he didn't handle it very well. Big deal. He never meant you a lick of harm. Yet three times you went to the police about him. Three times, for god's sake.'

Anna shone her torch into each of the storerooms as she passed them. None offered the slightest hope of concealment, bare as they were, and with their floors underwater, though at least she was soon out of that.

'He was mortified about your abduction,' said Oliver. 'He *hated* you thinking it was him. He'd have told you so himself if you'd let him anywhere near you.'

She'd thought maybe to hide inside one of the large earthenware vessels, but the moment she saw them again, she realised she'd been kidding herself. Even if she could have climbed inside one without shattering it, which she doubted, Oliver would be sure to check.

'You should have seen how grateful he was when I promised to pass you his note. You'd have been touched, honest you would. He wasn't great with words, though. I had to help him compose it.'

The armouries now. Anna tried to pick up an ancient sword by its hilt, but its blade simply crumbled into rusted fragments. She tried another. That fell apart too. Her eyes moistened. She wiped them dry. Self-pity wouldn't save her.

'What's this?' shouted Oliver gleefully. 'Footprints! Fresh wet footprints! That was a bit careless, wasn't it?'

She reached the end of the passage, as she'd somehow known she would. The antechamber was small and bare and offered nowhere to hide. The treasure chamber then. She clambered through the hole her uncle had torn, landing painfully on her elbow and hip. She found places for her feet between the tubs and chests and caskets then stood up and shone her torch around in search of a dagger or something else that she might wield. She tried one of the dislodged bricks, but it was lighter and softer than she'd have liked, closer to pumice than flint, and cumbersome too. Even if Oliver was foolish enough to give her a shot, she lacked the power to do him the necessary damage.

'I'm getting *cloh*-ser.'

She needed something harder and heavier. A casket filled with rings and brooches had handles on either side and a clasp lid. She lifted it above her head but its thin handles cut into her fingers and made it too unwieldy. She set it back down and looked around once more. There was nothing. Despair filled her. She felt helpless. Almost by accident, as she turned this way and that, her weakening beam fell upon William Marshal as he sat astride his chestnut charger, his squared shoulders and broad chest and purposeful expression.

Anna had never intended to write her thesis on Marshal. She'd wanted to write instead about Eleanor of Aquitaine, celebrated wife of Henry II. But Eleanor had been done to death; she hadn't been able to find anything new to say. She'd been looking for another idea at the time of her abduction, which episode had left her dreadfully depressed, longing to believe that not all men were like that, that some were good and brave and noble. And so she'd settled on Marshal, in large part because of an incident early in his career, when, as an obscure young knight errant, he'd escorted Eleanor herself through hostile territory, only to be ambushed by a party of Poitevin knights seeking to take her hostage.

Despite the fearful odds against him, Marshal had stayed behind to hold them off, buying Eleanor the time she'd needed to make good her escape. The wound he'd taken that day had almost killed him, but his courage and loyalty had also brought him to her notice, so that she'd not only secured his freedom, she'd also persuaded her husband to appoint him mentor to their son the Young King, putting him on the first rung of his long climb to the regency. For that was the thing about Marshal. He'd never backed down. He'd always faced danger head-on, and he'd almost always triumphed too.

Her failing torchlight shrank until it lit up only his face.

Poison was no weapon for such a man. It was the choice of cowards, and no one had ever accused Marshal of that. No. She refused to believe it of him. His charmed life had been the result of who he was, an extraordinary man touched by the gods, the kind who went through life with a kind of aura about them.

That was when Anna realised.

Marshal *literally* had an aura about him.

EIGHTY-TWO

It would take Quinn a while yet to check her traffic cams, and Elias had no time to waste. He went over to the BMW, placed a hand upon its bonnet. Stone cold. They'd been gone a while. He shone his torch around. The woods were thick but the trampled-down nettles, ferns and grasses showed which way they'd gone. He cupped his hands around his mouth, called out Anna's name. An owl hooted. Another bird flapped away. He gave it a few moments then called out Merchant's name instead. Silence fell once more. He tried to think it through. They'd been on good terms earlier. They were surely here in search of the source of the silver pennies, rather than for anything more sinister. No reason, then, to fear that Anna was in imminent peril.

Yet he feared it nonetheless.

He took out his phone and called for backup, but the nearest station was miles away, and it would be at least several minutes before anyone arrived. He couldn't bring himself to wait. The trail was easy enough to follow, the path of least resistance made even more so by the freshly broken branches and the stamped down undergrowth. He paused to call out their names every few seconds, keeping his voice as calm as he could. He kept thinking of the brutal injury done to Dunstan Warne. He'd never forgive himself if something similar happened to Anna. A tangle of brambles blocked his path, such as it was. He edged around it and saw a pair of short pine planks lying beside a hole in the ground. He knelt and shone his torch down an open shaft, its beam glittering off the ridged rungs of an aluminium ladder whose bottom two sections had been pushed high up off the floor. This baffled him for a moment until he realised a possible reason why. Merchant had pushed them up from beneath in order to trap Anna down there, which implied that not only did she now know the truth about him, but that he knew she knew it too.

He got his phone back out to call in his precise coordinates. Then he tucked his torch into his waistband and set off, pushing down the lower sections of the ladder with his foot as he reached them. Metal shrieked against metal, announcing his arrival like a faulty doorbell. He carried on anyway, stepping off the bottom rung onto a rubble mound in a pillared hallway. There were footprints on either side, one set of which were markedly smaller than the others. Those had to be Anna's. To his right, they went away and then came back again. To his left, they only went away. That was where she was. He took a deep breath for calm and courage, then – holding his torch out ahead of him – he set off.

EIGHTY-THREE

It wasn't just William Marshal who had an aura about him, Anna now saw. St Maur had one too. And there were more such seams around the knights behind, and around the baggage carts too. Which meant that the mural hadn't been painted directly onto the raw bedrock, as she'd initially assumed. No. It was another fresco. And a fresco meant plaster. And plaster created the possibility of something else behind.

'Don't you have *anything* to say for yourself?' called out Oliver. 'Anything at all?'

The two huge silver platters against the back wall looked almost like a pair of gates. Anna tipped one of them up onto its end to expose the plaster behind. It was in far worse condition near the floor – cracked, crumbling and bubbled by pockets of air. She pressed one of the bulges with her thumb. It was soft and loose and came away in a series of fat flakes when she picked at it with her nail.

'I mean Christ, you should have seen yourself that night. A skirt that short, you were begging for it. Honest to god, if it hadn't been me, it'd have been someone else. You might not have survived them either. Think about *that*. I may actually have saved your life. You should be thanking me.'

She pulled away more flakes until she was rewarded by a first thin line of mortar. She quickly exposed the outline of a limestone brick some six inches above the floor. It was hard to get at though, what with all the chests and caskets in the way.

But she ignored their sharp corners and edges even as they cut into her thighs and ribs.

'I see you broke those two wonderful old swords. Some historian you are.'

She pinched the brick between her fingertips and jiggled it like a loose tooth until she'd reduced the old mortar to a fine dust that made her eyes water and forced her to clear her throat quietly into her fist before it made her cough. She couldn't get enough purchase to pull it towards her, however, so she pushed it instead. It ceded reluctantly at first but then went in a rush, dropping with a low thud onto the floor behind. She put her torch to the hole but couldn't see a thing.

A little lamplight fluttered outside. Oliver had arrived at the entrance to the antechamber. She was out of time, yet the hole was still too small. She pushed the neighbouring brick with all she had. It yielded more easily than the first, and took the ones above with it too. She winced at the clatter they made as they thudded into the floor behind.

'Here I come, ready or not!'

She turned onto her front and wriggled through the narrow opening, her chest scraping against the stone. She drew her legs in after her then looked back out. Oliver was advancing cautiously through the antechamber, aware that Anna couldn't retreat any further and would therefore have to stand and fight. She rose to her knees and reached back out for the upended silver platter, and was lowering it back into place when Oliver shone his lamp like a lighthouse beam across the treasure chamber. She froze and held her breath, her hand trembling beneath the platter's weight. But thankfully he didn't see anything amiss, for instead he set his camera down on the antechamber floor to leave his hands free for his assault on the treasure chamber. And it gave her the time she needed to set the platter gently back down, praying he wouldn't notice the slight scraping noise it made, or the fact that it had moved.

She rose to her feet and edged quietly away. Her fading torchlight was barely stronger than a struck match by now, yet it still gave her some idea of this new space. A dusty white marble staircase led upwards, each step lined by religious artefacts: a pair of golden candelabras, heavy gold crosses studded with colourful gems, phylacteries of scrolls and gorgeously-wrought reliquaries containing the purported bones of saints or fragments of the true cross.

She reached a platform at the top, laid with pink-veined marble. A huge golden throne upholstered in dusty red velvet sat in pride of place, with a set of three gilded tables of diminishing size set out like wings on either side of it, their legs sculpted into caryatid angels, and each bearing a single precious object. A richly jewelled golden crown lay on each of the largest two tables. Then came a pair of ornamented sceptres and finally two golden wands, the one to her left with a dove perched upon it, the one to her right topped by a lion. And she couldn't help but notice how beautifully these treasures had been laid out, as opposed to the clutter in the outer chamber. But then crown jewels weren't just jewels any more than a king was just a man.

Crown jewels were sacred.

'What the fuck?' muttered Oliver, though to himself rather than to her, presumably on discovering she wasn't in the treasure chamber. Yet his voice brought Anna back to hard reality. He'd find her soon enough, if only by elimination. She needed a weapon of some kind. She picked up each of the sceptres in turn, holding them like a club, but they were simply too heavy for her to wield effectively. She tried the wands instead. They had the opposite problem, of being too light to cause sufficient damage. She felt like crying.

A ragged purple canopy behind the throne had gilded poles at each corner, to be held over the king's head during a royal procession. On the floor beside it stood a matching pair of oak chests, reinforced by rusted iron brackets and silver studs. The first contained an ermine-lined cloak, a tunic of red samite and various ceremonial robes in astonishingly good condition, while the other had gloves and belts and even a pair of shoes, beautifully embroidered and set with gemstones and precious metals. But nothing she could use.

'Don't think you can get away,' shouted Oliver. 'You're down here somewhere, I know you are. I'll find you, even if it takes me—' But then he broke off.

Anna glanced around, fearful he'd found her refuge. But there was no sign of it. And now she heard a second voice, so distant, faint and echoey that it barely reached her at all. 'Anna!' he was shouting. 'Anna!' Her heart gave a little skip. Elias. She'd known he'd come for her in the end, but she'd never imagined it would be so soon. Unfortunately, he'd only succeeded in putting Oliver on alert, meaning that he'd be walking straight into an ambush. She turned towards where she imagined him to be. And that was when she saw it, not on a table but in a crucifix-shaped niche in the wall that had clearly been specially cut for it. She went over to it. A ceremonial sword in a gorgeously-jewelled scabbard. The Sword of Tristram, it had to be. The Sword of Mercy.

She braced herself for its weight as she took its scabbard in one hand and its hilt in the other. Its blade caught for a moment as she drew it, before releasing with the low hiss of a threatened snake. She drew it all the way out and held it up. Yes, there was the famous broken tip that had earned it its nickname. Its blade was astonishingly bright and gleaming, as though it had just been oiled. She ran her forefinger along its edge and, though it didn't break her skin, let alone draw blood, she felt its strength and sharpness. Its tip might be broken, as the stories said, yet it still carried a real threat. For it hadn't only been known as the Sword of Mercy, after all.

No. It had been called the Sword of Justice too.

EIGHTY-FOUR

Elias had always prided himself on his courage. It was the trick he used to keep himself brave. But his stock of it had already been called upon heavily today, and he felt sick with fear as he made his way through this winding ancient necropolis in the knowledge that a murderer could well be waiting in ambush for him behind any of these raised tombs, or lurking on the other side of each doorway. It grew so draining that he told himself that it was okay to stop and wait for backup, that nothing bad would happen in the extra few minutes it would take. Yet he kept moving forward all the same.

He reached an ancient morgue with columns of tombs cut into its walls, and skulls, ribs and long bones scattered like spillikins across its floor, the whiteness of their joints suggesting that they'd only freshly been pulled apart. Anna would never have done such a thing, or even countenanced it, meaning that Merchant had done it himself, presumably while hunting for her. Maybe, then, he didn't have time to waste.

He tiptoed between the bones, doing his best not to touch them, yet carrying the burden of them into the next crypt and beyond. He began hurrying ever faster, goaded by the memory of how Anna had, without a second thought, left the comparative safety of the Twin Otter's cabin for the platform step, to press the stun gun against Andrei's cheek and so save his life. And suddenly he found himself blurting out her name, less to let her and Merchant know that he was on his way than to remind himself of why he was doing this. And having done so once, destroying any small hope of surprise, he called out her name again and again, a battle cry to give himself heart.

He left the necropolis behind, arrived at a fan of stairs down into a flooded chamber still rippling slightly from a recent disturbance. Two pairs of shoes and socks had been left on the steps, confirming that both Anna and Merchant had been this way and were likely down here still. He didn't bother to take off his own but simply plunged into the water and waded over to the first of the two accessible passages. But it proved to be an ancient chapel, and the water in it looked so undisturbed that he turned and went back the other way instead.

'Anna!' he shouted. There was no answer, so on he marched, sending waves splashing against the walls and then rebounding to clash with the ones behind, creating confusing patterns of light that kept making him think someone was right behind him, so that soon he was turning circles. 'Anna!' he shouted again, despite the anxiety in his voice advertising not just his presence but his state of knowledge too.

He hurried along a passage of empty storerooms, its gentle gradient soon taking him out of the water. His shoes began to squelch. He kicked them off and continued in his socks. He could see wet footprints on the dusty stone floor. The smaller ones were almost dry but the larger ones were still fresh. He was getting close.

'Anna!' he cried.

More storerooms. An ancient armoury. His shirt and trousers were clinging wet and chilly enough to make him shiver. He had to stoop as the passage neared its end. A final storeroom. This was it, he was sure of it, if only from the frantic pounding of his heart. He stood outside its doorway and pointed in his torch. It looked as empty as the others, except for the gaping hole in its far wall. He didn't call out any more. He tried not to make any sound, indeed, though his torchlight had surely already betrayed him. If Merchant was in any mood to come forward, he'd have done so by now. No, he was waiting in ambush either on the other side of this outer doorway or more likely in the chamber beyond.

'I've got more people coming,' shouted Elias. 'They'll be here any moment. Give yourself up while it still matters.'

His words echoed back at him, then fell to silence. He gave it a few more seconds then crouched down low to roll his torch along the floor into the outer chamber. He put his forearms up over his head and went charging in. But the outer chamber was empty. He picked his torch back up. He'd have felt absurd had he not been quite so scared. He approached the hole in the far wall on the balls of his feet, like being back in the ring again, his senses zinging, his reflexes sharp as knives. The fear somehow left him too, displaced by a concentration so intense that it felt like nothing could disturb it. But then he arrived at the far wall and his torchlight fell upon such an astonishing array of treasures that it robbed him of his focus for just a moment, and he reached his torch forward to shine it left and right before he could quite stop himself.

Everything then happened in a blur. A limestone block came slamming down upon his wrist, knocking the torch from his hand. Pain arrived in shocking waves. He cried out and tried to snatch back his hand, but Merchant was too fast. He grabbed hold of his forearm and tugged him so violently forwards that he found himself tumbling head-first through the hole, crashing onto an earthenware bowl that shattered beneath the impact, scattering gemstones across the floor, while his fallen torch rolled back and forth among them, casting kaleidoscopic colours onto a pair of silver platters leaning against the back wall, and from there up at the ceiling.

He rose to his knees and threw up his forearms to protect his head, only for the next blow to smash into his already injured wrist, crushing it against his skull and knocking him back down. A third blow now. He twisted around so that it caught him on his shoulder rather than his cheek. He heard as well as felt his collarbone snap. Merchant came to stand over him, panting hard from exultation as much as exertion. He was holding a limestone block in both hands and he crouched closer to Elias before swinging it a fourth time, bursting through his feeble defences and catching him on his temple.

Merchant tossed the block aside then knelt upon Elias's shoulders and clasped his hands around his throat. Elias tried to twist and buck him off, but he was too heavy and too strong, his thumbs digging into his windpipe, making him struggle and writhe for air. He scrabbled at his wrist with his left hand, then flung a fist at his face, but it was hopeless. He couldn't breathe. He couldn't breathe. The strength drained inexorably from his arms. His hands flopped uselessly to the floor. His mind began to drift. He had the strongest sense that his beloved son Marcus was standing nearby, in clothes as sodden as his own. Tears streamed from his eyes. This was what he deserved. It had been a long time coming, that was all.

His vision grew increasingly blurred. He couldn't tell any more what was real and what was hallucination. His torch was still casting its gemstone colours onto the two platters, only now he had the strangest impression that those platters were parting like the silver gates of heaven, as if in welcome. And then, impossibly, Anna appeared between them, her tousled loose dark hair tumbling to her shoulders as she stood up tall and hoisted a gleaming long blade with a broken tip high above her head, for all the world an avenging angel come to deliver justice. Now Merchant heard her too. He turned and saw her face and the fierceness in her eye, and he realised what it meant. He saw her face and, with a groan of dread and knowledge, he froze for the vital moment that might yet have saved him.

And then it was too late.

EPILOGUE

It was a chill, grey, winter morning as the mourners gathered for Dunstan Warne's funeral – appropriate weather, perhaps, for bidding such a man farewell. From fear of an empty church, Anna had called everyone she thought might possibly attend. It astonished and heartened her, therefore, to see the place so packed that latecomers had to stand against the sides or at the back.

Royston Flynn was there, and impeccably dressed for once. Gregory Scott was there as well, holding hands with Priya Kapur, while Penny Scott glared daggers at them from two pews back. There were plenty of other faces that Anna remembered from her time here too, some no doubt drawn by the sensational recent events, yet enough of whom paused on their way in to share stories about Uncle Dun for her to realise that it wasn't just her own life that he'd touched for the better.

He'd secured his own burial plot many years before, next to his wife and daughter. He'd chosen his own reading too: Ecclesiastes 3:14. Though he'd not been a notably religious man, he'd loved the language of the *King James Version*. So she made sure to keep her voice slow and solemn, to give that language its due.

To every thing there is a season, and a time to every purpose under the heaven:
A time to be born, and a time to die. A time to plant, and

a time to pluck up that which is planted.

Warne Farm was hers now. But what to do with it? She couldn't take it on herself, not with her PhD to complete. Yet she couldn't bring herself to sell it either, partly out of loyalty to the family, but also – to put it bluntly – because too many bodies had been found beneath its fields for it to fetch what it was worth right now. Maybe in a year or two. Fortunately, the big farming conglomerates were neither superstitious nor sentimental, so she was in negotiations to lease out the fields and the barn, and to rent out the house separately, while she decided on what next.

A time to kill, and a time to heal; a time to break down, and a time to build up.

The healing had come more quickly than she could have dared hope. In truth, she was still waiting for her first nightmare from killing either Andrei or Oliver. Oliver in particular should have haunted her, for the wound she'd inflicted on him had so closely matched the one he'd done her uncle. Yet she'd been sleeping better than for years. So completely had she put it all behind her, indeed, that she even wondered if she wasn't some kind of sociopath.

If so, kudos to sociopathy. It suited her just fine.

A time to weep, and a time to laugh; a time to mourn, and a time to dance.

Such weeping and mourning as she'd done, she'd done for her uncle – save, that was, for a strange morning in Nottingham with the parents of her one-time stalker Harry Kidd. Anna had felt so bad about him being wrongly accused of her abduction that she'd written to them to ask permission to visit his grave as a way of making peace. And they'd been so relieved to have their son cleared of that particular charge that they'd all gone together to grieve their separate losses.

A time to love, and a time to hate; a time of war, and a time of peace.

A number of women had come forward since Oliver's death with horrifying accounts of abuse suffered at his hands. They'd actually found films he'd made of some of it on thumb drives in a safety deposit box at a local bank, from which they'd also recovered a bag filled with the brooches, coins and other treasure that her uncle had stolen to plant around his fields. Anna found herself torn between sympathy for the ordeals these women had suffered, and anger that they hadn't spoken up before. But it was all done with now. She'd earned her time of peace.

Peace was hardly the word, though, for she found herself constantly fending off requests for interviews of one kind or another, while a well-regarded Hollywood screenwriter kept pestering her to collaborate on a script. She'd said no to them all, however, for to her delight she had her old energy back. Her appetite and ambition. She *wanted* things again. To have fun and make friends. To enjoy success and adventures and romance.

Most of all, however, she'd regained her interest in her thesis, even though she hadn't yet decided what to say about William Marshal and the curious deaths of all those kings. At times she thought she had him nailed as England's most consequential serial killer. The King of Assassins, as Royston would doubtless dub him. The Assassin King. But then she'd realise how thin and circumstantial her evidence was and decide to settle instead for a wry footnote or two about the weird coincidence of it all. Though even that made her feel bad, because she owed Marshal a great debt, for being there for her at a time when she'd needed to believe that not all men were monsters.

Thankfully, she didn't need him for that any more.

***

Elias's right hand had been brutally injured by Oliver's assault, as though mangled in some terrible industrial accident. His surgeons had done what they could, mending bones, reattaching tendons, repairing veins. But it would take more operations and months or even years of physiotherapy before he regained its full use. Not that he'd have been able to use it much right now anyway, for his arm was in a sling to help heal his shattered collarbone.

With driving out for the moment, WPC Maria Quinn had kindly brought him to the service. They stood together at the back, having surrendered their seats to an elderly couple Anna didn't recognise. They stayed all through the interment too, even after the worsening rain drove most of the others off. She went to thank them for coming. Quinn was thoughtful enough to make her excuses after a minute or two, allowing Anna time alone with Elias. Or perhaps she simply wanted to get out of the wet. A good idea anyway, what with the rain now hammering down, so the two of them hurried to take shelter in the church porch.

'I brought you a gift,' Elias told her, handing her the key to her uncle's van.

'You're done with it?' asked Anna. 'For good, this time?'

'For good. To be honest, we'll hardly even need it, what with how de Bruin and Wharton have turned on each other. They're toast, along with all their mates. We're going to be cleaning up the county, thanks to you. Some of my more excitable colleagues think we might even have as much as a week before the next lot move in.'

'And your old boss? He's out of prison, yes?'

Elias nodded. 'Back home again and planning his future, whatever that might be. He made me promise to thank you.'

'Whatever for? That bit was all you.'

'Yeah, but he's in an Oscar-winning kind of mood.

Thanking everyone he can think of.'

Anna laughed. 'Best Miscarriage of Justice. Truly the king of awards.' They gazed fondly at each other for a few moments. When you'd saved someone's life, and they'd saved yours, it created a special kind of bond. You couldn't help but take an interest in them. Their successes became yours. Their troubles, their joys, their enemies, their loves. 'Seen much of the kids?' she asked.

He gave a grimace. 'Julie's got a new man. Works for one of those car servicing chains. They want him to run one of their depots, apparently, and she means to go with him, wherever that may be. So who the hell knows? Except that I can't be too far away from the twins. I just can't.'

'You're a good dad,' she told him. But his eyes only watered, so that she realised too late what it was she'd said, and why it hurt. She reached out to touch his hand. 'You are,' she said. 'You're a good dad.'

'Yeah, well,' he said.

Anna shook her head. 'I keep thinking back to that first day, when you picked me up from Peterborough Station. I can't believe what an arse I thought you.'

'I was an arse, to be fair.'

'You're forgiven.'

'That's good. I've seen what you do to men who act like arses.'

'They did worse than that. They tried to kill my friend.' A rare warmth blossomed suddenly in her chest, a mix of affection, friendship and sadness at their imminent parting. She took half a step forward and put her arms lightly around him, careful of his injuries. He hugged her gently back. They stood like that for several moments, bringing to her mind that day in the Twin Otter, plunging weightless towards the sea – how, in that moment of disaster, she'd found such comfort and consolation in his embrace. But then she realised she was causing him pain, so she let go and stepped back again. A York historian. A Lincolnshire detective. How little overlap their lives should rightly have. Yet it hurt crazily to say goodbye. 'You'll keep in touch, yes?' she asked.

'Of course,' he said.

'Men always say that. And then they never do.'

But he only smiled at that, as though she'd said something funny. 'I'll keep in touch,' he told her. 'Count on it.'

AUTHOR'S NOTE

I first heard about King John losing his crown jewels in the Wash when I was a boy, though mostly because it made for such a bad pun. But I'd never really looked into it until recently, largely because I didn't think there was enough mystery about it to carry a whole book. But, as so often happens in my job, the more I read about it, the more intriguing it became, and the more possibilities opened up.

I hope I've done these possibilities justice, and that at least some readers enjoy the story enough to find out more – in which case I'd warmly recommend The Mystery of King John's Treasure by Shirley Charters and The Lost Treasure of King John by Richard Waters. There are, of course, countless good books on both King John and William Marshal. For casual readers, I'd recommend Marc Morris for the former and Richard Asbridge's The Greatest Knight for the latter.

ABOUT THE AUTHOR

Will Adams

Having pursued multiple careers over the years, Will finally deciding to concentrate on his lifelong dream of writing fiction. His books have been translated into over twenty languages and have appeared on bestseller lists around the world.

Printed in Great Britain
by Amazon